"Don't do this," he said. "Don't marry a man you do not care for when you and I . . ." He took a deep breath to steady himself against the on-slaught of emotions that whipped through him at the thought of having to relinquish all hope. "You cannot deny that there's something between us—something more than what is usual between two people who have only just met."

Jaw clenching, she tilted her head backward and looked him squarely in the eyes, saying, "While your company has been charming, I fear I must disappoint you, for I noticed no such thing."

She was lying. Anthony had seen the flash of concession that marked her features for a second, before she'd managed to train them.

"Is that so?" he asked as he backed her further up against the bookcase, jolting the heavy piece of furniture enough for one of his figures to fall over.

Miss Smith gasped, her eyes startled and her body grown stiff. She would *not* deny them their happiness, Anthony decided, though she clearly needed reminding of how he affected her.

"I do believe I am about to prove you wrong."

Capturing her head with his hands, he then lowered his mouth over hers . . .

By Sophie Barnes

Novels
THE TROUBLE WITH BEING A DUKE
THE SECRET LIFE OF LADY LUCINDA
THERE'S SOMETHING ABOUT LADY MARY
LADY ALEXANDRA'S EXCELLENT ADVENTURE
HOW MISS RUTHERFORD GOT HER GROOVE BACK

Novellas
MISTLETOE MAGIC
(from FIVE GOLDEN RINGS:
A CHRISTMAS COLLECTION)

Coming Soon
THE SCANDAL IN KISSING AN HEIR

SOPHIE BARNES

THE TROUBLE WITH BEING A DUKE

At the Kingsborough Ball

AVON

An Imprint of HarperCollinsPublishers

AVON BOOKS
An Imprint of HarperCollins*Publishers*
10 East 53rd Street
New York, New York 10022-5299

First Avon Books mass market printing: September 2013

Avon Trademark Reg. U.S. Pat. Off. and in Other Countries, Marca Registrada, Hecho en U.S.A.
HarperCollins® is a registered trademark of HarperCollins Publishers.

Printed in the U.S.A.

10 9 8 7 6 5 4 3 2 1

For Hanne,
whose appreciation for Jane Austen rivals my own,
and for Erling,
with the fondest memories of time spent together
in Spain, Denmark, and Ghana.

Acknowledgments

When my first editor, Esi Sogah, called me in May 2012, offering me a three-book deal for Avon Books on the basis of an idea I'd had for *Five Golden Rings* (the anthology published by Avon Impulse in December 2012), I was ecstatic! A lot of work lay ahead, of course, especially since turning what should have been a novella into three full-length novels was no simple task. In the end, I feel as though *The Trouble With Being a Duke* came together the way I envisioned it. However, the journey from concept to publication is far from a solitary one. To start, I'd like to thank Esi for opening the door of opportunity—it's been such a pleasure working with you, and I wish you lots of success in your future endeavors.

Changing editors can be a worrisome experience, but my lovely new editor, Erika Tsang, assured me that there was no need for panic and that I was in safe hands—she was so right. Together with the rest of the Avon Books team, which includes (but is far from limited to) editorial assistant Chelsey Emmelhainz, publicists Pam Spengler-Jaffee, Jessie Edwards and

Caroline Perny, she ensured a smooth and painless transition. My sincerest thanks to all of you for being so wonderful!

And to Carrie Feron for being so generous with your books—thank you!

I would also like to thank Nancy Mayer for her assistance. Whenever I was faced with a question regarding the Regency era that I couldn't answer on my own, I turned to Nancy for advice. Her help has been invaluable.

My family and friends deserve my thanks as well, especially for reminding me to take a break occasionally, to step away from the computer and just unwind—I would be lost without you.

And to you, dear reader—thank you so much for taking the time to read this story. Your support is, as always, hugely appreciated!

Once in a while, right in the middle of an ordinary life, love gives us a fairy tale.

ANONYMOUS

Chapter 1

Kingsborough Hall, Moxley, England
1817

"It's time, Mama," Anthony Hurst, the seventh Duke of Kingsborough, said as he strode toward one of the tall windows in his mother's bedroom and pulled aside the heavy velvet curtains, flooding the space with a bright beam of sunshine. Pausing for a moment, he looked out at the garden. The crocuses were beginning to bloom, adding a cheerful display of yellow and lilac to the dreary winter landscape.

"Why must you disturb me?"

Anthony turned at the sound of his mother's voice, gritting his teeth at the lifelessness in it. He hated the morose atmosphere that had swamped Kingsborough Hall for the past year, and he hated how difficult it was proving to move past it. "It's been thirteen months, Mama—that's long enough."

His mother, still dressed in her widow's weeds,

sighed from her seat in the corner, her light blue eyes squinting in the brightness as he pulled aside yet another curtain. Black did not suit her—it made her look pallid and brought out the silver streaks of gray in her hair. She had aged dramatically during the final stage of her husband's life. It was almost five years since the first symptom of illness had surfaced—a lump in the former duke's armpit. Three physicians had been consulted, all of them advising immediate surgery, and with no desire to meet a speedy end, the Duke of Kingsborough had complied.

Anthony knew it had been a painful procedure, and yet it had only been the first of several. So it had come as no surprise when his father had eventually called him into his study to say that he had refused further treatment—but it had still been bloody hard to hold back the tears in the face of such defeat, knowing without doubt what his father's decision had meant.

A month later, however, the condition hadn't worsened, and Anthony had begun to hope that perhaps it never would. But then, as if from one day to the next, his father's health had declined with startling rapidity. Nothing could have been worse than looking on helplessly while a loved one had withered away and died, his body wracked by pain at every hour of both day and night. Even the memory of it was unbearable.

"Is that all?" His mother's tiny voice was weak, forcing a wince from Anthony as he went over to her and gently took her delicate hand in his. "It seems like an eternity."

"Mama," he whispered, kneeling beside her, his heart aching for the woman who had once been so full of life. "So much more reason for us to end this."

Her eyes met his with the same degree of hopelessness that he too had felt for so long. His father had always been so strong and healthy—the sort of man that everyone had thought would outlive them all. Suffering through his deterioration, inheriting his title and eventually taking his place as duke had been far from easy for Anthony. It was now more than a year since they had laid him to rest, and Anthony had decided that it was finally time for all of them to start living again. With that in mind, he had an idea that he hoped would capture his mother's enthusiasm. "We shall host an event," he announced, in a voice that sounded too old and serious for his own liking.

"An event?" His mother looked as if she'd much rather crawl back into bed and draw the covers over her head than listen to one more word of what he had to say.

"Not just any event, Mama," he said, determined to make her listen and even more determined to uncover the woman who lay dormant somewhere beneath her beaten-down exterior. He knew she was there— somewhere. "It's the end of February already, but if we hurry, we can probably manage to arrange a house party in time for Easter." He saw that his mother was about to protest and quickly added, "It could commence with one of your infamous balls."

She stilled for a moment as she stared back at him, time stretching out between them until he doubted she would ever respond. He was trying to think of something to say to break the silence when he saw her stir, understanding flickering behind her eyes. "We haven't had one of those in years, Anthony. Do you really suppose . . ." Her words trailed off, but not with defeat this time. Anthony couldn't help but notice a slight crease upon her brow. She was thinking—quite furiously, judging from the fact that she was now chewing on her lower lip. Her eyes gradually sharpened, and she leaned forward in her seat. "Perhaps it will help bring the family back together."

Anthony certainly hoped so.

When his father had stopped fighting for his life, it had not taken long before his sister Louise had married and removed herself to her new home. Anthony had not questioned her motives at the time. She had been of a marriageable age (though perhaps a bit young), the Earl of Huntley had clearly been in a position to offer her the standard of living she'd been raised to expect, and Anthony had given the couple his blessing without much thought on the matter.

The truth of it was, compared to everything else he'd been faced with at the time—his father's imminent demise, the payment of physicians' bills that kept arriving daily, and his ever-increasing duties in regard to running the estate—his sister's hasty decision to marry had been more of an inconvenience than anything else.

It was not until after his father had died that he'd wondered if she'd perhaps been looking for a means of escape, some justifiable reason not to face the devastating truth looming over them all on a daily basis. Of course she'd visited a number of times, but she'd given herself a viable excuse to leave whenever she'd had enough. Anthony couldn't blame her. There had been times when he had longed to flee from it all himself.

His brother, Winston, had been more reliable. He was two years younger than Anthony, had married Sarah the vicar's daughter at the age of only twenty, and was now the delighted father of twin boys. To support his growing family, he ran a small publishing house that he'd started with the financial support of their father. Of course there had been those who'd disapproved of a gentleman making such a career choice, but Winston's love for books had prevented him from swaying in his decision, and his father had given his support—a clear sign that he'd considered his son's happiness more important than seeking the approval of his peers and a perfect example of the sort of man he'd been.

Though based in London, Winston had still managed to make the three-hour journey to Moxley once a week throughout their father's illness. But with Papa now gone, Winston was busy applying himself to the growth of his business, and he didn't visit Moxley as often as he had. Anthony understood his brother's reasoning, of course. He just missed him. That was all.

"I must speak with Mrs. Sterling immediately," his mother suddenly pronounced, startling Anthony out of his reverie. His eyes focused on her, and he noticed that there was a rather resolute expression about her eyes.

Anthony blinked. A moment earlier, she had looked as though a single puff of air would have overturned her. Now, instead, her back straightened and she gave a firm nod before pulling her hand away from his and rising to her feet.

This was what he had hoped for, but he had never imagined how quickly his mother would rally when faced with a project so large that it would require her immediate attention. To be honest, he had feared she might feel overwhelmed and that it would only serve to cripple her even further.

Clearly this was not the case, for not only had she already rung for her maid but she had also begun pacing about the room, checking off on her fingers all the items that would need addressing, all the while complaining about the limited amount of time Anthony had afforded her to prepare for such a grand event.

"We shall have to send out invitations immediately," she gushed between mention of a possible ice sculpture and her thoughts regarding the flower arrangements that would have to be ordered.

Anthony's head began to hurt, but he was pleased with the result of his plan. What he hadn't mentioned, simply because he'd had no desire to excite his mother any further, was that he intended to use the event as a means to improve his acquaintance with the young ladies his mother undoubtedly meant to invite. His father's demise had put everything into perspective for him, forcing him to realize just how fragile life could be. He needed an heir, and there was really no better time to start planning for one.

"Come, gentle night, come, loving, black-brow'd night, give me my Romeo; and, when he shall die, take him and—"

"Stop that right now," Isabella's mother warned as she lifted her gaze from her embroidery—a new set of pillowcases that the butcher's wife had ordered, with flowering vines trailing along the edges.

Isabella was supposed to have been practicing her cutwork, but she was finding the process incredibly tedious and had paused to read a little instead. She had just gotten started on her favorite passage when her mother had cut her off as usual—at the exact same point. "But it's the most romantic thing ever written, Mama." Isabella should have known better than to goad her mother like this, but she could not help it—it was much too easy.

"Romantic?" Her mother frowned, her mouth scrunched in a manner that warned Isabella of the derision that lay ahead. "You *are* aware that the hero and heroine both die because of some ridiculous misunderstanding, are you not?"

"Of course, but —"

"Not to mention that the passage you're presently reciting starts not only with Juliet considering her dear heart's demise but the prospect of having him chopped up and—"

"Cut up, Mama—into little stars, so that—"

"Honestly." Her mother shook her head as she returned her attention to the rose petal she was stabbing with her needle, as if it had been Shakespeare himself and she meant to make him pay for subjecting her to his play. "I've never understood why anyone would think it romantic for a young couple to kill themselves in the name of love."

Isabella stifled a grin as she set the book aside and reached for her cutwork. "I do believe you're the only person I know who can criticize the loveliest play ever written as if Mr. Shakespeare had penned it with the sole purpose of offending you. Considering how much you love Papa, I would have thought you'd be more romantically inclined, yet I'm beginning to wonder if you even know what romance is." She said it in jest, but when she looked up, her mother's eyes had widened and her jaw had gone slack. "I'm sorry," Isabella quickly muttered. "I didn't mean to upset you."

Her mother took a deep breath, held it, and then released it very slowly before bowing her head once more to her work. "No," she said. "I don't suppose you did."

Drat it all, Isabella thought as she drew her needle through the piece of white linen she was holding. It had been neat and crisp when she'd started on it, but it had long since taken on the appearance of a crumpled rag. She shook her head at her carelessness—not in regard to the fabric but because of her mother. She'd unintentionally hurt her feelings, and not for the first time. She really ought to have learned her lesson by now. Glancing at the book she'd been reading, she made a mental note not to bring it into her mother's presence ever again. It only resulted in trouble.

She let out a small sigh. All she wanted was a confidante—someone with whom to share her dreams of true love and a happily ever after. In spite of what she'd said, she knew that her parents were happy. It was obvious from the way they looked at each other and the manner in which they addressed each other with cheerful smiles.

Isabella wished for that, but she also wished for more—she wished for magic. Lord knew she had spent hours on end, dreaming about meeting a gallant stranger—a prince, perhaps—who would declare his undying love for her before carrying her off to his castle on a magnificent white stallion . . . or perhaps in a golden carriage similar to the one she'd imagined Cendrillon riding in the fairy tale she'd loved so dearly as a child.

"Isabella?"

Isabella blinked, realizing her mother must have been telling her something that required her attention. "Sorry, Mama, my thoughts were elsewhere. You were saying?"

Her mother frowned. "I know how fond you are of *Romeo and Juliet*. I didn't mean to mock it in any way, it's just . . . while I do appreciate Shakespeare's talent, his notion of romance is, in my opinion, lacking—at least in this instance." Tying off a thread, she folded the pillowcase and placed it in her embroidery basket. "Sacrificing yourself for the sake of love is not romantic, Isabella—it's rash, thoughtless, and completely meaningless. Real romance comes from small and selfless gestures, from private moments spent in one another's company or a shared kiss when no one else is looking. It's showing the person you care about that they're just as important to you as you are to yourself, if not more so. Most importantly, it's what tells them that you love them, without the need for words."

Isabella stared at her mother, suddenly feeling she wasn't entirely the person Isabella had always thought her to be. There was a more sensitive side to her than Isabella had ever imagined, or perhaps it was just that this was the first time her mother had ever talked openly about her own thoughts on the subject of romance. Of course Isabella knew that her mother wasn't a cynic when it came to matters of the heart, for her devotion to her husband bordered on the ridiculous. It was just that her mother did not understand why anyone would choose to write poetry rather than tell the person in question how they actually felt about them, and the idea that any lady might enjoy a piece of music written in her honor seemed silly to her—or at least that was what she'd once said.

Isabella was about to question her mother about the most romantic thing her father had ever done, but just as she opened her mouth, her mother rose to her feet and said, "You'd better ready yourself in time for Mr. Roberts's visit. You know he's never late."

It was true. Timothy Roberts was the most predictable man Isabella had ever known. Not that this was necessarily a bad thing—after all, Marjorie, their maid-of-all-work, always knew precisely when to put the pie in the oven so it would be ready in time for his visit. And he had been visiting a *lot* lately. Every Sunday afternoon at precisely three' o clock, for an entire year.

There was very little doubt about his intentions at this point (though he had yet to propose), and Isabella's parents were overjoyed. Her father, who'd arranged the whole thing, was quite proud of himself for securing such a fine match for his daughter. He should have been too, for while they were bordering on a state of impoverishment, Mr. Roberts was a wealthy man who'd struck up a business specializing in luxury carriages.

Isabella's father had worked in his employ for the past five years, test-driving each vehicle before it was delivered to the client, and while Isabella wasn't entirely sure of what her father might have told Mr. Roberts about her, the man had one day appeared for tea, and had continued to do so since.

With a sigh, Isabella gathered up her things, feeling not the least bit enthusiastic about Mr. Roberts's impending visit. Not because she didn't like him (it was difficult to form an opinion due to his reserve), and certainly not because he had done anything to offend or upset her. On the contrary, he was always the perfect gentleman, adhering to etiquette in the most stringent manner possible.

No, the problem was far simpler than that—she just did not love him, and what was worse, she had long since come to realize that she never would.

Chapter 2

"**I** really must commend you on the pie, Mrs. Chilcott," Mr. Roberts said as he picked up his napkin, folded it until it formed a perfect square and dabbed it across his lips with the utmost care and precision. "It is undoubtedly the best one yet—just the right amount of tart and sweet." The slightest tug of his lips suggested a smile, but since he wasn't a man prone to exaggeration, it never quite turned into one.

Isabella stared. Was she really doomed to live out the remainder of her days with such a dandy? Mr. Roberts was unquestionably the most meticulous gentleman she'd ever encountered, not to mention the most polite and the most eloquent. In addition, he never, ever, did anything that might have been considered rash or unexpected, and while there were probably many who would think these attributes highly commendable, Isabella couldn't help but consider him the most mundane person of her acquaintance. She sighed. Was it really too much to ask that the gentleman who planned to make her his wife might look at her with just a hint of interest? Yet the only thing that Mr. Roberts had ever looked at with even the remotest bit of interest was the slice of apple pie upon his plate.

Isabella wasn't sure which was more frustrating—that he lacked any sense of humor or that he valued pie more than he did her. The sense of humor was something she'd only just noticed recently. Unable to imagine that anyone might be lacking in such regard and taking his inscrutable demeanor into account, she had always assumed that he favored sarcasm. This, it turned out, was not the case. Mr. Roberts simply didn't find anything funny, nor did he see a point in trying to make other people laugh. This was definitely something that Isabella found herself worrying about.

"You are too kind, Mr. Roberts," her mother replied in response to his praise. "Perhaps you would care for another piece?"

Mr. Roberts's eyes widened, but rather than accept the offer as he clearly wished to do, he said instead, "Thank you for your generosity, but one must never overindulge in such things, Mrs. Chilcott, especially not if one desires to keep a lean figure."

Isabella squeaked.

"Are you quite all right, Miss Chilcott?" Mr. Roberts asked.

"Forgive me," Isabella said. "It was the tea—I fear it didn't agree with me."

Mr. Roberts frowned. "Do be careful, Miss Chilcott—it could have resulted in a most indelicate cough, not to mention a rather unpleasant experience for the rest of us."

Isabella allowed herself an inward groan. The truth of the matter was that she'd been forcing back a laugh. Really, what sort of man would admit to declining a piece of pie because he feared ruining his figure? It was absurd, and yet her mother had nodded as if nothing had ever made more sense to her. As for the threat of a cough . . . Isabella couldn't help but wonder how Mr. Roberts would fare in regards to their future children. He'd likely barricade himself in his study for the duration of their illnesses—all that sneezing and casting up of accounts would probably give him hives otherwise.

Her father suddenly said, "Have you heard the news?"

"That would certainly depend on which news you're referring to," Mr. Roberts remarked as he raised his teacup, stared into it for a moment and then returned it to its saucer.

"More tea, Mr. Roberts?" Isabella's mother asked, her hand already reaching for the teapot.

"Thank you—that would be most welcome."

Isabella waited patiently while Mr. Roberts told her mother that he would be very much obliged if she would ensure that this time, the cup be filled precisely halfway up in order to allow for the exact amount of milk that he required. She allowed herself another inward groan. He'd just begun explaining why two teaspoons of sugar constituted just the right quantity when Isabella decided that she'd had enough. "What news, Papa?" she blurted out, earning a smile from her father, a look of horror from her mother and a frown of disapproval from Mr. Roberts. A transformation Isabella found strangely welcome.

"Apparently," her father began, taking a careful sip of his tea while his wife served him another generous slice of apple pie, "the Duke of Kingsborough has decided to host the annual ball again."

"Good heavens," Isabella's mother breathed as she sank back against her chair. "It's been forever since they kept that tradition."

"Five years, to be exact," Isabella muttered. Everyone turned to stare at her with puzzled expressions. She decided not to explain but shrugged instead, then spooned a piece of pie into her mouth in order to avoid having to say anything further.

The truth of it was that the annual ball at Kingsborough Hall had always been an event she'd hoped one day to attend—ever since she was a little girl and had caught her first glimpse of the fireworks from her bedroom window. She hazarded a glance in Mr. Roberts's direction, knowing full well that a life with him would include nothing as spectacular as the Kingsborough Ball. In fact, she'd be lucky if it would even include a dance at the local assembly room from time to time. Probably not, for although the life she would share with Mr. Roberts promised to be one of comfort, he had made it abundantly clear that he did not enjoy social functions or dancing in the least.

Perhaps this was one of the reasons why he'd decided to attach himself to *her*—an act that she'd always found most curious. Surely he must have realized by now that they had very little in common, and given his current station in life, he could have formed a favorable connection to a far more prosperous family. Of course he would probably have had to attend a Season in London in order to make the acquaintance of such families, and his reluctance to do so certainly explained why he was presently sitting down to tea in her parlor instead of sending flowers to a proper lady of breeding.

Isabella had on more than one occasion brought the

issue regarding Mr. Roberts's displeasure for social-izing to her mother's attention, complaining that her future would consist of few diversions if she were to marry him, but her mother had simply pointed out that the only reason young ladies attended such events was with the direct purpose of drawing the attention of the gentlemen present. Once married, there would be little reason for Isabella to do so and consequently no point in engaging in anything other than the occasional tea party. And as if this had not been enough, her mother had added a long list of reasons why Isabella should be thankful that a man as respectable and affluent as Mr. Roberts had bothered to show her any consideration at all. It had been rather demeaning.

"Well, it's nice to see that they seem to be recover-ing from the death of the duke's father," Isabella heard her mother say.

"I couldn't agree more," Isabella's father said. "It must have been very difficult for them, given the long duration of his illness and all."

"Indeed," Mr. Roberts muttered without the slight-est alteration of his facial expression.

A moment of silence followed until Isabella's mother finally broke it by saying, "Now then, Mr. Roberts, tell us about that horse you were planning to buy the last time we saw you."

And that was the end of the conversation regarding the Kingsborough Ball—but it was far from the end of Isabella's dreams of attending. In fact, she didn't spare a single thought for anything else during the remainder of her tea, though she must have managed to nod and shake her head at all the right times, for nobody appeared to have noticed that her mind had exited the room.

"Was afternoon tea as delightful as always?" Jamie, Isabella's younger sister, asked when they settled into bed that evening. At thirteen years of age, she was a complete hoyden and just as mischievous as any boy her age might have been, getting into every scrape imaginable. After deliberately sneaking a frog into Mr. Roberts's jacket pocket three months earlier, she'd been barred from attending Sunday tea. Her punishment for the offense had included two weeks of confinement to her bedroom, as well as some choice words from Mr. Roberts himself. Needless to say, Jamie's approval of the man had long since dwindled.

"It was better, considering I was hardly aware of Mr. Roberts's presence at all."

Jamie scrunched her nose. "Honestly, Izzie, I don't know why you suffer the fellow. He has no sense of humor to speak of, is much too reserved to suit your vibrant character, not to mention that there's something really queer about him in general. I don't think you should marry him if he offers."

Isabella attempted a smile as she settled herself into bed, scooting down beneath the covers until she was lying on her side, facing her sister. They each had their own bedroom, but with the nights still cold, Jamie often snuck into Isabella's room so they could snuggle up together, talking about this and that until sleep eventually claimed them. "I have to think rationally about this, Jamie. Mama and Papa are struggling to keep food on the table, and there's also you to consider. I want a better life for you than this, with more choices than I've been afforded."

Jamie shook her head as well as she could, considering she was lying down. "I don't want you to sacrifice yourself for me. I'll never be able to forgive myself for being the cause of your unhappiness."

There were tears in her young eyes now that made Isabella's heart ache. Isabella loved her sister so dearly and knew that her sister loved her equally. "It's not just you, Jamie, but Mama and Papa as well. Mr. Roberts will ensure that they want for nothing."

"And in return, you will probably have to kiss him." Jamie made a face.

Isabella's hand flew up to whack her naughty sister playfully across the head. "What on earth do you know of such things?" Was there anything more appalling than talking with one's kid sister about kissing?

"Enough to assure you that you might want to think twice before giving that particular right to a man like him."

With a sigh, Isabella rolled back against her pillow and stared up at the ceiling. Jamie was right, of course, but what was Isabella to do? Her family's future depended on her seeing this through to the end. Really, what choice did she have?

"So, what did you daydream about this time?" Jamie asked, changing the subject entirely.

"What do you mean?"

"You said before that you barely noticed Mr. Roberts's presence during tea. I assume your thoughts must have been elsewhere."

"Oh!" Isabella sat up, turning herself so she could meet her sister's eyes. "The Kingsborough Ball. Papa says they're hosting a new one. Oh, Jamie, isn't it exciting!"

Jamie jumped up. "You have to attend."

"What?" It was preposterous—absurd—the most

wonderful idea ever. Isabella shook her head. She would not allow herself to entertain the notion. It would only lead to disappointment. "That's impossible," she said.

"Why?" The firm look in her sister's eyes dared her to list her reasons.

"Very well," Isabella said, humoring her. "I have not been invited, nor will I be."

"We'll sneak you in through the servant's entrance. Cousin Simon can help with that, since he works there."

Isabella rolled her eyes. Trust Jamie to have that problem already worked out. "I'm not an aristocrat—they will notice I don't belong," she countered.

Jamie shrugged. "From what you've told me, the Kingsborough Ball is always masked, is it not?"

"Well, yes, I suppose—"

"Then no one will notice." Jamie waved her hand and smiled smugly. "Do go on."

"I . . . I have no gown that I could possibly wear to such a function, and that is the deciding factor. No gown, no ball."

"Ah, but you are wrong about that," her sister said, meeting her gaze with such cheeky resolve that Isabella couldn't help but feel a growing sense of apprehension. "There's always the one in the attic to consider, and I'll wager—"

"Absolutely not," Isabella said. She knew exactly which gown her sister was referring to, for it was quite possibly the most exquisite thing Isabella had ever seen. It had also given rise to a string of questions that would probably never be answered, like how such a gown had found its way into the Chilcott home in the first place. Fearful of the answer and of the punishment they'd likely have received if their parents had discovered they'd been playing in a part of the house that had been off limits, they'd made a pact to keep their knowledge of the gown a secret.

"But Izzie—"

"Jamie, I know that you mean well, but it's time I faced my responsibilities as an adult. The Kingsborough Ball is but a dream that will never amount to anything more."

"A lifelong dream, Izzie," her sister protested. Jamie took Isabella's hand and held it in her own. "Wouldn't you like to see what it's like living it?"

It was tempting of course, but still, wearing a gown that had in all likelihood been acquired under dubious circumstances, as it was one her parents couldn't possibly afford, would be harebrained. Wouldn't it? After all, it had probably been hidden away for a reason. Her mother had never mentioned that it existed, which was also strange considering it would make an excellent wedding gown for Isabella when she married Mr. Roberts. No, there was something about that gown and its history. Isabella was certain of it, for the more she considered it, the more wary she grew of what she might discover if her questions were one day answered.

In any event, she couldn't possibly wear it to the Kingsborough Ball. Could she? She would be betraying her parents' trust by doing so. It would certainly be the most daring thing she'd ever done. And yet . . . this would be her last chance for a fairy-tale experience. Closing her eyes, she made her decision. She would do it. Isabella would seize a moment for herself—one night of adventure that would have to last a lifetime. She only hoped that she wouldn't one day look back on it with longing and regret.

Chapter 3

"Lady Frompton! So good of you to join us this evening," Anthony said, completing his salutation with an elegant bow. He straightened himself so he could shake hands with the gentleman at her side. "And Lord Frompton, there's a cigar for you in the gaming room."

"The card tables have been readied, Your Grace?" the old earl asked, his voice muffled as he leaned a little closer to Anthony.

"Indeed they have, my lord," Anthony replied quietly.

Lord Frompton gave a nod of approval before taking his wife by the arm and leading her inside the ballroom, allowing Anthony to welcome his next guest. It was a tedious affair, not to mention a tiring one. Standing up like this while two hundred people paraded past him was *not* his idea of fun. His back ached and his feet were practically begging for him to remove his shoes. They looked good—all shiny and black—but Lord, did they hurt! He tried to ignore it as he greeted the Earl and Countess of Rockly and considered his mother, who stood beside him as regal as ever. She looked radiant in a stunning creation of burgundy silk and without the slightest hint of fatigue in either her posture or features.

Pulling himself together, Anthony smiled at the Rocklys' five daughters, who were presently staring up at him as if their eyelids had been pulled to the back of their heads. It was flattering, of course, in a peculiar sort of way, though Anthony could have done with less snickering on their part. He smiled back at them, complimented the ribbons they'd chosen for their hair and had promised them each a dance by the time they followed their parents to the ballroom.

"It looks like a smashing success," Casper Goodard, Anthony's longtime friend, said as he came to stand across from Anthony after all the guests had arrived. There were so many that there was only room for the closest friends and family to stay at Kingsborough Hall. The rest would either journey home the same evening, depending on how far they had to travel, or remain at one of the other estates in the area as overnight guests.

"Mama definitely put a lot of time and effort into outdoing all the previous balls she's ever hosted."

"I take it this explains the carriage that's shaped like a pumpkin?"

Anthony nodded and tried not to smile too much. When his mother had told him that she had selected the theme of *Cendrillon* for her ball, he'd thought it a novel idea. He never would have imagined that she would go so far as to have a special carriage designed for the occasion. The vehicle (which had thankfully *not* been fastened to any horses) offered a place for people to sit while a sketch artist drew their portraits. "Did you happen to see the glass slipper?" Anthony asked as he nodded toward the refreshment table, where a dainty shoe stood fashioned in ice.

Casper nodded. "She's certainly invested herself in this affair, hasn't she? It's all rather practical, really, now that I think of it. Don't young ladies adore fairy tales—all that romance with a prince and so forth?"

Anthony smiled. "Are you suggesting that we use this to our advantage?"

"You must admit that it's a wonderful conversation starter."

"Certainly, but I have already promised to dance with five young ladies this evening, so I'm really not in need of any more female company. You know that I cannot flee the ballroom, but I am doing whatever I can to avoid eye contact with any more eager mamas."

Yes, he was hoping that making the acquaintance of some of the young ladies present might lead to an attachment, but that did not mean that he wished to exhaust himself by participating in each and every dance—especially when he wasn't all that fond of dancing to begin with.

"If that is the case, then I really must suggest that you try a little harder. Lady Snowdon has just cut across the entire ballroom with her daughter in tow—the one with the limp, not the other one. She's bearing down on us as we speak."

"Lady Georgina?"

"The very one," Casper confirmed.

Well in that case, there was nothing for it, Anthony decided. He would simply have to dance with one more lady, because there was no bloody way that he was going to turn down Lady Georgina. The poor woman had suffered enough rejections thanks to her mother.

Really, Lady Snowdon ought to know better than to subject her daughter to the constant scrutiny of others. From what he knew of Lady Georgina, she was a lovely person, but the world was a cruel place with too many people looking to mock those they deemed inferior.

Taking a deep breath, Anthony closed his eyes for a moment before turning around to face the ladies in question. They were approaching at quite an alarming speed—Lady Snowdon looking as though she would not hesitate to push aside anyone who happened to step in her way, while her daughter kept doing an awkward hop and slide in order to keep pace.

"Your Grace," Lady Snowdon gasped as she came to a halt before him. "I hope you will forgive us for being late, but we were forced to have one of our carriage wheels changed just as we were ready to set out."

"That's quite all right, Lady Snowdon—I would have done the same had I found myself in your position. It's always best to keep one's safety in mind."

"Oh, indeed it is."

"I see that you brought Lady Georgina along with you this evening," Anthony said as he offered Lady Snowdon's daughter a smile. The young woman, who wasn't all that young anymore (rapidly approaching her thirtieth year, if memory served), attempted a curtsy. Anthony bowed before adding, "And your husband, the earl? Is he here too?"

"Yes, yes, I believe he's having a word with your dear mama," Lady Snowdon replied. "Georgina and I were speaking to her as well, but then I spotted *you* and well . . . we simply had to come right over and thank you for inviting us here this evening—so kind of you."

"Think nothing of it," Anthony replied. He gestured toward Casper, who had otherwise kept completely silent during the exchange, no doubt in the hope of going unnoticed. Well, Anthony wasn't about to allow that to happen and said, "Have you perhaps had the pleasure of making the acquaintance of my very good friend, Mr. Goodard?"

Lady Snowdon's eyes narrowed ever so slightly, and then she turned her head in Casper's direction until . . . "Oh, I say!"

Anthony was finding it damn near impossible to keep a straight face. Apparently the poor woman had been so focused on *him* that she'd failed to notice the man he was with—a man many a young miss had claimed to be the handsomest man they'd ever seen. It wasn't something that had ever stood in the way of their friendship though. Anthony was certain that it had always bothered Casper more than it had him, but with his blonde hair and blue eyes, Casper was the sort of man who invariably turned heads. In short, he could probably have had any woman he wished regardless of the fact that he lacked a title.

"Ladies," Casper said as he reached for Lady Georgina's hand first and placed a kiss upon her knuckles. He repeated the gesture with her mother, who immediately turned a bright shade of pink.

Hoping to bring them all back to level ground, Anthony made the suggestion that he knew Lady Snowdon would try and coax out of him. He hated groveling, though, and decided therefore to avoid her pleas on her daughter's behalf altogether. "Lady Georgina. Would you do me the honor of dancing a quadrille with me?"

"Certainly, Your Grace," Lady Georgina replied,

looking terribly bashful as she dropped her gaze to the floor and shifted uneasily from side to side.

And then, much to Anthony's surprise, Casper chimed in. "If you still have room on your dance card, Lady Georgina, I would also appreciate the opportunity to dance with you—a waltz, perhaps?"

Lady Georgina's gaze snapped back up to stare at Casper in wonder while her mother let out a squeal of delight beside her and clapped her hands together for emphasis. "That is very kind of you, Mr. Goodard. Thank you."

And then the two women took their leave—Lady Snowdon undoubtedly eager to prepare her daughter for the big moment ahead of her. Anthony turned to Casper. "Feeling charitable?"

Casper shrugged and took a sip of his champagne. "Not particularly. Actually, I'm not sure what came over me other than that I felt a need to stop her mother from making things worse for her."

Anthony knew precisely what he meant, for he had felt the exact same way the few times he'd happened to find himself in Lady Snowdon's presence. He was just about to make another comment to that effect when he caught a glimpse of a woman edging her way along the periphery of the room until she came to a halt beside a pillar on the far side of the dance floor. Her face was turned slightly away from him, so it was difficult to get a proper look at her with all the people that kept blocking his line of vision, yet something about her caught his interest—she looked stranded. It was most peculiar, really, because she appeared to be dressed elegantly enough, yet instinct told him she didn't quite belong. It must have been in the way she carried herself—she simply didn't possess the same degree of aloofness as the rest of the guests.

Like Lady Snowdon and her daughter, she must have arrived late, for he had not seen her in the receiving line—he would have remembered if he had. And then she turned her face toward him and smiled, a smile so full of inner purity and goodness that for a moment he forgot to breathe. "Casper," he muttered, jutting his chin in the mystery woman's direction. "Who is that?"

"Who?" Casper asked, straining his neck as he tried to find the person to whom Anthony was referring. "There are a lot of people present—you'll have to be more specific."

"The woman over there by the pillar, just to the left of the orchestra—the one in the yellow gown."

Casper moved his head a bit and then his eyes suddenly widened. "I've no idea, Anthony, but if you don't ask her to dance, then I will." He frowned as he turned to face his friend. "Forget what I said—I'll ask her to dance regardless of whether or not you do."

Anthony was just about to protest when he felt someone pat him on the shoulder. "You're looking sharp as always." Turning his head, Anthony found Winston smiling back at him.

"A miracle, really," Anthony remarked as he stopped a passing footman so Winston could take a glass of champagne. "I've never understood why jackets have to be so bloody snug. If I had it my way I'd have a looser one made, though I do believe my valet would have an apoplectic fit."

"It's not so bad," Casper said. "One does get used to it, you know."

Anthony found himself tugging at his cravat. "It's

restrictive, that's what it is. I'll wager that most gentlemen here are finding it a nuisance, but they're too cowardly to do anything about it—keeping up appearances and all that. In fact, I think I'm going to take my jacket off. I'll be the most comfortable man here and consequently the envy of one and all."

"Don't you dare!" came a soft female voice. Anthony groaned. It was Louise, who'd made her approach together with her husband. "You know how important this is to Mama—you will not cause a scandal by allowing the guests to see you in a state of undress."

A state of undress?

"It's just a jacket, Louise. I would still be wearing my shirt and cravat." He turned to her husband. "What say you, Huntley?"

Glancing at his wife, whose firm expression suggested that she'd taken it upon herself to defend the laws of fashion come what may, Huntley replied, "I believe I must concur with her ladyship on this, Kingsborough." He leaned a bit closer to Anthony and whispered, "One must pick one's battles wisely."

"I heard that!"

"Perhaps that was my intention," Huntley said, eyeing his wife, whose countenance had turned to one of suspicion.

Anthony shook his head and turned to Winston. "Where's Sarah? I haven't seen her since the two of you arrived earlier in the day—she hasn't taken ill, has she?"

"Oh no, not at all," Winston replied. "She was detained by Lady Deerford at the refreshment table. With little desire to hear about her ladyship's latest acquisition, I wasted no time in excusing myself, so here I am."

"Latest acquisition?" Casper asked. "Is she perhaps a collector?"

"Surely you must have heard," Anthony said, surprised that such a bit of information might have slipped by his friend.

Casper responded with a blank stare.

"It doesn't look as though he has," Winston murmured, sounding intrigued.

"That hardly seems possible," said Louise as she turned to her husband. "How could he not have heard?"

Huntley shrugged.

"Heard what?" Casper hissed, looking all but ready to pummel the lot of them if that was what it would take to get the information out.

Anthony wondered how much longer he could keep a straight face. He and his siblings were notorious for irking Casper in precisely this fashion—a skill they'd perfected with many years of practice. "Very well," he relented, taking pity on his friend. "Lady Deerford collects dolls."

"Oh."

Anthony frowned, not in the least bit satisfied with Casper's response. Clearly he would have to elaborate. "I don't believe you understand—Lady Deerford is reported to have over one thousand dolls. She doesn't just collect them, Casper, she obsesses over them—buys expensive gifts for them and such. Frankly one has to wonder about her ladyship's sanity, but then again, I do believe she suffered a terrible blow when her daughter went missing all those years ago."

"Well, that would explain it," Casper said as he tossed back the last of his champagne and gazed out at the crowd. "It looks as though the orchestra's getting ready for the next set—isn't it time for you to find one of your partners, Anthony? You'll never get through six dances in one evening at the rate you're going."

"Six dances?" Louise stared up at him in surprise. "But you don't even like to—"

"I'm the host, Louise. I have responsibilities tonight, and besides, I've no desire to disappoint Mama."

"That's very admirable," Winston said as he snatched another glass of champagne from a passing tray. "I do believe I'll help. Anyone particular you'd like me to ask?"

Seizing the opportunity to tease Casper, Anthony said, "There's a woman, just over there—the one in the yellow gown and the gold mask standing just to the left of the orchestra."

Casper moved as if to step forward, but Anthony held him back. "Ask her to dance, Winston, and while you're at it, find out who she is."

Winston's face brightened. "A mystery! I do so love a good mystery."

As he crossed the ballroom, Casper turned to Anthony with a glower. "You're a fiend, you know."

Anthony nodded. "You're probably right, but then again, I did see her first, and with looks like those"—he made a gesture that encompassed Casper's entire figure—"you have to admit that it's only fair of you to give me a chance to catch her interest before you make a move."

"And yet the fact that you're suddenly so keen only makes me want her more," Casper sighed.

It was Anthony's turn to glower.

"Besides, you can't possibly make time for her with six dances ahead of you. While *I,* on the other hand, have only the one with Lady Georgina." Casper smiled his signature smile—the one that was meant to disarm even the most stubborn lady. "That ought to give me a two-hour advantage with our mystery woman."

"You wouldn't!"

"Best get on with it is all I can say." Turning toward Louise, who'd been following the exchange with rapt interest, he gave a slight bow, said something humorous yet meaningless to Huntley and then sauntered off as if he'd been King Midas and everyone present his subjects.

Anthony watched him go, finding it impossible not to smile. It was just like the good old days at Eton when the two of them had placed the oddest bets against each other.

"The man has a point, you know," Louise said a moment later, "though I would encourage you to consider the Hampstead move—it's a classic."

"Louise, you're a veritable gem!" If it hadn't been for Huntley, Anthony would probably have picked her up and twirled her about to show his enthusiasm, but some things just weren't done when one was in the presence of the lady's husband and with all eyes of the *ton* preserving each false move to memory—not even if you happened to be her brother. So instead he said, "I'll ask Cook to make crêpes for you every day while you're here."

Louise smiled. "Just best Casper and I'll be happy enough."

"Why, Louise, it almost sounds as if you hold a grudge."

"Croquet, six years ago—that's all I'm going to say on the matter."

"And here I was thinking you'd forgiven him for that long ago." Anthony turned to Huntley, who was looking terribly confused. "Goodard indirectly caused my sister to break her ankle one year, leaving her bedridden for the entire summer."

"And you've been waiting all this time to exact your revenge?" Huntley asked as he took a small step away from his wife.

Louise smiled. "One ought to pick such a moment carefully."

Huntley's eyes grew wide. "Remind me never to cross you, my dear." He suddenly frowned. "What exactly happened, anyway?"

"I'll tell you all about that later, but it basically involved a hole and a squirrel." Huntley's mouth opened as if he planned to ask for further explanation, but Louise gave him no chance as she quickly turned her attention back to Anthony and said, "Now get a move on, will you? Your competitor's no novice, so unless you hurry up, he'll undoubtedly depart for Gretna Green with your prize before you have so much as a chance to speak with her."

With one last tug at his cravat, Anthony handed his empty glass to a footman and went in search of his first dance partner.

Chapter 4

Whatever her imaginings, nothing could possibly have surpassed the opulence that greeted her as she entered the Kingsborough ballroom. Ladies dressed in the finest silk and lace, their gems sparkling beneath the thousands of candles that filled three massive chandeliers. Gentlemen garbed in elegant evening black, their shoes buffed and their cravats tied to perfection, all carrying themselves with the utmost grace.

Spotting a vacant corner close to the orchestra, Isabella moved toward it. She was in no hurry to socialize just yet, for that would mean lying, and while she was prepared to do so, she was more than happy to wait a while as she enjoyed the scenery. No one was dancing yet—they all looked as if they were far too busy chatting with one another, creating a steady hum of voices that rose to compete with the soft rise and fall of the music.

Allowing her gaze to roam, Isabella noticed that there were large vases filled with daffodils and hyacinths strategically placed throughout the room. Even the refreshment table boasted a magnificent floral arrangement of pinks, purples and yellows. Isabella couldn't help but smile. She loved daffodils, for they were such happy flowers—a true testament to spring.

"Excuse me," came a voice from behind her right shoulder.

Isabella jumped. She'd been so engrossed in her own thoughts that she'd failed to notice that someone had walked up behind her. Turning around, she came face-to-face with a sweet-faced lady who was in possession of a very welcoming smile. She was not alone however. Beside her stood a dark-haired gentleman who looked equally pleasant.

"I do hope you will forgive me for startling you," said the woman, "but we couldn't help but notice that you were standing here all alone, and immediately decided that you might enjoy some company. I am Lady Winston, by the way, and this is my husband."

"I'm very pleased to make your acquaintance," Isabella replied. "My name is Miss Smith." She'd deliberately chosen one of the commonest names that England had ever known as her pseudonym in the hopes that it would fit at least one of the names on the guest list.

"Of Flemmington?" Lord Winston asked.

Flemmington?

Isabella had never heard of a place by that name, but it did appear to offer her the perfect alibi, so she quickly nodded and said, "Yes, that's it—Flemmington."

A momentary look of surprise registered on Lady Winston's face, but it quickly vanished again as her husband continued with, "I've never had the opportunity to visit it myself, but I've heard that it's particularly lovely this time of year."

"Winston," said his wife. "I don't think—"

"The lake is rumored to be surrounded by crocuses, and there are supposedly boats that you can hire if you wish to sail out to the small island in the middle for a picnic."

"How romantic," said Lady Winston.

"Have you ever done that, Miss Smith?" asked Lord Winston. "Gone rowing on Flemmington Lake?"

What a relief that this was a masked ball, for Isabella could feel the heat rise to her face out of sheer and utter mortification. She'd always hated liars, and she hated herself for standing there now and being so blatantly dishonest with these people. Well, at least she could be honest about taking a boat out on Flemmington Lake. She shook her head. "No, I'm afraid not."

Lord Winston frowned. "Do you not swim?"

His question was rewarded with a sharp nudge in the ribs from Lady Winston. "What?" he asked his wife. "It's a perfectly legitimate question in light of the fact that Miss Smith has never been out on Flemmington Lake before."

"As a matter of fact, I quite enjoy swimming," Isabella said. Perhaps she should have stopped there, but feeling the need for more honesty, she added, "And I've been in a rowboat before as well—just not on Flemmington Lake."

It looked as if Lord Winston might have had more to say on the matter, but he was cut off by a petite, older woman who approached their small group with a "There you are, Winston. I was wondering what happened to you."

"Mama!" Lord Winston stepped aside to give way to his mother. He then turned back to face Isabella. "You are acquainted with the Duchess of Kingsborough, of course?"

The Duchess of Kingsborough? Good heavens!

Isabella had never before longed for a quicker means of escape than she did right now. Her eyes darted from one individual to the other. "Then you are . . . ," she said, looking at Lord Winston. "And you must be . . . ," she continued, her gaze shifting to Lady Winston. "I mean . . . I . . . er . . ."

The duchess frowned a little and said, "I don't believe I—"

"This is Miss Smith," said Lord Winston. "Of Flemmington."

The duchess's frown deepened and she opened her mouth to speak, only to be cut off once again by her son as he said, "Such a delightful town, though it's really a shame that Miss Smith has never been out on the lake." He then changed the subject of conversation entirely. "Sarah, didn't you mention that you were hoping to ask Mama for some advice in regards to the governess?"

Lady Winston nodded. "Indeed I did."

"Right," Lord Winston continued cheerily. He returned his attention to Isabella. "Are you interested in the subject of governesses, Miss Smith, or would you prefer to dance?"

There was no need for Lord Winston to ask twice for her to know the answer to that question, but how could she possibly say that she would rather dance than participate in the duchess's and Lady Winston's forthcoming conversation?

Thankfully, she was saved from saying anything at all by the duchess herself. "I shan't take the least bit offense if you would rather dance," she said with a kind smile.

"There," Lord Winston exclaimed. "You have been

granted permission by the highest authority." He then performed a most elegant bow. "Miss Smith, would you care to dance the next set with me?"

Unable to keep from smiling, Isabella nodded and said, "I would love to, my lord—if your wife approves."

It was Lady Winston's turn to smile. "I do, Miss Smith, for my husband simply loves to make me dance with him to the point of exhaustion. I'm indebted to you for allowing me a moment's reprieve."

Lord Winston leaned closer to his wife and said, "Fear not, Sarah. The first dance of the evening has yet to commence, so I promise you that there will be ample opportunity for you to partner with me later." He then winked at her, offered Isabella his arm and began leading her in the general direction of the dance floor, saying over his shoulder, "Oh, and don't forget to tell Mama about Flemmington—I don't believe she's very familiar with it."

As evenings went, this had to be the strangest. Two hours had passed since her arrival at Kingsborough Hall—a feat she'd accomplished, just as Jamie had suggested, with the help of her cousin Simon. He'd met her by the stables at a designated hour and led her through a back entrance that had bypassed the entire receiving line. None of the servants had stopped them to ask questions—they'd all been too busy attending to the many guests.

No more than half an hour after her arrival, Isabella had met not only the Duchess of Kingsborough's son but the duchess herself as well. It was incredible. Yes, there had been a moment when Isabella had been sure the dowager duchess would call her bluff, but Lord Winston had averted that catastrophe with his enthusiasm for Flemmington. Heaven help her but she'd never talked to someone for so long about a place she'd never been to, never mind heard of before.

She regretted the lie, but what choice did she have? If she told the truth—that she wasn't even gentry but merely the daughter of a carriage driver—they'd waste no time in tossing her out on her backside. Of this she was certain.

Thankfully, her appearance was serving to persuade them that she belonged, because however fantastic the gown she was wearing had looked in the dim candle glow of her room, it looked even more incredible now in the brightly lit ballroom. Heading toward the refreshment table after finishing yet another reel, Isabella was just about to pick up a glass of lemonade when a deep voice gave her pause. "You're quite the success this evening."

Turning slightly, she found herself gazing at a face more handsome than any she'd ever seen before. Her breath caught in her throat and she felt her cheeks grow warm. "I . . . er . . ." He looked precisely like the sort of trouble her mother had always warned her to stay away from, and the fact that he'd approached her without being formally introduced to her first only confirmed this.

"Mr. Goodard at your service." He smiled, and Isabella couldn't help but admire his beauty. But then he looked beyond where she stood, frowned and muttered, "Blast!"

Isabella instinctively turned her head to see what had caused the outburst, only to find yet another gentleman striding toward them with quick determination. His gaze was intense, his mouth drawn tight as if ready to start a quarrel, his hair dark and slightly ruffled, and his cravat in severe danger of falling into disarray.

Isabella felt her stomach tighten. Of the two, there was no doubt that Mr. Goodard was the handsomer one, if one favored the more classical and well-polished features. But Isabella had had enough of that in the form of Mr. Roberts. She was sick of it, in fact. The man approaching, on the other hand, appeared to be everything Mr. Roberts wasn't, and Isabella's pulse quickened in response.

"I never would have imagined you'd stoop so low as to apply the Hampstead move—especially given the fact that *I* invented it," Mr. Goodard said a bit too nonchalantly for Isabella's liking, since the other gentleman in question looked eager to engage in an altercation.

"You were determined to have your way, so I felt the need to delay you a little."

Mr. Goodard frowned. "At least you had the decency to pick some very agreeable ladies for your little scheme."

The other gentleman chuckled. "We are friends, are we not?" He didn't wait for a reply but turned to Isabella instead, bowing ever so slightly as he gazed into her eyes. Lord help her, she was in trouble. "I hope you will forgive the lack of etiquette and allow me to introduce myself. I am your host, the Duke of Kingsborough."

The time had come for Isabella to find a chair and sit down before she collapsed on the floor in a dead faint. Before her stood not only the most perfect man she'd ever seen—a man who appeared to be everything Mr. Roberts wasn't—but he was a duke as well, and he had bowed before her as if she'd been a princess. Heaven above, she ought to curtsy. So she did—as graciously as she could manage given the flummoxed state she was in.

Rising to her full height again, she realized that there was only one flaw to this magnificently spectacular moment—she was a nobody, and dukes did not associate with nobodies.

"Miss Smith, is it?" the Duke of Kingsborough asked as he reached for a glass of lemonade and offered it to her. "I believe my brother had the pleasure of dancing with you earlier."

"Yes, Your Grace." The duke said nothing further, so Isabella decided to add, "I also enjoyed a conversation with your mother and sister-in-law—two very lovely ladies."

The edge of Kingsborough's mouth edged upward to form the beginnings of a smile. "I'm glad you think so."

"Bloody hell."

Isabella's eyes widened, and Kingsborough's face grew taut. He turned toward Mr. Goodard. "Such language has no place in a lady's presence."

"My apologies," Mr. Goodard, said, taking her hand in his and placing a kiss upon the knuckles. "It's just that I suddenly realize I've lost my chance."

Isabella wasn't sure what he meant by that, and she was afforded little time to ponder it before he took his leave and Kingsborough in turn asked her to dance. Everything from that point onward happened in a daze. It was as if she'd been drifting toward the dance floor on puffy clouds, her whole body humming with anticipation while her heart hammered against her chest and her stomach tickled.

The music started, and Isabella realized that the dance they were about to engage in was a waltz. She almost lost her nerve. She'd never danced one before, and from what she'd heard, it was the most scandalous dance there was. She couldn't possibly go through with it. If her mother somehow found out . . . Oh, dear Lord, why on earth did she have to think of her mother at a moment like this? Her hands began to tremble and she felt ill, but then a thought struck her. "From what I understand, a lady requires permission to dance the waltz, Your Grace. Unfortunately, I have no such permission. Perhaps we could take a turn about the room instead?"

Taking her hand in his, the duke pulled her toward him. Heat swept through her body in a torrent until her mouth grew uncomfortably dry, and she found herself licking her lips. Kingsborough's eyes widened. "Then it is fortunate that we are in the country, where people are less inclined to notice. *And* this is a masquerade— they may not even recognize you."

He had her there, but she decided to ignore the point, saying instead, "But they are the same people who will flock to London for the start of the Season, are they not? Propriety and etiquette are the very backbone of the world they live in. If there is just the slightest bit of deviation they will surely notice—you cannot possibly think otherwise."

"I never said they wouldn't notice, merely that they would be less inclined. Besides, I don't believe my mother invited any of Almack's patronesses, so nobody will be the wiser until they happen upon them in another week or two, at which point our dance will be quite forgotten."

"You are certain of this?"

The duke sighed. "Miss Smith, if I were you, I'd concentrate a bit more on enjoying the dance rather than worrying about everyone else's opinion of you. Besides, it's unlikely that anyone in Flemmington will care."

Isabella gasped. Not only had she not realized she'd been twirling around the dance floor with the duke holding her firmly in place (how this was possible, she couldn't imagine) but she also thought it a bit harsh of him to suggest that her family and friends wouldn't care if they discovered she'd participated in an un-authorized waltz—even though they did come from Moxley instead of Flemmington, but that was beside the point.

"I can see that I've offended you, for which I'm sorry." He tightened his hold on her. "I only meant that as strict as the rules of Society are, they do tend to be a bit more lax and forgiving in the country."

"I see." Isabella tried to relax. After all, she might as well, because it really was unlikely that her mother and Mr. Roberts would ever find out. She was there to enjoy herself, and she'd been given the opportunity to do so in the company of a duke. Surely she had to be the envy of all the other ladies present, and that thought alone was enough to make her worries slip away. Tilting her head back a little so she could look up at the duke, Isabella said, "What's the Hampstead move?"

A slow smile snuck its way across his face while his eyes brightened with boyish mischief. "It's a means of distraction that my very good friend Mr. Goodard performed for the first time five years ago at the Hampstead Ball—hence the name."

"And what does it entail, if you don't mind my asking."

Kingsborough's smile widened as he swept her past the orchestra. "I'm not so sure it would be wise to tell you."

"Why ever not?"

He dipped his head to whisper in her ear. "Because it would disclose far more about my intentions toward you than I am prepared to at this point."

A shiver raced down Isabella's spine, all the way to the tips of her toes. The man was speaking of intentions now—toward her, no less. The sentiment was certainly flattering, not only because he was a duke but also because she liked him. She couldn't help herself, really—not just because of his looks, which were so elementally delicious that Isabella wished she could feast her eyes on him forever, but because he didn't seem aloof or arrogant but rather grounded instead. It was refreshing—*he* was refreshing—and the carefree way in which he carried himself only served to make Mr. Roberts's neatly folded handkerchiefs and perfectly groomed hair look so much more ridiculous.

Isabella bit back a groan. She was meant to marry Mr. Roberts one day. Even if he had yet to propose, the point was clear. He was much too proper to allow himself to become a permanent fixture in her parents' parlor without eventually doing what everyone had come to expect. All of this—the glistening ballroom and the man whose company she was presently enjoying—would have to end the instant she returned home. She was dancing with a duke, for heaven's sake!

A man so far above her on the social ladder that there was no point at all in making the wish that was starting to form in her mind.

If only . . .

"Are you all right?"

Isabella blinked. How long had she been woolgathering? "Forgive me," she said, "my thoughts were elsewhere."

"I don't suppose you'd be willing to share them with me?" The smile he gave her as he spoke was of the more crooked variety, dimpling his cheeks in a way that made him look terribly roguish.

For just about the millionth time since making his acquaintance only ten minutes earlier, Isabella felt her heart flutter in her chest.

Trouble was the word that came to mind.

She knew that whatever dreams she dared entertain of a man like Kingsborough courting her would remain exactly that—a dream. As regrettable as it was, she would have to be honest if she wished to avoid heartache, or at least as honest as she could be under the circumstances. "Actually, I was wondering what my fiancé would say if he were to discover that I danced with a dashing duke this evening." There, she'd told him about Mr. Roberts and would now be able to enjoy the rest of the evening with a clear conscience and without worrying that the duke might show more interest in her than he already had. He would do the honorable thing and walk away—she was certain of this.

But the dance had not yet ended, and rather than let her go, the duke tightened his hold on her and frowned. "Fiancé?"

"Yes." The tone of his voice did not fill her with the

confidence she'd hoped for but rather with despair. "I thought it best to inform you that I am practically engaged to a very respectable gentleman—an entrepreneur, to be exact."

The crooked smile returned to Kingsborough's lips. " 'Practically'?" Isabella had recognized her error the instant she'd spoken, but it was too late for her to take that one word back now. "Then you're really not engaged at all, are you?"

Swallowing hard, she tried to think of something else to say that might deter him. She could of course tell him the absolute truth about her identity. She'd surely find herself escorted off the premises without further ado, but at least it would save her from the risk of getting to know the duke further, from becoming more fascinated than she already was and, most importantly, from the prospect of falling in love with a man she could never, ever hope to marry.

It was the wise thing to do, and yet she found herself doing quite the opposite. "I suppose not—not yet, that is." Oh, how she wished she could give herself a good whack. Was she a complete idiot? And the way it sounded to her own ears . . . good heavens, but Kingsborough would have every right to think she was flirting with him. It was likely her most embarrassing moment to date.

The duke raised an eyebrow as the music faded and they glided to a stop. "Not yet," he murmured, his smile turning into something of a wolfish grin. Was he laughing at her or pondering the thought of devouring her whole? Neither prospect was in the least bit reassuring.

Dropping a curtsy in response to his bow, Isabella accepted the arm he offered her and allowed him to lead her off to the side. She was desperately wracking her brain for an excuse to escape his company and had just considered telling him she needed to visit the ladies' retirement room when he leaned a bit closer to her and said, "It's a lovely evening outside. Would you care to join me for a stroll on the terrace?"

Isabella knew she ought to refuse, make her excuse and leave his company immediately. There was just one massive flaw to her plan—the lack of will to do so as he stood there, gazing into her eyes and waiting for her response as if the stability of the planet hinged on her agreement. If only he knew that her agreement might actually cause it to fall off its axis.

Taking a deep breath, she decided to ignore her better judgment and do what she wanted to do instead—however temporary it might be and however much she might regret it later. This was her chance to experience the fairy-tale magic she'd wanted for so long, and with the Duke of Kingsborough unwittingly playing the part of her own Prince Charming. "Yes," she said, her stomach working itself into a tight knot in response to the look of pleasure that swept over his handsome face. "I would like that very much."

And as he guided her out of the ballroom to the drone of music and laughter, Isabella couldn't help but imagine that it was the sound of the fates mocking her.

Chapter 5

It was warmer than usual for that time of year, and with not even as much as a breeze to speak of, it was downright pleasant being outside—especially when compared to the stifling heat of the ballroom. In fact, Anthony had to admit that his cravat and his jacket didn't bother him nearly as much now as they had earlier. He eyed his companion, realizing that she might have been finding it chillier than he, what with her flimsy evening gown and no shawl to speak of. "If it's too cold for you . . . ," he began, but he stopped when she shook her head.

"Not at all—it's quite a relief actually." She nodded toward the ballroom. "As spectacular as it is in there, I'm happy to be able to get a bit of fresh air."

"All the same, I do hope you'll let me know as soon as you wish to venture back inside."

She smiled brightly and Anthony felt his spirits soar. "I shall do so without hesitation," she promised. "You have my word on it."

It was Anthony's turn to smile as he turned toward the far end of the terrace and began leading her forward at a leisurely pace.

Who was this woman he was talking to, and what was it about her exactly that captivated him so? He pondered the question for a moment, but, truth was, he had no idea. What he *did* know, however, was who she wasn't. She was not Miss Smith—or at least he didn't believe her to be—and she did not herald from a town by the name of Flemmington. He could easily drive himself mad speculating about the matter for the remainder of the evening, but he decided to opt for a much easier solution instead.

Anthony stopped in his tracks, bringing her to a standstill as well. He turned his head just enough to gaze down at her. "Tell me, Miss Smith, who are you really?"

He'd never seen anyone pale so quickly before. "It's quite all right—there's no need for alarm," he felt compelled to say for fear that she might actually collapse in a dead faint. "It's just that there was nobody on the guest list by the name of Smith, and with Flemmington being a fictitious location conjured by my brother's overactive imagination, the fact that you readily agreed that this was where you were from only suggests that you've no desire for anyone to know your true identity. Am I correct?"

She stared back at him for what must surely have been a full minute before her mouth eventually closed. She looked up at him from beneath her long lashes and gave an ever so slight, almost imperceptible nod. "What will you do?" she asked.

"I shan't have you evicted," he said, realizing from her heavy sigh of relief that this was what she'd feared most. "After all, with your attire taken into consideration, you must at the very least be gentry—no lowborn person would ever be able to afford such a costly garment."

"I . . . er . . . ah . . ."

"Oh, I see," he continued, feeling the urge to tease her a little with the hopeful prospect of easing the tension that had descended upon them. "You are a noblewoman's stepdaughter, locked away for countless years and forced to tend to your stepsisters' every demand. But when you heard of the Kingsborough Ball, you stole one of their gowns and snuck away to attend. Am I right?"

"Right enough," she whispered, smiling just enough to encourage him to continue.

Anthony felt his heart quicken. He wasn't sure why, but her willingness to play along with this game sparked his interest in her even more. Of course he wondered who she really was—it was impossible for him not to—but for some curious reason, it didn't seem like the most important thing at the moment. Especially not if she had her own personal reasons for keeping her identity secret. After all, she had mentioned an *almost* fiancé. What if she simply didn't want the man to discover she'd come to the ball? It was a possibility.

They started down the steps. After a moment's silence, she asked, "Why am I still here? You know that I'm an imposter, so why have you not decided to have me escorted off the property? Why, even your brother and mother know the truth, and yet none of you have acted as I would have expected."

Reaching the bottom of the stairs, Anthony turned to look at her. It was difficult for him to discern her expression with the mask she was wearing, but he could see her eyes, and there was something so honest, yet desperate, hidden there that he found it impossible to look away. She was mesmerizing, and whatever reason she had for being there, he knew that it was vitally important to her, that attending the ball was not without risk. "You intrigue me," he said, for it was the truth.

"And yet I've just told you that I have a fiancé."

"An *almost* fiancé, I believe you said."

The spark in her eyes dwindled. "Nevertheless—I will marry him. This . . ." She swept her arm in a wide circle to indicate their extravagant surroundings. "It cannot possibly last."

Her voice held such a degree of sadness that Anthony felt his heart break for this lovely woman before him. Instinct told him to put his arms around her and hug her against him. He wanted to keep her safe, to prevent her from marrying someone she so obviously had no desire to marry. It must have been something her parents had arranged—a match that would serve all parties most favorably, except of course for Miss Smith. "Have you told your parents that the prospect of marrying this man makes you unhappy?"

She looked at him, wide-eyed. "How did you—"

With a gentle tug, he began leading her toward the pumpkin carriage, the gravel from the walkway crunching ever so softly beneath their feet as they approached the grass. "You may not have said, but it is clear in both your voice and the expression upon your face—your eyes especially."

She shook her head a little. "It's a very fortuitous match actually—one that will benefit my family greatly." She gave him an awkward smile and a shrug before adding, "We do what we must."

The idea of it made him sick to his stomach. Nobody deserved to marry out of obligation. A thought struck him. What if *he* courted her? He was a duke, so her parents should have no qualms about approving the match, and besides, he *was* looking for a bride. Of course, there was no way of knowing if Miss Smith would not just be going from one undesirable fiancé to another. They'd only just met, and there was no way of knowing that he stood a chance of making her any happier than the man she was currently attached to.

And of course there was the slight detail of not knowing who she was. If she was prepared to sacrifice herself on the marriage altar, then perhaps there was something severely wrong with her—something this other gentleman was prepared to overlook, or worse, something he was not yet aware of.

Anthony cast a sideways glance in Miss Smith's direction. Surely a woman with such delicate features, such clear blue eyes and such a delectable figure had to be perfect in every other regard. It was damn near impossible to imagine otherwise.

Sensing Miss Smith's desire to avoid any further discussion of the matter, Anthony suggested they have their portraits drawn by the sketch artist instead, and with an eager nod of approval from the lady, he helped her up into the pumpkin carriage after Lord Shelby and a woman who was *not* his wife had vacated it. Anthony wasn't usually one to judge (especially given his own history of rakish tendencies), but as it happened, he rather liked Lady Shelby and was therefore unable to keep himself from saying, "Ah, there you are, Shelby." He eyed the woman Shelby was with—a widow who was notorious for sleeping her way into gentlemen's pockets. "I say, is your wife aware of the company you keep, old chap?"

"No . . . er . . . I . . . that is . . . ," Lord Shelby sputtered.

Anthony served him a strict frown. "I suggest you part ways with one another here, and none shall be the wiser—I've no desire for a scandal to ruin an otherwise pleasant evening."

"I couldn't agree more, Your Grace," Shelby replied, abandoning the widow posthaste and hurrying off toward the house.

The widow gave Anthony a spiteful glare. "Was that really necessary?"

"I apologize for ruining your fun, Lady Trapleigh, but I suggest you keep your talons away from the married gentlemen this evening, or I shall have you removed from the property."

She gave him a condescending smirk—her eyes darting toward Miss Smith in a predatory fashion as she took a step toward him, reached out and ran a long finger down his chest. Miss Smith gasped and Lady Trapleigh chuckled. "Perhaps I should offer my services to you instead?"

Years ago he would probably have accepted her proposal with a wicked smile to boot, but things were different now—*he* was different—and he wanted to do whatever he could to honor the memory of his father. Additionally, he did not want Miss Smith to think poorly of him. Lowering his voice to a near whisper he said, "That you would even imagine I might be interested in whatever it is you have to offer is only a testament to your own poor judgment." Leaning toward her he added, "We both know that the only reason you were even invited here this evening is entirely out of respect to the friendship your late husband shared with my father."

Lady Trapleigh opened her mouth as if to speak but wisely closed it again before storming off, her anger evident in every aspect of her being. Anthony watched her go before turning back to Miss Smith. "My apologies," he said. He felt like an ass for administering such a set down in her presence, especially knowing that his father would have handled the situation with more class. "But I cannot abide people like that."

Miss Smith smiled as he sat down next to her across from the sketch artist. "Really, Your Grace? Judging from your tone, I was under the impression that you were quite fond of her."

Sarcasm, eh? A rare commodity in a young lady and one that Anthony definitely approved of. It was impossible for him not to laugh as he leaned back against the seat, only to discover that whoever had designed this vehicle must have done so with much smaller people in mind. It was practically impossible for him not to touch the entire length of Miss Smith's body as they sat there, squashed together. "I'm so sorry," he muttered.

"Why don't you move your arm, my lord?" said the artist as he waved his piece of charcoal in the general direction of Anthony's left appendage. "Lift if up a bit . . . just like that . . . yes, there you go, that's much better."

Anthony could have sworn he heard Miss Smith gulp as he raised his arm and placed it against the top of the seat, but he wasn't sure. All he knew was that their thighs were touching and that the curve of her breast was much too close for comfort. Dear Lord, but it was impossible for him to relax—especially when Miss Smith kept shifting from side to side and adding to the friction between them.

It was the closest he'd been to her since they'd met, and he found that it stirred to life an awareness of her that he couldn't possibly ignore. Her scent was sweet—as if she'd recently bathed in the nectar of honeysuckles. Anthony winced. The thought of her bathing was probably one he should avoid at the moment. Dropping his gaze to her naked arm, he marveled at how unblemished it was—not as much as a freckle marred the milky whiteness of it. Unfortunately, said arm was directly perpendicular to her breasts. Anthony tried to do the right thing and stop his gaze from wandering, but his eyes were apparently less noble and refused to listen, which in turn led to a rather uncomfortable situation a mere second later.

Anthony hastily crossed his legs and looked back up at the artist, only to find the annoying little man grinning right back at him. Thankfully he held his tongue and returned his attention to his work, finishing the sketch with merciful rapidity so that Anthony could finally distance himself from Miss Smith. But in his eagerness to prevent any further inappropriate contact with the woman, he shot to his feet so quickly that he bumped his head on the roof of the carriage, lost his balance and landed right back in his seat. This alone might not have been such a disaster had he not placed his hand upon Miss Smith's right thigh in an attempt to stop his fall.

Anthony learned a number of interesting facts about Miss Smith in the moment that followed. First, she was not too easily startled, for although she'd emitted a squeak of surprise at the moment of initial contact, she'd refrained from yelling or hitting him (for which he was very much obliged). Second, she possessed the ability to remain calm when faced with unusual circumstances. Third, and perhaps most memorable of all, was the way she felt. Anthony had never considered himself the shallow sort, and he was well aware that the first two elements were of equal, if not greater, importance because they pertained to her character, but he also knew that he could never deny the way his body responded to the softness of her. It was as if molten hot lava had surged up his arm, filling his entire body with a pulsing heat unlike any he'd ever felt before.

It confounded him to such a degree that he found himself at a complete loss for words. After all, it wasn't as if he had no prior experience with the female sex. Truthfully, he had ample, for until his father's health had begun to decline, he'd led the same life of debauchery as every other young and unattached gentleman. Casper could attest to this. In fact, it was probably the only cause for tension between them, because while circumstance had forced Anthony to grow up and become the responsible adult he was destined to be, Casper refused to abandon his roguish ways, declaring that it would be wrong to meddle with nature's intent.

As for Miss Smith . . . Anthony removed his hand from her thigh and hazarded a glance at her, expecting a reprimanding frown. Instead, he found her looking down at the exact spot where his hand had just been. Even in the dim light of the carriage he could see that her cheeks were flushed. She lifted her gaze to meet his, her eyes wide with wonder and her lips slightly parted as if she wished to say something but failed to find the right words. It was a moment that Anthony would never forget, for as he looked into her eyes, he knew that she had been just as affected as he.

"Your portrait, Your Grace."

Anthony blinked, turned away from Miss Smith and accepted the piece of paper that the artist was holding out to him. With the spell broken, he voiced his thanks and alighted from the carriage before offering Miss Smith his hand. She quickly accepted and was on the ground beside him a moment later.

"There you are!" Anthony recognized the voice immediately as that of his mother. Looking over his shoulder, he found her walking toward him with Casper at her side. "I've been searching everywhere for you—the food is about to be brought out, so I thought it might be an appropriate time for you to make a toast."

For the briefest of moments, Anthony considered asking his mother to do it instead, but he knew that would never do. He was the duke, and the making of toasts was his responsibility no matter how much he disliked the prospect of speaking to a room full of people. Being on public display like that made him uncomfortable—it always had—and was the reason why he'd delayed taking that dreaded seat of his in Parliament. But, in light of the fact that this was the first ball hosted at Kingsborough Hall since his father's death, he couldn't help but agree with his mother: saying something was the right thing to do. "Of course," he said, managing a smile that he hoped would mask his nervousness.

"Thank you, my dear," his mother said. She cast a quick glance in Miss Smith's direction before returning her gaze to him. "And if you wouldn't mind mingling a little with the rest of your guests for a while after, I think it would help reassure everyone that you're taking your new role as duke seriously."

The implication could not have been clearer if she'd spelled it out for him word by word. His mother knew, just as well as he did, that the woman whose company he'd been enjoying for the past hour was not only an imposter but also, perhaps, even unsuitable for him to associate himself with. It annoyed him—mostly because he knew she was right. He couldn't remain absent from the ballroom too long without the guests wondering where their host had disappeared to, and since his mother would be the one to suffer most from any potential rumors, he had no choice but to do as she asked.

"Don't worry," Casper said with an impish smile. "I'll be more than happy to keep Miss Smith entertained while you see to your ducal duties."

Anthony had no doubt that he would, but knowing his friend's devilish ways, he didn't feel the least bit reassured by his willingness to help. Not when it came to Miss Smith. He was trying to think of an excuse to prevent Casper from spending any time with her when the lady herself said, "How kind of you, Mr. Goodard."

"It's settled then," his mother declared as she took Miss Smith by the arm and started leading her back inside.

Anthony waited until they were out of earshot before he turned to Casper and said, "If you so much as look at her in an inappropriate fashion, I'll call you out."

Placing a hand upon his heart Casper said, "I promise I'll be on my best behavior."

Anthony frowned.

"Your lack of confidence wounds me," Casper said with exaggerated sadness.

Anthony's frown deepened.

"Look," Casper said with a sigh. "Miss Smith is clearly more interested in you than she ever was in me—though I cannot begin to imagine why. Regardless of my reputation, I have never once risked ruining our friendship for the sake of a woman, have I?"

Forced to concede the point, Anthony shook his head.

"And I've no desire to do so now. If she's so important to you, then I won't ruin it for you—you have my word on that."

"Thank you," Anthony said with a nod as he started after his mother and Miss Smith. "I realize how strange it must seem to you, given everything we've been through together, but there's something special about her, and I . . . well, I suppose I'd just like to keep her to myself for the remainder of the evening—find out if there's a chance for anything more." Considering what he knew of her, he somehow doubted that she would agree, and yet he couldn't shake the feeling that their paths had crossed for a reason.

Keeping pace with him, Casper raised an eyebrow. "More? You're not thinking of reverting to your sinful ways with Miss Smith, are you?"

"God no," Anthony said. He realized a moment later that Casper had stopped walking, and he stopped as well so he could turn to look at him.

"Surely you're not contemplating marriage!" Casper was staring at Anthony as if his head had just fallen off his shoulders. "You barely know her!"

"Casper," Anthony warned. "I have no intention of

marrying anyone . . . yet. So if you don't mind, I'd greatly appreciate it if you'd refrain from hollering about it for the entire world to hear."

"My apologies," Casper whispered. "I can't imagine *what* came over me."

Anthony rolled his eyes before adding, "I happen to like Miss Smith." *Her soon to be fiancé aside.* "And since I *am* entertaining thoughts of marrying in the not so distant future, I've decided to start looking at all potential candidates."

Casper gaped at him. "Are you serious?"

"Quite. In fact, I've never been more serious about anything else in my life, and while you may be correct in that I don't know Miss Smith well enough yet to propose to her, I do know that she's very forgiving and has a splendid sense of humor." And before he was tempted to tell his friend more about the time he'd spent in Miss Smith's company, he hurried up the steps and strode inside the ballroom.

Chapter 6

"**H**ave you met my daughter, the Countess of Huntley?" the dowager duchess asked as she guided Isabella along the periphery of the room.

"No, I have not yet had the pleasure," Isabella said, eyeing the duchess. She felt as though she ought to address the topic that was hanging over them like a storm cloud waiting to burst. Apologizing for her unauthorized attendance would be the proper thing to do—especially since her host and hostess had not yet tossed her out. That in itself was a miracle to be marveled at. Determined to do the right thing, Isabella placed a staying hand upon the duchess's arm. The older woman slowed, stopped and turned to look at her expectantly. "I hope you will forgive my intruding on your festivities this evening. Should you wish for me to leave, I will do so immediately."

The duchess watched her silently for a moment before saying, "After all the trouble you went to? I don't know who you are or how you managed to get in without detection, but I should hate to be the one to ruin your evening if being here is so important to you." She waved her hand to indicate Isabella's attire. "Besides, you're not lowborn or you wouldn't have been able to afford such a gown. At the very least, you are gentry, perhaps you are even nobility, though I have to admit that if that is the case, then I am even more curious about your desire for anonymity." She leaned closer to Isabella and lowered her voice to a whisper. "You wouldn't happen to be one of Lord Jouve's illegitimate children, would you? It is my understanding that he has several. Perhaps—"

With no desire to lie again, Isabella shook her head. "No," she said. "It's nothing like that. If you'll forgive me, I simply have my own personal reasons for not wanting to disclose my identity." Giving her a sympathetic smile, the duchess nodded. "Your secret is safe with me, *Miss Smith*." She chuckled and shook her head bemusedly. "Come, I'll introduce you to my daughter. We can watch the duke's toast together."

A few minutes later, Isabella found herself standing across from a lovely brunette, her hazel-colored eyes visible from behind her green mask.

"Louise, I'd like to present to you Miss Smith," the duchess said. She turned toward Isabella with a smile. "Miss Smith, this is my daughter, Lady Huntley, and her husband, Lord Huntley."

"It's a pleasure to make your acquaintances," Isabella said, executing a graceful curtsy.

"Oh, the pleasure is all ours," Lady Huntley said, her lips curving upward and dimpling at the corners. "Isn't that so, Peter?"

"Most assuredly," Lord Huntley murmured as he reached for Isabella's hand, leaned over it and placed a soft kiss upon her knuckles.

"You see, my brother—"

The ringing sound of metal striking glass stopped Lady Huntley from finishing her sentence. Isabella realized then that the music had ceased and that all the guests had turned toward the steps leading out of the ballroom, where the duke stood staring down at the crowd.

He looked devilishly handsome with his cravat slightly loosened and a few locks of stray hair brushing against his forehead. But he also looked terribly serious with that frown he was wearing upon his brow—not at all like the easygoing man she'd strolled with in the garden. He took a deep breath. Exhaled it and . . . took another. Good heavens. Was he nervous? Surely not.

"He's always disliked being the center of attention," Lady Huntley whispered. Addressing the duchess she said, "Mama, was this your idea?"

"This is his first public appearance as duke," the duchess whispered back. "I thought it prudent for him to assert himself by saying something. Besides, he can do with the practice. As it is he avoided taking his seat in Parliament last year, claiming exemption due to his state of mourning. He won't be able to use that excuse this year."

Lady Huntley let out a small groan. "I only hope he doesn't embarrass himself by fainting. Look, he's tugging at his cravat again and rocking from side to side like he always does when he's nervous."

Isabella cringed. The duke might command an air of confidence when he was on equal footing with everyone else, but speaking aloud with all eyes pinned on him was clearly not his forte. Sending up a silent prayer that he would somehow garner the sense of calm required, she thanked her lucky stars that she was not the one standing in his shoes.

"I would like to thank you all for coming here this evening," the duke finally said, his voice growing in strength as he spoke. "The title of duke is not one I had hoped to assume at such a young age, for it has come to me at a terrible cost. I miss my father every moment of every day, and can only hope that I may one day be as great a man as he was.

"But life must go on, and I now have duties to attend to. It is for this reason that my mother and I have invited you all here this evening; to usher in a new era here at Kingsborough Hall as we commemorate my father—a man who will never be forgotten by any of us." Raising his champagne flute, he then said, "To the sixth Duke of Kingsborough."

"To the sixth Duke of Kingsborough," the crowd echoed his salute as they raised their glasses in unison.

"That was pretty good," Lord Huntley said as the music started back up and the chatter of the guests resumed, "for a man who doesn't care for public speaking."

Isabella had to agree. In fact, she'd found the toast both heartfelt and moving, leaving her with no doubt that Kingsborough was well on his way to becoming a very fine duke indeed. His eyes had met hers right after he'd finished, and he'd stepped down from his vantage point on the steps with (she suspected) the intention of joining her. The duchess wasn't likely to approve if he did, for although she'd been nice enough to Isabella, she'd been far from subtle in her suggestion that her son had other guests to see to as well.

"As I was saying before," Lady Huntley said, drawing Isabella's attention toward her. "My brother seems quite taken with you." She leaned closer to Isabella. "Tell me more about yourself, Miss Smith."

"I . . . er . . ."

"She's from Flemmington," the duchess said, leaping to Isabella's rescue. Why she would carry on what she knew to be a lie with her very own daughter went beyond Isabella's realm of comprehension. She could only deduce that the duchess's desire for discretion outweighed any thoughts she had of being honest.

Lady Huntley frowned. "I don't believe I've ever heard of it. Is it far?"

"Very far," the duchess replied before Isabella had a chance to, "though it is my understanding that there's quite a grand lake there with ducks and such—lovely for boating."

"How charming," Lady Huntley said. "We shall have to visit you sometime, shan't we, Peter?"

"I suppose we can try," Lord Huntley said, his eyes shifting between the duchess and Isabella. There was no denying that he was not as easily convinced about Isabella's place of residency as his wife was.

"How delightful it is to see you again, Miss Smith!" The voice belonged to Mr. Goodard, who, Isabella discovered as she turned to her right, was standing directly beside her. "I was hoping you'd be willing to dance the next set with me."

"You're very eager this evening," Lady Huntley said as she stepped around Isabella to better face Mr. Goodard. "Your dance with Lady Georgina was particularly entertaining. I do hope that you enjoyed it."

"As a matter of fact, I did." Mr. Goodard frowned while Lady Huntley's eyes narrowed into two tiny slits.

They stood like that, staring at each other for a moment in awkward silence until Mr. Goodard's eyes suddenly widened and he stepped back, pointing an accusing finger at Lady Huntley. "It was *your* idea!"

"I haven't the slightest notion of what you mean," the countess replied primly.

"*You* suggested the Hampstead move, didn't you?"

Lady Huntley shrugged. "Maybe."

"Aha! I knew it!" Mr. Goodard turned to Lord Huntley. "Do you have any idea how devious your wife can be?"

"I'm beginning to have an inkling," Lord Huntley murmured.

"If you ask me, I'm quite impressed with her patience and surprised she didn't exact her revenge sooner," the duchess said.

"Revenge?" Mr. Goodard looked well and truly stumped. "What on earth for?"

"Stand perfectly still, Louise," Lady Huntley said in what was presumably meant to be an imitation of Mr. Goodard's voice—a very poor imitation at best. "There's a squirrel nibbling on your skirt."

Isabella stared at the countess, as did everyone else in their small group, including Lord Huntley. It was as if everyone was holding their breath, waiting to see how the situation might unfold, each of them reluctant to speak for fear that doing so would put a rapid end to what had quickly turned into a most entertaining exchange.

Mr. Goodard gaped at her. "Are you serious? That was years ago, not to mention that you should have known better than to believe me."

"You know that I have an innate fear of rodents," Lady Huntley protested.

"But squirrels are so cute," Isabella couldn't stop herself from saying.

Lady Huntley gasped. "Cute? They are no such thing, Miss Smith. In fact, they are no more than rats with bushy tails! Remove the tail and I tell you, it's a rat, and I abhor rats."

"I see," Isabella murmured.

"Nonetheless," Mr. Goodard said, "you can't possibly mean to blame me for stepping into that hole and breaking your ankle—that was entirely your own doing."

"I wouldn't have done it if I hadn't been frightened of a fictitious squirrel," Lady Huntley said between clenched teeth.

"Well, you'll be happy to know that your attempt to delay me from enjoying Miss Smith's company was quite successful," Mr. Goodard said. Lady Huntley finally smiled. "However, I am here now and only too happy to comply with the duchess's desire for me to entertain Miss Smith for a while."

Lady Huntley turned to her mother. "Mama, I'm not sure that would be a good idea." She lowered her voice and added something else that Isabella failed to hear.

"Not to worry, my dear. Mr. Goodard has promised to be on his best behavior this evening." The duchess pinned the gentleman in question with a dangerous stare. "Isn't that right, Mr. Goodard?"

"It most certainly is, Your Grace."

"There, you see?" the duchess said in her usual, gentle voice. "There's nothing to worry about. Besides, it's not as if we won't be keeping an eye on him." She wagged a finger at Mr. Goodard. "You're to stay indoors where we can see you. Is that clear?"

"Absolutely," Mr. Goodard said with a nod of confirmation as he reached for Isabella's hand, placed it upon his arm and began escorting her through the crowd and toward the dance floor.

"I take it that your reputation leaves much to be desired," Isabella said a short while later as she and Mr. Goodard stepped nimbly forward between the colonnade of expectant ladies and gentlemen who'd chosen to participate in the country dance.

Mr. Goodard smiled as he glanced down at her. "You are correct in your assessment, though the fact that you don't consider my name to be synonymous with the devil clearly indicates that you must have led a rather sheltered life. Not fond of the City, Miss Smith?"

Isabella averted her gaze. "Not particularly," she said. Thankfully, they were forced to part from one another and take up their respective positions at the end of the colonnade, preventing Mr. Goodard from prying further. Looking sideways, Isabella spotted the duke. He was saying something to an older gentleman, but then, as if she'd called his name, he turned toward her. His eyes met hers, and there was a hint of a smile behind them—nothing overt, but an inner warmth that flowed across the space between them.

Isabella gave herself a mental shake and returned her attention to her dance partner. He was strikingly handsome—too much so, no doubt—and yet Isabella felt no more for him than she did for Mr. Roberts, whom she was destined to marry. An awful acknowledgement, she told herself, since this made Mr. Roberts no more dear to her than a man she'd just met.

The duke, on the other hand . . . well, she'd known

him for an even shorter duration than she had Mr. Goodard if one considered that Mr. Goodard had made his acquaintance known to her first. But there was something about the duke that Isabella was finding hard to resist. It was an eagerness to know who he was as a person, what his childhood had been like and which experiences had made him the man he was now. A crazy sensation, she realized, but one she could not seem to rid herself of regardless of how much she tried to focus on Mr. Goodard's handsome face instead. It was no use. Her thoughts invariably returned to the duke.

Isabella sighed.

"Are you all right?" Mr. Goodard asked as he stepped toward her, took her hands in his and spun her around while the other dancers waited for them to resume their places. "You don't look as if you're enjoying yourself, which is unusual, since ladies in my company *always* look as if they're enjoying themselves."

That brought a smile to Isabella's lips. "I imagine you must be used to blushes and batting eyelashes wherever you go." She made an attempt at a lovesick gaze. "Is this better?"

Mr. Goodard frowned. "Now you're just mocking me."

"I wouldn't dare," Isabella quipped as she gave him a sly smile. She accepted his hand again, and they moved past the other dancers.

Mr. Goodard raised an eyebrow. "Sarcasm? No wonder he likes you."

"Who?" Isabella asked, instantly aware that her dance partner had just said something that he'd probably not intended for her to hear. The look of surprise on his face confirmed it.

"What?" He looked about as if seeking a means of escape, but of course there was none—not unless he planned on being particularly rude.

They returned to their places as the music faded, and Mr. Goodard bowed, while Isabella curtsied. He then offered her his arm and led her away from the dance floor.

"Who likes me?" Isabella asked, determined to squeeze that little bit of information out of him.

"I've no idea what you're talking about," Mr. Goodard said as they walked across to the refreshment table.

"But you just said . . . I mean, when we were dancing . . ." Mr. Goodard raised an eyebrow as he picked up a glass of lemonade and handed it to her. She breathed a sigh of defeat. "Oh, you're insufferable."

A cheeky smile graced Mr. Goodard's lips. "I know," he said. He looked away from her and added, "Oh look, there's Kingsborough right now. He's coming our . . . oh, dear."

"What is it?" Isabella asked, craning her neck in an attempt to catch a glimpse of the duke.

"It looks as though he's been detained by Lady Deerford." Concern crept into his eyes. "From what I've been told about the lady, I do believe this could take a while."

Disappointment flooded Isabella. It was ridiculous. She barely knew the duke, had spent no more than an hour in his company and would never see him again once the evening ended. Hoping for something more with him was impossible, and if he ever discovered who she really was—a lowly woman who lived in a simple cottage on the wrong side of town—he'd never

forgive her. Especially not if she continued this charade and allowed him to think that the only thing
standing in his way was a man she wasn't even engaged to yet. No, she had to find a way to avoid his
company for the remainder of the evening—for both
of their sakes. She turned to Mr. Goodard. "Then how
about if we pass the time with another dance? Is that
not a quadrille starting?"

Mr. Goodard hesitated a moment and then smiled
with mischief. "Indeed it is, Miss Smith. Shall we show
the others how it's done?"

There was humor in his eyes as he spoke, which
brought an instant giggle from Isabella. "Most definitely," she said as she placed her hand upon his arm
and allowed him to guide her back to the dance floor.

Isabella enjoyed the quadrille immensely, mostly
because it allowed for more conversation time with Mr.
Goodard than the country dance had done. Desperate for a bit more information about the man whose
company she really craved, she turned to Mr. Goodard
for answers. She worried he might be reluctant to say
too much, but she quickly discovered that once Mr.
Goodard started talking about his childhood exploits
with the duke, there was no stopping him. It was de-
lightfully entertaining, especially when he spoke of
the treasure they'd buried in the garden one time while
playing pirates. The gardener had dug it up years later
and believed it to be real.

"I do believe we ought to go and save him from
Lady Deerford's clutches," Mr. Goodard suggested as
soon as the dance ended and he finished another story
involving a trench they'd dug around the duke's tree
house one year, pretending that it had been a moat.

Determined to ignore her better judgment, Isabella was just about to agree when a gentleman she'd not yet met appeared, blocking their path. He was just as tall as Mr. Goodard and almost as handsome, though there was something in his eyes and the way he smiled that put Isabella immediately on edge.

"Ah, Lord Starkly," Mr. Goodard said in a bored tone of voice. "I was rather hoping to avoid you this evening."

Pinning Isabella with his gaze, Lord Starkly didn't as much as glance in Mr. Goodard's direction as he said, "Yes, I imagine you were. But then again, it's not you I'm here to see but the lovely lady whose company you've been keeping. Perhaps you'd be so good as to introduce me to her."

Heat scurried across Isabella's flesh. Not the good sort of heat that she'd felt in the duke's company but rather the kind that made her feel like a little trapped rabbit, about to be flayed. She sensed Mr. Goodard's indecision, but propriety apparently won out, because he finally managed to say, "Miss Smith, this is Lord Starkly—Lord Starkly, I present to you Miss Smith."

"A pleasure," Lord Starkly murmured as he took her hand in his, raised it to his lips and kissed her knuckles, lingering there for one second . . . two seconds . . .

Mr. Goodard coughed and Lord Starkly straightened himself, releasing Isabella's hand with a roguish slowness that could only be defined as most outrageous.

"Would you please do the honor of partnering with me for the next dance, Miss Smith," Lord Starkly asked, the corner of his mouth rising to form a crooked smile.

Heaven above, she'd never seen someone look more arrogant in all her life. He knew she could not refuse him without being rude, for he was a nobleman while she was a mere "Miss." She turned to Mr. Goodard, gazing up at him as she prayed he'd see the imploring look in her eyes that said *Please rescue me from this scoundrel.*

"I don't believe that's possible," Mr. Goodard said as he looked about the ballroom. "For she has already promised to dance the next set with another gentleman."

"Oh? With whom?" Lord Starkly asked, his eyes narrowing as he leaned toward Mr. Goodard.

"With . . . er . . ." Isabella watched as Mr. Goodard continued to look about, realizing that he was trying to find somebody for her to partner with. "With me."

"What?" Both gentlemen turned their gaze on Isabella. She wasn't surprised, for her question had sounded like a croaked squeak.

"That's right," Mr. Goodard announced. "We were simply taking a small reprieve to quench our thirst, but since you've delayed us, I daresay we'll have no time for that. Come along, Miss Smith."

Finding it difficult to believe what had just transpired, Isabella stumbled after Mr. Goodard, leaving behind a very angry-looking Lord Starkly. "You cannot do this," she said as they arrived back at the dance floor. "We've already danced twice. People will think . . . it's unseemly and—"

"What was I supposed to do?" Mr. Goodard hissed. "I couldn't allow you to dance with that man—he's a renowned womanizer."

"And you're not?" She regretted the words as soon as they were spoken, for there was suddenly something deadly in Mr. Goodard's eyes.

He leaned toward her. "Think what you will about

me, but at least I treat women with decency and respect. I don't toss my mistresses out without a penny the instant I tire of them or, worse, get them with child. No, Miss Smith, I am nothing like Lord Starkly—please don't make the error of presuming that I am."

Isabella shuddered. "I'm sorry. I didn't—"

"I know the consequences of dancing more than twice. Had it been up to me, you would have danced with someone else, but Lord Winston, as you can see, is about to dance with his wife, as is Lord Huntley. As for Kingsborough . . . I've no idea where he is, for I cannot see him anywhere." He met her gaze. "Fret not, Miss Smith. This is a masquerade, after all, we are in the country and you are not familiar to anyone. In fact, it won't surprise me in the least if after this evening none of us here ever lays eyes on you again."

Isabella stared back at him, shocked by his observation. She swallowed hard and then nodded. Whatever the case, dancing three sets with Mr. Goodard was surely more favorable than having to dance a single one with Lord Starkly. Taking up her position for what unfortunately promised to be another waltz, she felt Mr. Goodard's hand upon her waist just as a deep voice rumbled from behind her.

"What the devil do you think you're doing, Casper?" It was the duke who'd spoken, and he did not sound the least bit pleased. Turning her head, Isabella gasped. He looked just about ready to kill somebody.

As if Mr. Goodard had just discovered that Isabella was infected with the plague, he released her and stepped back. "Thank God you're here," he said, his features relaxing with visible relief. "I was beginning to fear for my freedom."

"Not as much as I was beginning to worry about your intentions. Really, Casper, you know three dances with the same woman is unacceptable."

"Of course I do, but what choice did I have with Lord Starkly preparing to pounce on her. Frankly, I can't imagine what you were thinking inviting him here in the first place. You know what he's like, and to submit poor Miss Smith here"—they both directed a gaze toward Isabella, who was feeling rather like a piece of rope in a game of tug-of-war—"was unthinkable. I tried to locate you, but you were nowhere to be seen, while both your brother and brother-in-law are occupied with their wives."

The duke averted his gaze from Mr. Goodard for a moment, frowned and said, "So they are."

"All in all," Mr. Goodard continued, "I think I did the right thing considering the circumstances, but now that you're here, I do suggest you take over while I enjoy a much-needed brandy. Miss Smith," he added, bowing toward Isabella, "thank you for your company. It was a delightful pleasure." And then he hurried off before either of them could say anything further.

"I hope you'll forgive me," the duke said as he pulled Isabella toward him, placing his hand against her waist as he guided her forward to the first tunes of the waltz. A flutter of nerves settled in the pit of her stomach in response to his closeness. And the way he was looking at her . . . there was an elemental possessiveness behind his eyes that made her heart beat faster and her legs turn to jelly. Thank God he was holding onto her, for she feared that if he hadn't been, she'd have collapsed to the floor. "As noble as his intentions might have been, Mr. Goodard was about to make a very serious mistake. I had no choice but to intervene."

"I see," Isabella said as he twirled her about. "Then it really is fortuitous that you were there to prevent it—particularly since I'd hate having to explain to Mr. Goodard that I'm practically engaged to someone else. I daresay it would have been detrimental to his ego, not to mention that it would in all likelihood have ruined my own reputation."

"It's not a laughing matter," he said, though the corners of his lips were beginning to edge upward. "I'm being quite serious."

"Oh, I know," Isabella replied, smiling sweetly. "So am I."

The duke laughed. "Miss Smith, what am I to do with you? You're unlike any lady I've ever met before—so free and spirited that I cannot help but wonder . . ." He stopped himself from saying anything further, but his hold on her tightened as he led her about in a wide circle. "Tell me," he continued. "This man you intend to marry—do you love him?"

She wanted to say yes, willed herself to do it even, for she knew that it would stop the duke from pursuing her any further. And yet the word wouldn't come. It remained on the tip of her tongue until she realized that she could not bring herself to say it. "It's complicated," she said instead, averting her gaze.

"I wish to court you." Anthony blurted out the words without thinking. Well, that wasn't entirely true, for he hadn't done much else *but* think—about Miss Smith, that was. He'd done as his mother had asked and had spoken to several of his guests—had even suffered through Lady Deerford's detailed description of her newly acquired doll. And yet, through it all, he'd been thinking of Miss Smith—her eyes, her smile . . . the touch of her thigh beneath the palm of his hand. He'd known her for less than a day, and yet he found himself smitten, though he thought he ought to clarify his sudden statement in case she thought him in love with her. That would be ridiculous—he barely knew her. "What I mean to say is that I'd like to spend more time with you—get to know you better."

She stared back at him from behind her mask, and he longed for nothing more than to tear it from her face so he could get a proper look at her.

"That's impossible," she said, breaking the silence with words he'd no desire to hear, in a voice filled with pain and regret.

"Why, Miss Smith?" He wanted to shake her and make her see that marrying someone she did not love was a terrible idea, no matter the reason for it. "Who is this man? Why do you feel yourself bound to him?"

"I cannot say," she muttered.

"Look at me," he said, determined more than ever to change her mind and suddenly willing to risk making a fool of himself in the bargain if that was what it would take. She was too special, too perfect, too . . . destined to be his. He felt it deep in his bones like nothing he'd ever felt before, a pure certainty that demanded he do whatever it might take to win her.

Where this notion came from, he couldn't imagine, but it was there, as real as the fact that he was dancing with her right now. It took a moment for her to comply, but then she did, and there was pain in her eyes that tore at his heart. "I'm a duke, Miss Smith. Don't tell me that if I come to call on you your parents will send me away. Don't tell me that should I offer to marry you, your father will say no, all because of an understanding you might have with some other gentleman."

The music faded and they glided to a slow halt. He bowed before her while she in return curtsied, but when he straightened himself, he noted that her eyes were glistening. Bloody hell, he'd made her cry. "Forgive me," he muttered as he steered her toward a set of open doors at the side and toward the hallway beyond. He had to speak with her in private . . . had to make her see that she was making a mistake—one that could still be averted.

Chapter 7

"**W**here are we going?" he heard her ask as he pulled her along behind him.

Her voice sounded wary, and rightly so. After all, he was leading her away from the ballroom with the inappropriate intention of getting her completely alone where no one would be likely to disturb them. "In here," he said, ushering her into a room as he swiftly closed and locked the door behind him. It was his library—his sanctuary—a place where he could just relax and be himself. Turning around, he found Miss Smith eyeing him as if he'd been a no-good pirate who'd just asked her to sail the seven seas. Not exactly the reaction he'd been hoping for.

Intent on putting her at ease, he said the first thing that popped into his head. "What's your favorite food, Miss Smith?"

He saw her frown, as if she was examining his motive for posing such an absurd question. But then her expression eased and she said, "Strawberries, Your Grace. Not baked in a pie or turned to jam, but fresh, plump, juicy strawberries."

Anthony stared back at Miss Smith—at her lips, to be exact. Her talk of strawberries only served to make him wonder what those lovely lips of hers might taste like, and worse, how he might go about discovering it.

He watched as she walked across to one of the bookcases and gave its contents a close inspection.

"What is all this?" she asked.

Anthony shrugged. "My collection, I suppose." He'd forgotten about it in his hurry for privacy—had intended to have it all moved upstairs to his bedroom so nobody else would see it. Not that he cared if anyone happened to think it strange that he liked turning bits of scrap into something more, but there was something personal and private about it that made him want to protect it from scrutiny. Casper was the only person outside his family who'd seen his work. He held his breath now, waiting for Miss Smith's evaluation.

"Did you make these?" she asked, looking over her shoulder at him briefly before returning her attention to an elegant lady that he'd fashioned from a crooked nail, two brass buttons, a bit of fabric and some twine. He'd had a devil of a time getting her face right, recalling how he'd had to wipe the paint away twice before it had looked just the way he'd wanted it to.

Scratching the back of his head as he stepped forward, he didn't answer right away but watched instead as she moved on to the next figure—a dog made from bits of folded newspaper and painted black. "Yes," he said, feeling much the same as when he'd had to make that dratted toast.

Again he found himself holding his breath, but then she turned around to face him, her eyes wide as she said on a whisper of breath, "They're splendid."

Splendid.

The sense of elation that buzzed through him, replacing the nervousness with warm pleasure, was heady indeed, for she had voiced her praise as though she'd been looking at a fantastic landscape painting complete with a castle, some mountains and a boat upon a lake, so vividly depicted that one might imagine stepping right into the scenery. Instead, she was merely regarding some odd bits and pieces that he'd glued, tied and pinned together to make some funny-looking characters. It was absurd really, and yet he couldn't ignore the admiration that shone in her eyes, for it was the first time that anyone had ever looked at him quite like that—as if he'd been capable of magic.

With renewed determination, he stepped forward and took her hand in his, enjoying her sharp intake of breath and the way her pulse fluttered against his fingertips. "Who are you really?" he asked, his eyes meeting hers as he moved even closer.

She shook her head. "I cannot say," she whispered.

"Why not?" he asked as he cupped her head with his hands, forcing her to look at him. "I won't tell a soul if you do not wish for me to do so. Your parents will never discover that you were here, and neither will your intended, but I need to know who you are . . . the name of the woman who's captured my interest."

"Please stop," she muttered as she tried to back away from him. She couldn't go far, for the bookcase was right behind her. "Whatever it is that you wish from me is impossible. You're a duke and I—" She clamped her mouth shut.

Anthony leaned toward her. "You're what, Miss Smith?" he asked as his eyes searched hers for answers.

There was fear there, the sort of fear that he could not begin to understand. What on earth would have her so worried?

"You will ruin everything for me," she said, avoiding his question. "My parents are counting on me to do the right thing and yet here you are, determined to make a mess of it. I won't let you."

"Is your father in debt to this man? Did he perhaps lose you to him in a game of cards?" Anthony asked, the desperation he felt at her rejection filling him with anger. "Because if that is the case, then let me talk to them. I can—"

"No," she said. One simple word that hung in the air between them, promising to tear away whatever dreams Anthony had of sharing a future with Miss Smith.

"Don't do this," he said. "Don't marry a man you do not care for when you and I . . . ." He took a deep breath to steady himself against the onslaught of emotions that whipped through him at the thought of having to relinquish all hope. "You cannot deny that there's something between us—something more than what is usual between two people who have only just met."

Jaw clenching, she tilted her head backward and looked him squarely in the eye, saying, "While your company has been charming, I fear I must disappoint you, for I noticed no such thing."

She was lying. Anthony had seen the flash of concession that had marked her features for a second before she'd managed to train them. "Is that so?" he asked as he backed her further up against the bookcase, jolting the heavy piece of furniture enough for one of his figures to fall over. Miss Smith gasped, her eyes startled and her body stiff. She would *not* deny them their happiness, Anthony decided. "I do believe I am about to prove you wrong."

Capturing her head with his hands he lowered his mouth over hers and moved closer until he was pressed up against her, the faint taste of the lemonade she'd recently drunk still present upon her lips. She felt rigid against his embrace, and he half expected her to start flailing him for his unsolicited advances. But since she wasn't hitting him yet, or even attempting to get away from him, for that matter, he decided to move ahead with his attempt at enticement and slowly ran the tip of his tongue along her bottom lip. She shivered. There could be no denying that. "Kiss me back," he whispered as he kissed his way along her jawline and toward her ear, licking the edge of her lobe just enough to—

"Oh God," she moaned, her arms reaching around him and tugging him against her as if she was drowning and he was her lifeline.

Everything that followed was a frenzy of movement, as if neither could get enough of the other. He'd done it—he'd acted on the rakish impulse he'd tried so hard to repress since making her acquaintance.

Suppressing the guilt that threatened to surge, Anthony allowed his hands to move down Miss Smith's back while his tongue roamed over hers, and all he could think of was strawberries. Plump and juicy strawberries, or even better, Miss Smith biting into said strawberries. He'd never considered the possibility that there could be something erotic about food, and yet Miss Smith had changed that for him—she'd spoken of strawberries with that delicious mouth of hers and he knew, beyond any shadow of a doubt, that strawberries would forevermore be reminiscent of something delightful and enticing.

Tilting her chin for better access, he kissed her neck, inhaling the sweet scent of her, though he couldn't quite place it. He'd thought of honeysuckles earlier, but that wasn't it. It wasn't roses or lavender either as was commonly used by ladies, but something entirely different—something pure, like the sunset in the evening or the dew upon the grass in the morning. "I love the way you smell," he murmured as he kissed his way along her collarbone. "Tell me, what is it?"

"Chamomile and honey—from the soap I use." Her breath was raspy as she spoke, her fingers twining through his hair, holding him against her with a desperation that matched his own. The pulse at her neck was beating fast—he could see it, that rapid thrum of excitement.

Encouraged by her response and by the way his own blood roared through his veins, he grew daring, allowing his hands to slide down her back until he cupped her bottom, squeezing her slightly as he pulled her against his own hardness. Her eyes widened, but her back arched as he'd expected, pushing her breasts forward and up until they strained against her bodice. "Make no mistake, Miss Smith. I want you more than I have ever wanted anything else before in my life. It may defy logic, but I am powerless to stop it." He deliberately lowered his eyes to her breasts, a helpless smile tugging at his lips. "Say what you will, but I know that you feel it too, as evidenced by your eagerness to—"

"How dare you?" she snapped, cutting him off as she wrenched herself away from him, killing the moment and surprising him in the process.

Anthony froze. What the devil was going on? Had she not just been cavorting in his arms as though her life was entirely dependent upon his kisses? Where was the anger coming from? For there was definitely anger. Plenty of it, in fact, as he caught a glimpse of her stormy eyes.

"You . . . you . . . argh!" With a hard shove she pushed him away, just enough for her to escape his closeness. She stopped at a reasonable distance and turned to face him as she held her hands up before her. "Stay right where you are," she warned.

Her breathing was still coming fast, and there was a blush to her cheeks that put Anthony more at ease, for it suggested that her temper hadn't flared because of his kiss or even because of what he'd said (though he felt sure she'd have a different opinion on the matter), but rather because she'd just realized that he was in fact right. She pointed an accusing finger toward him. "I had everything worked out before I met you," she said. "I knew my life wasn't perfect, but it was one I was willing to accept. My mother was right to warn me about the stories I chose to read. Fairy tales are for children. As adults, we must think rationally and without dreams of the impossible clouding our judgment. I know this, and yet I was still determined to come here this evening—some deep-rooted wish to experience the fairy-tale splendor of the legendary Kingsborough Ball—before I lost the chance forever. The memory of this evening was intended to last me a lifetime. But then I met you and—"

"And?" Anthony asked carefully as he moved hesitantly toward her.

She let out a quivering sigh, and when her eyes met his again, there was desperation there—like that of a trapped animal. "And I found myself hoping for more—wishing for something that isn't meant to be.

Don't you see? You've ruined my life by kissing me, for it will be impossible for my future husband to live up to what we just shared, and because of that, I will have to live with the regret of what might have been had things been different, as will you."

It was bloody difficult not to smile with male pride in response to her words, but he attempted a serious expression anyway, hoping for a look of concern. "It doesn't have to be like this. We *can* be together if you'll only tell me who you are so I can speak to your father. I'll ask for permission to court you and—"

"I've already told you it's impossible, so please, stop making this more difficult than it already is," she said. Her shoulders slumped, and she gave him a sad little smile. "I should probably go."

"And miss the fireworks?" Anthony asked, knowing full well that he was trying to find any reason to hold on to her for just a little while longer. Perhaps if they spoke some more she'd let something slip—some small detail that would help him find her again, because whatever ridiculous reason she thought there might be for denying his courtship, he was confident he'd be able to fix it once he knew what it was. He saw her pause and decided to press his advantage. "You really can't say that you've attended the Kingsborough Ball without seeing the fireworks."

She looked skeptical but eventually nodded. "Very well, Your Grace. I will agree to watch the fireworks, but as soon as they are over, I really must take my leave. Are we in agreement?"

"Certainly, Miss Smith," Anthony said, knowing full well that it was the best deal he was likely to get at that moment.

Chapter 8

"**W**here on earth have you been?" Louise hissed as she drew up next to Anthony with her husband following dutifully on her heels. With a quick glance in Miss Smith's direction, Louise narrowed her eyes. "Honestly, I thought you'd changed, but that is clearly not the case, is it?" As much as her words hurt (more so because of the truth in them), Anthony had no intention of having that particular discussion right now and decided to remain silent instead, eliciting a disappointed shake of the head from his sister. "Just so you know, people have been asking about you."

"What people?" Anthony asked blandly as he stopped a passing footman and began handing a glass of champagne to Miss Smith before giving one to his sister and Lord Huntley.

"The guests, you numbskull, or have you forgotten that you're supposed to be in the process of hosting the grandest ball of the year, and with the fireworks about to begin—Mama had to make the announcement herself! She was absolutely frantic, and rightfully so."

Louise hit him on the arm, much like she'd done as a child whenever he'd annoyed her.

Anthony groaned and took a sip of his drink. He knew his absence from the ballroom had lasted too long and was unlikely to go unnoticed, especially not by his mother, who was counting on him for support. "I'd best try and find her," he said, determined to make it up to her. This evening was mostly for her benefit after all—a means by which to help her recover from her loss. Taking Miss Smith's arm and linking it with his own, he then stepped forward while his sister followed behind with her husband.

With two hundred people cramming together on the terrace, it took a while for Anthony to locate his mother—particularly since it turned out that she wasn't on the terrace at all but on the lawn below with Winston, Sarah and Casper. There were a few other people milling about down there—especially in the vicinity of the pumpkin carriage. With Miss Smith beside him, Anthony made his descent, arriving at his mother's side a moment later. "I hope you will forgive my tardiness, Mama, but I was otherwise detained and lost track of time."

"Lost track of your sanity, I'd say," Casper muttered, to which Winston elbowed him in the ribs.

"I had hoped that you were past this sort of thing, Anthony," his mother said, glancing briefly at Miss Smith. "You know all eyes are upon you this evening. To sneak off with any young lady is not only uncouth but could also result in permanent damage to the young lady's reputation. You must try to be more civilized—you have responsibilities now."

As if he hadn't known that. His mother's words

grated, for if anyone had undergone a change of character from one day to the next, it was surely he. Casper could attest to that, as could Winston, for they had both been shocked when he'd said good-bye to his three mistresses, though Winston had been more pleased about it than Casper. This seemed insignificant now however, considering how easily he'd allowed his newly adopted righteousness to slip this evening. "I realize that, Mama."

"After all," his mother continued with a note of despair, "the invitation did say midnight fireworks. I waited as long as I could for you to return, but the guests were getting restless and—"

"I'm sorry, Mama," Anthony said, and he meant it. She'd always had her husband at her side whenever she'd hosted such events. This was her first public appearance without him, and Anthony had thoughtlessly abandoned her in favor of kissing Miss Smith. He felt like an ass.

His mother sighed, shook her head a little and then smiled. "Considering your lovely toast, I do believe I'll accept your apology. Thank you for that, by the way—I know it was difficult for you."

Difficult?

Nightmarish was more like it. His hands had started to sweat, his cravat had felt tighter than a hangman's noose, and he'd felt his heart beating closer to his knees than to his chest. Not to mention that the pressure of saying the right thing and *not* making a fool of himself in front of everyone had made him feel faint. In fact, he was quite certain he'd lost all sensation in his toes for the entire duration of the ordeal.

His thoughts were interrupted by a bright burst of

color in the night sky as the first firework exploded with a popping sound. Glancing down at Miss Smith, he saw her eyes light up as she watched the display, and it filled him with deep satisfaction knowing that he'd contributed to this small moment of happiness for her.

"I used to watch this from my bedroom window as a child," she said, her voice so low and dreamy that Anthony wondered if she was aware that she'd spoken her thoughts aloud.

He held quiet, hoping that she might say more, but she didn't, so he eventually whispered, "Your parents didn't mind you staying up so late?"

She didn't turn her head to look at him, but he could see that she was smiling. "They didn't know," Miss Smith said. "They would put me to bed at a decent hour, but I would stay awake, imagining the extravagance of the ball while I waited—the pretty gowns, the dancing and the soft, flowing music. By the time the firework display began, I almost felt as though I was at the ball myself, amidst the splendor."

There was a wealth of information to be found in what she'd just told him, and as shrewd as it might have been, Anthony decided to press the advantage that the moment offered. "Did you enjoy growing up in Moxley?"

"Oh, yes, I . . ." She looked at him then, her eyes unblinking and her lips slightly parted to form a startled expression. And then she frowned, and that frown turned to something else entirely—something sad and defeated that in turn made Anthony feel like a cad. She hadn't wanted him to know, but he'd tricked her into telling him anyway. He regretted it, and yet he didn't, because now he finally stood a chance—*they* stood a chance. If she lived close by, he would find her, no matter what.

"Kingsborough!" a deep voice called from behind him. Anthony turned to find Lucien Marvaine, the Earl of Roxberry, striding toward him, accompanied by the lovely Lady Crossby, recently widowed, a particularly sad affair, since she'd been left alone with the couple's six-month-old daughter, Sophia.

Anthony smiled as they approached. He'd always gotten on well with Roxberry. He had an adventurous streak that Anthony found particularly entertaining. Stepping forward, he was just about to voice his own greeting when from the corner of his eye he saw a flash of movement and then two things occurred at once. Anthony turned his head to see Daniel Neville dancing his way toward him with a lady he did not recognize. They were just coming up beside Lady Crossby and Roxberry when another firework exploded, a loud bang sounded and Neville's dance partner screamed.

All else forgotten, Anthony ran forward to where Neville stood, his eyes wide open in shock as he held the limp lady in his arms. "Oh Jesus!" His eyes met Anthony's in a frantic plea for help. "Someone shot her. Someone bloody shot her!"

Seeing the red patch of blood at the lady's shoulder, Anthony knew he was right. "Get her on the ground," he said as he removed his jacket for her to lie on. Next, he undid his cravat, bundled it into a tight wad and shoved it toward Neville, who was now kneeling at the lady's side together with Roxberry, Winston and Casper, who'd all come to offer their assistance. "Put this on her wound, add some pressure, and try to stop the bleeding. Winston, I'm leaving you in charge here while I try to find out what the devil happened."

Without a backward glance, Anthony started toward the steps leading up to the terrace. The majority of his guests were still congregated there, gazing up at the sky in expectation of the next firework, oblivious to the fact that a woman had just been shot. Taking the steps two at a time, Anthony quickly reached the terrace. He stopped to look around, searching the crowd for any sign of a perpetrator. Whoever had fired the pistol would have had to stand right at the edge of the terrace, up against the railing where the crowd was most dense.

Signaling a footman, he told the man to alert the guards and close off all the exits. He then pushed his way past the first few people and made his way toward the front, looking around as he went, but nothing struck him as strange or unusual. *Damn*. Whoever he was looking for had probably run off already. Seeing Lord Frompton, Anthony patted him on the shoulder, drawing his attention. "There's been an incident. One of my guests—a woman, to be precise—has been shot."

"Good Lord," Frompton muttered. "Is she dead?"

"I've no idea. I left my brother and a few others to tend to her while I went in search of the villain. The lady in question was shot in the shoulder as she was turned in this direction, indicating that whoever did it must have been standing up here amongst the rest of you. Did you happen to see anything unusual? Someone's sudden departure?"

Frompton shook his head. "I'm afraid not, but I'll help you look. I'll just inform my wife."

Grateful for the extra bit of assistance the earl offered, Anthony gave him a curt nod before making his way over to one of the stone benches that lined the periphery of the terrace. Climbing up, he scanned the crowd again, but nobody was in a hurry to depart. In all likelihood, the would-be assassin had already left the grounds.

Jumping down, Anthony marched toward the doors leading back inside the ballroom. "Don't let anyone else in," he ordered the footman that he'd stationed there, "unless they're a member of this household."

Back inside, he didn't break his stride as he glanced briefly at the orchestra—nothing out of place there. Hurrying onward, he ran up the grand staircase leading up to the foyer, saying, "Did someone else just come this way, Phelps?" to the startled butler.

"A lady, my lord, about ten minutes ago. She'll be long gone by now though—her carriage was ready and waiting."

"Christ! One of my guests has been shot." At this Phelps blanched. "Please dispatch two footmen to fetch the constable along with Doctor Harper."

"Yes, Your Grace," Phelps said stiffly as he turned about and hurried off.

Heading back toward the ballroom, Anthony was met by Neville, who was carrying the shooting victim in his arms, his face pale and filled with a desperation that Anthony had never before seen in the reprobate. He was accompanied by Winston, his mother and . . . Lord and Lady Grifton? Why on earth were they hurrying after Neville with such sour expressions?

Anthony frowned. He'd never cared for how miserly, selfish and arrogant they'd proven themselves to be in the time he'd known them, but their estate was close to his. It would have been badly done not to invite them.

Now was not the time to deliberate, however—there would be time for explanations later. Instead, it was imperative that they did whatever they could to help the woman who'd been shot. Looking beyond them all, he saw that the footman he'd stationed at the ballroom doors was starting to have trouble turning the guests away. It wouldn't be long before someone pushed the man aside, demanding entry. "This way," Anthony told Neville as he switched directions and began heading toward the green parlor. Ushering everyone inside, he closed the door behind him. "You can set her down over there, Neville. I've sent for a doctor, but in the meantime . . ." He hesitated before asking the dreaded question. "Is she alive?"

"It appears so," Winston said while his mother—whom Anthony would have thought to be beside herself in light of how her perfect evening was turning into a rapid disaster—walked across to where the lady now lay and began pulling her sleeve down over her shoulder.

"The least we can do is try to clean this," she explained. "Would you please give me some brandy and another cravat? This one's soaked through."

Anthony blinked, momentarily taken aback by his mother's air of command. It had been years since he'd seen her like this. Eager to help in any way he could, he quickly poured a measure of brandy into a glass and placed it on the table next to where she knelt just as Winston and Neville both handed him their cravats. He gave one to his mother, who dipped the length of fabric into the glass of brandy, then pressed it against the lady's open wound. Her mask had been removed, he realized, revealing a face he hadn't seen since . . .

well, he couldn't quite remember since when, but he suddenly understood why Lord and Lady Grifton were present.

"I thought she was—"

"Quite," Lady Grifton snapped. "Apparently she pulled the wool over all of our eyes."

Trying to find an appropriate response to that and failing miserably, Anthony decided to go in search of Miss Smith. "I ought to explain the situation to our guests, but I'll be back soon. Can you manage until I return?" It was partly true of course—the guests had looked quite disgruntled at being kept outdoors. Deep down inside, however, there was no denying that it was an excuse to find Miss Smith and at the very least bid her a good night before she left.

But when he returned to the ballroom, it was clear that panic had begun to unfold. The rest of the guests must have realized what had happened and were now worried for their own safety. Ignoring the jumble of nerves that tumbled through his stomach at the thought of addressing everyone, Anthony stuck two fingers in his mouth and whistled—rather uncivilized perhaps, but it worked immediately, drawing the attention of one and all.

"Will she be all right?" Louise asked, coming up to him as soon as he'd assured his guests that the shooter had already vacated the premises and no longer posed a threat to any of them. Determined to be hospitable, he ended by saying that the music would resume and that dancing would continue, though he secretly hoped they'd all depart within the next half hour. There was much for his family to attend to; more so once the doctor and constable arrived. "I hope so," he told Louise while her husband stood silently at her side. "It's Lady Rebecca, by the way—the Earl of Airmont's daughter."

The surprise on Louise's face was unmistakable. "The mad one?" This was spoken in a whisper of disbelief.

"Precisely," Anthony said. He still had to figure out what she was doing at the ball. He hadn't invited her, and judging from Lord and Lady Grifton's expressions, they were equally surprised by their niece's attendance.

"If you need assistance, I'd be happy to help," Huntley said.

Anthony nodded his appreciation. "Thank you. I was actually hoping to find Miss Smith. I don't suppose either of you have seen her since you came back inside?"

"She left," Louise said matter-of-factly. "It was right before you returned, so I suppose you must have been—"

"In the green parlor," Anthony muttered, his heart feeling suddenly heavy. He met his sister's gaze. "I don't suppose she said anything significant to you before her departure?"

Louise shook her head, but then she suddenly frowned, and Anthony knew she'd thought of something important. "She rushed past me, saying something about how late it was and that she had to hurry home."

"She did thank you for a lovely evening," Huntley put in.

"Yes, she did, but she'd barely gotten out the door before the Deerfords appeared and . . . ah, here they are again."

It was too late for Anthony to beat a hasty retreat

without being deliberately rude, but he really didn't have time to listen to what either of them might have to say. Lady Rebecca had just been shot in his home, and he'd left his mother and brother to tend to her. He really ought to be getting back to the parlor so he could supervise and offer his support, not to mention the fact that he had quite a few questions for Lady Rebecca and the Griftons.

"Your Grace," Lady Deerford began. She sounded as if she was struggling for breath. "You must tell us who she is—the blonde with the yellow gown—your sister says her name is Miss Smith, but surely you must know something more, like where she lives? How did you address her invitation, Your Grace? It's of the utmost importance that we find her."

"Are you able to tell me why?" Anthony asked, his curiosity piqued.

Wringing her hands together, Lady Deerford glanced at her husband before saying, "When my husband mentioned the startling resemblance Miss Smith's gown bore to the one our daughter wore when she disappeared all those years ago, I was skeptical." She made a nervous little chuckling sound that held an underlying note of sadness. "It's been so long I dared not hope, but then I caught a glimpse of her myself. Upon closer inspection it was clear that she was wearing the exact same gown that our Margaret wore the night she vanished."

Yet another development Anthony hadn't anticipated; the night seemed full of them. Wishing to find out more, yet determined to keep Lady Deerford's peculiarities in mind, Anthony said, "As far as I recall, your daughter went missing when I was but a child.

Perhaps the gown was simply similar—after all, it would be difficult to recall the exact fabric and cut after so long."

"Not at all," Lady Deerford said, a deep pink coloring her cheeks. "I helped my daughter select the fabric myself and . . ." She took a moment to compose herself as she drew a deep breath. "After she went missing, I had a precise replica made for one of my dolls. There's no mistaking that it was the exact same gown."

Anthony stood as if frozen. Lady Deerford's proclamation was truly shocking, for it meant that . . . Well, he wasn't entirely sure of what it meant exactly, except that Miss Smith had somehow come to possess Lady Margaret's ball gown. Could she have found it somewhere? Stolen it perhaps? Or had Lady Margaret given it to her at some point in time? All were important questions that needed answering.

As for the Deerfords—he understood their desperation. They'd lost a daughter whom they'd probably long since accepted they'd never see again, only to be faced with proof of her existence in the form of Miss Smith. He had to find her, not just for himself anymore but for them as well. And she had said . . . "I don't know her exact location, but based on my conversation with her, I don't believe she's far. I'll do what I can to help you find her."

"Thank you, Your Grace," Lord Deerford said, his voice cracking just enough to convey how emotional this was for him. His wife was beyond speaking and merely nodded her appreciation.

"Now, if you will please excuse me, there is a matter of some importance that I must attend to." Addressing his brother-in-law he said, "Will you please see to it that the Deerfords receive some refreshments, Huntley?"

"Certainly," Huntley said, signaling a footman while Anthony strode off in the opposite direction, hoping desperately that Lady Rebecca's condition had not worsened during his absence. If only the doctor would be quick to arrive.

Chapter 9

With the skirt of the gown hugging her legs, Isabella hurried along the path that would take her back to her cottage. It was a long and tedious walk, for although she lived in Moxley, Kingsborough Hall was a good two miles outside of it. Removing her slippers, Isabella picked up the pace. She was used to walking, just not in a highly impractical evening gown.

The sound of horses approaching filled the air, and she moved hastily to the side of the road, crouching down in the hope that she wouldn't be seen. A moment later a carriage tumbled past—most likely filled with guests departing the ball. Her own departure had been hasty, not to mention quite ill-mannered considering that she'd failed to thank either of her hosts for a delightful evening, especially after they'd allowed her to stay knowing she'd not been invited.

But what choice had she had? When an elderly couple had approached her asking about her gown, she'd panicked. They'd wanted to know who she was, where she was from, who her parents were and especially where she'd gotten her gown from—all questions that she couldn't possibly answer without giving herself away and betraying her parents in one clean sweep.

Dear Lord, her mother would never forgive her if a lord and lady came knocking at their door demanding answers. Her mother, who spoke the word *aristocrat* with particular emphasis on the *-rat* part, would find herself humiliated by their accusatory questions. And they would be accusatory, for although Isabella knew that they were mistaken in their belief that the gown was familiar to them, they believed they were correct in their assumption—she'd seen it in their eyes.

The duke would undoubtedly become involved in the whole process as well then, discovering who she was and that she lived in nothing more than a measly cottage. The thought of that happening was unbearable. It was better never to see any of them ever again, to prevent tarnishing His Grace's good opinion of her, to avoid seeing the truth she knew in her heart reflected in his eyes—that his confidence in finding a way for them to be together had been misplaced and was, as she had told him, impossible.

It was with a heavy heart and aching feet that she arrived home, entering the garden through the back gate. She'd left the kitchen window unlatched, and, nudging it open, she climbed through it. It was a tight squeeze, given that she wasn't the skinniest girl in the world, but she managed it all the same, stepping carefully down onto the counter. Marjorie would be livid if she saw— she was hysterical about scrubbing and cleaning and would not take well to knowing that Isabella's dirty feet had occupied the same space as the food for the Chilcott household.

Having considered this beforehand and knowing

that it would be dark upon her return and consequently difficult to see what she was doing, Isabella had prepared a bowl of soapy water, which stood to one side. Taking the cloth she'd laid out beside it, she soaked it, wrung it, and quickly washed away any evidence that Marjorie might discover in the morning. She then gathered up her slippers and exited the room.

Arriving in the hallway, Isabella started making her way across the floor to her bedroom door, but a sliver of light coming from under the door to the parlor caught her attention, and she froze. Her heart pounded in her chest. Somebody was awake, which could only mean that her absence had not gone unnoticed, for her parents never stayed up late.

Remaining completely still, she considered her options. She could either go back the way she'd come, or she could risk discovery and move forward. If nobody noticed her, she could wake up the following morning and claim she'd been unable to sleep and had gone for a walk—a stretch perhaps, but one that would be hard to dispute.

Sucking in a breath, she stepped slowly forward, balancing herself on her tiptoes. One step . . . two steps . . . creak. Isabella stopped midstride. She was right outside the parlor door now. Her heart hammered in her chest and her legs began to tremble, and then the worst possible thing happened. She sneezed. Footsteps sounded and then the parlor door opened, revealing her mother, who was standing there in her dressing gown, staring back at her with the sort of disapproval that only a disappointed parent can emanate. At that very moment, Isabella wanted nothing more than to run out the front door and never look back. But the steel in her mother's eyes warned her against further disobedience, forcing her to enter the parlor instead, where she silently took a seat.

Her mother closed the door behind her. "This is not the sort of behavior I would have expected from you," she said, her voice slicing the air like a knife. Her mother could be gentle and loving, but when she was angry, she was absolutely terrifying, her voice eerily calm while her eyes took on a frosty glare.

"I'm sorry, Mama, I—"

"Have you any idea how worried I've been? Any number of things could have happened to you, but you decided to sneak off with no regard for anyone other than yourself. Even your sister, as recklessly loyal to you as she is, refused to tell me anything when I woke her, though I can well imagine what you've been up to given the way you look. Really, Isabella, I've half a mind to throttle both of you for this harebrained scheme of yours, and with my gown, no less."

"I had nothing else to wear that would have been appropriate," Isabella muttered, feeling wretched for deceiving her mother like this. She'd suspected that the gown had been her mother's, but she hadn't been certain until now. In spite of the awful situation at hand, her curiosity got the better of her, and she found herself saying, "I can't help but wonder where you got such an exquisite gown. How did you . . . I mean, it must have been very expensive."

Her mother's eyes closed momentarily, and when she looked at Isabella again, there was something shining there—an emotion so strong that it took Isabella's breath away. "If you must know, I bought it from a peddler before you were born so I'd have something decent to wear when I married your father. I never gave much thought to where he might have gotten it and have no intention of doing so now." Her mother's eyes darkened. "You will take it off immediately and return it to the trunk in the loft, is that understood?"

Isabella nodded and muttered a weak "yes." It was impossible for her to look her mother in the eye after what she'd done, and yet she felt the need to say something—to offer some sort of explanation in the hope that she might understand. "I'm sorry I betrayed you, Mama. It's just . . . I've always dreamed of attending that ball, and once I marry Mr. Roberts it's unlikely that I'll ever—"

"You should hope and pray that he never finds out about this, Isabella." There was a note of impending doom in her mother's voice that sent shivers down Isabella's spine. "After all of our efforts to steer his attention in your direction, all will be for naught if he ever discovers that you're the sort of woman who enjoys midnight escapades. He'll never stand for it, and you know it."

Isabella did.

"He's your best chance at a happy future," her mother went on, relentlessly hammering on as she always did whenever Isabella showed the slightest sign of disapproval toward Mr. Roberts. "A man who's not only wealthy but also keenly aware of the importance of dressing properly, he'll be sure to supply you with however much money you need to fill a new wardrobe."

"He doesn't desire me for me, Mama. He wants me only because I'm convenient and because you've assured him how easily I can be molded into the trophy he truly wants—one that he can parade about town when need be and then return to the shelf as soon as we arrive home."

Her mother's nostrils flared. "Not only is that untrue but it is also an unkind thing to say about a man who is willing to pluck you out of the gutter and turn you into a swan."

It was Isabella's turn to get angry. "We may not be very well off, Mama, but we certainly don't live in a gutter. Papa works very hard to support us, and there's nothing shameful about his profession either, so don't you dare belittle his efforts!"

"I meant no disrespect toward your father, Isabella," her mother said, walking wearily toward the sofa and sitting down with a loud sigh. "I just don't think that you fully realize how difficult life can be. Why do you think I work so diligently at my embroidery every day? Because I enjoy it?" She shook her head. "Necessity can steal the joy from any task, but I have no choice—we need the extra bit of money the embroidery can fetch.

"Even so, it's not as if we're the poorest people in England, and it's true that we do have Marjorie in our employ, but I want more than that for you, Isabella, for Jamie too when the time comes for her to marry. I want you to have beautiful gowns to wear and to ride in a magnificent carriage—to live in comfort and without having to worry about whether or not you'll have to cut back on a few things in order to have enough money for food. I know what that's like. The first few years with your father were a desperate struggle for survival—one that I wish to protect you from."

"But you love each other, Mama," Isabella said softly.

"Yes, we do. And I have every confidence that you will grow to love Mr. Roberts too. He's a good man, Isabella. You mustn't be too hard on him." Reaching for Isabella's hand, she took it in her own as she met her gaze. "This is part of the reason why I object to all of these fairy-tale romances that you like to read. I believe you've long since conjured an image of the ideal man; a man who doesn't exist, except in your own imagination—a man that nobody else can possibly compete with."

It was true, except for the startling fact that he did exist. Isabella had met him that very evening, had spoken to him and danced with him. Her mother was right. Nobody would ever hold a candle to him—least of all Mr. Roberts.

Chapter 10

"**I**'m sorry about the way the evening turned out, Mama," Anthony said as he stood by the sideboard and poured himself a glass of brandy. He raised an empty glass toward Winston and Huntley, who were each occupying their own armchairs while their wives sat next to Anthony's mother on the sofa. "Would you care for some?"

Both gentlemen nodded, so Anthony proceeded to pour for them as well.

"It wasn't your fault," his mother said, her voice sounding tired. "Not unless it was your idea to have Lady Rebecca shot on my lawn in front of everyone."

"What a thing to say," Louise gasped. She looked at Anthony. "Pour her a sherry, will you? And while you're at it, Sarah and I would like one too."

Anthony hid a smile. He loved his sister dearly and knew that she meant well, which was part of the reason why he rarely asserted himself whenever she tried to take charge. Not unless she was being unreasonable. Stubborn and willful best described her—traits that had resulted in her marrying Huntley when the alternative would probably have been a deep depression. Anthony knew she'd left not because she hadn't cared but because she'd cared too much. Watching their father's daily digression would have killed her—Huntley had offered her the excuse for escape, and as far as Anthony could tell, the two were getting along well enough, for which he was both grateful and relieved.

"The Griftons didn't look very happy," Winston muttered. "But then I suppose that's to be expected. To believe that Lady Rebecca had remained behind at Roselyn Castle, locked away in her chamber, only to find her here, the center of a dramatic event."

"For someone declared to be as mad as a March hare, she did sound rather succinct when I spoke to her," Anthony said, handing the ladies their drinks.

"Neville sounded shocked when her condition was mentioned—as if he'd realized no such thing," Winston said, accepting the glass that Anthony gave to him.

"All things considered," Huntley remarked, "it would probably have taken a great deal for Neville to notice whether or not Lady Rebecca had a few bats loose in the belfry. He's not very levelheaded himself."

"That's true," Anthony heard his mother say as he strode back to fetch the final glass for Huntley. "He's always been too carefree for his own good—much worse than Anthony and Mr. Goodard ever were, and that's saying something."

"I still can't imagine who would do such a terrible thing," Sarah said as she took a careful sip of her drink. Anthony watched her with the same sense of wonder he'd always reserved for his sister-in-law. Everything she did, from the way in which she moved to the way in which she spoke, was done with the same amount of care that one might apply to a piece of artwork. It was most peculiar.

"It's very strange," Anthony's mother said, her brow knit in a tight frown.

"She can't possibly have any enemies," Louise said, looking to her husband, then to Winston and finally to Anthony for an answer.

Huntley shrugged. "It does seem unlikely. Perhaps it was an accident."

"An accident?" Louise's voice pitched. "One does *not* bring a loaded pistol to a ball and then proceed to fire it by accident."

"Huntley's right," Anthony said. All eyes turned to him in surprise and, he surmised, expectation. "What if the bullet wasn't meant for Lady Rebecca but for someone else entirely?"

"She was dancing with Neville at the time," Winston said, following his statement with a large gulp of brandy.

"Now there's a man that many would likely wish dead," Anthony's mother said as she shook her head a little sadly. "His uncle has his work cut out for him, reforming that boy so he can one day inherit. I certainly don't envy him."

"And I don't envy Anthony," Louise said. She gave her brother a look that was filled with genuine sympathy. "Not only are you faced with the challenge of solving an attempted murder but you also have Miss Smith to find."

"As grateful as I am for your consideration, Louise," Anthony felt compelled to say, "the constable will hopefully locate our villain with the help of law enforcement in other parishes, if necessary, which means that all I really have to do is discover Miss Smith's whereabouts. I'll begin tomorrow."

"I say," Winston remarked with the hint of a cheeky smile upon his lips, "she must have left quite an impression on you. I haven't seen you this eager about a woman since I can't remember when."

"It does seem a bit rash," his mother added.

Anthony rolled his eyes. "I am not engaging in a search for her because I'm smitten," he said. At least that wasn't his only reason. "But because the Deerfords are of the opinion that the gown Miss Smith was wearing was the very same one their daughter wore the night she disappeared."

Silence.

"In my opinion it's ridiculous," he continued, pausing only to take a healthy sip of his brandy. "What on earth would Miss Smith be doing with Lady Margaret's ball gown? It's absurd."

"Then again," his mother said, her gaze coming to rest upon Anthony's face, "we don't really know anything about Miss Smith, not to mention that she did adopt Winston's ridiculous idea about being from Flemmington."

"I thought it was rather clever, unveiling her that way," Winston said as he smiled across at Sarah, who was looking at him as adoringly as ever.

"It didn't offer us much information about her though, other than her desperate desire to remain unknown," the duchess said. She leaned slightly forward in her seat and looked at Anthony. "Whoever she may be, she attended this evening without invitation and proceeded to lie to us directly. The only reason she wasn't escorted out was because you developed a weak spot for her. I can understand it in a way—her looks, coupled with that bit of mystery—most men would grovel for her attention."

"I never grovel for anything," Anthony said. His annoyance made the words come out harsher than he'd intended.

"Nevertheless, your interest in her was what kept her here—that and her attire, which indicated that she was every bit the gentlewoman she pretended to be. And I do mean pretend, Anthony, especially given the latest bit of news about the Deerfords. Heavens, she might be someone's maid, for all we know." The duchess's lips twisted into a bit of a pout. "It promised to be such a lovely evening, and now . . . this."

"It could be worse," Sarah said, surprising them all with the sound of her smooth voice. "Lady Rebecca could have died while Miss Smith vanished without a trace. From what I gather, however, Miss Smith cannot be far from here. I was standing close to her when she mentioned seeing the fireworks as a child from her bedroom window."

"How very observant of you, my dear," Winston said, his eyes shining with pride.

"You are right," Anthony told her. He then looked around at everyone else. "She must live within a ten-mile radius to have seen them clearly. If I go into Moxley tomorrow and visit the various homes—"

"You cannot possibly," his mother gasped. "There are hundreds of houses, Anthony—Moxley may not be the biggest town in England, but it's not exactly a village either."

"I can help," Huntley said, "if you wish it."

Winston nodded. "So can I, and if we enlist the help of the footmen too, then it ought not take more than a day to visit all the homes."

"Thank you, both of you." Anthony reached for his brandy. "I'll ask my valet to visit the peripheral homes—that should save us some time." Tossing back the remainder of his drink, he rose to his feet. "If you'll forgive me, it's been a long day, and tomorrow promises to be quite grueling. I'd like to retire to my chambers and get some rest."

"A wise decision," his mother said, nodding. She looked as if she planned to say more but stopped herself.

"What is it?" Anthony asked.

Her eyes met his with such intensity that Anthony found himself taking a step back, hitting the heel of his foot against the chair behind him as he did so. "I know it's been difficult for you the last few years, but I want you to know that I'm so proud of the way in which you've handled it all. I'm sorry about what I said earlier—about needing to take responsibility." She sighed, a sad little smile playing upon her lips. "You've faced your obligations without the least bit of hesitation, and you've reformed. Most men would not have accomplished such a growth of character in so short a time."

"I only did what was necessary, Mama," Anthony said, feeling somewhat bashful from all the praise.

"Perhaps," his mother conceded. "But that makes it no less impressive. I hope you find happiness for yourself, as Louise and Winston have done, for you deserve it. Perhaps Miss Smith—"

"A moment ago you were opposed to her," Anthony said, surprised that his mother would mention Miss Smith in regards to his future.

"I only mean to caution you against acting rashly—at least until we discover more about her and why the Deerfords say they recognized her attire, though I must agree I think they're mistaken in this regard. Don't take me wrong, Anthony—I'm not in the least bit happy about Miss Smith's deceit. Be that as it may, I can't deny that I enjoyed her company—she's a very likeable young lady."

"She's engaged," Anthony muttered, then added, "*almost* engaged."

"What on earth do you mean?" Louise asked. "Is she or is she not? It makes a big difference, you know."

A moment ago, he'd been off to bed. Now he had some explaining to do. Resuming his seat, Anthony said, "I believe there's a long-standing agreement, though the gentleman in question—whoever he may be—has not yet proposed."

"Well then," his mother said with a determined set to her jaw, "it's not too late if she's the one you want, though I can't say I approve of a woman who sneaks around behind the back of the man she's meant to marry, regardless of whether or not their attachment is formal."

"She doesn't wish to marry him," Anthony said. He was tired, and now that they'd embarked on this topic and he was forced to address all that he had learned about Miss Smith during the course of the evening, he was beginning to feel discouraged. "But in spite of that, she kept saying that she *had* to and that anything else would be impossible. I think it's a match arranged by her parents, and for whatever reason, she believes it to be final."

"Whatever the case," Winston said, "you're a determined fellow. You also know how to seduce a woman. If I were you—"

"That's enough," the duchess said, her head turning toward her youngest son in dismay. "That you would even suggest such a thing is reprehensible, and in front of ladies no less. It's so unlike you, Winston, whatever were you thinking?"

"Merely that my brother might consider drawing on some of the experience he garnered before he reformed," Winston said, looking mildly uncomfortable. He'd always been the one to do as he was told and never stray from the dictates of Society, making his career choice all the more surprising. "I'm sure he can manage to charm both her and her parents into accepting a courtship. He is a duke after all."

"My social standing didn't seem to sway her opinion when I brought it up earlier this evening," Anthony muttered. His eyes were beginning to hurt—he really ought to get some sleep. "She still insisted that I should dismiss any ideas I might have of seeing her again, courting her or marrying her. In truth, I don't believe I've ever encountered a woman more bent on turning me down."

"If that's the case, perhaps it would be wise to do as she asks and stay away," Huntley said.

"That's impossible. Especially now that the Deerfords are involved. No, I have to find her, if only for their sake." But he knew he was lying to everyone, including himself, as he said it. The Deerfords were just an excuse. Once he saw Miss Smith again, it would be impossible for him to walk away from her without a fight. The sort of connection they'd shared, however brief it had been, could not be ignored. He'd been with countless women, so he knew—knew as well as he knew his own name—that there was something special between them, something most people never had the fortune to experience. He'd be damned if he was going to let it slip through his fingers.

Chapter 11

The following morning was bright and beautiful. It took a bit of organization to ready the search party, given that the staff was not informed of it until Anthony mentioned it to Phelps as he was heading in to breakfast. He asked that everyone be ready to leave within the hour, which put a bit of a strain on the butler's features, but, being the dutiful servant that he was, he simply said, "I'll see to it right away, Your Grace," and then departed, leaving Anthony to enjoy his eggs and ham with Winston and Huntley.

It was nine o'clock by the time they set out, the horses as eager for a burst of fresh air as the men who rode them. Having made a simple plan during breakfast detailing who would cover which parts of the town, Anthony, accompanied by a footman, rode toward the eastern side of Moxley, while Winston, Huntley, and the rest of the footmen veered off in other directions.

Arriving at a neat row of houses, all white with black roofs, Anthony handed the reins to his accompanying footman and proceeded to climb the front steps. A butler answered, and, having stated his purpose, Anthony showed the man the sketch that the artist had made of him and Miss Smith the previous evening, inquiring if he recognized the woman. A shake of the head indicated that he did not, so Anthony moved on to the next house, where the process was repeated.

And so it went all morning, without the slightest bit of luck. Granted, the picture that Anthony had of Miss Smith was one where her face was partly obscured by the mask she'd worn, but he felt certain that anyone who knew her well would recognize her anyway. He let out a sigh of frustration, for it did seem as though the ground had somehow swallowed her up.

"Any luck?" he asked Winston and Huntley when they rendezvoused at the Sword and Pistol tavern in the middle of the day.

"None at all," Winston said, chasing the sandwich he was eating with a gulp of ale. "Nobody has recognized her based on the drawing, and if you ask me, it's a pretty good drawing, even though our copy was traced from the original."

"We still have a few parts of town left to visit," Huntley said, sounding optimistic. "I wouldn't give up hope just yet."

"You're right," Anthony agreed. Still, he couldn't ignore the sense of doubt that settled over him. They'd visited all the homes belonging to the gentry, which meant that if Miss Smith did indeed reside in Moxley, it was becoming increasingly unlikely that she was of noble birth, or even the daughter of an affluent business owner. Unless of course her butler had deemed it necessary to protect her and had given no indication that he knew her.

Anthony sighed. It was possible—butlers were notoriously protective of their masters and mistresses. Of course it might also have been possible that her family had fallen on hard times and had been forced to move into cheaper accommodations. That would explain her need to marry a man who didn't appeal to her taste, although, if that was the case, Anthony saw no reason why she couldn't as easily marry him.

Something stood in the way—to her mind at least. Only two solutions presented themselves. She or her parents had either made a promise that she felt honor bound to keep or . . . Anthony steeled himself. What if the Deerfords were right? What if the gown she'd worn *had* belonged to their long-lost daughter? He had no idea how Miss Smith might have happened upon it, though he supposed she might have received it as a gift from someone—perhaps Lady Margaret had been in need of money and had sold it. Miss Smith's suitor might then have bought it, offering it as a gift. No, that would be inappropriate. Perhaps Miss Smith had stolen it then? Whatever the case, Anthony found himself unable to dismiss the possibility that Miss Smith was a simple woman from a simple family—a lowborn ignoble, to put it bluntly.

With renewed determination, Anthony kicked his horse into a trot and headed toward the less affluent part of town, his heart filled with a mixture of certainty and apprehension. He was a duke. He couldn't marry just anyone, could he? Determined not to worry about it until his suspicions had been confirmed, he tried to relax. He'd always enjoyed a good challenge. Even if Miss Smith turned out to be the daughter of a blacksmith, he'd still find a way to make her his. He wasn't sure how he'd do it, but he would. Somehow.

Two hours later, he'd visited every house situated between Mill Road and Hill Street. He'd walked down Church Lane and was now turning onto Brook Street, exhausted and lacking the hope he'd had when he'd set out in the morning. It was entirely possible that Miss Smith had only lived in Moxley as a child and had since moved away to another neighboring town. If this was the case, it would be near impossible to find her.

Leaving the footman to keep an eye on the horses, Anthony unlatched the gate leading into the front garden of a small thatched cottage that sat apart from the rest, on the very edge of the town. It was a quaint little place, with daffodils and hyacinths filling up the flowerbeds. Anthony stopped to stare at them, then looked toward the cottage. Miss Smith had spoken fondly of daffodils—they were her favorite flowers. A coincidence perhaps, but one that demanded further investigation.

Shoulders back, Anthony strode up the pathway toward the front door and knocked. Nobody answered. He knocked again. Still nobody answered. Discouraged by his lack of success, he turned to go, but paused at the sound of a door slamming somewhere toward the back. Someone was there; there was still hope that this last person would be able to give him a useful bit of information—unlikely perhaps, but possible.

Skirting the building, he rounded a corner to discover a maid who appeared to be busy at work in the vegetable garden. It looked as if she was digging up new potatoes and tossing them into a basket. "Excuse me," Anthony said, keeping a reasonable distance so as not to frighten her.

The woman looked up and then immediately rose,

bobbing a curtsy while she hastily tried to brush the soil from her hands.

"I hope you'll forgive the intrusion, but nobody answered the door when I knocked, so when I heard a noise coming from back here, I thought I'd see if anyone was at home—save myself the trouble of having to return at a later hour."

"My apologies, sir, but the Chilcotts are not at home right now. You're welcome to wait of course, or leave your calling card if you prefer."

Anthony didn't bother to correct the maid's improper form of address. She'd no way of knowing that he was a duke, and detesting the thought of acting like a pompous aristocrat, he determined to keep quiet about his heritage. "It's been a long day," he said, feeling suddenly overcome by a heavy feeling of weariness. All he wanted was to go home and sit in his favorite chair in the Kingsborough Hall library and enjoy a glass of brandy. "I will be back tomorrow. Perhaps you can recommend a more convenient hour for me to call."

"If it's Mr. Chilcott you're seeking, he's hardly ever here except during the evenings and on Sundays."

Anthony really didn't feel like waiting or venturing back out later in the day. He gave the maid a pleasant smile. "Well, perhaps you can help me then. You see, I'm looking for a woman who attended the Kingsborough Ball last night. If you'd please take a look at this drawing, I'd be most obliged."

Holding the piece of paper up for the maid to see, Anthony watched her frown. She took a moment, but eventually shook her head. "She holds no resemblance to anyone I know," she said.

Well, so much for that.

Thanking her, Anthony slipped the drawing back inside his jacket pocket, turned, and began making his way back toward the front of the cottage when something caught his eye—a piece of fabric stuck in a window. It fluttered slightly, and Anthony watched it shimmer as the yellow threads captured a bit of sunlight. Leaning forward, Anthony reached out and gave it a gentle pull, freeing it. A smile tugged at his lips as he straightened himself. The maid had clearly lied to protect her mistress, for it did appear as though he'd just discovered Miss Smith's whereabouts after all.

Tucking the fabric safely away in the same pocket as the picture, and with more of a spring to his step than he'd managed all day, Anthony continued back to where the footman stood waiting. "Let's go home," the duke said, feeling both cheerful and relieved. He had plans to make now—plans involving a proper social call to Mr. Chilcott and flowers to . . . Miss Chilcott? He couldn't be sure of her real name just yet, though it was fair to assume that she had to be Mr. Chilcott's daughter. He would have to discuss it with his mother of course. She'd probably swoon at the thought of a lowborn woman becoming his duchess, while the gossip-rags would have a splendid time writing about it all in every detail—a price he was willing to pay nonetheless.

"Do you have a moment, miss?" Marjorie asked shortly after Isabella's return from the shops.

As usual, Isabella hadn't bought anything—she never did, she simply liked to browse. And after everything that had happened last night, she'd been in desperate need of some fresh air, as well as something to distract her from all the guilt she felt at betraying her mother, her hasty departure from the ball, lying to everyone and getting her sister into trouble for helping her do all of these things.

And then of course there was Mr. Roberts to consider. He'd be joining her for afternoon tea tomorrow. However would she look him in the eye without feeling like the most wretched woman to have ever walked the earth? She could picture him now, all proper and perfectly starched as he sipped his tea, oblivious to the fact that the woman he meant to marry had snuck out of her house in the middle of the night, traipsed across the countryside, kissed a duke *and,* most deplorably of all, lost her heart to said duke.

She pushed the thought aside and eyed her maid. "Certainly," she said, growing curious as she noted Marjorie's troubled expression. "Right this way."

They entered the parlor, where Isabella took a seat while Marjorie remained standing. "A gentleman came to call today," Marjorie said without preamble. It was one of the things Isabella liked best about her—she was always direct.

"Oh? And did he have a name?" Isabella asked, frowning. The only gentleman who ever came to call was Mr. Roberts, but Marjorie knew him, so it had to be someone else. A growing sense of uneasiness began to tickle her skin.

"He didn't give me one, but he showed me a picture, miss—one that looked an awful lot like you, if you don't mind my saying so. I might be mistaken of course, given that there was a mask covering part of the face, but I'm familiar enough with your features to be sure." Her gaze dropped to the floor and she quietly said, "It was a very good drawing."

Isabella sucked in a breath. *Good Lord!* She swallowed hard as she tried to collect herself and stop her hands from trembling. "What did you tell him?" She grasped the fabric of her skirt and twirled it between her fingers.

Lifting her gaze, Marjorie looked directly at Isabella. "That I didn't recognize the woman in the picture." She paused momentarily before adding, "I think he believed me, for he seemed rather disappointed and left shortly after."

Isabella nodded. "You did the right thing by not telling him that I live here. Thank you."

The corners of Marjorie's mouth tightened into an odd little smile. "There's something else you ought to know, miss. He said he'd be back tomorrow."

"*What?*" This wasn't happening, it simply was not.

"Forgive me, but he'd already inquired as to when it might be more likely for him to encounter Mr. Chilcott before I realized that he was looking for you. I'm sorry if this puts you in a difficult position."

"It's all right, Marjorie." Isabella's voice sounded faint to her own ears. She felt light-headed and on the verge of falling into a state of panic. "You didn't know."

"Once again, I'm truly sorry," Marjorie said, bobbing a curtsy as she exited the room, closing the door behind her.

Isabella sat in perplexed silence for a long while after. He'd found her, and all because he'd caught her off guard the previous evening during the fireworks display. She was sure that had to be it, because she'd been careful otherwise.

Blast!

Her mind whirled as she tried to think of how best to address the situation. He might be back tomorrow, but he still didn't know that he'd found her. Perhaps she could talk to her father—warn him of the duke's impending visit. And, she decided, she'd have to tell her mother as well. Isabella dropped her head into her hands at the thought of it and groaned. After their argument the previous evening, she'd rather hoped to avoid having to discuss the Kingsborough Ball with her again—had hoped that they could just carry on as if it had never happened. She didn't want to tell her mother any more lies though.

With a deep sigh of resignation, she pulled herself together, rose to her feet and headed for the kitchen. She'd ask Marjorie to help her prepare a cup of hot cocoa. Cocoa made everything better—especially when it was served with scones topped with cream and strawberry jam.

"**O**f all the stupid things you could possibly do," Isabella heard her mother say as they sat across from one another at the dining room table that evening. Her father, seated at the head of the table, was being his usual nonconfrontational self and had said nothing as of yet. "Have you no pride?"

"Of course I do, Mama. This has nothing to do with that. The duke—"

"I beg to differ," her mother said, cutting Isabella off and pointing her fork directly at her daughter as if it had been a sword. "You've made a mockery of the Kingsboroughs by sneaking about the way you did, acting as if you had a right to be there. I daresay the duke will be incensed when he discovers the truth about you, and then where will we be? Only the Regent holds more power than a duke, Isabella. What if he decides to have you arrested? I'm sure he can find a way if that's what he wishes, or worse, he might insist on making you his mistress."

Isabella blanched. "He would never make such a demand," she muttered. "He was kind toward me even though he knew I'd told him a Banbury tale. He knew me to be an imposter, and yet he allowed me to stay, as did his mother."

"Hmf!" her mother retorted, taking a sip of her wine. "And that doesn't worry you? You're a bigger fool than I thought, Isabella."

Isabella had been in the middle of cutting a piece of chicken, but she paused at her mother's words and slowly raised her head to look at her. "What do you mean?"

Her mother took a deep breath. "Hasn't it occurred to you that he should have tossed you out?" Her mother's eyes narrowed. "Did he make any advances on you?"

Isabella dropped her gaze. Her cheeks were burning as she quietly said, "He kissed me."

"And you let him?" Her mother's tone was sharp and accusing.

"I . . ." A sigh of defeat escaped Isabella's lips. "Yes."

"Then I am right—as unfortunate as that is. He has designs on you. That's why he didn't ask you to leave. His mother's wishes would have been inconsequential. He's the duke, and judging from what you've just told us, it's quite clear that he was—"

"That's enough!" Isabella watched in stunned silence as her mother froze, her mouth dropping open in response to her husband's outburst. She turned her head toward him. Isabella turned too. "Nobody is going to make a mistress of my daughter," he said, his voice deep and rough and desperately protective. "I'll meet with the duke and explain the situation properly to him. I'm sure he'll understand." He looked at his wife. "And I would like to caution you, madam, against speaking of such things when there are children present—it's unbecoming."

They all turned to look at Jamie, who was seated opposite her father at the other end of the table, eyes wide with interest. She looked vastly entertained by the discussion taking place, but she wisely fixed her attention on her meal, quite possibly hoping that this would make her invisible.

"I only meant to draw attention to the severity of the situation," Isabella's mother said, her tone a little softer than before as she turned her gaze away from her youngest daughter and regarded her husband instead. "It's obvious that she's caught the duke's attention, so if he's out looking for her, it's also obvious that he *wants* her."

"He's known to be a reasonable man, love. I'm sure he'll leave Isabella in peace once I've had a word with him."

Isabella doubted it. After all, she'd told him repeatedly that they couldn't be together. As if to confirm this fear, her mother said with incredulity, "Reasonable? He's one of the worst rakes this country's ever seen! Why, he and that friend of his were notorious for leaving a blazing trail of ruined maidens behind them in their youth."

Isabella saw her father frown. "I believe that's highly exaggerated, my dear, not to mention that the duke is older now and has proven himself quite responsible these past five years or however long it's been . . . I forget."

"All I can say," Isabella's mother said, "is once a rake, always a rake, and a duke is a dangerous man to meddle with to begin with. You know as well as I that these sorts expect to have their way."

There was a look in her mother's eye that Isabella couldn't quite place as she stared back at her husband—as if the two of them were sharing a silent exchange.

Jamie's fork clattered against her plate as she accidentally dropped it, distracting Isabella from her pondering. "What if she's right, Papa?" she asked in a muted tone. "What if he won't listen?"

"Then we may have to resort to different measures."

"Such as?" Isabella's mother asked, her eyes still riveted upon her husband.

"Such as encouraging Mr. Roberts to propose right away. Once you're married, the duke will have no choice but to abandon all thought of you."

It was true, and a simple plan. Yet Isabella felt her shoulders slump as she expelled a deep breath. There was a feeling of emptiness inside her that she feared might never be filled. Pushing back the tears that threatened at the thought of marrying a man she did not love when the man she truly desired had declared himself eager to court her, she stabbed a piece of chicken with her fork. It was a fate she would have to accept. Social standing would make it difficult for the Duke of Kingsborough to show any interest in making her his duchess, and it was unlikely he'd wish to once her father spoke to him. Her mother was right. If he still wanted her after discovering that she was nothing more than the daughter of a carriage driver, he'd want her as his mistress. It was disheartening to consider, but in this instance she had to agree with her mother—being realistic was of far greater importance than being romantic.

Chapter 12

As was to be expected, Mr. Roberts appeared at precisely three o'clock the following day, dressed in a moss green velvet jacket and a pair of dark brown buckskin breeches with newly buffed Hessians to match. "Miss Chilcott," he said, bowing toward Isabella as he entered the parlor. "You look lovely today. I see that you took my suggestion of tying a cerulean blue ribbon in your hair to heart."

He did not smile as he said it but managed to maintain the perfectly bland expression that Isabella had come to expect from him. The ribbon had been her mother's suggestion, since Isabella had no recollection of him having mentioned any such thing—probably because he'd said it during one of her woolgathering moments. And although she hated having ribbons tied in her hair (they always got in the way or came loose to dangle in one's eyes), she had submitted herself to her mother's command. It was vital that she got Mr. Roberts to offer for her as soon as possible, and given his character, this was more likely to be accomplished if Isabella showed herself to be agreeable. "Yes," she heard herself say as they took their seats on the sofa across from her parents. "I believe it was very sound advice."

With a nod of approval, Mr. Roberts's gaze slid sideways. "Ah, the infamous apple pie," he said. "It looks even better than I remember."

Isabella stifled a groan while her mother did the honor of serving them all a slice and pouring tea.

"I trust you have all been well since I last saw you," Mr. Roberts said, following a bite of pie with a sip of tea.

"Very much so," Isabella's mother said. Her voice was completely level, and she even managed what looked to be a genuine smile. There was absolutely no trace of the tension that was surely strung as tight as a bow inside her. "And you, Mr. Roberts? Has business been good for you this past week?"

"It has been acceptable—not too busy and not too slow." He set his cup on its saucer, leaned back against the sofa and folded his hands in his lap, saying nothing further.

Isabella reached for the pie. She'd already had one piece, but she felt the need to occupy herself with something, and eating pie—even though it was apple and she'd grown quite tired of that particular flavor—felt like a useful way to accomplish this. But just as she picked up the knife, Mr. Roberts said, "Not that I mean to pass judgment, Miss Chilcott, but I do wish you would have a care for your figure."

Her grip on the knife tightened. Would it be so terrible if she stabbed the man to death right there on the sofa?

Feeling her mother's eyes upon her, Isabella took a

calming breath, set the knife aside and turned her head to look at Mr. Roberts directly, saying, "I was actually hoping that you might like to go for a stroll with me after tea." This had been her parents' idea, for they had deemed it safer for Isabella to be out of the house in case the duke stopped by. It would also offer her a bit of alone time with Mr. Roberts, which was meant to encourage him in his pursuit of her.

Mr. Roberts nodded thoughtfully as he plucked a piece of lint from his jacket. "Yes, that would be most agreeable—the weather is ideal for a stroll about town. Perhaps we can find a new pair of gloves for you."

Isabella frowned. "That's very thoughtful of you, but I already have a perfectly good pair."

His grimace was so subtle that Isabella probably wouldn't have noticed it if she'd been sitting a little further away from him. The message was clear—he did not approve of the gloves she currently owned, which caused her to wonder what else he might disapprove of and, more to the point, how much of herself she'd have to change in order for him to find her acceptable. After all, two criticisms in the space of one minute were hardly indicative of a happy future.

The duke had taken no issue with her appearance—on the contrary, his appreciation for her had shone in his eyes. True, she'd been wearing an evening gown, but she'd begun to suspect that no matter what she wore, she'd never elicit a look of desire, longing or anything that even bordered on the emotional from Mr. Roberts. He was like a statue—perfect, but cold.

"Consider it a gift," he said as he rose to his feet in one fluid movement. "Besides, a lady ought to own more than one pair."

Isabella rose as well and accepted the arm Mr. Roberts offered her. He thanked her parents for their company, assured them that he would take exceptionally good care of their daughter and then proceeded to escort Isabella down the garden path and out the front gate.

"Lovely weather, don't you think?" Mr. Roberts asked as they made their way along Brook Street.

"Yes, it is," Isabella agreed. Trust Mr. Roberts to commence their conversation by discussing something as mundane as the weather. *Typical.* They continued on in silence until they reached Church Lane, when, feeling as if she ought to try to discover something more meaningful about Mr. Roberts, Isabella said, "Do you read?"

"Certainly," he said. "I read the papers every morning."

It was difficult for her not to roll her eyes at that response, particularly since she knew he was being serious. "I am speaking of books, Mr. Roberts—do you enjoy reading books?"

His face looked suddenly strained, as if he found the question uncomfortable in some way. "If you're referring to novels, Miss Chilcott, I must admit I've never bothered with the stuff—waste of time if you ask me."

Isabella's heart sank. They had less in common than she'd dared imagine.

"I hope you're not the sort who likes to while away the hours by reading all those ridiculous tales," he continued. "For if you are, I'll have no choice but to insist you stop doing so once we are married. There will be far more practical things for you to attend to, such as the daily running of the household, our wardrobes, which must be renewed seasonally, and of course the matter of . . . ahem . . . producing children."

Isabella had been certain that her heart had dropped as far as it possibly could with his previous statement. She'd been wrong. In one halfhearted remark, Mr. Roberts had alluded to their marriage as a certainty even though he had not yet proposed and she had not yet accepted. Additionally, he had a very clear notion of what he expected of her once they were married, and the thought of having to give up on reading as well was more than she could bear. "I cannot imagine a life without books in it," she muttered, more to herself than to him.

He heard her anyway, for he gently patted her hand with his and said, "You'll adjust soon enough, for I do believe that your chores will keep you much too busy to even consider lazing about with a book—at least not with *those* kinds of books. If you wish to read the ledgers, then that's another matter."

Feeling a desperate urge to scream but knowing how little that would accomplish, Isabella clenched her jaw tightly and took a deep, steadying breath. He might have had the means to dress her in costly gowns and jewels, but she was quickly becoming aware that life with Mr. Roberts would be the very opposite of comfortable—indeed, it promised to be hell.

Her options were few however. Dreaming about the duke was pointless. He wouldn't want her as his duchess, of this she was certain. And if she didn't marry Mr. Roberts, she'd likely end up becoming a spinster unless she married a man with a lower status and income.

Her parents would be terribly disappointed with either of these results, not to mention that she'd have difficulty helping them financially. And they needed help. As it was they could barely afford Marjorie, but her mother insisted that proper ladies did not involve themselves in the preparation of food, nor did they clean. So her parents managed as best they could, hoping that Isabella would marry well.

There was also Jamie to consider. Isabella desperately wanted her to have more of a choice than she herself did once the time came for Jamie to marry. No, she really couldn't allow herself to be selfish when it came to her future. There was too much at stake.

"Come along," Mr. Roberts told her as they turned on to Main Street. "Stop dragging your feet. A lady should keep a decent pace—neither too slow nor too fast. If you follow my lead, you'll manage quite nicely, I believe."

The tempting thought of hitting Mr. Roberts over the head with her reticule flashed through Isabella's mind. She forced a smile instead. "I shall endeavor to please you, Mr. Roberts," she said, hoping that her tone didn't really sound as sarcastic as it did to her own ears.

"Splendid," Mr. Roberts said as he guided her across the road toward the glove shop on the other side. "I knew I could count on you to be agreeable—it's one of the things I like best about you."

Isabella winced. In her opinion, *agreeable* was one of the worst descriptions a person could attach to their character, for it indicated weakness and a willingness to submit to the needs of others. She hated how well it suited her current state of being, especially since she didn't usually consider herself the agreeable sort; she was much too argumentative by nature. But, in regards to Mr. Roberts, she had no choice but to suppress her instinct to argue, or he might decide to cast her aside like a dishrag, and as desirable as such an outcome might be to her, she knew it would put a strain on her family.

"Here we are," Mr. Roberts said when they arrived in front of the shop. He opened the door and held it while Isabella stepped inside. Following her he added, "If I recall from my previous visit, the gloves are on the shelves behind the counter."

It wasn't a large shop, and with three other customers inside, Isabella thought it a bit cramped. "Perhaps we should come back another time," she suggested.

"Nonsense," Mr. Roberts replied. "Here, why don't you have a look at the selection of reticules over there while we wait?"

Having little else with which to pass the time, Isabella walked over to the display case that stood up against the shop window. A reticule made from deep red satin and trimmed with black beadwork caught her eye. It was bold—too bold for an unmarried woman to have in her possession, yet Isabella fell instantly in love with the item, most likely *because* of that. In fact, she was so busy admiring it that she failed to notice that there was someone else looking back at her from the other side of the window—until the person moved.

Looking up, she caught only a brief glimpse of the back of a man's jacket before the door to the shop opened and a little bell rang, announcing the arrival of yet another customer. Turning to look, Isabella found herself assaulted by a rush of heat, for there before her stood none other than the Duke of Kingsborough—the very man she'd hoped to avoid.

It was her. Anthony was absolutely certain of it. Having decided to take advantage of the lovely weather, he'd chosen to leave his horse at the Sword and Pistol and walk to the Chilcotts' home from there. It was more convenient anyway, since he intended to bring flowers with him, and flowers always looked better when one arrived on foot than on horseback.

Passing the glove shop, he automatically turned his head to look at the items displayed in the window and froze. He couldn't believe it. The upper part of her face was obscured by the shop sign, which read Burton's Fine Goods & Accessories, but he recognized those lips . . . the curve of that jawline. . . . He'd pictured them in his mind's eye repeatedly since the night of the ball. There could be no mistaking it—he'd found Miss Smith. Turning away from the window, he went to the door, pulled it open and stepped inside.

"Ah, Mr. Roberts," he said, recognizing the only other gentleman present. "What a pleasant surprise. Again, I must thank you for the curricle you had delivered to my estate—I still don't know how you manage to make them faster and sturdier than other designs. It's a remarkable bit of engineering, really." Anthony hoped that a bit of light conversation would allow for an air of casualness while he discreetly regarded the woman who stood by the window. She'd turned to look at him as he'd entered, her eyes had widened and then she'd quickly looked away.

Mr. Roberts nodded, his face as bland as usual. Anthony had always thought him an odd fellow, though he had to admit that the man knew how to dress. In fact, he couldn't recall seeing him in the same ensemble more than once, which, for a man who wasn't nobility and had inherited no fortune from anyone, could only be considered a testament to his success.

"I'm glad that you're pleased with it, Your Grace," Mr. Roberts said, glancing sideways. He returned his gaze to Anthony. "As it happens, I'm developing a new design for a faster and more luxurious landau. Perhaps I can tempt you?"

They moved aside to allow the other three women who had now finished with their purchases to pass so they could exit the shop.

"I might have to visit your facilities one of these days," Anthony agreed, his gaze shifting to the woman who'd drawn him into the shop in the first place. It was the first time he'd looked at her properly. His heart began beating faster in his chest. When he'd last seen her she'd been wearing a mask, and while he'd known she'd be beautiful without it, he hadn't expected her to be quite so breathtaking.

"How terribly rude of me," Mr. Roberts said. "I've quite neglected to introduce you to Miss Chilcott. We were hoping to find a new pair of gloves for her—that's why we're here. Miss Chilcott, please join us."

With a growing sense of uneasiness, Anthony watched as Miss Chilcott stepped toward them. She looked perfectly calm and collected, save for her hands, which were clenched in tight fists at her sides. She looked at Mr. Roberts, who immediately said, "May I present you to His Grace, the Duke of Kingsborough?"

Anthony waited while Miss Chilcott dropped into a deep curtsy. "It is an honor, Your Grace," she said, her head bowed toward the floor.

She rose, and Anthony reached for her hand. Bowing over it, he lifted it to his lips and placed a gentle kiss upon her knuckles, his eyes meeting hers from beneath his lashes as he did so.

The blush in her cheeks was unmistakable. "What a coincidence," Anthony said. He'd begun to suspect that Mr. Roberts was the man she intended to marry, for it would be unusual for them to shop for gloves together otherwise—especially with Mr. Roberts's character taken into account. Consequently, Anthony found himself quite unable to stop himself from adding a little more to Miss Chilcott's state of discomfort. "As it happens, I was on my way to the Chilcott residency just now to meet with your father."

"Oh, so you know them then?" Mr. Roberts asked, seemingly oblivious to the pallor of Miss Chilcott's face.

"Not yet," Anthony said, smiling at Miss Chilcott. She was really taking the whole thing remarkably well, all things considered. "My interest in them pertains to some information regarding a missing person—it has come to my attention that Mr. Chilcott might be able to help."

Miss Chilcott coughed. "Beg your pardon," she said. "If you don't mind, I do believe I'll take a look at the gloves."

"Well," Mr. Roberts said, "I do hope you find this person you're looking for."

"Thank you," Anthony muttered, his eyes still on Miss Chilcott. The lady had a lot of explaining to do. Just to be sure that he'd made the right assessment, he turned to Mr. Roberts, lowered his voice to a whisper and said, "Forgive me, but I can't help but wonder if congratulations are in order?" He nodded toward Miss Chilcott, who stood with her back toward them, her right hand inside a dark green glove.

"Not yet, but soon, I believe. Her parents are quite eager, and besides, the sooner we marry, the sooner I can tell Mrs. Jenkins that she's free to retire."

"Mrs. Jenkins?" Anthony asked, frowning.

"My housekeeper. She's a lovely woman but too old for all that's required of her. Miss Chilcott is young and spirited—she'll do marvelously well, I'm sure."

"As your housekeeper or as your wife?" Anthony couldn't believe he'd just asked such a question, but what Mr. Roberts had suggested was far too outrageous to be ignored.

"I see no reason why Miss Chilcott cannot fulfill the duties of a housekeeper *and* a wife. I am not expecting her to scrub the floors after all, but I don't desire a woman who is of the opinion that it is her sole purpose in life to sit on a chair and look pretty. Besides, having a housekeeper is an unnecessary expenditure when one's wife is perfectly capable."

"I see." It did sound logical, but the way he said it . . . something about it convinced Anthony that Miss Chilcott was destined to live a grueling existence if she married Mr. Roberts. He didn't like it one bit. There had to be a way to stop him from offering for her. As it was, he did seem a bit too much like a dangle after, though Anthony couldn't for the life of him imagine why he was taking so long in coming up to scratch. Had *he* been in Mr. Roberts's shoes, he and Miss Chilcott would have been well on their way to expanding their family by now.

"What do you think of this pair?" Miss Chilcott

asked, turning just enough to hold up a pair of dark blue gloves for Mr. Roberts to see.

Anthony liked them and was about to say as much when Mr. Roberts said, "I don't think that's a very good color for your hands—the green ones were better."

Miss Chilcott blinked, and so did Anthony. What an absurd comment. Anthony considered saying as much but stopped himself. As far as Mr. Roberts was concerned, Anthony had no reason to defend Miss Chilcott, and for the present, it was best it remained that way. So he held silent instead while Miss Chilcott frowned, sighed and nodded as she told the woman behind the counter that the green pair was better.

It was a dratted business really. When Miss Chilcott had mentioned her impending engagement on the night of the ball, it hadn't occurred to Anthony that he might actually know the man. For some reason he'd thought it a simple enough task to steal her away from whoever he turned out to be. That the man was Mr. Roberts complicated the matter significantly, not just because Anthony knew him (however little that might be), but because he lived in Moxley and Anthony would have to face the very real possibility of happening upon him on a regular basis. Really, was there anything much worse than passing the man whose fiancée you'd stolen in the street?

Anthony sighed. He'd speak to Mr. Chilcott first and *then* decide how best to deal with Mr. Roberts. And then of course there were the Deerfords, who needed contacting. That would be yet another delicate matter. It would probably be best if he first discovered if (a) the gown Miss Chilcott had worn to the ball was in fact the same as the one belonging to Lady Margaret and (b) if it was, then how such a thing could be possible.

If he could only answer these questions, he felt certain that everything would be made a lot simpler.

"Do you plan to stop anywhere else before calling on the Chilcotts, Your Grace, or would you like to walk with us? We're going there directly." Mr. Roberts said as he took Miss Chilcott's parcel for her and offered her his arm. She did not look at Anthony as she took it, but she did not have to for him to know how awkward she felt—it was radiating from her entire person.

"Thank you. I'd be happy to join you," Anthony said, deciding that he'd have to abandon his idea of buying flowers—if anything, it would make the situation more difficult than it already was. He would have to slow down a bit instead. Especially since he didn't wish to embarrass anyone, and he had to admit that arriving at the Chilcotts' front door with flowers for Miss Chilcott when Mr. Roberts was in attendance would be humiliating for everyone, not to mention exceptionally badly done.

"After you," Mr. Roberts said, gesturing for Anthony to lead the way.

They stepped back into the street and began walking. Nobody said a word for a while until Miss Chilcott, much to Anthony's surprise, suddenly said, "I was wondering, Your Grace, do you enjoy reading?"

Anthony considered asking if it was some sort of a trick question, considering how unexpected it was.

"I don't th—," Mr. Roberts began, only to be silenced by Miss Chilcott, who continued with, "You see, Mr. Roberts and I were discussing the matter earlier—reading, that is. Not your reading habits, of course, since that would be absurd considering we've only just met, but relating to ourselves." She drew a deep breath while Anthony struggled to hide his grin. Apparently Miss Chilcott liked to speak when she was nervous.

"And what, pray tell, did you discover?" Anthony asked. He tipped his hat to an elderly lady and stepped aside so she could pass.

"That reading is an indulgence that only serves to distract from more important things in life." This statement came from Mr. Roberts.

"Such as?" Anthony asked.

"Such as the improvement of oneself, of one's household and of one's business."

Trust Mr. Roberts to think like that.

"Well, I do like to enjoy the occasional book," Anthony said, deciding that this was as good a time as any to start making Miss Chilcott aware of the ways in which he would make a better match for her than Mr. Roberts. "The library at Kingsborough Hall is vast, so I often find myself passing the evening with a bit of poetry or a novel."

There was an unmistakable sigh from Miss Chilcott, and Anthony found himself smiling. It didn't matter—he was walking in front of them, so they couldn't see.

"To each his own, I suppose," Mr. Roberts said. "But I for one have always considered the arts a complete waste of time. All it really is, is a bunch of people who've decided not to work but to take advantage of the rest of us instead by profiting on their hobbies. Painting, writing books and playing music . . . if all these so-called artists would only make themselves useful by doing actual work, the world would have advanced much further by now, of that I have no doubt."

That settled it. If there had been the slightest bit of uncertainty in Anthony's mind about continuing his pursuit of Miss Chilcott now that he'd discovered that he actually knew the man she planned to marry, it had just been completely and utterly dismissed.

The man was obviously an idiot. More than that, he'd actually told Anthony that Miss Chilcott would be taking on the duties of housekeeper once they married. If that didn't spell frugal when even Anthony was aware that Mr. Roberts made a substantial amount of money, then Anthony wasn't sure what did.

But for Miss Chilcott—the vibrant and cheerful woman he'd met the night of the ball—to be subjected to such a dreary existence was not only unfair but would also probably be harmful to her character. Mr. Roberts would break her, whether he intended to do so or not, and Anthony realized that it was no longer only about his wish to be with her; it was also about a deep-born need to save her.

None of them said anything further until they arrived at the Chilcotts' cottage. "Mama, Papa," Miss Chilcott said as she opened the door to what Anthony soon discovered to be the parlor, "we have returned from our walk and have brought with us the duke, who said he wished to meet with you, Papa."

Following Mr. Roberts into the room, Anthony spoke a greeting and bowed toward Mrs. Chilcott, who didn't look the least bit happy to see him. He turned to Mr. Chilcott and put out his hand. The older man hesitated only a moment before accepting it in a firm handshake. Like his wife, however, he did not smile, which could only mean that whatever they imagined the reason for his visit to be, it wasn't good.

Well, he'd just have to prove them wrong, that was all.

"If this is an inconvenient hour for you, sir, I can return at another time," Anthony said, mostly because he felt it would be the polite thing to say—not because he really wanted to leave only to come back again later. He wanted the whole affair to be over with.

"This way if you please," Mr. Chilcott said as he directed Anthony through to another, much smaller room that was sparsely furnished with a wooden table that could seat up to six people, and a credenza that stood tall against one wall. This was clearly their dining room. Closing the door behind Anthony, Mr. Chilcott gestured to one of the chairs. "Do have a seat."

"Thank you, Mr. Chilcott." Anthony sat, adjusted himself so he was comfortable and then reached inside his jacket pocket to pull out the drawing of himself and Miss Chilcott. "I met a woman the other day—at the Kingsborough Ball, to be exact—but she departed very suddenly while I was attending to some business. I'd like to find her again if possible and was hoping that you might be able to help me in that regard."

He handed the drawing to Mr. Chilcott, who studied it for a moment before he finally shook his head. "I'm sorry, Your Grace, but I have never seen this woman before."

Anthony sat frozen. He could not believe that Miss Chilcott's own father was denying that it was his daughter in the picture. "How can you say that, sir, when it is obvious even with the mask she's wearing that this is—"

"Nobody I know," Mr. Chilcott said firmly. "And in case you are implying otherwise, my daughter was here, asleep in her own bed that night. I know, because she and I played chess together that evening while we waited to watch the fireworks display—which was beautiful, by the way."

Anthony was stunned. He was being deliberately shut down. Either that, or Miss Chilcott wasn't the woman he'd danced with at the ball after all. Perhaps he'd just wanted her to be Miss Smith so badly that he'd convinced himself that they were one and the same.

They looked alike, based on the drawing, but then again there was the mask to consider. He shook his head. No, it wasn't possible. Miss Chilcott *was* Miss Smith—she *had* to have been. He felt it deep in his bones. Whatever his reason, Mr. Chilcott was lying. Discussing the possibility of a courtship, not to mention the Deerfords, would have to wait. Anthony had to think about everything he'd learned first, and in order to do so properly, he would have to go home. His mother would be able to help perhaps, Winston and Casper too. Yes, he would have to invite Casper over, because when it came to women, he always knew what to do when faced with a problem. The fact that he was a rake was no coincidence—it was a vocation that came naturally to him.

Chapter 13

"**M**r. Goodard is waiting for you in the library, sir," Phelps announced as soon as Anthony returned home.

He handed the butler his hat and gloves with a smile. How convenient that Casper had decided to call exactly when Anthony wished to speak to him. It was probably no coincidence though—his friend would want to know about Anthony's progress regarding Miss Smith.

"I was planning to send you a dinner invitation," Anthony said as he walked into the library and spotted his friend, who was comfortably seated in one of the deep leather armchairs with a book in his hand, "but you've saved me both the paper and the need to dispatch a footman. Thank you for that."

Casper grinned. "Truth be told, I'm desperate to discover if you've found Miss Smith."

Anthony nodded and walked over to the side table. "I thought you might be. Care for a drink?" He held up a crystal carafe filled with brandy.

"Please."

Turning his back on his friend, Anthony prepared a glass for each of them. "What are you reading?" he asked as he strode across to where Casper was sitting, placed the glass on the table in front of him and sat down opposite his friend.

"*Candide,*" Casper replied, handing it to Anthony. "Love the sarcasm."

"Hm . . . trust you to find the one book I've hidden away." Anthony put the book aside and took a sip of his brandy.

Casper followed suit. "That's not entirely true—there's also the *Memoirs of a Woman of Pleasure* that you've so diligently placed behind Chaucer."

Anthony coughed. "Yes, well . . . my mother would probably have a fit of the vapors if she discovered either one of them." Getting up, he took the book and returned it to its rightful place—behind Defoe.

"Even with *Candide*?" Casper asked, frowning. He sounded unconvinced.

"She considers it blasphemous, which I suppose I can understand—in a way."

Casper shrugged. "So tell me—did you find the elusive Miss Smith?"

Hesitating a moment, Anthony considered what he'd discovered. He then met Casper's gaze and nodded with slow deliberation as he walked back to his seat. "Yes, I did."

"And?" Casper's eagerness for information was most apparent not only from his tone of voice but from his posture as well, for he was now leaning forward in his seat as if the act of doing so would elicit a quicker reply.

"And her name is Miss Chilcott. Her father is employed at Roberts' Exclusive Carriages." He reached for his brandy. God how he needed it with everything he'd learned today.

"Well, I hate to state the obvious, old chap, but she's hardly duchess material then. Society dictate will want you to marry a lady and . . . Miss Chilcott, was it?" Anthony nodded morosely. "Why, she may be lovely to look at and more charming than most, but she's not even the daughter of a baronet!"

"I am aware of that small detail, thank you very much. However, there's no law preventing me from courting her or from marrying her should I choose to do so."

"It will be social suicide if you ask me," Casper muttered. "You're a duke, which unfortunately for you and Miss Chilcott means that you have a standard to uphold."

Anthony knew this of course, but that didn't mean he liked it. "Hang Society," he muttered, tossing back the rest of his drink. "Besides, it's not as if this family hasn't done the unconventional before. Winston has still not been accepted back into some circles because of his business, but at least he's happy with the choice he made."

"If I were you, I'd marry the daughter of an earl and make Miss Chilcott your mistress," Casper said, ignoring Anthony's comment. "Besides, you know what these highborn ladies are like—too prim to be stroked, much less . . ." He allowed the sentence to trail off. "So if you do marry one, you'll require someone else on the side to satisfy your needs." Anthony scowled, but Casper blithely continued with, "You may have abandoned your rakish ways, but men like us have appetites, and that's not something that ever goes away."

"You're disgusting," Anthony said, though he had to admit there was some truth to it. How often had he submitted to his own hand in the course of the past five years? Thousands, perhaps more. And since he'd met Miss Chilcott . . . if she only knew what he'd done as he'd thought of her luscious body these past two evenings since the ball.

Casper smiled. "Say what you will, but I can see it on your face. Make Miss Chilcott your mistress and I'm sure she'll—"

"Stop right there!" Anthony warned. "Miss Chilcott is a decent woman, Casper. She's not the sort with loose morals, and I won't allow you to speak of her in such a degrading fashion."

Casper held up his hands. "Fair enough."

The door opened and Anthony, turning his head, found both Winston and his mother entering the room. "I hope we're not intruding," his mother said. She was wearing a rusty orange day dress that went well with her coloring, her black and gray completely abandoned, much to Anthony's relief.

"Not at all," Anthony told her, rising and waving them both over. Stepping around the table, he kissed his mother lightly on the cheek. "We were just discussing my investigation regarding Miss Smith, otherwise known as Miss Chilcott."

"Oh, so you found her?" Winston asked as he poured himself a drink at the side table. "Would you care for some sherry, Mama?"

"Just a small one," the duchess replied.

"And please bring the carafe with you over here, Winston," Casper said as he leaned back in his chair and crossed his legs. "Your brother and I are in need of a refill."

"So, tell us about Miss Chilcott, Anthony. Is she the

unwanted stepchild of a countess, hidden away so that none shall know of her beauty?"

Anthony rolled his eyes. "You read too many fairy tales, Mama."

"Not anymore." There was an edge of sadness to her voice. "But I used to when Louise was little. To be honest, I always did enjoy those happily ever afters—they don't happen often enough in real life."

"Well, it looks as though it's unlikely to happen for me either," Anthony said. "Miss Chilcott is a driver's daughter, and as Casper has correctly pointed out, it would be difficult for me to make her my duchess—socially speaking, that is."

"That explains her belief that she cannot share a future with you, though I'm not entirely sure of how it affects *your* decision, Anthony. When did you begin caring about what Society thinks?" his mother asked as she took a careful sip of her sherry, the tiny glass balanced perfectly between her elegant fingers. "Because if you ask me, you never gave much of a damn about anyone's opinion until recently. I'd be greatly saddened to see you do so now, when so much depends on you doing the complete opposite."

All three men stared at the tiny figure of a woman who sat before them. Anthony could not recall her ever using profanity before—it was so unlike her. She, on the other hand, looked completely unaffected as she looked right back at them. She eventually shrugged. "There's little joy to be had in growing older, but having the freedom to say as you please is most assuredly one of them."

"And here I was advising him to make her his mistress," Casper said. "I'd no idea that you were so liberal in your way of thinking, Duchess."

"Casper, surely you have been a friend of this family long enough now to know we're not as conservative as most. It is my very deepest wish that my children will be as happy in their choice of partners as I was with my husband. If Miss Chilcott is the woman Anthony wants, then I have no intention of standing in his way. The rest of Society will give both of them a hard enough time—I see no reason to make the situation more difficult."

Anthony felt his heart swell with a bit of hope—the only bit of hope he'd had all day. "Thank you, Mama. I really appreciate your support in this. However, there is a complication that you ought to know about."

"Please don't tell me that she has a child out of wedlock," his mother said, concern marking her drawn features.

"No, it's nothing like that." Taking the carafe Winston offered him, Anthony poured a measure into Casper's glass before adding another to his own. He'd already told his family that Miss Chilcott was planning to marry someone else—that he believed she felt duty-bound to do so. "I happened upon her this afternoon in Moxley as I was on my way to meet with her father. She was buying gloves."

His mother raised both eyebrows. "I approve."

Anthony sighed. "She was not alone but in the company of Mr. Roberts, who was acting as her escort—*he* is the man she intends to marry."

Both his mother and Winston frowned.

"The carriage maker?" Casper asked.

Anthony nodded. "The very one."

"I thought the name sounded vaguely familiar," Winston said. "Didn't you acquisition your new curricle from him, Anthony?"

Anthony gave his brother a tight smile. "You see my dilemma?"

"Not particularly," Casper said, looking annoyingly calm.

Trust Casper to change his view on the matter just so he could argue the point. "A moment ago, your opinion was quite pessimistic," Anthony told him.

"That was before I discovered how open your mother is to the idea of having Miss Chilcott for a daughter-in-law," Casper said, directing a sweet smile at the duchess.

"I'm not particularly fond of toadies, Casper, though I do appreciate the consideration," the duchess remarked, sipping delicately at her sherry.

"Whatever your opinion," Anthony said, deciding he'd had enough of their backscratching, "the fact remains that I know Mr. Roberts, perhaps not personally, but enough to feel some remorse at the thought of stealing Miss Chilcott away from him."

"Then you're a better man than I," Casper said.

Anthony grinned. "I believe that goes without saying." They saluted each other with their glasses before proceeding to take a healthy gulp.

"There is also the question regarding the gown," the duchess said, breaking the silence. "However would the daughter of a mere driver have come to possess such an expensive item?"

"I cannot give you an answer to that yet," Anthony told her. "But I don't believe Miss Chilcott to be a thief. Whatever the case, I think there's an honest explanation. Until I discover it though, I've no intention of alerting the Deerfords. I trust you'll make no mention of it to them either."

"You have our word on it," Winston told him seriously. "And if there's anything at all that we can do to help . . ."

Anthony nodded. "Thank you, but I can't think of anything right now. It's good to know that I have your support though. Now, if I can only convince the lady herself." He frowned, realizing he'd neglected to tell them how his visit to the Chilcotts had actually gone. "When I spoke to her father and showed him the drawing of his daughter, he denied recognizing her. For whatever reason, they're insistent upon marrying her off to Mr. Roberts, though I cannot for the life of me understand why."

"Could they be indebted to him somehow?" Winston asked.

"I've wondered that myself," Anthony said as he leaned forward, put his elbows on his knees and placed his chin in his hands. "I suppose it's possible. Her father is in Mr. Roberts's employ."

"The father of the woman you wish to marry is her fiancé's driver?" Casper asked, looking undecided about whether to laugh or frown. He picked the latter.

Anthony nodded. "He test-drives the carriages that Mr. Roberts manufactures."

"Well, then perhaps Mr. Roberts is blackmailing the poor man in some way?" the duchess suggested.

"That would certainly explain a lot," Anthony agreed, "but Mr. Roberts, as peculiar as he may be, doesn't seem like the sort of man who'd resort to such baseness of character."

"I agree," Casper muttered. "It takes an evil-minded person to bend someone's fate to their will. If Mr. Roberts had it in him, you'd know."

"But if all the Chilcotts are looking to accomplish is to marry off their daughter to an affluent man—which Mr. Roberts is, by the way—then I see no reason for them to deny you, Anthony," the duchess said, her tone taking on a defensiveness unique to a proud mother. "You're a duke, for heaven's sake! She should be thanking her lucky stars that you've paid her any attention at all."

"Unless of course she's in love with Mr. Roberts," Winston pointed out.

"She's not." Anthony's voice was clipped as he spoke. "She believes she has to marry him—that she has no choice in the matter. I mean to prove her wrong. I will speak to her father again, and when I do, I will be very clear about my intentions."

"And if they still refuse you?" Casper drawled, his gaze meeting Anthony's.

"Then I may have to whisk Miss Chilcott off to Gretna Green." He was joking of course. He would never force a woman to marry him against her will, but he did feel as though he was being brushed aside too easily. Perhaps it would be good to assert himself a bit more—remind Miss Chilcott of what they'd shared the night of the ball. Seeing his mother's horrified expression, he couldn't help but add, "Let's not forget that I used to excel at seduction. Perhaps a rake is precisely what Miss Chilcott needs."

Smiling to himself, he drank deeply from his glass just as his mother muttered faintly, "Heaven forbid."

Chapter 14

Anthony set out for the Chilcott home the following afternoon. He was tired, having suffered yet another restless night with thoughts of Miss Chilcott, and he still wasn't sure of what he would say to Mr. Chilcott—how best to make his case so that he wouldn't be turned away yet again. Pondering this, he trotted along at a leisurely pace, his horse's hooves stamping the road that led toward Moxley when suddenly, in the distance, he saw someone walking toward him. As he got closer to the individual, his heart rate picked up in realization of who that person was.

It was Miss Chilcott—there could be no mistaking it, even though her face was downcast as they approached each other, leading Anthony to suspect that she'd determined his identity as well and was probably hoping he wouldn't notice her. As if such a thing had been possible.

As he came closer to her, he pulled his horse to a complete stop and tipped his hat in salutation. "Good afternoon, Miss Chilcott."

She looked up at him, her hand shading her eyes

against the afternoon sun. "Oh, Your Grace—what a surprise!"

Did the color in her cheeks just deepen, or was he imagining things?

"What brings you all the way out here? You must be at least a mile from town."

"I . . . er . . ." As if unaware of where she actually was, Miss Chilcott looked both left and right before returning her gaze to Anthony, who was trying his damndest to keep his expression straight. "I was on my way to visit my aunt with a pie." She held a small basket up for him to see.

"Does she live far from here?" Anthony asked, a little concerned that a woman of Miss Chilcott's beauty was roaming the countryside on her own. Had she no inkling of the sort of danger she was placing herself in?

"Another mile perhaps—there's a turn up ahead that will take me straight there."

Looking down at her, Anthony considered his next move. She looked dazzling with the sunlight casting a golden glow upon her hair. Her gown was simple and white, yet so much more enticing than the more elaborate ones he'd seen ladies in London wear. And then of course there was her bosom, of which he was afforded a very clear view from his vantage point.

His stomach was not the only part of him to tighten as he thought of what it might be like to bare it. Bloody hell, Casper was right—he might have stopped behaving like a rake, but his mind was not so easily controlled.

Taking a tight hold on the reins with his left hand, Anthony swung himself down onto the ground, landing right in front of Miss Chilcott. He turned to face her, noting the look of surprise and . . . was that dread in her eyes? "Allow me to accompany you."

"I cannot possibly," she gasped. "It's . . . it's not proper."

Intrigued by her level of discomfort, Anthony leaned toward her. "How so?"

"We have no chaperone." She looked around again, like a naughty child who feared being caught. "If anyone saw us together, it would make things quite difficult for me. You see, I am to marry Mr. Roberts, in case you were not aware. Whatever will he think if he hears I've been out walking *alone* with you?"

"I imagine he'd thank me for seeing to your safety," Anthony said. As reluctant as she was for his company, he was enjoying their discussion. Determined to win, he added, "Besides, if anything were to happen to you—a sprained ankle perhaps, or, God forbid, something worse—I'd quite simply never forgive myself."

Letting out a deep sigh, Miss Chilcott nodded. "Very well then," she acquiesced. She started walking again while Anthony kept pace, leading his horse by the reins.

"Do you often go for walks like this? On your own?" he asked.

Turning her head, she met his gaze, her deep frown alluding to her displeasure at the question. "I suppose you're about to tell me that you don't approve."

Sensing she would not respond well to overprotectiveness but feeling an elemental need to keep her safe, Anthony shrugged and said, "The world can be a dangerous place, Miss Chilcott. I merely mean to caution you."

Looking at her, he could tell she was struggling with

what to say. Her voice was low when she eventually spoke—so much so that he had to strain to hear her. "Thank you, Your Grace. I shall take your concern under advisement."

Well, she'd certainly taken the high road, which of course only served to increase his admiration of her. "So, what sort of pie are you taking to your aunt?" he asked after a moment's silence.

Miss Chilcott didn't turn to look at him as she said, "Apple," her eyes fixed firmly upon the horizon.

"Something tells me you're not so fond of apple pie yourself," Anthony prodded.

She gave him a wary look, held silent for a moment and then said, "To be honest, I've grown tired of the flavor. I enjoy variety in my food, you see, but this past year Mama has been particularly fond of serving apple pie for Sunday tea."

"I'm more partial to blueberry myself," Anthony confided. "Or something entirely different, like chocolate—I must admit I'm very fond of chocolate."

Miss Chilcott finally relaxed and chuckled. "It appears I've just discovered one of your indulgences. Am I right?"

"I suppose so," he said.

"What else do you enjoy, Your Grace, besides eating chocolates?"

Talking to you . . . better yet, kissing you.

"Many things, especially horseback riding, the company of friends, the opera—"

"The opera?"

"Does that surprise you?"

"I don't know. I've never been myself, but it's always been my understanding that gentlemen went only for the sake of accompanying the ladies—not because they actually *wanted* to."

Anthony smiled. "I think it's an acquired taste—you either like it or you don't. Believe me, Miss Chilcott, I've seen many sleepy-eyed ladies at the opera as well. One mustn't generalize."

"No, of course not," she agreed.

Eyeing her, he took in the soft slope of her nose, her high cheekbones flushed a delightful shade of pink, and her deep, rosy lips. A lock of hair had torn itself free from its fastening and was presently blowing across her cheek, tempting Anthony to pull it away and tuck it behind her ear. He resisted the urge and asked instead, "What are your enjoyments, Miss Chilcott?"

She tilted her head to look at him. "As you already know, I love to read." Her eyebrows rose a little as she added, "But if you want me to be more specific, then *Romeo and Juliet* is my favorite—I know it by heart."

"So you're a romantic by nature," Anthony said and was rewarded with a smile.

"Undoubtedly, though it's not always the most beneficial trait to have. I often wish I were more practically inclined."

"You think life would be easier then?"

She brushed a strand of hair away from her eyes. "I have no doubt that it would. Romantics have a bad habit of dreaming of things they cannot have and later of what might have been had things been different."

"And what are your dreams, Miss Chilcott?" He knew he was being bold, but he couldn't help himself—it was too tempting.

She breathed deeply, her features tightening around the edges, and he knew that she was aiming for indifference. Shaking her head, she said, "*That,* Your Grace, is irrelevant." And then, as if to deter him from pressing the matter further, she smiled brightly and added, "Did I mention that I can split an apple in half by twisting it?"

"Really?"

He must have sounded very dubious, for her smile turned to one of mischief. "You don't believe me," she stated matter-of-factly.

"I've just never seen anyone do something like that before, and frankly, it does sound a bit unlikely."

Her laughter went straight to his heart, urging it to beat faster. "It has nothing to do with strength, you know, but rather with skill."

"The skill of picking an apple soft enough, no doubt," Anthony muttered.

She stopped walking, eyes narrowing. "Are you suggesting I'm a charlatan?"

"Not at all, Miss Chilcott—I wouldn't dare." But the memory of her deception at the ball hung in the air around them, and he knew that she had to be just as aware of it as he.

They continued on in silence for a few more minutes when she suddenly stopped, turned toward him and said, most seriously, "I know you came to my house hoping to find Miss Smith. I'm very sorry that you didn't."

Anthony steeled himself for a moment. Did she really wish to go on pretending that she didn't know that *she* was Miss Smith? It was absurd to his way of thinking, and yet he found himself submitting to her game. "I couldn't agree more, for I felt a true connection with her . . . as if we were meant to be together no matter what, but she obviously didn't agree, or she wouldn't have run off the way she did."

"Perhaps she was scared?" Miss Chilcott suggested, her voice barely more than a whisper.

Scared?

"I cannot imagine what she might be scared of," he said, hoping she'd say something more.

"You have done an admirable job of turning your life around, Your Grace, but be that as it may, your rakish reputation is not so easily forgotten. It would be difficult for any young lady to associate with you without tarnishing her own good name and that of her family in the process. No, I can understand Miss Smith's way of thinking—she probably means to marry a reputable gentleman who can offer her respectability and comfort."

Anthony gritted his teeth. He'd been the perfect gentleman toward her at the ball—well . . . *almost* perfect. He hadn't planned on kissing her. Surely that had to count for something. Besides, it could have been worse. He could have submitted to his urges and had her right there in the library.

Recalling how lost she'd been in their kiss, he felt certain she wouldn't have stopped him. The thought of it sent a wave of heat surging straight to his groin. He winced as he felt himself harden. "I have behaved most honorably since becoming a duke and without the least bit of wrongdoing." It was the truth. What surprised him was how much he enjoyed this new way of life he'd chosen. For the first time since he could remember he felt a calm togetherness, as if his life was finally on the right track, though he was certain that it would be much improved with Miss Chilcott at his side. She was also the only person who threatened to bring out the rake in him, not for the sake of ruining her but to win her, and he heard himself say, "But after meeting Miss Smith . . . I find my resolve wavering." He paused, watched as she sucked in a breath, and then took a step closer. "She encourages me to abandon all thoughts of propriety, to stop acting like the decent gentleman who never thinks of what it might be like to hold her . . . touch her . . . kiss her in the most wicked way I know how. If anything, Miss Chilcott, it is *I* who should fear Miss Smith, for I do believe it is *she* who poses a threat to my reputation, and not the other way around."

"How can you say such things?" she gasped. "It's entirely inappropriate."

Keeping his eyes trained on hers, he began removing his gloves with slow deliberation. Reaching up, he then touched his hand against her cheek, allowing his fingers to trail along the soft skin until they reached her lips. Her eyes widened, her breathing turned shallow, and a deep flush rose to her cheeks.

But she did not turn away, or even move as he ran his fingers over the plump, strawberry-colored flesh. And when he pressed her lower lip down, suggesting she grant him entry, her eyes closed and her lips parted, letting him in. It was the most erotic thing he'd ever experienced, watching her take his finger in her mouth . . . feeling the wetness of her tongue as it brushed against him. Heaven above, he couldn't believe he'd been so forward—could not believe that she had accepted such an advance. What on earth were they thinking? This was an act she would surely regret.

They weren't exactly kissing, and yet there was something far more intimate about it . . . something very suggestive that led to thoughts of tossing her on the ground and burying himself inside her until this unbearable yearning went away.

He knew better though. The sort of need he felt for her was not the kind that would ever go away even if he was fortunate enough to act out his every fantasy with her. No, it was only going to grow stronger—become more and more demanding. Pulling his finger away from her mouth, he tugged her against him, his arms encircling her in a tight embrace. She opened her eyes but said nothing—just gazed back at him with eyes that begged, *Kiss me.*

So he did. His mouth closed over hers, and he was delighted to discover that she was ready to meet him, her lips parted to allow him immediate entry. And as their tongues swept over and under each other, Anthony heard her sigh, whimper and groan. He heard himself groan too, the pleasure she offered so rich and full that it was impossible for him not to.

There was a soft thud against the ground and Anthony realized she must have dropped her basket, for in the next moment, her arms came around his neck, pulling him closer—urging and enticing him. He ran his hands slowly down her back, pausing at her waist before allowing them to roam lower still, across her bottom. She responded with another groan as he gently squeezed and forced her up against him.

Abandoning her mouth, he kissed his way along her jawline until he reached her ear. Allowing himself the pleasure of pushing up against her, he held her firmly in place as he whispered, "You were correct in your assessment of me, *Miss Smith,* for though I may appear to have abandoned my sinful ways, my thoughts of you are most wicked indeed."

Isabella did not doubt him for a second. She could still feel the proof of his desire as it pressed against her. The worst of it was that she *liked* it. Good Lord! It was deplorable, unseemly, scandalous and about a dozen other awful things. To her horror, she couldn't stop her errant mind from thinking it absolutely wonderful as well. Heaven help her, she was no better than a doxy— whatever must he think of her? Based on what they'd just done and what he'd told her, that she was the sort of woman whom he could take some rather alarming liberties with. The thought did not sit well with her at all. Placing her hands against his chest, she gave him a small push.

To her surprise, he disengaged himself from her immediately and stepped back, leaving her with a sense of abandonment that failed to allow the feeling of relief she'd been hoping for to take root. "Forgive me, Your Grace, but what we just did . . ." She looked around, fearful that someone might have seen them, but there was nobody else on the road. She let out a deep sigh. "I hope you'll try to forget this ever happened. I am to marry Mr. Roberts, and I will not have you ruining the chance of that happening."

"He hasn't even proposed!" The duke sounded well and truly agitated as he crossed his arms over his chest and stared back at her with defiance.

"He will," she said. "It's only a matter of time."

He stepped toward her again, looming over her with his broad shoulders, dark eyes and tousled hair. "Don't do it, Miss Chilcott. Don't marry him."

"I must, for the sake of the security he offers to me and my family."

Something deep and dangerous ignited in the duke's eyes. "He cannot offer this." And before Isabella knew what was happening, she was in his arms again, his lips were on hers and her arms had found their way around his neck once more. It was the safest course of action really, considering she'd probably collapse on the ground if she didn't hold on to him with all her might. No, she couldn't imagine Mr. Roberts being so seductive. In fact, she couldn't imagine him being seductive at all.

Their intimate encounters with one another would probably be meticulously scheduled, and whatever they would do, it would not have anything to do with passion but everything to do with the production of a child in mind. Pushing the thought aside, Isabella tried not to think of it, willing herself to enjoy the kiss the duke offered instead. But then it ended—much too abruptly for her liking—and she found herself standing alone once more with a decent amount of space between them.

"Marry me," the duke said, a raw longing emanating from his eyes. "Marry me, and I will promise to give you this every day for the rest of your life."

Swallowing hard, Isabella blinked. She felt faint. Had she just received a marriage proposal from the Duke of Kingsborough in the middle of a dirt road? Her mind reeled at the possibility of his offer, even though she knew, sadly, that she could not accept. Instinct told her to fling herself into his arms and say *Yes, with all my heart, yes,* but instead she just stood there, until slowly, she shook her head. Her throat closed at the look of anguish and disappointment that filled the duke's every feature at her rejection, and it was sheer willpower that forced the words from her throat. "Forgive me," she said, choking back the tears of despair that she feared would overcome her.

"Why?" His words were softly spoken, but when she found herself unable to answer for the knot in her throat, his voice rose to a near roar as he repeated the question. "Why?"

"My father has made an agreement with Mr. Roberts—it is the honorable thing to do."

He stared back at her in disbelief and eventually shook his head. "It is a stupid thing to do—an action you will come to regret many times over."

"You cannot possibly know that," she said, annoyed by his accusation.

"Of course I can," he insisted. "For the minute you marry him, you'll find yourself waiting on him hand and foot. He doesn't give a damn about your needs or your desires, but only about his own. I believe your question yesterday about reading will attest to that. You like to read, but he doesn't. Consequently there will be no more reading for you once you marry him. Is that really the sort of life you desire? One where your husband will dictate each detail of your existence for you just so he can take you out in public on occasion, the way other men might take out their horse?"

Shocked by his statement and pained by its accuracy, her hand flew across his face in a hard slap. Her blood was boiling she was so enraged—at Mr. Roberts for wishing to deny her freedom, at her parents, who'd made the match, at herself for being too honorable to reject Mr. Roberts's attention and at the duke for making her doubt a decision she'd long since come to terms with.

For a moment they just stood there staring at each other, their breathing coming hard as they fought for control. "I will not allow you to speak of Mr. Roberts in such a manner," she said. If she was to hold on to her sanity, then she had to believe that marrying Mr. Roberts would not be as bad as she feared, and the duke was not being the least bit helpful in that regard. "Being a duke has obviously led you to believe that you can toy with people's lives as you see fit, that you can have whatever you wish for regardless of the consequences."

He didn't respond, but there was no mistaking the dangerous glint in his eyes as he stood there staring back at her. Clenching and unclenching his jaw, he finally said, "I advise you to think very carefully about your decision to marry Mr. Roberts." His anger abated and his voice grew softer and gentler as he spoke. "I should hate to see you sacrifice yourself in such a meaningless way."

"There is nothing meaningless about it, Your Grace." Whether he wished it or not, his words riled her.

"Yes, there is." He reached for her hand, and she was powerless to pull away as the heat of his touch seeped under her skin. "You have an alternative in me. As you have just pointed out, I am a duke, Miss Chilcott. Don't tell me I do not trump Mr. Roberts's offer any day. Whatever reason you think there is for having to choose him over me—the agreement he has with your father as you claim—is exaggerated, I assure you. But the matter will not be made easier once he makes his offer, which is why I would strongly urge you to make it clear to him now that you will not accept him."

"Why?" she asked, unable to believe that *he* would be willing to sacrifice himself for her—a mere nobody—when he could have any woman he desired. "Why would you wish to marry me? We hardly know one another."

Tilting his head to one side, he appeared to consider her question quite thoroughly. "True." He paused for a moment before saying, "May I speak plainly?"

"I would encourage you to do so," she said, curious about what he planned to confide.

"Very well then . . . to be quite blunt, I am seven and twenty years of age. My experience with women has not been . . . limited." Isabella felt herself blush, but, sensing the importance of what he was about to divulge, she kept her eyes on his in spite of her embarrassment. "But then I met you, and I felt something different than what I've felt for all the rest—a connection that made all my prior experience inconsequential. I know that it may sound strange to you, but trust me when I tell you that whatever it is that binds us together is rare. It's not something that I can turn my back on with ease, for I know I'm unlikely to find it again with someone else."

What on earth could she possibly say in the face of such a declaration? This was the fairy-tale moment she'd always dreamed of, and yet, tragically, it couldn't be hers. She shook her head with sadness. "Even if I turn Mr. Roberts down, my parents will never allow me to marry you." She didn't have to look at him to know he had to be thoroughly confused.

"What are you talking about?" he asked, confirming her thoughts. "Any other parent in the world would be thrilled at the prospect of a duke paying court to their daughter. Why would they possibly be against it?"

She couldn't look at him as she spoke, her words reflecting her sadness. "It is my mother, to be precise. She hates your kind and will never allow me to wed you."

Silence filled the air with a crispness that crackled around them. Unable to stand it any longer, Isabella looked up at him and saw the incomprehension in his eyes. He shook his head and blinked. "She doesn't approve of my history as a rake." He spoke as if this had to be the obvious meaning behind Isabella's words. "Surely she must know that I've given up on that life, but if not, I shall just have to prove myself to her."

"It's not that," Isabella said, eliciting a frown from the duke. "She hates the nobility and everything it stands for."

"Well," he said, bringing her hand to his lips and placing a tender kiss against her knuckles, "then it is fortunate that your father shall be the one making the decision. I will speak to him."

And I will pray for a miracle, Isabella thought, keeping silent this time, reluctant to say anything that might instigate another argument. She knew that he was right—that it was her father he would have to speak with, but that was only a matter of convention. When it came to actual decision making, her mother had some very firm opinions, and her father never resolved anything of importance without consulting her first. No, in order to marry the duke, she would have to elope with him, and that was something she could not do.

One late-night escapade behind her mother's back was one thing, betraying both of her parents' trust in her was entirely a different matter. She nodded, but there was no conviction behind it. "Get his approval, and you shall have mine."

She watched him smile—the smile of victory close at hand. If he only knew the obstacle that awaited him in the form of her mother. He had no idea. Reluctant to ruin his good mood, however, she accepted the arm he now offered her and recommenced walking. They had lingered enough already. It was time she delivered the pie to her aunt.

Chapter 15

It was not without apprehension that Anthony arrived at the Chilcott home later that day. He'd put on a confident smile for Miss Chilcott's benefit, but her words of defeat worried him. After escorting her all the way to her aunt and uncle's doorstep, where she had, to his great consternation, proven herself capable of splitting an apple in half with the mere twist of her hands, he'd returned to Moxley, assured by Miss Chilcott's aunt that her uncle would take her home in his buggy.

Rapping on the door, he now waited for it to be opened by the same maid he'd met on his previous visits. "Is Mr. Chilcott at home?" he asked, hoping she'd respond in the affirmative.

She did, much to his relief, leading him quickly inside to wait for his host in the parlor. "Mr. Chilcott will be with you shortly." She gestured toward a beige armchair that stood as part of a larger seating arrangement. "Please have a seat."

Thanking her, the maid bobbed a curtsy, then exited the room, leaving Anthony alone. Looking around, he was just preparing to take his seat when the door to the dining room opened, revealing the man himself. "Your Grace, I am honored once more by your visit." Anthony straightened himself, accepting the hand Mr. Chilcott offered him in a firm shake. "Do have a seat—tea will arrive shortly."

Thanking Mr. Chilcott for his hospitality, Anthony placed himself in the beige armchair while his host took a seat on the sofa across from him.

So far so good.

"I apologize for coming unannounced like this," Anthony began. "But there is a matter of grave importance that I must discuss with you—indeed, I have a moral obligation to do so."

Mr. Chilcott frowned as he leaned back against the sofa and crossed his arms. "That sounds rather serious. Do continue."

Anthony steeled himself. The nerves in his stomach were in utter uproar. What if he failed? He wanted Miss Chilcott at his side—needed her in such a profound manner that he felt quite desperate at the thought of losing all hope. Swallowing his misgivings, he trained his features into a mask of utter confidence and said, "I wish to ask for your permission to court your daughter, sir."

Mr. Chilcott blinked. "I'm sorry—what?"

Taking a deep breath, Anthony directed his intense dark eyes squarely at Mr. Chilcott and pressed on, attempting to choose his words with care. "I know that it was she who I met at the ball—the mystery woman whom I've been searching for—that it was her I danced with, spoke to and . . ."

Kissed.

Mr. Chilcott raised an eyebrow.

"She's a remarkable woman," Anthony continued, hoping he wouldn't be asked to elaborate on what he'd just left unsaid, "and I am confident that she will make an excellent duchess."

Mr. Chilcott frowned again—more deeply this time. "What makes you so certain? You cannot possibly know that you will get along well with one another in the long run—you barely know each other, for heaven's sake!" The words were barely out before Mr. Chilcott's eyes widened with alarm. "Don't tell me you've been romancing her in secret and that she went to the ball specifically to meet with you. Good God! Has she been compromised? If you've—"

"It's nothing like that—I assure you." The corner of Anthony's mouth edged upward to form a crooked smile. "Regarding the length of our acquaintance however, which, for the record began on the night of the ball, I think you should know that your daughter made the exact same point."

Mr. Chilcott's eyes narrowed and Anthony shifted a little in his seat. He might have been a duke—a man whose presence most men would tremble in—but for the moment, he was nothing more than a man laying bare his deepest wish to the father of the woman he hoped to marry. Mr. Chilcott might have been nothing more than a carriage driver, but Anthony was wise enough not to underestimate the power he had to turn down Anthony's proposal.

The door to the parlor opened, admitting the maid, who'd returned with a tea tray. She poured a cup for each of them in turn, bobbed a curtsy and departed once again.

"What did you tell her?" Mr. Chilcott asked as soon

as she was gone and the door had been closed behind her once more.

Leaning forward in his seat, Anthony stared into his teacup for a long moment, recognizing that what he was about to say would be detrimental to both his and Miss Chilcott's future. He eventually looked up and, meeting Mr. Chilcott's serious gaze, he said, "That I cannot explain the connection between us, but that I know it is there, so powerful that I cannot ignore it. I know she feels it too, for I can see it in her eyes." He swallowed hard before adding, "She is marrying Mr. Roberts for your sake alone—not because she wishes to. It is a sacrifice, Mr. Chilcott, in every possible sense of the word, for she will have to abandon herself in the process."

"What are you talking about?" Mr. Chilcott had been reaching for his tea but froze in response to Anthony's words, spearing the duke with a hard stare instead. "Mr. Roberts may be a bit . . . reserved, but he will offer my daughter a most comfortable life, complete with a grand house to live in, beautiful gowns and countless servants. What more does she possibly need?"

Respect?

Instead of saying as much, Anthony raised an eyebrow. "I do believe Mr. Roberts neglected to tell you that he intends for her to earn her keep."

"What's that supposed to mean?"

"His housekeeper will retire as soon as he's married, and, considering it an unnecessary expense in light of the fact that his wife will be more than capable of taking on the task, he has no intention of hiring another." Feeling more confident in the face of Mr. Chilcott's shocked expression, he went on with, "I do not know him all that well, I admit, but I do know this—the man is a snob. He will not treat your daughter well, for to his way of thinking, she is far beneath him socially. Therefore, one must wonder at his reasoning. I believe he is quite aware of her beauty and imagines that she would make a fine accessory."

"How dare you speak of my daughter in such a degrading fashion?" Mr. Chilcott's words were spoken beneath his breath and with little force behind them, but his eyes had grown dark.

"Because I care about her and should hate to see her shackled to someone so lacking. She deserves better than that."

A smirk presented itself on Mr. Chilcott's lips. "You, perhaps?"

Anthony closed his eyes as he took a deep breath. This was not going as well as he'd hoped. "I know how this must seem to you, sir." He opened his eyes and looked back at the man opposite him. "I assure you that my first concern is for your daughter's happiness, and to be frank, I feel she stands a better chance for that if she attaches herself to me. I have more money than I know what to do with, so she shan't be lacking and neither will you. I will not dictate to her what she can and cannot do with her free time, provided that such activities are appropriate for a young lady to enjoy. Forget about Mr. Roberts and let me court her. Please."

Mr. Chilcott sat completely unmoving for a long moment before finally saying, "I shall have to speak to my wife."

Bloody hell.

Hadn't Miss Chilcott told him that her mother would

never give her consent? Anthony felt as if the ground was falling away beneath his feet. He was doomed.

Running his fingers through his hair, he expelled a deep breath and reached for his tea. If only he had a brandy instead. He was in dire need of something stronger than flavored hot water. "I don't understand it," he muttered as the tepid liquid flowed down his throat. "Your daughter is receiving an offer of courtship from a duke, and not a single one of you is responding with the degree of elation that one might expect under the circumstances. There's something you're not telling me."

"I assure you that there is *not*," Mr. Chilcott said, his voice a notch tighter than it had been before. "Perhaps our lack of enthusiasm is merely based on your sudden appearance upon our doorstep, your eagerness to court our daughter based on one fleeting encounter with her, during which, according to you, an incomprehensible connection was formed between the two of you—one that urges you to hasten to the altar with her at the first available opportunity. Forgive me, Duke, if I am not as willing as you would have liked me to be in offering my nod of approval, but your argument is quite fantastic, not to mention rank with suspicion. Are you quite certain that you did not compromise her in any way?"

"You have my word on it, Mr. Chilcott," Anthony promised. He had to admit that the man had a point. He hadn't made a very convincing case by attempting to explain his motives for wanting to court Miss Chilcott by trying to make sense of his feelings toward her. It sounded unlikely to his own ears, and if the situation had been reversed, he'd probably have thought that the so-called *connection* he spoke of was nothing more than pure lust.

It wasn't though. Anthony knew all about lust, and whatever it was that drew him so strongly to Miss Chilcott was a different beast entirely. Deciding he had to say something more to make Mr. Chilcott understand, he asked the most absurd question he'd ever imagined himself asking another man: "Do you believe in love at first sight, Mr. Chilcott?"

Mr. Chilcott choked on the tea he'd unfortunately just taken a sip of. "I hope you're jesting," he said once he'd composed himself again. "Love at first sight? That's the stuff of fairy tales, Duke."

"Yes," Anthony agreed. "And I'm not suggesting that I've fallen in love with your daughter, but rather that for the first time in my life, I have glimpsed the possibility for it with her."

Something in Mr. Chilcott's gaze shifted, and as Anthony looked back at him, he knew he'd managed to say the right thing, that as unlikely as it was, Chilcott understood.

"It is this possibility that I wish to explore," Anthony continued. "I know how rare it is for anyone to experience such . . . oneness with another person and how fortunate I am to have done so with your daughter that I cannot—nay I will not—relinquish the chance of a love match with her."

"How very noble of you, Your Grace." The words came from the doorway, and Anthony turned his head to find Mrs. Chilcott standing there dressed in a violet gown that suited her complexion immensely. A matching ribbon had been twined about her hair, reminding Anthony of the Greek style that so many upper-class women were presently fond of.

Anthony rose to his feet without pause and approached her, executing a polite bow as he reached for her hand and brought it to his lips. "A pleasure to see you again, Mrs. Chilcott," he said as he straightened himself.

She did not smile—not even a little bit. Instead, her lips remained drawn in a tight line while her eyes assessed him slowly from head to foot and back again. Without comment, she swept past him and took her seat upon the sofa next to her husband. With a deflated feeling of having just been cut by the woman he hoped might one day become his mother-in-law, Anthony hesitantly returned to his own seat, upon which Mrs. Chilcott said, "I strongly advise you to abandon this ridiculous notion at once."

Caught off guard by her curt remark, Anthony stared back at her for a long moment before managing to find his tongue. "There is nothing ridiculous about it," he said, looking to Mr. Chilcott for a bit of support. Before Mrs. Chilcott had arrived, Anthony had been certain that he'd managed to convince him of his plight. Now, however, the man appeared to have retreated inside himself, his eyes trained stubbornly on his teacup.

"Of course there is," Mrs. Chilcott went on, her eyes narrowing as she leaned toward Anthony. "You are mistakenly romanticizing your own beastly instincts by using some emotional attachment you wish for us to believe you have developed with our daughter as an excuse. Well, allow me to unravel your feelings for you, since you are clearly incapable of doing so yourself. Considering how little the two of you know each other, there can be no doubt that what you speak of is desire. If you say otherwise, you are being dishonest. All this talk of love or the possibility of love is nothing more than a means by which to make a gross elaboration of the truth."

Anthony blinked. He didn't know what shocked him more—Mrs. Chilcott's blatant rudeness or her swift dismissal of what he felt. "It is more than desire," he ground out, determined not to let this woman have a say without fighting back. "I am no stranger to desire, madam, and I assure you that this is something more— something much more permanent."

"He wishes to court her," Mr. Chilcott muttered.

Without a change to her demeanor, Mrs. Chilcott said, "Then I must inform you that your wish, Duke, has been declined. Our daughter will marry Mr. Roberts. They have known each other for almost a full year and I have every confidence that they will be very happy together."

Incensed by her quick dismissal, Anthony rose to his feet, stared down his nose at her and said, "It appears, Mrs. Chilcott, that you are completely blind when it comes to the affairs of your daughter. Either that, or you simply do not care. Good day." And with that, he exited the parlor and the house, taking what little pleasure he could from slamming the door behind him as he left.

Chapter 16

"You look fairly miserable."

Looking up from the tiny figure that was standing before him on his desk, Anthony met his brother's gaze as Winston entered the study and moved toward one of two empty chairs that stood on the opposite side of the table.

Anthony shrugged as his brother lowered himself onto one of the seats. "Just busying myself with my latest project," he said. He'd no desire to talk about the conversation he'd had with Mr. and Mrs. Chilcott earlier in the day, for the experience had left him not only drained but also with a sense of hopelessness that he was finding hard to shake. They were all against him, including Miss Chilcott. Reaching out, he picked up the figure he'd made of her using an old teaspoon, some wire and a bit of horse hair. He'd fashioned a gown from the piece of torn fabric he'd found and painted her face to the best of his ability on the spoon. Twirling her gently between his fingers, he met his brother's gaze. "I should probably just give up."

Winston raised a brow. "Is it that hopeless?"

Anthony sighed. Reluctant though he was, he knew that he might as well tell his brother everything, so he did, as accurately as he could manage but without any mention of the intimate moment he'd shared with Miss Chilcott on the way to her aunt's house. Some things deserved to be kept private. When he was done, he couldn't help but note the look of disbelief on his brother's face.

"Mrs. Chilcott said that to you?" Winston asked, gaping. He frowned as he shook his head, as if trying to make sense of it. Anthony understood him—he'd been trying to comprehend the woman's boorishness since the moment he'd left her house. "She clearly has no respect for your title, Anthony."

"That goes without saying," Anthony said dryly. He paused for a moment before adding, "Her daughter claims she hates the nobility and all it stands for. I just hadn't expected her to be quite so . . . difficult to deal with."

"One cannot help but understand her reasoning though."

"Whose side are you on?" Anthony growled as he set the figure of Miss Chilcott down and glared across at his brother.

Winston rolled his eyes. "Yours, of course, you idiot, though you have to admit that your talk of having found some profound connection with Miss Chilcott that you believe will lead to true love—all in the space of one evening—does sound just a little bit unbelievable."

"You think I'm being fanciful," Anthony blistered. He'd had a headache since leaving the Chilcott's, which had abated during the course of the evening, but he could feel it threatening to return now in full force.

"I would prefer to think of you as hopeful. However, all I am saying is that it would be odd if Mr. and Mrs. Chilcott would welcome you with open arms on the basis of such a claim, agreeing to end their daughter's acquaintance with a suitor who, while he may not be the ideal match for her and might be a cold fish with some rather peculiar notions, is firmly grounded in reality—the Chilcotts know what to expect of him."

"Are you saying that I am not realistic?" Anthony asked. He spoke slowly in an attempt to keep his rising temper at bay.

Winston regarded him for a moment. "I've always thought you were," he eventually said. "Being a rake and all that . . . Well, you know how it is—rakes don't usually believe in love, or at the very least, they don't plan to find themselves immersed in it. But you've changed over the last few years, and now, with this whole business regarding Miss Chilcott, I daresay you've taken on quite the romantic streak, and we all know that romantics are *not* grounded in reality, Anthony."

Anthony frowned. "That's not true."

"Of course it is," Winston countered. "Romantics are dreamers, and dreams rarely have anything to do with reality."

"What the devil are you talking about? You married Sarah, didn't you? And Lord knows you dreamed of her for an eternity before anything came of it."

"True, but I never would have presumed that she'd accept my proposal or that her father would give us his blessing unless they'd been certain that my intentions were honorable and that I wanted her for *her* and not for something more . . . devious . . . though of course I did." Winston grinned broadly at that, which could only suggest that there was real passion between him and his wife.

"Would you please speak plainly?" Anthony said, crossing to the sideboard to pour two glasses of brandy.

"What I'm trying to say is that you might have more success at convincing them by avoiding whatever feelings you have for their daughter until you can speak of them without sounding as though you merely wish to toss her on your bed."

"I alluded to no such thing!" Anthony turned abruptly in response to his brother's words and the brandy sloshed over the side of one of the glasses, wetting his hand. He handed the other glass to Winston and pulled a handkerchief from his pocket so he could wipe away the liquid.

"Of course you did," Winston protested. "How else do you suppose they might interpret your talk of being inexplicably drawn to their daughter? You need only look to Mrs. Chilcott's response—inappropriate though it may be—to find your answer."

Silence filled the room while the two brothers stared back at each other. Anthony eventually raised his glass to his lips and took a deep sip before sitting back down on his chair. "I've made a mess of this, haven't I?"

Winston sighed. "Honestly, I can't say. It's possible that they would have turned you away regardless, but I do believe you might have stood a better chance if you'd done it differently. You should probably have romanced the mother to get to the daughter—flowers, chocolates and such."

"Hmmph . . . I doubt that would have made a difference. I'm a duke, Winston, most parents would be thrilled at the prospect of their daughter marrying so well. Not the Chilcotts though. From what I gather they'd be more accepting of me if I were a laborer, which of course is absurd. In any case, using my title for leverage is having no effect at all—quite the opposite. I believe I'll have to find another way."

Winston nodded. "Well, I wish you the best of luck." There was no need for him to say that Anthony would need it. The implication was abundantly clear, the only problem being that luck was something Anthony was beginning to feel he had in short supply. What he really needed, was a miracle.

"Lady Crooning and her daughter are here to see you, Your Grace," Phelps announced the following morning as Anthony and his secretary were going over some of the duke's investments. He wanted to finish quickly so he could spend some time with his houseguests, who'd been entertained entirely by Winston, Louise and his mother for the last few days while he had been traipsing after Miss Chilcott. It really wouldn't do. So, he'd arranged for a picnic down by the lake, hoping that this would serve to prove that he hadn't neglected his visitors, as well as allow him the afternoon free to seek out Miss Chilcott's company again. He had to spend more time with her if they were to further their acquaintance, and, by doing so, he hoped to weaken whatever objections she had toward him until she had no choice but to accept the obvious—that they were meant to be together.

Reluctant to waste precious time on a countess whose company he wasn't particularly fond of, not to mention her daughter, whom he liked even less, Anthony requested that Phelps ask his mother to do the honors. "She is better acquainted with Lady Crooning anyway," he added.

Phelps remained stubbornly in the doorway however. "The duchess is already with them, Your Grace. It was she who requested that I ask you to join them."

Damn!

It was with great reluctance that Anthony rose to his feet, muttering a few words to his secretary before following Phelps from his study. Pausing just outside the parlor, he pasted a bright smile on his face before nodding for Phelps to open the door. "What a wonderful surprise," he said upon seeing Lady Crooning and her daughter Lady Harriett perfectly poised upon the sofa, each gracefully holding a teacup. Anthony bowed toward the ladies, then turned to his mother, leaned down to place a kiss upon her cheek and whispered, "I should have your head for this."

The duchess responded, as he had expected, with a deep chuckle as she waved her hand with delight. "Do join us, Your Grace—we've been so looking forward to your company."

"Is that so?" Anthony asked as he planted himself in one of the other armchairs and regarded his mother in the hopes of eliciting an explanation from her.

"We wished to thank you for your hospitality the other evening. The ball was a grand success," Lady Crooning said as she placed her teacup delicately upon its matching saucer.

If one ignores the attendance of two uninvited guests, one of whom was shot, then yes it was, Anthony thought dryly. "Thank you," he said instead, "but you didn't have to trouble yourselves by coming all the way out here and offering your appreciation in person—a simple note would have sufficed."

"Yes, well . . ." Lady Crooning's face took on a strained expression. "We thought we might take the opportunity to invite you to visit us for dinner one evening and," she added, smiling a bit too serenely for it to be genuine, "to take a look at Harriett's watercolors. She's quite the artist, you know."

"I'm sure she is," Anthony muttered, removing his gaze from Lady Crooning and looking straight at Lady Harriett, who immediately blushed. He should have known that the countess was trying to unload her daughter on him, for she'd never been a close friend of his mother's and could have had no other reason for visiting. He only wondered why in God's name his mother hadn't told the blasted woman that he wasn't available to receive her. "As much as I appreciate your offer, I must regrettably decline. You see, I still have houseguests to entertain. It would be rude of me to abandon their company for an evening. Surely you understand."

"Yes, yes of course," Lady Crooning said, looking not the least bit pleased about his rejection. She quickly brightened again however, which put Anthony immediately on edge. "Not to worry though. The Season will begin soon enough, isn't that so? And with the Darwich Ball to kick it off no less—our invitation arrived yesterday. Now, we all know how boisterous these things can be and what a trial it is to seek your dance partners upon arrival. It would be so much simpler if one had already secured at least one dance in advance."

Oh, no.

"Which is why," Lady Crooning continued blithely, "we've had the splendid foresight of bringing Harriett's dance card with us. I'm sure you won't mind adding your name to it, Your Grace, considering how fond you are of dancing."

Anthony could have kicked himself for having danced all those dances the other evening. It wasn't that he had a particular aversion to the activity, especially not when he considered the waltzes he'd enjoyed with Miss Chilcott, but it had armed the countess with the ammunition she required to corner him into agreeing to dance with her daughter. He had no choice—not unless he wished to be frightfully rude. So he smiled and said, "It would be an honor."

No sooner were the words out of his mouth than Lady Crooning and Lady Harriett exchanged the smuggest smiles he'd ever seen. They clearly viewed him as prey to be caught and devoured. Accepting the dance card that Lady Harriett had removed from her reticule and thrust in his direction while her eyes shone with victory, Anthony quickly scribbled his name, hoping he would have secured Miss Chilcott's hand in marriage by the time the Darwich Ball came to pass. A monumental task, it seemed, given the resistance he'd met with so far. However, he wasn't about to give up just yet—especially not with Lady Harriett looking at him as if she'd been a cat who'd just found a mouse on which to pounce.

Annoyed by their audacity, Anthony picked up his teacup and leaned back in his seat. "I wonder," he then drawled in a pensive tone, "if you are familiar with the Chilcotts?" Out of the corner of his eye he saw his mother gape, but he chose to ignore her.

Lady Crooning frowned. "I don't believe I know them, Your Grace. Do they live in Moxley?"

"Yes—at the end of Brook Street, if I'm not mistaken."

"Oh," Lady Crooning remarked, scrunching her nose a little. "No, we never venture over to *that* part of town."

"Really?" Anthony asked, feigning innocence as he lured the countess further into the trap he was weaving. "And why is that?"

The countess shifted in her seat, while her mouth worked from side to side as if she wasn't quite sure of how best to explain herself. It was her daughter who eventually raised her hand to the side of her mouth, leaned forward and whispered, "That's where the poor people live. We prefer to stay away so as not to be affected by their inferiority."

Anthony raised his eyebrows a notch and turned to his mother with a pointed look. "Did you hear that, Mama?"

His mother nodded unblinkingly and Anthony returned his gaze to Lady Crooning and Lady Harriett, offering them both his most benign expression. "What a pity that you would think so." They looked immediately wary, as well they should have, for no matter his smile, Anthony was now quite furious with both of them. "You see, I intend to make Miss Chilcott my wife, but since you think her beneath you . . ."

Both ladies gasped, but rather than apologize, the odious Lady Crooning had the nerve to say, "You cannot be serious. You're a duke and she . . . she's a . . . a . . ."

"A what?" Anthony asked, his face now tight with irritation and lack of patience.

Lady Crooning didn't finish that sentence however, saying instead, "Society will flog her."

"I'm sure they shall," Anthony said, enjoying the look of surprise on the ladies' faces. "It's not the first time this family has taken on the *ton,* however, and while there are those who will disapprove of my choice in wife, I've never really been one to care about the opinion of others. I'd much rather be happy."

"You cannot mean that." The countess and her daughter spoke in unison.

Anthony didn't even bother to hide his distaste for the two women any longer. "I most certainly do. I have no wish to surround myself with snobbery, and as far as Society goes, I'll have you know that Miss Chilcott's character is superior to most of those dolts who think themselves grand on the basis of a title they did nothing to earn." He moved to rise. "Now, if you please, I should like to return to my study. There is still—"

"Well I never," the countess said, her cheeks reddening as she rose to her feet, yanking her daughter up with her.

"If you wish to leave," Anthony said unflinchingly, "I will call for Phelps to show you out." He could sense his mother's tenseness as if it had been his own and knew he'd have to apologize to her profusely for subjecting her to such rudeness, but he simply couldn't bear listening to Lady Crooning or her daughter for one more second. He wanted to strangle them—the fact that he'd only given them a set down was really a testament to the level of command he had over his own actions.

"Thank you for the tea, Your Grace," Lady Crooning said tightly, acknowledging the duchess with a halfhearted attempt at a curtsy before stomping toward the door with her daughter in tow.

Much to Anthony's surprise, they stopped in the doorway and turned back to face him. "I trust you will not forget the dance you promised Harriett," Lady Crooning said.

It was Anthony's turn to be shocked. Had the woman no self-respect for herself or her daughter? He looked at Lady Harriett, who appeared oblivious to how degrading it ought to have been for her that her mother was practically begging a duke to dance with her. He nodded however and said, "I am a man of my word."

And then they were gone, and Anthony allowed himself to breathe a sigh of relief. He turned to his mother, who, he noticed, did not look the least bit pleased. "That was completely unnecessary," she said. "Not to mention incredibly embarrassing for all of us."

"I'm sorry, Mama, but she is the one who wormed her way into our home, expecting me to fall on my knees for her daughter. You should have known better than to ask me to help entertain them."

His mother shook her head a little sadly. "You know that I lack the strength of character required to deal with a woman like her. If you hadn't come, we would in all likelihood be dining at their home this very evening."

Reaching for her hand, Anthony gave it a tight squeeze. "You're a duchess, Mama—she is nobody compared to you."

The corner of his mother's mouth edged upward a little. "Who's being a snob now, Anthony?"

"I only wish to encourage you to be more confident, Mama. You should have no trouble putting women like that in their rightful place."

"Your father always did say that I was too polite for

my own good," she muttered, her eyes glistening a little at the mention of the old duke.

Feeling the need to comfort her, Anthony pulled her into a tight embrace—something he hadn't done since the day his father had died. "There's nothing wrong with being polite," he whispered, "but there are those who will see it as a weakness and try to take advantage. You must learn to sort these people out from the rest, and you must learn to be firm with them."

She shook her head against his chest. "When did you become so wise?"

"I am merely offering you the same advice that Papa once gave to me," he whispered, his own eyes beginning to burn at the memory of the man who'd filled such a large part of his life. He knew there were many aristocrats who spent little time with their children, allowing nannies to do all of the work instead. Not his parents though. His father had taken an immense interest in his upbringing—had designed the tree house that had been placed in one of the large oaks in the garden himself.

They'd played pirates there together, his father giving him treasure maps with impossibly difficult riddles to solve that he must have spent hours concocting in the evenings after Anthony went to bed. Yes, he'd had tutors, but his father had always taken the time to sit down on the library floor with him, books scattered all around them as they'd pored over the atlas, the works of Plato, Aristotle and Socrates, Motte's translation of Newton's *The Mathematical Principles of Natural Philosophy* and a hundred other works that his father believed essential to a young boy's education.

Stepping out of the embrace, the duchess wiped her

damp eyes with the back of her hand, made an attempt at a weak smile and said, "I miss him so desperately much, Anthony."

Fearing his voice would crack if he tried to speak, Anthony just nodded.

"I still expect him to walk through the door any minute, you know," his mother continued. She heaved a great sigh, then leveled Anthony with a frank expression. "I've never been a very strong person, Anthony. Your father—he was my rock. With him gone I . . ." Her voice broke and she looked away.

"You have me, Mama," Anthony told her gently. "And you also have Winston and Louise. If you need anything—anything at all, we're here for you."

"That's why I called for you to join me for tea with Lady Crooning, though I do think you overstepped a little." She grinned slightly. "You were awfully rude to her."

Anthony couldn't help but smile. "I was rather, wasn't I?" To which his mother nodded. Anthony shrugged. "Well, she deserved it."

"Perhaps she did, but that doesn't make it all right," his mother said. "You must try to show a bit more grace and restraint in such situations. Had your father been here—"

"He would be disappointed in me, wouldn't he?" Regret filled him at the realization of how differently his father would have handled the situation. Anthony had to do better if he wished to live up to the former duke's name.

His mother was serious as she met his gaze. "Your memories of your father are not from when he was young like you. I know that you idolize him, but he made his own mistakes too. You make a fine duke, Anthony, and I have no doubt that your father would be proud of you."

Clenching his jaw to stop the sob that was trying to work its way out of his throat, Anthony nodded and turned toward the side table. "Would you care for a drink?" he asked as soon as he felt capable of speaking without his voice cracking.

"I wouldn't mind a sherry," his mother replied. He could hear her moving about as he poured a glass for each of them, selecting a cognac for himself. "You really think she's the one, don't you?"

Anthony stiffened for a moment and then turned. "I do." Stepping toward his mother, he offered her her glass.

Taking it, she stared down at it, her brow knit in a serious frown as she said, "Then you must stop at nothing to win her." She looked up at Anthony, and there was such encouragement in her eyes that Anthony knew without doubt that she was just as determined as he in turning Miss Chilcott into the Duchess of Kingsborough. In case he had any doubt however, she raised her glass toward his and said, "You have my full support."

They clinked their glasses together, and Anthony silently reflected on how important a moment it was. His mother might not have had the strength of character required to give women like Lady Crooning a proper set down, but she was kind and loving to a fault, and the fact that she trusted him so completely with something that he barely understood himself meant the world to him. Now, if he could only convince Miss Chilcott and her parents, everything might just work out the way he hoped after all.

Chapter 17

Five days had passed since the Kingsborough Ball, and Isabella's mind was more muddled than it had ever been before. She was being courted by Mr. Roberts, who *still* hadn't proposed, *and* she was being pursued by a duke.

She let out a sigh of despair. She didn't care for Mr. Roberts in the least—especially not now that he had revealed what her marriage to him would entail. But she knew that her father had done all in his power to encourage his suit and consequently feared that denying Mr. Roberts at this point would not only incur his wrath but also make a mockery of her father.

On the other hand, the man she felt drawn toward was so far above her on the social ladder that she felt such hopelessness at even considering the possibility of that working out. Besides, her mother hated his kind and everything they stood for, which would not lead to very joyous family reunions.

The duke seemed not to mind her station in life, which only endeared him to her further. He might have been a man of power, but he was good and kind, or he would have started by trying to make her his mistress instead. He had not, however, and while he seemed terribly convinced that a union between them would work, Isabella still worried.

She didn't know him very well after all, and he didn't know her. What if this . . . *thing* . . . they felt for each other wasn't enough? What if it faded? He hadn't called it love, much to her relief, since she would have thought him presumptuous if he had, but rather the *promise* of love. And yet . . . what if all it was, was a need? She'd heard of such unquenchable desire before, and judging from the way he'd kissed her at the ball, not to mention their interlude on the road three days ago . . . She felt herself grow unbearably hot at the reminder and went to open the window.

Lust.

She allowed the word to form in the privacy of her mind and took a moment to consider it. Was that what it was? A breeze swept past her face, toying with her hair, and she sighed as she looked at the piece of paper she held in her hand. Marjorie had brought it up to her in secrecy, and she'd waited for the maid to depart before tearing open the seal to read its contents—an invitation from the duke to meet him later that afternoon by the Kingsborough barn, located quite conveniently on the same road that she would have to take to go to her aunt's house.

Isabella felt her heart flutter at the very thought of accepting such a liaison. It spelled trouble, and yet the note said that he only wished to talk to her. Instinct warned her that he would want to do a whole lot more, but the sound of her heart beating was drowning out her voice of reason.

She wanted to see him again, if only to say good-bye. The very idea of having to do so was terrifying, but unless she ran away with him, she had no choice. She didn't want to disappoint her parents, to humiliate her father or, for that matter, to tell Mr. Roberts that he'd wasted so much time on her. It just wasn't in her.

But just because she'd determined to sacrifice herself for the sake of others did not mean she should be denied one last afternoon of happiness with the man she . . . She decided not to finish that thought, for not only was it ridiculously romantic, even for her, but it would also lead to further heartbreak if she allowed herself to believe it to be true.

Donning a plain white cotton gown, Isabella picked a bouquet of daffodils in the garden, then announced to her mother that she would be taking them over to her aunt. Fortunately, her mother was in the middle of her correspondence and barely batted an eyelid, waving Isabella off instead as she wished her a pleasant walk.

"Can I come with you?" Jamie asked just before Isabella reached the garden gate.

"No," Isabella said, turning to meet her sister's inquisitive gaze with a pointed look.

Jamie smiled cheekily and whispered, "You're going to meet him, aren't you?"

Isabella had of course shared with her sister every detail about the Kingsborough Ball—except for the kiss—and, like the duke, Jamie was of the opinion that the two should marry, claiming that all of Isabella's reasons against doing so were ridiculous.

"I'm going to end whatever is between us," Isabella said, trying to sound convincing.

Her sister looked dubious, then shook her head.

"It's one thing for you to lie to everyone else, but to lie to yourself, Izzie . . ." She scrunched her mouth as if thinking how best to continue. "I never thought you such a coward."

Filled with the kind of indignation one could feel only at receiving such a blunt appraisal from a younger sibling, Isabella opened her mouth to protest, except that her sister was already marching back toward the house. "Give my love to Aunt Rosalyn and Uncle Herbert, will you?" she called over her shoulder, stopping Isabella from saying whatever it was she'd meant to say a moment earlier.

Isabella stared after her.

Was Jamie right? Was she a coward? She wouldn't have thought so, considering everything she was giving up for the sake of those she loved. But emotionally . . . It wasn't a thought she wished to entertain at present, so with a brisk step, Isabella quickly left Moxley behind her and headed toward the rendezvous point, her heartbeat quickening when she spotted the brown building in the distance.

"You can do this," she told herself, squaring her shoulders and clenching her teeth as if she'd been on the verge of facing an army in battle rather than a simple man, though she had to admit that there was nothing simple about him. In fact, nobody had ever complicated her life more.

As she came closer, she looked over her shoulder to ensure that there was nobody else on the road who might see her. Not even a stray dog could be seen, and Isabella wasn't entirely sure if she felt worried or relieved by this, for there was no longer any excuse not to turn off the road, walk into the field and around to the back of the barn, where one of the doors stood slightly ajar.

Pushing it open just enough to squeeze through, Isabella stopped and allowed her eyes to adjust to the dim interior. It was warm inside—the sort of dry warmth one feels on a bright sunny day—and it smelled richly of hay. A fluttering sound reached her ears, and she looked up to see a bird preening its feathers up under the rafters, where narrow gaps in the wood roofing allowed beams of sunshine to pour through, bathing the hay in a golden glow.

She was just about to step further inside when a strong arm snaked its way around her waist, pulling her back against a solid chest. She would have screamed in startled surprise, but a large hand covered her mouth instead. "It's just me," a deep, familiar voice whispered against her ear.

She relaxed, and he removed his hand. "Was that really necessary?" she asked, moving to escape his grasp. He spun her around instead so they were facing each other, and she reluctantly sucked in a breath. How was it possible for him to be handsomer than when she'd last seen him? Logic told her it wasn't so, yet she couldn't deny that her recollection of his appearance had been unjust—a clear sign of her own denial.

"I didn't mean to frighten you—just surprise you a little, that's all." He brought his hand up and ran the inside of his thumb along her cheek. "I've missed you."

Isabella felt her heart hammer against her chest at the deep sincerity that glowed in his eyes. "Your Grace, I—"

"Anthony," he muttered, still stroking her cheek.

Isabella frowned, her mind not at all its usual alert

self with him caressing her. "I beg your pardon?" she managed, the feel of his arm tightening around her waist sending a shiver down her spine.

The duke smiled, and it was the sort of smile that was filled with the promise of pleasure, sin and mischief all rolled into one. Isabella felt her legs grow weak—the man was completely irresistible with his hair all mussed and his cravat slightly askew, as if he didn't give a damn about propriety. Isabella's heart skipped a beat. "I have kissed you twice, Miss Chilcott, and I am about to do so again. I believe it's time we dispensed with formality, wouldn't you agree?" And then, before Isabella was afforded the chance to voice a response to that question, the duke lowered his mouth over hers, and it was almost as if the ground fell away beneath her feet.

It was gentle at first, with their lips just grazing, but then he captured her lower lip between his teeth, tugging at the tender flesh, and she gasped, her arms reaching around his neck and pulling him closer. She was a fool, but she couldn't stop herself, couldn't think of anything else—didn't want anything but this, right here, right now, with him.

The kiss grew deeper, more urgent, and Isabella ignored the voice in her head that called for her to stop and walk away. She was powerless against him and gave herself up to the kiss instead, parting her lips and allowing him entry. His tongue swept inside her mouth without hesitation, rolling over hers as he tasted her in the most sensual way possible.

Not knowing how it happened, she suddenly found herself pressed up against the barn wall, her breasts flattened against his chest as he pushed up against her.

He abandoned her mouth, kissing his way along her jaw instead, straight toward her ear, where he flicked his tongue against her lobe.

A shock of heat shot straight through her, she felt her breasts tighten and then . . . an unbearable longing between her thighs. Dear God, she had to get away from him before she started begging him to do his worst with her. What a surprise that would be for Mr. Roberts on their wedding night. She groaned at the thought of it—a reaction the duke apparently took as a welcome, for his hands slipped between them, his fingers seeking her hardened nipples, then squeezing.

She groaned again, but this time it was from complete and utter pleasure.

"Tell me your name," the duke whispered against her neck, sending yet another wave of heat straight to her groin. "Please," he added.

"It's . . ." Dear Lord, he'd managed to make her forget even that. She fought for control of her wits. "Isabella," she gasped as his head dipped and he proceeded to lick his way along the edge of her neckline.

He paused. "Beautiful," he murmured as he gave her bodice a slight tug. "The woman as well as the name—so utterly beautiful."

Isabella allowed her head to fall back against the barn wall. She closed her eyes and sucked in a breath, knowing what he was looking at. There was no corset, since she rarely wore the uncomfortable thing, and her chemise was loose. Anthony had no trouble pulling both it and her gown down just enough to reveal her breasts in their entirety, and she was too caught up in the moment to stop him. It was mortifying.

Common sense spoke to her from a faraway corner

of her mind, and she thought to push him away—to put an end to this folly before it was too late. But then he did the unspeakable. The wicked man grazed his teeth against one of her nipples, nipping it gently, and Isabella practically buckled. "So responsive . . . ," she heard him mutter. "So passionate." And then he took her entire breast in his mouth and suckled.

Oh, dear Lord!

What was happening to her? Her whole body was humming with expectation, there were tingly sensations in the most unspeakable places and she felt restless—as if she wanted something but couldn't quite put her finger on what that something might be.

Blast!

The next thing she knew, she was in his arms and he was carrying her across the floor to a large pile of hay, his gaze hot and determined, which should probably have scared her to death but didn't. Something about this man made her feel safe and comfortable. She trusted him, and the way in which he looked at her was enough to make her want to forget about all else. This was a sacred moment they were sharing, and nobody was going to intrude on it or ruin it for them.

Sitting down in the hay, Anthony leaned back with Isabella on his lap and hugged her against his chest. He wanted her in every way imaginable, but that was not the reason he'd come here. In fact, he really had meant only to talk to her, but then he'd seen her standing there with the scattered beams of sunlight brightening her hair and skin and he'd been unable to control himself. She'd looked so divine and tempting.

His hands reached for her breasts again and she groaned as he molded the soft, pliable flesh, feeling them swell with excitement. No, he would not deflower her so primitively in a barn, though it would not be for lack of wanting but because he knew she deserved better than a tumble in the hay—literally.

She wriggled against him and he belatedly realized that the deep, guttural groan he heard, so foreign to his ears, had come from somewhere deep inside himself. Again she moved, submitting him once more to the same sweet torture he'd felt a moment earlier as her bottom had rubbed against him. "Stop," he muttered, his hand grabbing at her thigh in an attempt to hold her still. Her thigh . . . how he'd contemplated it for endless moments since accidentally placing his hand against it in the pumpkin carriage the night of the ball; the way it had felt to his touch—so soft and curvaceous—so sensual and womanly.

He felt her tense beneath him. "What . . . what is it?" she asked, her breathing low and heavy. "What's wrong?"

"Nothing, except that you're driving me mad, and I'm not sure how much of that I can bear before I . . ." He coughed to mask his discomfort and decided to steer the conversation back to more comfortable ground, focusing on her needs instead of his own. He squeezed her thigh and kissed the side of her neck. "I wonder . . . if you've ever . . ." His fingers trailed up over her leg, bunching the fabric of her gown as they travelled across her hip and settled between her thighs. "Touched yourself . . . here."

She probably would have jumped to her feet and run out the door if it hadn't been for the fact that Anthony held her firmly in place. At least that was the indication her very loud "no" gave him. She then started prattling on about what sort of doxy he must think her to be, that she must have been mad to be there with him and what could she possibly have been thinking.

Unable to silence her with a kiss due to their present position, he decided to move his hand against her instead. "Then allow me to show you what magnificent pleasure can be found in a mere touch."

Her hips rose to meet him, as he'd known they would, and though she sighed and groaned, she muttered, "No," and then, "You mustn't."

He stilled, unable to advance unless she asked him to. Whatever people thought of him, he'd never so much as kissed a woman without her granting him permission. So he turned his attention to her shoulder instead, nibbling there as his hands found her breasts once more. "Are you quite certain?" he asked as he tugged at one of her nipples, eliciting a throaty cry of pleasure from her.

God, he was hard for her. He'd never in his life been more aroused than he was now, to the point when it was causing him actual physical pain. He squeezed his eyes shut and tried to concentrate on what mattered. This was about her—about showing her what he could give her if she'd only let him.

"No," she murmured again, and Anthony reined in his passion and started to pull away—to do the right thing—when she grasped his hand and said, "I mean no, I'm not certain I wish you to stop."

Anthony chuckled. "Then you wish for me to continue?"

"Yes," she rasped.

It was all the permission he needed. Caressing the smooth surface of her belly, his hand drifted lower, over the soft curls guarding her womanhood, tickling her gently on their downward journey. She stiffened, and he sensed that she was holding her breath. "Relax, Bella, and let me show you," he said. And then he did—his fingertips slowly skimming her tender flesh.

"Oh, God," she moaned as her hips rose to greet him. "Please . . ."

"Please stop . . . or please continue?" Anthony asked, his words soft against her ear as he gently parted her and ran one finger along her center, reveling in the slick wetness that welcomed him.

"Don't stop," she murmured, arching her back and grasping his legs with her hands. "Don't ever stop."

She was his. Anthony was sure of it, for her passion was such that he knew Mr. Roberts would be incapable of satisfying her, and now that Anthony had unleashed her inner wanton and made her aware of her desires, she'd know that she would have no choice but to pick him over that fool.

Besides, Anthony thought as he circled the hard nub that would lead her to fruition, he had to have her for himself if he was to preserve his own sanity. No other woman would do—not anymore—and the mere thought of Isabella . . . Bella . . . left him hard and aching. Living out the remainder of his days in such an unfulfilled state would be torturous.

Self-conscious as she was of her own body, Isabella was thankful for the privacy her gown offered, for though she'd tossed her inhibitions aside a while ago and no longer cared that her breasts were bared and her skirts hiked up across her hips while the duke . . . Anthony . . . fondled and petted her, she was comfortable knowing that what he saw of her body was limited. He stroked her again, the feeling incredible—unlike anything she'd ever experienced before—and she wanted all of it.

Hoping to offer him some measure of encouragement, she raised her hips against him once more, but it wasn't enough—he wasn't doing enough to satisfy this crazed feeling that swept through her. Not the best at being passive and idle, she decided to do something—something that would leave him with no doubt about how exactly he was to proceed. After all, she was a country miss and not in need of coddling like she imagined some of the London ladies would be. So, lifting her legs, she swung each of them over each of his, opening herself up wider.

"I didn't think I could possibly want you more," he muttered against her cheek between kisses. "But seeing you like this—so free and so inviting . . ." His words trailed off as he dipped one finger inside her.

Heaven.

Sensing that this was what she'd been seeking, Isabella lifted herself toward him again.

"You want more, don't you, Bella?" His voice sounded hoarse as he said it, and as if to add to her torment, he removed his finger just enough to leave her wanting.

"Yes," she said on a gasp of air, and his finger returned, moving inside her, then joined by another, increasing the fullness—in and out as she moved against him.

"That's it, Bella," he murmured. "Take your pleasure, find your release, and imagine me joined with you—how good it would feel to have me thrusting inside you."

Isabella couldn't speak. It was as if her mind and body were no longer her own but belonged entirely to him—his scandalous words making her hotter and needier as she reached for something just within her grasp. "I know you want me," she heard him say as the first tingles swept up her legs. "Marry me, Bella, and I'll give you pleasure beyond your wildest imaginings." He pushed his fingers inside her again and a wave of pure ecstasy crashed over her, leaving her spent and breathless.

But there was something else going on as her mind began to clear and she was able to consider her actions—his actions and his words—with greater clarity. A feeling of intense anger swept over her, so strong that she found herself leaping away from him as she did what she could to adjust her dress. How could she have been so stupid as to fall for such a backhanded trick? "You, sir, are no gentleman," she said as she stared down at him with an accusatory finger pointed in his direction.

The man had the audacity to smile as he said, "And it would seem that you're not much of a lady either."

Isabella's mouth dropped open. Was he seriously going to act so cavalier about this? "How could you?" she asked with a small shake of her head.

He frowned, got up and stepped toward her, but she edged away, determined to keep her distance. He shrugged. "How could I not when you were so willing?"

Of all the things anyone had ever said to her, this was the worst—partly due to the fact that his words rang true. She'd encouraged him in the worst possible way. Clearly she'd lost her mind somewhere between entering the barn and now. It was the only logical explanation. And then it dawned on her. "This was your plan all along, wasn't it? You wouldn't take no for an answer, so you decided to give me a taste of what I can have if I marry you."

He didn't deny it, asking instead, "Did it work?"

Staring back at him, she felt an uncontrollable urge to scream. She was furious with him for trying to force her hand this way and furious with herself for letting him. What purpose had it served? Nothing but a means by which to add to her misery. She would marry Mr. Roberts, except now, on top of everything else, she would be acutely aware of what she was missing, because there was no question that Mr. Roberts would not be willing or capable of giving her the same unparalleled bliss that Anthony had just done.

Instead, she would live out the remainder of her days knowing what she might only otherwise have suspected—that her marriage was lacking in a very key element. "This was a mistake," she said, turning her back on Anthony and walking across to where her basket was lying crooked on the floor.

"How can you say that?" he asked. "Don't you know how incredible this was? You cannot possibly tell me that you can walk away and forget this ever happened."

She turned back to face him, the anger she felt coiling around her until she feared she might explode. "No. I cannot forget. That is the problem, you idiot. I will forever know what I am missing now."

He looked back at her in disbelief. "You're still going to marry him," he said as if it was the most absurd thing he could think of.

"Of course I am. My parents won't let me marry

you, and even if they did, I'm not entirely sure I'd be willing to subject my father to the sort of humiliation he'd surely face at the prospect of telling Mr. Roberts that his suit is no longer wanted. And that is without considering that you just tried to force my hand by turning my own body against me."

He came toward her in one brisk stride, grabbing her by the arms before she had a chance to pull away. Startled, she met his fiery gaze. "Don't you dare pretend as if you didn't like it," he ground out.

"Of course I liked it," she said as she clenched her jaw and balled her hands into two tight fists. "The problem is that you methodically seduced me in the most calculating way and with no thought of anyone but yourself. You knew I'd be putty in your hands. You knew that I would be unable to turn you away and that I would have allowed you to do as you wished without thought for the consequences. I didn't, because no one has ever made me feel the way you do—as if nothing else exists but you. Except now the moment is gone and I have to face reality again, only now it's worse thanks to you. You should have stopped when I still had the will to say no."

"Perhaps," he acquiesced. "And I would have if you had repeated the request or even sounded more convincing. But then you started begging for more and I . . . I'm sorry if I overstepped."

A sad laughter erupted from Isabella's throat.

Overstepped?

You could say that again.

"Please let me go," she said, tugging a little at her arms. He released her slowly and with obvious reluctance, and she bent down to pick up her basket.

"I should have compromised you completely," he muttered, taking what little calm she'd retained and snapping it in two.

Rising to her feet with her basket in hand, she resisted the urge to strike him and glared back at him with pure fury instead. "How dare you!"

"I'm sorry, I—"

"No, I don't believe you are. You were a rake once, so I don't believe it would be beneath you to take a woman's innocence if it served your own agenda." She watched as he clenched and unclenched his jaw, but he didn't respond, so she turned away instead.

"The gown," he suddenly said. "The one you wore to the ball. Where did you get it?"

Pausing in the doorway, she looked steadily back at him, her eyes narrowing with suspicion. "Why do you ask?"

He shrugged. "I suppose I'm just curious, considering that it did seem rather expensive and—"

"I didn't steal it, if that's what you're thinking," she said. "My mother bought it a long time ago, from a peddler, if you must know." She refused to allow him to see just how humiliating she found this admission, for it only served to compound how different her world was from his. Keeping her back rigid, she raised her chin before saying, "If that is all, I have some flowers that I must deliver to my aunt, and if it's not too much trouble, I should like to ask that you refrain from contacting me again. I hope that you will respect at least that much." And then she left.

Anthony stood there for a long moment just watching the door through which she'd departed. If he could only hang himself up under the rafters and give himself a good flogging. He'd acted abominably and completely without thought for what she would think or of what the consequences might be.

It hadn't been his intention for it to turn out the way it had, but he'd stupidly allowed himself to get carried away. What the hell was he going to do now? He'd turned a difficult situation into an unsalvageable one. It was a mess, and he was to blame. He was the one who had taken a moment that should have been precious to both of them and used it as a means by which to prove his superiority over Mr. Roberts—and in the most primitive way possible. He was a cad—a complete and utter cad—and he loathed himself.

Grumbling a string of self-deprecating oaths, he strode across the floor, yanked the door open and stepped out into the sunshine. He didn't even bother to look for Isabella, knowing well enough that she would be long gone by now. Christ, he needed a drink, and then he would find his mother and confess everything. That was precisely the sort of punishment he deserved after acting so despicably, though on second thought an account of his escapade would surely offend his mother's sensibilities. Perhaps he'd talk to Winston instead. Yes, Winston would give him the proper lashing he deserved—he was absolutely certain of it.

Chapter 18

Isabella started at the sound of someone knocking on her bedroom door. It had been two days since she'd walked away from Anthony after their tryst in the barn, the thought of which still sent waves of heat rushing through her. *Blasted man.* She'd arrived home after delivering the daffodils to her aunt and had immediately removed herself to her room, too angry to enjoy the company of even her own family.

"Enter," she said, expecting to see Marjorie carrying a tray of food or tea or some other substance meant to soothe her.

To her astonishment, the door opened to reveal her father instead, his expression most grave as he glanced around the small space she inhabited before meeting her gaze. "It can't possibly be good for you to remain cooped up in here," he said. "I'd like you to come and join us for supper."

"Thank you, Papa, but I fear I must decline. You see, I'm not feeling at all well and would much rather remain in bed." However, her voice did not sound weak, as it should have if she'd truly been ailing, but clipped with frustration instead.

"I see," he muttered. His eyes narrowed. "I don't suppose this decline in health would have anything to do with a certain duke?"

"Not at all," Isabella murmured, hoping he'd believe her.

"I don't believe you," he said, right on cue.

Isabella sighed. "I never should have gone to that ball," she said as she pulled a blanket across her shoulders and nodded toward a chair, prompting her father to sit, which he did. "Now I . . ." She shook her head. "Everything's such a terrible mess, Papa."

Her father expelled a deep breath. "You really like him, don't you?" he asked.

Isabella reluctantly nodded. As angry as she still was with Anthony's seduction, she couldn't deny what was in her heart.

"And you don't care much for Mr. Roberts at all, do you?" he pressed.

"Not in the least," she confessed, not daring to look her father in the eye—afraid of the disappointment she'd see there.

"Then the situation isn't very complicated at all, my love," her father said.

"Of course it is," she said, more confused than ever by his change of stance. "I am forced to marry a man I don't particularly like because I *cannot* marry the man I do like. How can you say that's not a muddle of the worst possible kind?"

Her father nodded. "You're right. Your mother and I have made your life quite difficult. It wasn't our intention—I hope you know that."

"I do," she said, wishing he'd go away and leave her in peace. She had little desire to talk about Anthony or Mr. Roberts right now. If only she could forget them both.

"If it's any consolation, I believe the duke cares very deeply for you."

"How can you possibly think that might console me?" she asked, gaping at him as if he'd been half mad. "Do you think it will make it easier when I marry Mr. Roberts, knowing that the man I care for holds as much affection for me as I do for him, but that Society, my ridiculous sense of honor and my own parents are what kept us from each other?" Her voice had risen to a shrill pitch, but she didn't care. She was so angry with everyone, including herself, that she found it impossible to contain it a second longer. "A duke wishes to marry me, Papa, but your ridiculous promise to Mr. Roberts and Mama's asinine dislike of the upper—"

"Careful, Isabella," her father warned. "I won't have you insulting your mother when you know nothing of what she's been through. You have no idea what she's had to suffer."

He rose and walked toward her, looking angrier than she'd ever seen him before. It was so unlike him, and she instinctively shrank back against her pillow. "Forgive me, Papa, I didn't mean—"

"You may think your mother harsh and demanding, but she loves you more deeply than you can possibly imagine. She would lay down her life for you in a heartbeat, Isabella. Whatever you may think, she would never try to stand between you and your happiness."

"Then why won't she let the duke court me? I know it's not you preventing him from doing so."

"Because she's afraid you'll get hurt!"

Isabella stared back at her father as if he'd been a complete stranger. He looked so impassioned as he stood there towering over her, defending her mother as if his life depended on it, and it dawned on her then, in the dim light that her bedroom had to offer, that she might not know her parents as well as she thought. "Why would she be afraid of that?" she asked in a low whisper.

Her father straightened himself and stepped back. "That is not for me to say."

"But I—"

"I will talk to her, Isabella."

"But that won't stop Mr. Roberts from turning against us. He'll never forgive any of us if I deny him now. You could lose your job."

"Let's deal with your mother first and with Mr. Roberts later," her father said as he reached for the doorknob. He paused and added, "Perhaps you're right—perhaps it would be best if you remained up here for the remainder of the evening. I'll ask Marjorie to fix a plate for you. Tomorrow, though, you're leaving the house—you need some fresh air, Isabella, and more importantly, you need to face your problems head-on."

"I love you, Papa," she whispered as the door closed behind him. She'd always wondered at her mother's relentless criticism of the aristocracy, for it had always been clear that it had nothing to do with envy. Considering what her father had said, as well as everything he'd left unsaid, she couldn't help but wonder if it might have something to do with the gown Isabella had worn to the ball.

Her mother had said that she'd bought it from a peddler, but what if that wasn't true? The more Isabella contemplated it, the more unlikely she found it. A thought struck her. Oh God! What if her mother had once been somebody's mistress? What if some earl or marquess had bought it for her—a favor in return for . . . Isabella swallowed hard, not daring herself to think such reprehensible things about her own mother. No, there had to be some other explanation that Isabella wasn't seeing. She could only hope that her father would somehow be able to convince her mother that it wasn't reason enough to prevent her daughter's happiness.

Determined to do as her father had asked, Isabella left her house the following morning and headed toward Main Street. Clouds had begun gathering in the sky, but Isabella felt confident that if it rained, it wouldn't be until much later in the day. Having spent a great deal of the previous evening thinking about what her life with Mr. Roberts would be like in comparison with what Anthony promised her, she'd decided to venture over to Browning & Co, the local bookshop. If Mr. Roberts meant to put a ban on reading, then she in turn had every intention of enjoying something by the scandalous Mary Wollstonecraft before saying her nuptials.

Stepping inside to the sound of a tinkling bell, she quickly surveyed the space, noting the elegant signs that marked the various categories along the bookshelves. Four large bookcases stood back to back in the center of the room, and Isabella was just about to advance on one of them when a short, gray-haired man stepped in front of her and said, "Is there anything I can help you with?"

"I . . . er . . . that is . . ." The man raised an eyebrow in anticipation of her response. *Drat*. She didn't wish to tell him what she was looking for, since he'd probably disapprove. Taking courage in the face of his assessing stare, she squared her shoulders and said, "No, thank you—I merely wish to browse."

He didn't budge. "I am sure you would, miss." He gave her a patronizing smile that she didn't care for in the least. "However, I do have a rather great appreciation for order, and since this is your first visit to my shop, I fear I cannot allow you to roam around unchaperoned."

Isabella gaped at him. "You think I will make a mess of your cataloging?"

His smile broadened. "Precisely."

"Why, that's preposterous!"

"Nonetheless," the man continued. He gave her a pointed look. "If you would please tell me what you're looking for, I shall be more than happy to find it for you."

Isabella clamped her mouth shut in annoyance. It seemed that wherever she turned, a man would be there instructing her on what to do. It was maddening. Well, she wasn't about to tell this little gnat that she desired to buy a book—any book—by that Wollstonecraft woman, so she shook her head instead and said, "Thank you, but that won't be necessary. In fact, I—"

"You really ought to stop scaring off your customers like that, Mr. Browning. It's terribly bad for business."

Isabella's heart leapt into her throat and she cringed. *Kingsborough*. Turning her head, she saw him stepping out from behind one of the large bookcases, looking as handsome as ever in a dark brown suede jacket, beige breeches and shiny black Hessians. His eyes met hers, and he smiled a cheeky smile that immediately had her reaching out to a nearby table on which to steady herself, except her hand missed its mark and she dropped to the floor instead. *Blast his dashing good looks*. He would have no choice but to think her a complete nitwit now.

He was beside her in a second. "Are you quite all right?" he asked, his voice filled with concern. He was probably frowning too, though she wouldn't know, since her eyes were squeezed tightly shut in a hopeless attempt to ignore him. After all, the last time he'd seen her she'd been most indecent and he'd been . . . She felt the heat rise in her cheeks.

"Please go away," she whispered.

"And leave you alone here, in distress and with no one but Mr. Browning to tend to you? Highly unlikely."

She felt his firm hand beneath her elbow, urging her upward until she was once again standing on her own two feet. Opening her eyes with a gradual slowness, she found Anthony staring down at her with a bit too much of a twinkle in his eyes. "Whatever makes you think I need tending to? I'm not some feeble female who cannot take care of herself."

He leaned toward her and whispered for only her to hear, "Come now, Bella, you practically swooned at the sight of me."

Oh, God!

"Mr. Browning," he then added before she had a chance to respond, "I shall personally see to it that Miss Chilcott here stays out of mischief and that she doesn't meddle with your order. This way if you please, Miss Chilcott."

With a muttered apology directed at Mr. Browning, who stood shaking his head—though he clearly lacked the nerve required to argue with a duke—Isabella allowed Anthony to lead her around the sturdy bookcases until they were shielded from anyone else who might enter the shop.

"Before we go any further," Anthony said, lacking all indication of his jovial demeanor from a moment earlier, "I would like to express my sincerest apologies. The way I . . ." He dropped his tone to a whisper. "The way I behaved toward you the other day was deplorable. Please know that there was no ill intent on my part, but that I simply got carried away. It was wrong—doubly so because I used it as a means to try and bind you to me. I'm sorry, truly I am, and can only hope that you will forgive me."

She knew she was probably blushing from head to toe as she stared back at him. It was true that he'd taken her by surprise, but he hadn't forced her in any way—if anything, she had encouraged him, and while she'd been angry and confused in the wake of it all, she'd had time to consider how both of them had behaved and had concluded that it would be unfair to place the blame on his shoulders alone. "We were both at fault," she said. "So there is really nothing to forgive."

He blinked, looking doubtful at first, but then another expression took its place, and Isabella recognized it as relief. Though she hadn't yet admitted to herself that she loved him, she acknowledged it then, in that brief moment as he silently told her without the use of words just how worried he'd been that he'd lost her.

She was still coming to terms with the notion as he took her hand in his and raised it to his lips for a kiss.

"Thank you," he said, his voice a further reflection of his appreciation. He straightened, regarded her for a moment, then said, "Now then, why don't you tell me what you're looking for so I can help you find it?"

Deciding that now was as good a time as any to determine where the duke stood on women's rights and whether or not he would consider her an equal, Isabella primly told him, "Anything really, as long as it is by Mary Wollstonecraft."

Silence.

Isabella shifted on her feet while Anthony just stood there staring back at her, leading her to deduce that she must have truly shocked him. But, just when she thought he'd tell her not to waste her time on such nonsense, he tilted his head instead and said, "Right. Mary Wollstonecraft it is then, though I don't believe you'll find any of her books here. Mr. Browning doesn't seem like the sort who'd approve.

"However, I do happen to have a copy of *A Vindication of the Rights of Woman* at home. You're welcome to borrow it if you like." He turned and moved to the far corner of the shop, where he ran a finger along one of the shelves, stopping at a slim book bound in dark green leather. Pulling it out, he held it toward her. "How about this in the meantime—*The Romance of the Forest,* by Mrs. Radcliffe?"

Isabella gave him a dubious look as she reached for the book. "Isn't she one of those Gothic novelists?"

Anthony shrugged. "I suppose you could say that, though I thoroughly enjoyed reading it myself. I'm sure you will too, for it is full of both intrigue and romance."

And then he waggled his eyebrows in a manner so suggestive that it was impossible for Isabella not to laugh. "Very well." She grinned. "I shall give it a try—thank you."

He bowed slightly in acknowledgement of her thanks and said, "I do hope you'll allow me to purchase it for you as a token of my appreciation."

"That's very generous of you," Isabella said. "But not in the least bit appropriate, I'm afraid—we're not even courting, and I couldn't possibly accept—"

"My dear Bella," he said in a tone so devilish that it flipped her stomach upside down. "I am well aware that we are not courting and that Mr. Roberts is the man whom you intend to marry. My feelings for you however are genuine, and consequently, I have every intention of doing what it takes to change your mind."

Isabella's heart knocked against her chest. She could feel her legs trembling beneath her own weight and automatically glanced around in search of a chair. She really ought to sit down before she collapsed to the floor—again. But when she turned back to gauge the distance between herself and Anthony, he was closer than before—so close she could feel his breath against her forehead. Her mouth grew dry and she reflexively licked her lips, only to catch him staring at her with that same hooded expression he'd had in the barn right before he'd kissed her.

She gasped at the thought of it. He couldn't. No, he wouldn't—not in the middle of a bookshop in broad daylight and for all the world to see. She squeezed her eyes shut, and the next thing she felt was his lips—not on her mouth as she had expected—but against her ear. "Do you know why I'm so determined?" he asked.

She shook her head, refusing to look at him.

"Because I want you for myself, Bella—in every conceivable way. Mind, body and soul—I want it all."

Isabella squeaked. It really was a miracle that she was still upright, considering that her legs had long since turned to jelly. Opening her eyes a little, she was surprised to discover him gone, and she immediately hastened around to the other side of the bookcase, where she found him paying Mr. Browning for her book. His ability to distract her was nothing short of impressive, not to mention frightening; she hadn't even realized he'd taken it.

"Now then, Miss Chilcott," Anthony said as soon as Mr. Browning had finished wrapping the book for him. "How about a cup of tea?"

Wary of keeping his company for fear of what people might think—or worse, of gossip reaching Mr. Roberts and her parents—Isabella shook her head. "Thank you, but I really ought to be getting home." She then headed for the door, suddenly quite desperate to get away from him.

Anthony followed her out, his hand stopping her in her path as he took hold of her arm. She spun back toward him, almost colliding with his firm chest, and it was just too much—her shortness of breath, the rapid beat of her heart, the heat that shot through her at the awareness of how she longed for him to pull her into his embrace. His effect on her was overwhelming, and she staggered backward and met his gaze, only to be stunned by the amusement she found in his eyes and the cheeky smile that played upon his lips.

The horrid man was enjoying her discomfort. She felt like pummeling him. And then he said, "I believe Mrs. Wilkes' Tearoom has strawberry tarts."

Isabella blinked. "I beg your pardon?" she managed.

"The tea shop over there," he offered by way of explanation as he nodded across the street. "I saw the tarts on display in the window on my way over here and immediately thought of you. I know how much you like them, though given the time of year, they'll be made with preserves no doubt, and not with fresh strawberries, as you would prefer."

She never should have told him about her fondness for strawberries, for he was clearly using it against her now and with his own devious motives in mind. She had to resist, no matter how tempting the man and the tarts might be. "Unfortunately I must decline." Something shifted behind his eyes at her refusal, but she wouldn't be swayed and pressed on instead, determined to do what she must. "My parents will be expecting my return. Good-bye, Your Grace."

He didn't release his hold on her, however, and she was halted once again. When she turned her head to look back at him, she was met with a most grave expression. "Your book, Miss Chilcott," he muttered, offering her the small parcel.

With a brief nod, she accepted the gift, his fingers brushing against hers as she did so, sending a pulse of energy straight through her. "I will call on you tomorrow," he said, his voice deep with promise.

She shuddered, drew a ragged breath and clutched the book to her chest. He released her then, allowing her to escape, which she did, hurrying away from him at a near run just as it began to drizzle. Her heart was still pounding when she reached her house, dashing inside with one singular purpose—to reach her bedroom without having to face Marjorie or her parents.

The last thing she wished to discuss at the moment was the unnerved state she was in. Why did their paths have to keep crossing like this? It was torture seeing him and knowing that he wanted her as much as she wanted him when such a thing was impossible. Why couldn't he just leave her alone and let her forget? No, she would never be able to forget him. He'd ruined her for anyone else, and when she said her vows to Mr. Roberts, she would forever carry the burden and regret of love lost in her heart. She let out a bitter sigh. *Why did life have to be so bloody unfair?*

Chapter 19

"**Y**ou have a visitor, miss," Marjorie announced the following morning as Isabella sat with her mother, each of them working on their embroidery.

Isabella's heart jumped. Surely it wasn't Anthony. He'd said he'd call, but would he come so early in the day? She wasn't prepared. "Who is it?" she asked, hoping her voice sounded calmer than it did to her own ears.

"A lady."

Isabella sensed the tension in her mother's posture. "Does she have a name?" she asked.

Marjorie shook her head. "She did not give me one but asked specifically to speak with Miss Chilcott."

"Well, by all means then, show her in," Isabella said, putting her needlework back in its basket as she wondered who this lady might possibly be. Lady Louise, perhaps?

"She asked that you come outside," Marjorie said, looking somewhat uncomfortable, "so you can speak in private."

Isabella stilled and glanced hesitantly at her mother,

whose brow was furrowed in a deep frown. "It seems we've been quite overrun with nobility these past few days," she said tightly, making her disapproval known.

Isabella rose and went to the door. It had to be Lady Louise, for she doubted the duchess herself would venture into this part of town, requesting a private conversation with her. "I'll just see who it is," she told her mother as she stepped into the hallway and opened the front door.

The woman she found waiting for her, however, was not Lady Louise. In fact, Isabella had no idea who she might have been, for she had never seen her before in her life. She was pretty, with light brown curls framing her face. Her figure was fashionably slim, and Isabella couldn't help but feel a stab of envy at her natural elegance. "May I help you?" Isabella asked.

The woman gave Isabella a head to toe inspection, then stared down her nose at her with the same amount of disgust and arrogance that she probably reserved for toads. "Frankly, I don't know what he sees in you."

"I beg your pardon?" Who was this woman, and what on earth made her think she had the right to speak to Isabella that way?

"The duke may have taken a momentary interest in you, Miss Chilcott, but you know as well as I that it is only a matter of time before he tires of you." Her lips curled upward and her eyes flickered with disdain. "Why, you're not even worthy of being his mistress, so why don't you stop your . . . whoring and save us all further embarrassment by staying away from him?"

Isabella could scarcely believe her ears, but she recognized the rage that swept through her at the other woman's insult. "I don't believe I care for your tone,

Lady . . ." She deliberately allowed her words to trail off, hoping this shrew would fill in the blank.

"Harriett," the lady said, and then, "the Duke of Kingsborough's fiancée."

Isabella could feel the blood draining from her face. "His fiancée?" she squeaked, hating how panicked she sounded.

Lady Harriett nodded as though she'd just conquered France. "It hasn't been formally announced yet, so I thought I'd use what little time I have before it becomes public knowledge to do a little housekeeping. It's one thing for the duke to have a few indiscretions—indeed, I expect nothing less—but what I won't stand for is when those indiscretions stop being discreet." She stepped toward Isabella with a sneer. "I saw you leaving his barn with your clothes and hair in disarray as I was on my way to Kingsborough Hall myself the other day, and I am well aware of his . . . appreciation of you."

Isabella felt sick.

"However," Lady Harriett continued in a brighter tone than before, "he knows his duty and will eventually accept that he must end his acquaintance with you. I merely thought to speed things along."

"If that is all," Isabella said, her voice clipped with anger, "then I would like to ask you to leave."

Lady Harriett gave her a hard stare. "Don't do anything foolish, Miss Chilcott, or I will see what little reputation you have ruined."

"Is that a threat, my lady?"

Lady Harriett shrugged as she moved toward the gate. "I only mean to caution you," she said, "unless of course you wish for the whole town to know what a harlot you really are. Good day!"

If only Isabella had had a rock in her hand, she would have happily tossed it at Lady Harriett's head, she was so enraged. The nerve of her to come to her home and . . . and accuse her of being a whore! She watched, her whole body shaking, as Lady Harriett climbed inside her awaiting carriage and drove away.

It couldn't be true, could it? Anthony would have said something, surely he would. He'd asked her father for permission to court her, for heaven's sake. Was it possible he'd changed his mind and offered for Lady Harriett instead? The woman had said that their betrothal was recent. Perhaps it had happened yesterday after she'd walked away from him on Main Street. He hadn't looked pleased, but he *had* promised he'd call on her. She took a deep, steadying breath and decided that the only reasonable thing to do at this point was to ask him herself. She certainly wasn't about to take that snooty Lady Harriett at her word.

"A letter, Your Grace."

Anthony watched from his side of the table as his mother plucked a letter from the silver tray that Phelps was holding toward her. His mood was somber at best after having told Winston about his meeting with Miss Chilcott in the barn. As he'd expected, his brother had looked at him as if he was unworthy of being a duke, and then he'd told him precisely how disappointed he was in his behavior. It had been nothing less than what he deserved.

"Thank you," his mother said, breaking the seal and pulling a neatly folded piece of paper from the envelope. She read, her lips parted and when she looked up,

Anthony immediately knew that something was amiss. "It's my sister," she explained, looking to each of her children in turn.

"Is she all right?" Louise asked, while Huntley, Winston and Sarah broke off their conversation to offer the duchess their undivided attention.

"She took a fall and . . ." Her voice broke. "From what I gather, she is not herself. I must go to her at once."

"I will escort you," Anthony said, placing his napkin next to his plate and rising. He signaled Phelps, who'd removed himself to the doorway. "Please tell the stable master to ready the landau."

The butler nodded and disappeared into the hallway beyond.

"Would you like me to come with you?" Winston asked.

"No," Anthony said. It was a kind offer, but he knew that his brother was eager to return home and pick up the reins of his business. Things never ran quite as smoothly as they did when Winston was there, and besides, Anthony didn't want to suffer his brother's glower for the entire duration of the carriage ride. There was no denying that he was still angry with him. "You have plenty to see to as it is."

"Huntley and I can join you if you like," Louise offered.

Anthony gave her an appreciative smile. "Thank you, but I know that you were planning to return home and close up the estate before removing yourselves to London for the Season. Don't worry—Mama and I will be fine." He turned to his mother, who was looking worried and pale. "If you can be ready to leave in an hour, we should be able to make it by nightfall."

She nodded quietly, acknowledging his words, and rose slowly to her feet. Louise was beside her in an instant. "Let me escort you upstairs," she said. "I'll call for your maid, and the two of us can help you pack."

Anthony watched them go before turning his attention back to Winston, Sarah and Huntley. "I'm sorry to leave you all in such a rush, but knowing Mama, she'll worry herself sick until she sees Aunt Cordelia."

"You mustn't concern yourself about us," Sarah said, her voice as soft as always. "Your mother needs you, and we completely understand. We just hope that your aunt will be all right, and like Winston said—if there is anything at all that we can do to help, by all means, let us know."

"Thank you, Sarah, that's very kind of you, but right now I just . . . I need to pack. If you'll excuse me." He left them then, heading to his study to collect enough money to sustain them on their journey. After that, he called for his valet, who accompanied him upstairs to help him pack. Half an hour later, he and his mother said their good-byes to Louise, Sarah, Winston and Huntley, climbed into the carriage and headed north.

"I'm sorry to burden you like this," his mother said as she turned away from the window to face him. They had left Moxley behind a while ago and were now galloping at full speed across the English countryside.

Anthony stared at her. "Your apology is completely unnecessary," he said, taking her hand in his and giving it a gentle squeeze. "I am only happy to help, surely you know that."

She attempted a smile and nodded. "Yes, but I feel as though you've been doing little else for the past five years."

"I don't mind it," he said, hoping to ease her concern. "It's my duty to take care of you, and even if it weren't, I'd still do it. You're my mother and you need me, that's all that matters."

Tears welled in her eyes. "I can't help but think that it has kept you from making a family of your own. You put your life on hold for all of us—for your father when he was sick, for Winston and Louise so they could be free of the burdens you chose to carry on your own, and for me. We've all been like rocks around your ankles, weighing you down and keeping you in one place."

Anthony shook his head. "You're wrong. I'm the oldest and I was here—managing the estate and taking care of you and Papa was my responsibility. Granted, it wasn't easy seeing Papa in such a state of decline, but I never considered any of it a burden."

She wiped the tears away with her hand and leaned back against her seat. "I'm glad you've finally met a woman whom you care about. Miss Chilcott—"

"Oh no," Anthony muttered, staring back at his mother with wide eyes. "I told her I'd call on her this afternoon, but I completely forgot with our haste to get on our way." Her expression was once again pained, so he hastily said, "Not to worry—I'll send her a letter as soon as we reach our destination. I'm sure she'll understand, given the circumstances."

His mother nodded. "You should invite her for tea one day, Anthony. I'd like to meet her when she's not masquerading as Miss Smith." Her smile was good-natured, and Anthony couldn't help but return it. What other mother would be willing to accept that her son had fallen for a woman who wasn't who she'd said she was? None, he wagered.

He contemplated her words and said, "Perhaps that's not a bad idea. One thing is for certain—I can use all the help I can get in convincing her to marry me instead of that wet towel Mr. Roberts."

"That's a bit possessive of you, don't you think? From what you've told me, Mr. Roberts has been courting Miss Chilcott for almost a year. You can't possibly expect her to just toss him aside from one day to the next just because you've suddenly come into her life."

Anthony glowered. He knew she was right, but that didn't make him feel any better. "I know she feels the same way as I," he grumbled.

"Even more reason for her to be backing away from you." She gave him a stare so frank that Anthony felt certain she saw the situation with far more clarity than he did. "I'm not familiar with Mr. Roberts, but if your description of him is accurate, then I very much doubt he's managed to elicit as much as a blush from Miss Chilcott, which would mean that if she's responding to you in the same manner that you're responding to her, well heavens! The poor girl must be terribly confused, perhaps even frightened by such an onslaught of emotion."

Anthony closed his eyes against the truth that shone in his mother's eyes. Her meaning wasn't much different from what Winston's had been the previous evening, but her words were kinder. God help him, he felt like an ass. Not only had he burst into Miss Chilcott's life with his sudden need to claim her as his own, seeking out her house, investigating her identity and meeting with her parents, but in the space of one week he'd kissed her three times and had fondled and pleasured her in a barn, for heaven's sake. He had single-handedly turned her life upside down, had acted on his baser instincts and had felt affronted when she'd asked him to walk away and leave her alone. "I've self-ishly pursued her with no thought for what she might be going through," he muttered.

"Well, I suppose the need for haste has been a factor for you, considering it really will be too late once she marries Mr. Roberts, and since he's already been courting her for a year, I daresay he'll propose soon—especially if he and the Chilcotts feel a need to act quickly."

"I've made a complete mess of it," Anthony said, looking at his mother as if she could somehow give him the answer he needed to make Miss Chilcott his. "I can't let her marry him, Mama—not with this . . . this bond that's between us. I know it sounds ridiculous, but I feel it inside me, drawing me toward her. If she mar-ries him, I'll . . ." He expelled a deep breath and shook his head. "I don't know what I'll do."

"There's nothing strange about the way you feel, Anthony, though I must admit that I'm a bit surprised by just how quickly you fell for her. It was the same for me and your papa, you know—we saw each other for the very first time across a crowded room and there was this inexplicable pull.

"We both denied it at first—after all, love at first sight is a fantasy—but then we were introduced, and the more time we spent in each other's company, the more impossible it became for us to ignore the way we felt about each other." She paused, tilting her head a little as she regarded her son. "You love her, Anthony, and the sooner you admit that to yourself, the better."

Anthony shook his head. "No, I . . . what I feel is the promise of love, Mama. I don't actually . . . I mean I—"

"Is she constantly in your thoughts? Do you ache to be near her? Do you worry for her and what will become of her if she marries Mr. Roberts instead of you? Have you pondered what life will be like with her at your side? What your children will be like? Would you risk your life to save hers? Would you sacrifice your own happiness for hers? And what if something terrible were to happen to her, would you recover from it and go on with your life, or would it cripple you?"

Anthony couldn't speak, so he just sat there staring back at his mother, who, in turn, offered him a knowing smile and nodded. "That's what I thought," she said.

He felt as if his chest was constricting—as if he couldn't breathe. This feeling that suddenly swamped him was not in the least bit pleasant. In fact, it terrified him to death knowing that what his mother said was true, because this was far worse than the promise of love. He'd actually gone and quite unwittingly fallen in love with a woman who, he doubted, felt the same way about him. Hell, he knew she was drawn to him, but love? What the devil was he going to do now? *Damn!*

By the time they arrived at his aunt and uncle's estate, it was dark. Two footmen came to greet them, each carrying torches to light the way. Anthony helped his mother alight, and together they climbed the steps to the front door, where the butler waited. "Good evening, Your Graces," he said, taking their hats and gloves and handing them to an awaiting maid. "The earl is in the library—right this way."

As they followed the butler down a dimly lit corridor, Anthony couldn't help but reflect upon the note of relief that had tinged the butler's voice as he'd greeted them. He understood, however, the minute they entered the library. Sitting in a deep armchair was his uncle, the Earl of Chester, staring off at some faraway place, concern and fatigue apparent in the dark patches beneath his eyes. He looked as if he'd aged a dozen years since Anthony had seen him last, only four months earlier, and he recognized in that instant the severity of the situation.

"Gerald," the duchess whispered as she stepped away from Anthony's side and approached her brother-in-law with tentative steps.

The earl didn't flinch—did not as much as acknowledge her presence as he spoke to the space beyond. "She fell . . . she just fell . . ."

"How did it happen, Gerald?" the duchess prodded, crouching next to his seat.

The earl turned to gaze at her then, the stricken look in his eyes so familiar to Anthony, for it was a look he'd seen in his mother's eyes three times before—when her husband's ailment had been announced, when he had given up the fight, and when he had drawn his final breath. It was a look of complete and utter hopelessness and loss of control.

"If you'll excuse me, Mama," Anthony said. "I shall just have a word with the butler."

They exchanged a knowing glance, upon which she nodded and he left the room. Though he had yet to see the state his aunt was in, one thing was clear—his uncle needed help, and Anthony knew precisely what to do. He'd done it all before, after all.

"Marsham," he addressed the butler who'd positioned himself close enough to the library door should they need him, yet far enough away to offer privacy. "A word if you will."

Marsham nodded and Anthony followed him back to the foyer.

"Have my cousins been informed about their mother's condition?" Anthony asked.

"Yes, Your Grace. Our first missives were addressed to them, but as you are probably aware, Lord Hillcrest and his sisters meant to continue on to London after attending your house party. It will take longer for them to arrive than it did you."

"Quite right, and since they left my estate three days ago, they will have arrived in London already. I doubt they'll make it all the way back until the day after tomorrow at the earliest." He considered the butler's stark expression. Marsham hid it well, but Anthony could tell that he was hoping for assistance. "Needless to say, my mother and I shall remain here until Lord Hillcrest arrives."

Marsham gave a curt nod. "Thank you, Your Grace," he said in his familiar, affected voice that betrayed not a single emotion.

"They are family," Anthony added. "And nothing is more important than that. Now, I assume a physician has been to visit the countess."

"Yes, Your Grace. He was here this morning and again this evening—he left shortly before your arrival."

"Very good, Marsham. I'll need to know exactly what he said, as well as what treatment he has prescribed." He stopped to think. "Has my uncle eaten his evening meal?"

"No, Your Grace—he has not moved from that chair since yesterday."

"Good God," Anthony exclaimed. "And you didn't think to serve him his food in the library? The man needs to eat, Marsham—he'll never get through this otherwise."

"We did try," the butler said, sounding not the least bit moved by Anthony's suggestion that he and his staff had shirked their duties.

Anthony raked his fingers through his hair as he paced the space. "Have Cook prepare something cold for all of us—some ham and some cheese with a few slices of bread. The duchess and I are hungry as well— perhaps if he sees us eat, he'll find himself tempted."

"A splendid idea, Your Grace."

Anthony eyed him and frowned. "Only if it works, Marsham."

"Of course, Your Grace. Will that be all?"

"Bring the food so we can eat, then you and I will discuss the doctor's visit, and when that has been completed I should like to take the duchess to see her sister. Does that sound reasonable?"

Only the slightest twitch of his lips betrayed Marsham's surprise at being asked rather than ordered, and by a duke no less. He nodded briefly, and with an "I believe so," he took his leave of Anthony and headed for the kitchens.

Chapter 20

He hadn't called on her—not today, not yesterday and not the day before that either. Isabella yanked a potato out of the ground and tossed it into a nearby basket. She'd pushed him too far with her stubbornness, and now he wanted nothing to do with her—and after he'd been so kind as to buy her that book. It was a good book too, with a definite flair for the dramatic.

No, he was probably showering Lady Harriett with attention instead. A fierce pang of jealousy sprang to life in Isabella's chest, so painful that she actually winced. What right did she have to feel that way? She'd rejected him—repeatedly—and he'd decided to move on. It was for the best really, and it was what she wanted. Wasn't it?

No, her inner voice screamed. The thought of him marrying someone else—of him touching any other woman the way he'd touched her—Dear God, she couldn't bear it.

Yanking another potato from the ground, she considered her options. Lady Harriett had told her that she and Anthony were betrothed, but something about her words and the way she'd spoken them had rung false. In fact, Isabella was willing to guess that Lady Harriett had taken an interest in Anthony and was trying to eliminate her competition, which would explain why she'd threatened her.

But before she hurried off to confront him about it, Isabella had to make a decision. Would she be the dutiful daughter everyone expected her to be, condemning herself to live unhappily ever after with Mr. Roberts? Or would she do what she knew would make her happy and marry the duke instead? If there was ever a time in her life when she ought to be selfish, then this was surely it. Her parents would undoubtedly be furious—might never speak to her again—and Mr. Roberts would be . . . well, he wouldn't be happy, that was for sure. But she and the duke would be, though they would not avoid scandal.

Standing there in the vegetable patch with her hands all covered in dirt, she finally made her decision—she would go to him and ask him about Lady Harriett, and if he denied any connection to the woman, Isabella would accept his offer of marriage. She'd run away with him if that was what it took for them to be together.

A weight was lifted from her heart in that moment. Hopefully her parents would not be too cross with her—especially once they realized how much easier their lives would be with the duke's protection. He would care for them, she was certain of that.

Finishing her task, she took her basket to the kitchen and gave it to Marjorie, after which she ran to her room, washing her hands and face at the washbasin and changing into a clean gown. Filled with excitement, she wrote a quick note to her mother explaining that she would be back later in the day, then left the cottage at a brisk pace.

It took her half an hour to arrive at the massive front door to Kingsborough Hall, and for a long while she just stood there, staring at it as she tried to calm herself. Taking a deep breath, she eventually stepped forward just as the door swung open, revealing none other than the odious Lady Harriett.

Isabella froze. What on earth was she doing here unless . . . No, it wasn't possible. Whatever the case, Isabella would not be made to feel inferior by such a vile woman, so, squaring her shoulders, she stood her ground, offered Lady Harriett a curt nod in greeting and then looked beyond her, at the butler. "I'm here to see the duke," she announced, trying very hard to ignore Lady Harriett's glare.

The butler peered down his nose at her and said, "The servant's entrance is at the back, miss, though I don't believe we're presently hiring."

Lady Harriett snickered, and again Isabella ignored her, determined to make her case. "I am not here as a servant but as an acquaintance of the duke."

The butler looked dubious but at least asked her name, which she gave him. He seemed to consider it for a moment before saying, "I don't believe I've ever heard mention of you. Besides, His Grace is no longer in residency."

Isabella's jaw dropped. "What?"

"He has left town, Miss Chilcott, and I am not at liberty to say when he will return. Now, if you will please excuse me, I have a job to do." And without further ado the door closed in Isabella's face.

"I thought I had made myself clear," Lady Harriett said. Isabella turned to look at her and was struck by the venom that shone in her eyes. Surely Anthony couldn't mean to marry such a creature. "He no longer wants you, and with the Season about to begin, I suspect it will be an age before he returns, and once he does . . . well, it shall be with me on his arm. We are to announce our engagement, you see. That is why I was here—to ensure that all will be ready for my arrival as duchess."

Isabella gaped at her. She glanced at the door, then back at Lady Harriett, who was looking far too pleased with herself. In that moment, Isabella lost hope. She'd pushed him away and he'd left without a single word of warning, to set up his residency in London, no doubt, where Lady Harriett would reconvene with him.

Isabella hadn't wanted to believe it, but the butler's concise dismissal of her made it difficult to deny what Lady Harriett had told her.

With a breaking heart, she straightened her back and addressed the woman before her. "I will stay away from him," she promised in a low whisper. "You have my word on it." And before Lady Harriett had a chance to see the tears that threatened to spill from her eyes, Isabella turned on her heel and strode away, hurt and angry. How could he? What kind of man chased after a woman, desperate to make her his wife, only to choose someone else without a moment's notice? One who clearly didn't feel for her what she felt for him. "I hate him," she muttered as she walked the long and tedious road leading back to Moxley.

In the space of one week, he'd made her long for something more than what was her due, he'd made her believe he cared, had given her a taste of passion and had, with his charm, his touch, his words, made her fall desperately in love with him. And then he'd left her—gone to London to prepare for the Season and the arrival of his fiancée. She'd never hated anyone as much as she hated him in that moment. What a fool she'd been to think that a duke would actually want anything more from her than a few laughs, some stolen kisses and . . . thank God she'd managed to preserve her innocence, or she might have been left to bring a child into the world on her own.

It was no wonder that her mother hated his kind. They were arrogant people who toyed with people's lives, as if doing so was a game to them. *She* had been a game to him. That much was clear now. She stopped for breath, her heart pounding in her chest as the tears flowed down her cheeks. She wiped them hastily away when she spotted a carriage rolling toward her. As it came closer it slowed, coming to an eventual stop as it drew up beside her. The door opened and Mr. Roberts peered out, tipping his hat in greeting. "Miss Chilcott, I've been hoping to speak to you. I trust you have fully recovered from your ailment?"

She nodded, recalling how she'd remained in her room when he'd called on her Sunday for tea. She'd been in no mood to entertain him—her meeting with Anthony in the bookshop earlier in the day had been too troubling to think of. "Yes, thank you," she said, smiling up at him.

"I'm glad to hear it, though I'm not the least bit pleased to find you trudging about the countryside like this. It really won't do. The future Mrs. Roberts must ride in a carriage."

There were so many things wrong with that statement that Isabella didn't know where to begin. For one thing, she'd received no proposal from him yet, nor had she accepted. Next, there was the fact that now he was prohibiting her from walking, which she might have been able to accept if, like Anthony's, his reasoning had been based on some concern for her safety. However, it was perfectly clear that the only thing concerning Mr. Roberts was that he keep a high standard for appearance's sake.

Nevertheless, it wouldn't do to offend him by saying any of those things, since she would soon be accepting his offer. Or at least she hoped so, for if he too decided to cast her aside, it would leave her family in dire straits indeed. So when he offered her his hand, she obediently accepted it, allowing him to help her up into the landau, where she took the seat across from him. "To Moxley," he then directed the driver. Turning to Isabella he said, "It's time we find you something decent to wear."

"I beg your pardon?" He'd said it as if she'd been a river rat that he'd just fished out of the Thames when in fact she'd worn her best gown, thinking she'd be seeing Anthony. She pushed all thought of him aside—as difficult as that was to do—and focused on Mr. Roberts instead.

"Well," he said, peering at her. "You can't expect me to make a proper proposal unless you look the part."

"The part," she reiterated, sounding daft to her own ears. Then again, the man whose company she was keeping had just claimed her unfit for a proposal given her present attire. It rankled her beyond imagining, but what choice did she have but to keep quiet?

"Of my future wife, Miss Chilcott." Good God,

could he possibly sound more patronizing? He leaned forward, narrowing his eyes on her as he tilted his head a little and asked, "Is there a problem?"

"No," she muttered, fearful that if she said what she truly thought, he'd toss her out in the road and never speak to her again. She couldn't afford that—not with Anthony gone, and with her parents and Jamie relying on her to make a sensible decision.

Mr. Roberts leaned back against his seat. "Good," he said. "Because the only reason that I am prepared to marry you, Miss Chilcott, is because your father gave the impression that you are capable of being both discreet and compliant. Based on my own assessment of you for the past year, I've had no reason to disagree with him. However, if something has happened recently, and you no longer feel yourself capable of being the wife I seek, then by all means, do let me know so that I may place my interests elsewhere."

Isabella trembled. He'd just given her a means of escape, but it was one she couldn't possibly accept, least of all now. She had to reassure him somehow. "Please don't misunderstand me, sir. I am exceedingly grateful for everything you've done for me and my family, and your offer to see me properly outfitted is very much appreciated." She forced herself to smile. "Considering your own impeccable taste in clothes, I know that I shall be in good hands, and I assure you that once we marry, you can count on me to be as discreet and compliant as you require. I know how important privacy is to you."

He didn't answer immediately, and Isabella found herself holding her breath while she prayed that he wouldn't see right through her. For the truth of the matter was that she had never in her life resented another person as much as she did this man. She needed him though, as unbearable as that was, and found herself relieved when he eventually said, "I believe I shall order a new jacket and trousers as well—to match your gown."

And no matter how ridiculous Isabella thought they might look garbed in the same fabric, she kept quiet this time, unwilling to say anything that might cause him to change his mind.

Anthony was in a state of panic. He'd been gone from Moxley for three days, and he'd forgotten to send a letter explaining his absence to Isabella. With a groan he stared out the window at the passing countryside. His mother had fallen asleep shortly after their departure from Chester House, which hadn't surprised him in the least, since she'd hardly slept at all during their stay there.

Neither had he, for that matter. He'd had plenty to see to, with an aunt paralyzed on her entire right side, an uncle in shock, a mother who hadn't stopped crying since seeing her sister in such a god-awful state, servants who'd gone adrift from lack of instruction, and a physician who'd seemed more interested in having his bills paid than in caring for his patient.

It had been a tremendous ordeal, and while he'd thought of Isabella a number of times, there had always been something to distract him from getting that letter written and mailed out. Thankfully, his cousins had arrived last evening and Anthony and his mother had been able to depart. They needed rest, if nothing else.

Closing his eyes, he saw Isabella's smiling face before him. She must have been livid, for he'd told her four days ago that he would call on her the day after. One thing was certain—he'd have to make a good apology, though knowing how attentive she was toward her own aunt, he felt confident that she would understand once he explained the reason for his sudden departure. With that thought lifting his spirits, he leaned his head back against the plush upholstery that the seat offered and allowed the sway of the carriage to lull him to sleep.

"Anthony," his mother's voice whispered from somewhere far away. "You must wake up."

He chose to ignore her, turning his head away from the direction of her voice as he attempted to hold on to his dream—one in which Isabella was walking toward him in a flowing white gown, her hair falling over her shoulders. It was a good dream—a happy dream—one that he wasn't prepared to part with just yet.

"Anthony," his mother's voice was louder—more urgent. "Wake up right now, do you hear me?"

He tried to wave her away, but she grabbed his arm instead and gave it a hard yank. "What the devil did you have to do that for?"

She gave him a tart look—no doubt in response to his profanity—then jutted her chin toward the window. Turning his head, Anthony looked out and discovered that they had returned to Moxley, the carriage at a standstill while a farmer passed with his cart. It took him a moment to figure out why his mother had woken him but once he did, he felt his jaw clench, for there was Miss Chilcott hanging on the arm of Mr. Roberts, gazing up at him and smiling as the two of them entered the modiste's.

Bloody, bloody hell!

"You have to do something," his mother said.

Like punch someone, Anthony thought. *Mr. Roberts would do nicely.* He nodded. "I couldn't agree more. I take it they didn't notice us?"

"Not as far as I can tell," his mother said. She looked away, and Anthony knew there was something she wasn't telling him. When she met his gaze it was with great hesitation. "It appeared as though Mr. Roberts was too busy telling Miss Chilcott about something, while she in turn was giving him her undivided attention. I doubt either one of them would have noticed if a parade of elephants had wandered by."

Not the answer he'd been hoping for. He felt his chest constrict. If he'd lost her to that bore, he'd . . . he'd . . . hell, he didn't know what he'd do. "I'll see you at home, Mama," he said, scrambling to get out of the carriage so he could hurry to the modiste's and intervene in Miss Chilcott's outing with Mr. Roberts. Once on the ground, he gave his mother an awkward smile. "There's something I must see to first."

She nodded her understanding and wished him good luck.

As he strode across the street, his heart was pounding, his hands felt sweaty and there was a jitteriness coursing through him that he didn't much care for. Truth was, he was terrified—terrified that Mr. Roberts had finally gone and proposed to her during his absence, terrified that she had accepted his offer, since Anthony had seemingly vanished, and terrified that she didn't reciprocate the feelings that threatened to overwhelm him with their power.

"Ho there, Kingsborough!"

Anthony stopped in his tracks and turned his head to find Casper striding toward him.

"I tried calling on you yesterday but was turned away by Phelps—thought you might have removed yourself to London already."

"No. I was called away on some family business."

"Nothing serious, I hope?" Casper said, frowning.

Anthony gave his friend a quick account of all that had happened in the last few days while his friend's frown deepened in response to every word. "I'm so sorry to hear it," he said once Anthony had finished. "How is your mother taking it?"

"As one would expect—she's devastated."

Casper nodded. "Perhaps it will be good for her to get to London and attend some social functions. The ball she hosted livened her spirits."

"I think you may be right. It's just . . ."

"Are you still chasing that Chilcott chit?" There was a look of amusement in Casper's eyes that Anthony didn't much appreciate. And then his friend said the one thing that Anthony couldn't dispute. "Good God, Anthony—you're completely besotted by her."

"Well . . . I . . ."

Casper barked a laugh. "You, of all people—a notorious rake! Well I'll be."

"A reformed rake," Anthony muttered, crossing his arms and standing his ground.

"I hear they make the best of husbands," Casper said. He was smiling so broadly that Anthony could see all his teeth. "And you're a duke, to boot. What an excellent catch for her."

"Perhaps you'd like to tell *her* that," Anthony grumbled. He and Casper had known each other since they were lads, so since they'd already embarked on this subject, Anthony saw no point in holding back.

Casper's face grew serious once again. He stared back at his friend in disbelief. "She won't have you?"

"Apparently she has some duty toward Mr. Roberts, and with me having been away for three days without giving her any hint of where I went and why, I'm inclined to assume the worst." He nodded toward the door to the modiste's. "They're in there together right now."

Understanding dawned on Casper's face. "You were going to happen upon them *accidentally,* weren't you?"

Anthony shrugged. "Perhaps."

"Come on then," Casper said. "I'll help you out."

"You will do no such—" But his friend stepped past him, opened the door and entered the shop before Anthony had a chance to finish his sentence. With a deep breath, he followed him inside, keeping close to the exit while he surveyed the space.

There were bundles of fabric everywhere, in all possible colors and nuances. Anthony had never seen anything like it, for he had all his clothes made in London. The tailor came to him, he'd select the fabric based on swatches and that would be the end of it. This . . . it was overwhelming.

Following Casper, he ventured further inside the shop, his hand deliberately reaching out to touch a shimmery blue silk that slipped between his fingers like water, and an image of Isabella dressed in the fabric, of his hands running over her body and of . . . The sound of her voice coming from the far corner of the room snapped him out of his reverie. "What about the lilac muslin over there?" she asked.

"Too dull," came Mr. Roberts's voice. "You need something more vibrant, like that amaranthine velvet, for instance."

Did he just sigh? Anthony met Casper's gaze, and, judging by his attempt to restrain his laughter, Anthony knew that yes, Mr. Roberts had just sighed over a fabric. What the hell was wrong with him?

"The purple one?" Miss Chilcott asked, her voice sounding not the least bit convinced. "It's a bit too bold, don't you think?"

There was a loud sigh, upon which Mr. Roberts could be heard saying, "It is important to recognize the exact hue, Miss Chilcott. 'Purple' is much too broad a descriptive for such a lovely shade, and no, it is not too bold. Imagine it trimmed with black and with a black spencer to match." His voice had taken on a dreamy note. "You'll look—"

"Like a plum?" Isabella offered.

It was Anthony's turn to press his lips together to keep from laughing.

"No, Miss Chilcott. Plum is an entirely different color."

"Why, hello, Miss Chilcott," Casper said as he rounded the display shelves that stood in the middle of the room, blocking Miss Chilcott and Mr. Roberts from Anthony's view. "And Mr. Roberts is here too, I see. What a coincidence, since I was just on my way over to call on you—thought I'd stop in here first to see if I might be able to find something appropriate for my . . . er . . . friend."

Anthony groaned. Was it really necessary for Casper to refer to one of his mistresses in front of Isabella? On the other hand, what other reason would he possibly have for visiting a modiste? He considered stepping forward and announcing his own presence, but he stopped himself when Casper continued. "I couldn't help but overhear your recommendation to Miss Chilcott—seems you're quite the expert with regard to fashion. Perhaps you'd be willing to help me out? There's a fine selection of laces over here."

"Yes . . . yes, of course, Mr. Goodard," Mr. Roberts said, taking the bait without the least bit of hesitation and sounding most flattered. "I would be happy to help."

Anthony heard them move and was about to do so himself when it must have occurred to Mr. Roberts that he was meant to be escorting Miss Chilcott. "That is, of course, if you do not mind," he said, addressing her as if she'd now become a nuisance.

"By all means," she said. "Take your time. I shall continue to admire the amanthine until you return."

"Amaranthine," Mr. Roberts corrected, his voice tinged with exasperation.

Another shuffle of feet sounded, followed by footsteps as Casper and Mr. Roberts moved to the other side of the shop. Anthony made his move, rounding the shelves.

There before him stood Isabella, her back slightly toward him as she looked down at the piece of fabric that lay spread out on a counter. Did Mr. Roberts really intend for her to wear that? It would never suit someone as gentle and kind as her—it was much too gaudy for a woman with such soft blonde hair and pale complexion. She needed something milder, like the silk he'd seen at the front of the shop.

Stepping forward, he moved closer until he was

standing at her right shoulder, but she was so lost in thought—serious thought, if the crease between her eyebrows was any indication—that she didn't register him at all. How he longed to smooth away her worries and distract her from all her concerns. "If it's any consolation, I would have said it was purple too," he whispered.

She spun toward him, eyes wide, and in one fraction of a second he saw the contents of her heart. Then she must have remembered his absence—that he hadn't called on her like he'd said he would and that he hadn't even sent her a note—for her expression became shuttered, and when she spoke, her voice was as cool as rime on a winter's morning. "I have nothing to say to you. Please leave."

"I'm sorry about the way I—"

He was cut off by her laugh—quite possibly the most sarcastic laugh he'd ever heard. "Sorry? Whatever for? You owe me nothing, Your Grace, least of all an apology." The struggle that raged within her was so painful to watch that Anthony was tempted to look away. He forced himself not to, took a deep breath and placed his gloved hand upon the one she was resting on the counter. It did not have the effect he'd been hoping for. Instead she snatched her hand away and glared up at him. "How dare you?" she seethed.

He felt himself stiffen as anger rose in him as well. He might not have acted very gentlemanly toward her, but he had his reason—a very good reason, in fact—yet here she was in Mr. Roberts's company, treating him with disdain when she'd not even listened to what he had to say. He opened his mouth to speak, when the tinkling of a bell announced the arrival of yet another customer and he heard both Casper and Mr. Roberts say in unison, "Lady Harriett, how do you do?"

What followed happened with such speed that Anthony wasn't entirely sure of what to make of it. One moment, Isabella was standing before him, the next she was dashing past him, only to trip over a bolt of fabric that had fallen to the floor and land in a heap with the grace of a sack of potatoes and a loud "umph."

Anthony stepped forward to help her up, taking her by the arm as he asked about her welfare.

"Please don't touch me," she whispered, attempting to shake him off as her eyes darted about with the fear one might expect from a rabbit chased by a hound. What the devil?

"Kingsborough!" a sweet voice chimed just then, and Anthony turned his head to find the detestable Lady Harriett smiling up at him with stars in her eyes. "I had no idea that you were back in town—what a lovely surprise. After our last conversation I hadn't thought I'd see you before the Darwich Ball, but since you're here . . ." Her words trailed off, and Anthony could have sworn that the look she served Isabella held some hidden meaning.

If only he could figure out what the bloody hell was going on. He wasn't afforded much time to consider it though before the lady continued by saying, "Perhaps you could help me find a suitable fabric for the gown I plan to wear that evening. You could have a waistcoat made to match—now wouldn't that be splendid!"

Anthony sensed Isabella stiffen by his side and realized what game Lady Harriett was playing at. She knew he had designs on Isabella because, like an idiot, he'd blurted out his plans without thinking what a woman like her might do when she discovered her adversary to be of such inferior rank.

He pulled himself up to his full height and opened his mouth to give the abominable creature the proper set down she deserved when Mr. Roberts came up beside Lady Harriett with Casper right on his heels. Casper gave Anthony a look of apology while Mr. Roberts stared at him in surprise. "Your Grace," he said. His gaze drifted to where Anthony's hand still gripped Isabella's arm before returning to Anthony's face with a frown of disapproval. "I didn't realize you were here as well." His features softened, but when he spoke, there was no mistaking the menace of his question. "I hope you're not planning to abscond with my fiancée."

Fiancée?

Had he proposed, then? More importantly, had Isabella accepted? She must have if Mr. Roberts was claiming her to be his fiancée. A pang of jealous rage poured through him at the thought of it, but he forced himself to remain still and in control of his features. There was no way he would allow any of the people present to know the weight of the blow that Mr. Roberts had just dealt him. Releasing Isabella, since this seemed the prudent thing to do, he said, "Miss Chilcott took a tumble—I was merely helping her up when Lady Harriett arrived. I hope you don't mind."

"Not at all," Mr. Roberts said, his assessing gaze still fixed on Anthony. "It is only too fortunate that you were here to assist. Thank you."

Anthony glanced at Isabella, hoping that something in her eyes—some truth she dared not speak—would answer the one question that he dared not, could not, ask. *Are you engaged to this man?* But he found nothing there to appease the uproar that had taken hold of him, and when Mr. Roberts announced that he had placed the order for the amaranthine velvet and that he and Miss Chilcott also had plans to visit the milliner's in pursuit of a new bonnet for Miss Chilcott, Anthony was left with no choice but to watch her walk away.

Nothing had ever depressed him more, but at least he'd handled the situation with the same degree of restraint his father would have shown. It was a small comfort.

"So, Miss Chilcott is to marry Mr. Roberts, then?" a vexing voice asked as soon as the couple had left.

"Lady Harriett . . ." There was no mistaking the warning in Casper's voice as he tried to silence the nefarious woman, but she stupidly added, "How disappointing that must be for you, Your Grace."

His name coming from her lips grated, and Anthony stared at her, his eyes trapping her with menace, all thought of the civility he'd shown a moment earlier forgotten. She gasped a little and took a retreating step backward, but he was too angry to care. "What did you do?" he asked, his voice filled with ducal command.

"I . . . I . . . I don't know—"

"That is *not* the answer I am seeking, my lady." He leaned toward her, taking perverse pleasure in watching her tremble as she leaned back until she hit the shelving unit. "Miss Chilcott was terrified of you, and you took the opportunity to imply that you and I have formed an attachment, so don't feign ignorance with me. I know a snake when I see one."

She gasped at the insult. "It was merely a bit of fun, really," she said, her gaze shifting imploringly to Casper, but she would find no help from him.

"Fun?" Anthony's words dripped with incredulity, and then the dam broke and he found himself yelling, "FUN?"

The shopkeeper came running to ask if everything was all right, but she took one look at Anthony and chose to retreat to a safe distance. Anthony forced himself to take a deep breath. He had to get himself back under control—dukes yelling at people in shops simply wasn't done—and to think how well he'd handled the situation with Mr. Roberts, only to lose his temper a second later. Closing his eyes to avoid having to look at the woman before him, he reined in his emotions. He couldn't be sure of what she'd told Isabella, but he had an inkling, and when he spoke again his voice was a deep rumble—the sort that demanded obedience in the most rebellious sorts. "Please stay away from her, Lady Harriett. Do not speak to her or approach her, for if you do, I cannot answer to the consequences."

There was a beat of silence, and then she asked, her voice snippy and completely lacking the respect that was his due, "Is that a threat?"

"You can bet your bonnet it is, my lady." Anthony turned on his heels and stormed out. Good Lord, he'd never considered resorting to murder before, yet there were suddenly two people whom he was now very keen to dispose of.

"I say, Anthony," Casper said from somewhere behind him. "That was very well done, indeed. Bravo!"

"That woman has overstepped," Anthony said as he marched along, his anger still coursing through his veins, putting his nerves on edge and tightening his muscles.

"I couldn't agree more!" Anthony could hear

Casper's footsteps quickening as he tried to keep pace. He said nothing more for a while, but when Anthony turned sharply onto Church Lane, he asked, "Where are we heading?"

"To Miss Chilcott's house."

"Do you think that's wise?" Casper asked, hurrying after him.

Anthony spun around to face his friend, stopping so abruptly that the two almost collided. "I need to know if Mr. Roberts spoke the truth when he referred to her as his fiancée, I have to tell her that whatever Lady Harriett has said to her is a lie, and I have to explain the reason for my absence."

There was sympathy in Casper's eyes as he regarded Anthony. "I don't mean to point out the obvious, but Miss Chilcott does seem quite determined to thwart your advances. Are you sure it wouldn't be best for you to direct your attentions elsewhere? If we go to London—"

"You don't understand," Anthony said, knowing how impossible it was for his friend the rake to comprehend the sort of power love could hold over a man. It was crippling, really. "It is either her or no one. I will not go to London to waste my time on women I don't give a flip about when the one woman who fills my every thought is right here. I need to make this right—this tangled mess that threatens to drive me insane."

"Well, you certainly don't lack determination," Casper offered with the barest hint of a smile.

Anthony held his gaze. "I'll do whatever it takes to secure her hand."

"Providing it's legal of course," Casper said, his eyes starting to sparkle.

Anthony deliberately hesitated just long enough to make his friend wonder before he responded, "Of course."

"Is there anything I can do to help?"

They'd started walking again, though at a more casual pace. Anthony pondered the question a moment before saying, "Yes, I believe there is. The Season is starting, and since I have no intention of leaving Moxley before I've settled this matter with Miss Chilcott, I'd be most obliged if you would see to escorting my mother to London for me. Louise and Winston will be better company for her right now than I, and as you mentioned earlier, attending a few social functions will do her good."

"I will be happy to help if she agrees. Just let me know when she will be ready for departure."

Anthony nodded. "She wished to invite Miss Chilcott for tea in order to further her acquaintance with her. If they meet tomorrow, then I see no reason why you cannot depart the day after that, but I will send a note around so you are made aware of the proceedings."

They came to a halt in front of Miss Chilcott's home. "You're quite optimistic," Casper remarked, "to think that you can pacify Miss Chilcott to the point where she will be willing to appear at Kingsborough Hall tomorrow. I suggest you pray for a miracle."

"No need," Anthony said, sensing that whatever miracle he needed had already occurred in the form of his mother's request. "I shall not be the one issuing the invitation, Casper—my mother shall, and I doubt very much that Miss Chilcott would turn down the Duchess of Kingsborough for any reason."

"My dear man," Casper chuckled as he dipped his head in admiration, "I fear your quarry may have underestimated her pursuer, but wouldn't it be better, then, to give her time to cool a little? Surely you can wait until tomorrow with your questioning."

Anthony shook his head. "No, for I wish to give her something to consider before we meet again, and besides, I doubt I'll get a moment's rest tonight unless I discover whether or not she has promised herself to Mr. Roberts."

Chapter 21

Having promised Casper to send word later in the day about his mother's decision to journey to London with him, Anthony bid his friend a good day, assuring him that the matter he now faced was one he must see to alone.

Unlatching the gate, he stepped inside the garden and started up the path that led to the front door. Once there, he took a moment to straighten his jacket before raising his fisted hand and giving the door three loud raps. It didn't take long before the door opened, revealing the same maid he'd encountered on his previous visits. "I'm afraid Mr. Chilcott is not at home," she said. "Would you like to leave a note?"

"I'm not here to see Mr. Chilcott," Anthony told her. The fact that she would make such an assumption rather than ask him to state his purpose was a sharp reminder of his current location. "It is Miss Chilcott I've come to call upon."

"She's not at home either," the maid responded.

Anthony hadn't expected her to be, considering Mr. Roberts had seemed quite keen on finding a fashionable bonnet for her. He'd probably insist that it match the purple fabric he'd selected for Isabella's new gown. Anthony shuddered. Poor Isabella—she was going to look positively ghastly in that color. "If you don't mind, I should like to wait for her—there is a matter that I wish to discuss."

The maid looked perplexed, and Anthony realized then that she had been informed to turn him away, except he was making it more difficult by giving her reasons not to. And then something that Isabella had said about her mother a few days earlier came to mind. *She hates your kind and will never allow me to wed you.* "In the meantime," he said, "if Mrs. Chilcott is available, I would be delighted to join her for a cup of tea." And then he did something he never would have thought himself capable of. Frustrated by the lack of success he'd had in winning the Chilcotts' favor, he decided to abandon some of the changes he'd made to his character and pushed his way past the maid without being granted entry. Not the sort of thing one might expect from a duke, and certainly not his proudest moment considering his efforts to live up to his father's good name, but enough was enough—he would not be turned away.

"Your Grace," the maid gasped behind him. "You cannot—"

But Anthony had already entered the parlor and found Mrs. Chilcott, who was sitting on the sofa with her embroidery in her lap, staring back at him with what could only have been described as deep loathing. Anthony smiled and executed a very ducal bow. "What a pleasure it is to see you again, Mrs. Chilcott."

"I cannot say that I return the sentiment," she said.

"Forgive me, Mrs. Chilcott," the maid spluttered. "I tried to send him away, but he insisted and—"

"That's quite all right, Marjorie," Mrs. Chilcott told her coolly. "It isn't your fault that the gentleman lacks manners. You may bring us some tea if you please."

The flustered maid bobbed a quick curtsy and dashed from the room.

"May I?" Anthony then asked, gesturing toward an armchair.

"By all means," Mrs. Chilcott replied, her voice still clipped. "At least it will save me from having to crane my neck."

Accepting the cue, Anthony stepped toward the chair and sat. Leaning back and making himself comfortable, he met Mrs. Chilcott's assessing gaze without the least bit of hesitation and said, "I would be most grateful if you would please explain your dislike of me." She didn't flinch, and yet there was a movement about her mouth suggesting she wasn't entirely comfortable with the question. Anthony decided to use it to his advantage. "You do not know me at all, and yet you are rather determined to think the very worst of me. Consequently, I am inclined to believe that you are drawing a parallel between your own experiences and those of your daughter."

"Your Grace! You are entirely too forward," Mrs. Chilcott snapped, but not before she'd revealed the fear that brewed beneath her otherwise placid demeanor. It shone in her eyes more brightly than the sun. "I should ask you to leave."

Anthony nodded. "Yes, you should, but I will not oblige you on that score—not yet—not until you tell me why you would rather throw your daughter into the arms of an undeserving scoundrel than see her happily married to me."

Mrs. Chilcott turned red and her eyes widened, but Anthony would not be cowed so easily, no matter how many rules of etiquette he had to break in the process. His and Isabella's future was at stake, as well as their mutual happiness. He intended to stand his ground.

"Mr. Roberts is a very respectable gentleman, whereas you . . ." Her words trailed off as the maid returned with a tea tray. She moved to pour, but Mrs. Chilcott waved her away.

When they were alone again and the door had been closed behind the departing maid, Anthony crossed his arms and leveled Mrs. Chilcott with a very direct stare. "Do go on," he said. "I believe you were about to tell me what it is about my person and character that you so blatantly disapprove of."

"For starters, how about the way in which you barged into my home without invitation, or perhaps the patronizing manner in which you're addressing me now?" Her voice was clipped, her eyes fierce as she spoke. Worst of all, she made an excellent point—one which could not be denied. "You think you have the right to do as you please because of your title, to treat the rest of us as if our opinions are inconsequential unless they align with yours." She waved her hand with distaste. "Hmpf! You're no better than a spoiled child determined to have his way and throwing a tantrum when you're told you can't. Frankly, *Your Grace,* your actions have proved you to be as arrogant as any other aristocrat and not the sort of man my husband or I will entrust our daughter to. Isabella will marry Mr. Roberts and you will leave them both in peace if you have any shred of dignity at all."

The verbal blow struck its mark, rendering Anthony speechless. He suddenly saw himself through her eyes, reflected on all his actions of late—the way he'd kissed Isabella at the ball without even knowing her name, seducing her in the barn to prove himself superior to Mr. Roberts, doggedly pursuing her although she'd asked him not to and his rude behavior toward Lady Crooning, her daughter Lady Harriett, and, worst of all, the Chilcotts. It was as if he'd abandoned all civility the moment he'd set eyes on Isabella, making him no better than the man he'd once been and diminishing whatever chances he'd ever had of success. The answer to his problem became clear: to win Isabella's hand in marriage, he would have to ignore the elemental urge to knock all obstacles aside and drag her away with him like a savage. Instead, he must resolve to be polite, considerate, honorable . . . qualities that would surely be rewarded with respect if nothing else. And if at the end of the day this proved insufficient in his plight . . . well, then he would have to accept defeat with grace.

He eyed Mrs. Chilcott, who was still regarding him in much the same way he suspected she'd watch a criminal. It was time for him to right his wrongs, and there was no better way in which to do so than simply apologize. "You're right," he said. "I've acted abominably, for which I'm well and truly sorry. I hope you'll accept my sincerest apologies."

As she stared back at him, her eyes widened, as if this was the very last thing she'd expected him to say. They remained like that for a beat or two, their gazes locked, with neither willing to look away, until she sighed and with a nod said, "Thank you, Your Grace, that is most kind of you." She hesitated before adding,

"I believe I've also said some things in anger which I hope you'll forgive. Please understand that I just want what's best for Isabella."

It was of course a comment to be expected from a mother who loved her daughter, and yet she spoke in a manner that was nothing short of enlightening. To her way of thinking, Mr. Roberts represented safety and security for her daughter, while Anthony did not. *She hates your kind.* Whatever experience Mrs. Chilcott had had with the nobility, it had not been positive.

"So do I," Anthony told her. "And I know that you believe you are doing so by encouraging her to marry Mr. Roberts, but you are wrong. Mr. Roberts has only his own interests at heart. I don't believe he will love her." He didn't wish to elaborate on his reasoning, since much of it was based on speculation. Still, his instincts were seldom wrong.

Mrs. Chilcott eyed him dubiously. "And you will?" She met his gaze with steel in her eyes as she leaned toward him and said, "I understand that you have tried to abandon your rakish ways—to reform, as they say— but that doesn't change who you are at heart. You are an aristocrat, Your Grace, and in my book, that is hardly something to be proud of, as evidenced by your actions thus far—actions which have lacked both honor and decency."

Though he'd just made a similar observation, he didn't enjoy the accusation. He felt compelled to say something in his defense, but Mrs. Chilcott continued.

"The way in which you've been chasing after Isabella is simply disgraceful. There's nothing honorable or respectable about it, and at the end of the day, you're doing not only her but yourself a great disservice." He couldn't deny that his actions toward Isabella had been rash, and he dreaded the thought of her mother discovering just how far he'd taken his advances. But he knew that what he felt for her was more than lust—something deeper and enduring. Perhaps he should say so? He opened his mouth to speak, but Mrs. Chilcott stopped him as she added, "Please leave her alone. Leave *us* alone." She stood, signaling an end to the interview.

"I'm afraid that's impossible," Anthony said, rising as well. "You see, I—"

"Margaret?" Mr. Chilcott's voice called from the entryway to the sound of the front door closing behind him. "Where are you, love? I . . ."

Anthony turned just in time to see Mr. Chilcott come to an abrupt halt in the parlor doorway, his mouth open in dismay as he registered Anthony's presence. With a sidelong glance in Mrs. Chilcott's direction, he noticed that her eyes had grown wide and that the blood had drained from her face. She'd completely lost her composure. Why? It took but a second for Anthony to realize the implication of Mr. Chilcott's words.

Margaret.

Surely not *the* Margaret—the one who had gone missing twenty years ago—the Marquess of Deerford's daughter? Anthony shook his head. Of course not. It was a ridiculous notion, and yet . . . Isabella had told him that her mother had bought the gown from a peddler, but what if that was untrue? What if the gown had belonged to Isabella's mother all along? It would certainly explain a lot, like the grace with which Isabella carried herself, not to mention her refined speech pattern. She'd been able to pass herself off as an aristocrat at his ball because she was one.

Turning his head slowly toward Mr. Chilcott, Anthony asked the one question that overshadowed the rest. "Does Isabella know?"

It was clear that Mr. Chilcott was trying to think of something to say that might dismiss all of Anthony's suspicions. Resignation eventually enveloped his features and he stepped forward, closing the parlor door behind him. "No," he muttered.

Good God!

"We wanted to protect her," Lady Margaret added. Her voice sounded weak now compared to the resolve that had underscored it just a few minutes earlier.

"By lying to her about her heritage?" They were mad, both of them.

"It was for her own good," Lady Margaret said as she perched herself on the edge of the sofa and poured an extra cup of tea for her husband before turning her attention to Anthony and offering him a fragile smile. "More tea, Your Grace?"

Struck dumb by the incredulity of it all, Anthony slumped back down on his chair and nodded mutely. Isabella was the granddaughter of the Marquess of Deerford and she hadn't the slightest idea. *Bloody hell*.

"We had our reasons for keeping this from her, you understand," Mr. Chilcott said. "It was . . . easier than telling her the truth."

Easier for whom? Anthony wondered. He swallowed hard as he tried to come to terms with it all. The deception was monumental, and he found his anger rising at the thought that these people could have lied so thoroughly to their children for so many years without any apparent shame. "Why?" he asked. "Why did you do it?"

There was a beat of silence before Lady Margaret responded. "Because I wanted to keep my girls safe from the humiliation of what happened to me and because I wanted to keep myself safe as well."

"From what I have been told, you were kidnapped." Anthony looked to each of them in turn to see if what he said was true, only to find Lady Margaret biting nervously on her lip while Mr. Chilcott lowered his gaze to his lap. Realization struck, and Anthony found it impossible to look away from the man who sat in the other armchair. "Good Lord. She ran away with you! What were you? A footman or her father's secretary— his valet, perhaps?"

"I was the stable master," Mr. Chilcott said. He looked up, and there was a shadow of torment in his eyes that could not be dismissed. "And just so we're clear, Margaret and I did nothing wrong. We love each other as much now as we did back then, probably more, but her father—"

"Is distraught, by the way," Anthony said. He returned his attention to Lady Margaret. "And so is your mother. Heaven above, did you even think to consider what your running away would do to them? They've been worried senseless about you."

"My father," Lady Margaret said, her words sounding measured, "is the reason behind all of this. If he wouldn't have . . ." Her words trailed off as a shadow crossed her face. It was obvious that she was wrestling with the decision of how much to divulge.

Reflex pressed Anthony to encourage her with words, but he thought better of it and decided to hold silent instead. He was desperate for answers now, but he sensed that he would be more likely to get them if he gave Lady Margaret the time and space she required. So he leaned back in his chair and waited.

When she finally spoke, it was in such a soft whisper that Anthony had to strain to hear her. "When I turned eighteen and had my coming out, my parents did all in their power to ensure a good match for me. I have no siblings, Your Grace, so my dowry was astronomical. Naturally, every bachelor in England came to call on me, expressing a keen desire to court me, or my money, to be more precise. To put it in perspective, I received no fewer than ten proposals that first week. My parents were ecstatic, of course, but I . . ." She paused momentarily as she fidgeted with her gown. With an almost shy smile about her lips she looked to her husband. "I had already made my choice. I'd fallen in love with Walter and knew that he loved me in return."

"Except he wasn't a man your parents could accept," Anthony muttered.

"No," she said, reaching for her teacup and taking a small sip. "But I knew I had to try and fight for what I wanted, so I told them about my feelings for Walter—that I loved him desperately and wanted to marry him. My dowry would have allowed us to live a comfortable life, but my father refused to listen. He was furious, in fact. First, he told me that I was insane to think that he would allow me to marry his stable master, then he gave me a seething speech about how love was for children and about how I had a duty to adhere to, and then he sacked Walter. I was devastated and refused to leave my room for a whole week.

"My father eventually came to make amends with me. He told me how sorry he was for his outburst but that I must realize what a shock I'd given both him and

my mother. Of course I could, so when he begged forgiveness for his rash response and told me he would
let me marry Walter after all if that was what would
make me happy, I believed him." Anthony tensed at
the sound of her ominous tone. "The Shrewsbury Ball
was to take place that evening, and my father suggested
we go together as a family. In the morning, he would
send for Walter and give him his blessing.

"As was to be expected, given my successful debut,
the gentlemen lined up to claim a dance with me the
moment we arrived. One of these gentlemen was Lord
Jouve. He was terribly charming with that crooked
smile of his, and when he spoke to me he didn't seem
to have that same eagerness about him that all the other
gentlemen had. He asked me to accompany him in a
reel, and I accepted, thinking nothing of it.

"Once the dance was over, we toured the periphery
of the ballroom together, during which he engaged me
in the most interesting conversation about the stars.
I was so enthralled by what he was telling me that it
didn't occur to me to say no when he offered to take me
outside and show me some of the many constellations.
It was terribly naïve of me of course, for he spared not
a moment before taking advantage, and who do you
suppose arrived on the scene just in time to witness my
ruin?"

Anthony knew, and yet it was far too horrid to con-
template.

"As it turned out, Lord Jouve was in dire financial
straits. He needed my dowry, so when my father went to
him and suggested he compromise me, the two forged
a plan that would see me married to an aristocrat just
as my father wanted, while Lord Jouve would reap the

benefits." Lady Margaret expelled a deep breath as her eyes met Anthony's. "I left home that same evening, still dressed in my ball gown."

Silence filled the room. What Lord Deerford had put his daughter through was unpardonable—the ultimate betrayal. And to mask the disgrace, he'd concocted the kidnapping story. It didn't surprise Anthony in the least that she'd stayed away all these years, though it must have taken great resilience for her not to have contacted her mother. Surely she must have suspected how deeply her absence had wounded Lady Deerford.

But, however regrettable Lady Margaret's past was, it didn't change the fact that Anthony wanted to marry her daughter. Society was still likely to frown—perhaps even more so with her blood ties to the infamous lady who'd taken up with the stable master so long ago. The scandal would probably rock the Kingsborough name, but there were also those who would stand by him, and besides, Anthony mused, it was worth the risk. "You have to tell Isabella," he said.

"*What?*" the Chilcotts said in unison.

"As sorry as I am for everything that has happened to you, my lady, you have no right to impose yourself on your daughter's future like this. Don't you see that in doing so you're doing to her precisely what your father did to you?" He saw the look of indignation on her face, but he pressed on before she had a chance to speak. "I love your daughter and have every intention of making her my wife, so if you don't tell her the truth, then I will. Hell, she thinks herself unsuitable to be duchess when nothing could be further from the truth. She's the granddaughter of a marquess, for heaven's sake!"

"I . . . I cannot bear the thought of seeing him again," Lady Margaret said. There was no doubt about whom she was referring to. "And I worry about what Isabella will say—what she will think of us when she learns the truth."

"The sooner you tell her the better," Anthony said. "And once that's done, I hope you'll give me your blessing. I'd like to propose to her before Mr. Roberts does."

"You know, I'm still not clear on why you disapprove of him so vehemently," Lady Margaret said. "Is there something we ought to know, or is your dislike for the man based purely on the fact that he's competing for her hand?"

Anthony looked to Mr. Chilcott. "You haven't told her, have you?"

"I must admit that I found your claim hard to believe and decided to confront Mr. Roberts directly. He assured me that he has every intention of seeing to Isabella's comfort."

Of course he did. What Mr. Chilcott had apparently chosen to ignore was that once Mr. Roberts married Isabella there would be nothing to stop him from doing as he pleased with her.

"Would one of you please enlighten me," Lady Margaret insisted.

Since Mr. Chilcott looked unlikely to do so, it fell on Anthony's shoulders to inform Isabella's mother that Mr. Roberts's definition of comfort was likely different from their own and that Isabella would in fact become his maid.

"I can't believe you knew this and failed to tell me," Lady Margaret said, addressing her husband.

"I know how fond you are of Mr. Roberts and didn't

want to place him in a negative light unless I knew that what His Grace had told me was true. But when Mr. Roberts denied the accusation I . . . well, I believed him."

Lady Margaret closed her eyes momentarily. When she opened them again she looked at Anthony. "Are you telling us the truth, Your Grace, or is this a trick to have your way?"

"On my father's grave, I swear to you that I am telling you exactly what Mr. Roberts told me." He paused, regarding them both in turn. "As I've said, I love Isabella with all my heart and know that she feels the same about me. Please don't get between us the way Lord Deerford got between the two of you, but give us your blessing and let us be happy—I beg you."

"We cannot let her marry Mr. Roberts," Mr. Chilcott murmured. He turned to his wife with distress. "I know that we have an agreement with him and that he won't be the least bit pleased if we go back on our word, but I cannot in good conscience allow Isabella to marry him when there's a chance he will demean her in such a way. If he's really looking to treat her like a servant, then it's no wonder that he was so adamant about her being the judicious and trustworthy sort when I initially suggested he court her. I'm sorry, my love, but I will not sacrifice her happiness like this—not even for you."

Lady Margaret held silent for a moment as she gazed back at her husband with misty eyes. Composing herself, she eventually said, "I haven't made your life easy, Walter. In fact, I've many a time wondered if you wouldn't have been better off with someone else . . . someone less spoiled." He shook his head and opened his mouth to speak, but she held up a staying hand.

"You've gone to great lengths to make my life as comfortable as possible, providing me with a maid when there were times when we could barely afford to put food on the table. And now, with Isabella, when you suggested we seek out my parents and ask them to aid us in finding her a good match and I refused . . . you gave in to my selfish demands—demands that should have no bearing on the lives of our children.

"What happened, happened to me, not to her. She deserves to know of her heritage, as does Jamie—they both deserve to marry whoever they want, the same way I did." She met Anthony's gaze then and, reaching out her hand, clasped Anthony's with her own. "We will tell her everything, and once that is done, you may make your offer."

The sigh of relief that Anthony expelled in response to those words was immense. "Thank you, both of you. I know how difficult it was for you to make this decision, and I am also aware that there are a few things that concern you. Rest assured that you will never want for anything, and neither will your daughters. We will be family, and as such, we will take care of each other." A thought struck him and he anxiously said, "Speaking of which, my mother asked me to extend an invitation for tea to Isabella on her behalf. Perhaps I can persuade you to join us?"

There was a wariness about Lady Margaret's eyes, telling Anthony that she wasn't quite ready to venture back into the upper crests of society. The lady within her, however, must have found it difficult to refuse without appearing rude, for she answered in the affirmative. "We would love to—thank you."

"And tomorrow afternoon I shall have a word with

Mr. Roberts and explain the lay of the land," Mr. Chilcott said.

"I'll be happy to join you for that discussion if you like." Anthony rose to his feet, eager to get home and tell his mother the good news. Offering Lady Margaret a perfectly executed bow followed by a handshake for Mr. Chilcott, Anthony headed for the door.

Pausing, he turned and said, "If you don't mind, I'd rather you don't speak of this to Isabella just yet—I'd like to ensure that everything regarding Mr. Roberts is aboveboard before we start celebrating her engagement to someone else. A courtesy, if you will." The Chilcotts both agreed and were complimenting his thoughtfulness when the parlor door opened and Isabella popped her head inside. Her eyes widened when she registered Anthony's presence. "Your Grace," she said as she entered the parlor and dropped a curtsy. "I didn't expect to see you again so soon."

Is that annoyance in her voice?

Yes, Anthony decided. *Yes, it is.* He offered her his most dazzling smile in return. "There was actually something which I wished to talk to you about," he said. "But since you weren't at home when I called, your parents were kind enough to offer me tea while I waited for your return. But now that you're here, perhaps you'd like to join me outside for a moment? The weather is beautiful, and I would love an opportunity to admire your garden a little closer."

Isabella's eyes flittered first to her father and then to her mother. Finding no help from either, her mouth opened in a gape.

Amused by her astonishment, Anthony stepped toward her and offered his arm. "Shall we?"

It took a second or two for her to react. Without a word, she gave a slight nod, placed her hand in the crook of his elbow and allowed him to escort her from the room while he thanked the Chilcotts for their hospitality.

Outside, the late afternoon sun was casting everything in a dreamy glow, including Isabella, whose hair shone with streaks of gold, while her face radiated a vitality reminiscent of the outdoors. Anthony's heart thudded in his chest as he stopped their progress toward a low stone bench and turned to face her instead, deciding that it was too chilly to sit. "You were very distressed at the modiste's earlier today," he said. "Would you like to tell me why?"

"Not particularly," she muttered, avoiding his gaze. Taking a deep breath, she expelled it with a loud sigh. "Why can't you just do as I ask and leave me in peace?"

"Because I believe you're worth fighting for," he murmured.

Her head shot up at that pronouncement and she stared back at him for a long moment, searching for an answer to some determining question.

"You resent me for leaving without a word of warning, I think. And I believe Lady Harriett also plays a part." She looked away again, cheeks flushed and jaw clenched. "First of all, the reason for my sudden departure was a family emergency. My aunt suffered a stroke, so my mother and I hastily went to see how she was faring. Since my cousins had not yet arrived, I took it upon myself to see to all the necessities until they were in a position to take over. I meant to write and offer an explanation, but I'm afraid I forgot, with everything else that was happening around me."

She was looking up at him now with quivering lips and watery eyes, and Anthony knew that she did not fault him for his actions. She was just as kind, selfless and loving as he knew she was. "I'm so sorry," she said, reaching for his hand and giving it a gentle squeeze of sympathy. "You're a good man, and I . . . I'm afraid I thought the worst of you."

A wisp of hair had come loose and was fluttering gently against her cheek. Anthony brushed it aside with his fingers and tucked it behind her ear. "You thought I'd abandoned you, is that it?"

She nodded wistfully.

"And I'm guessing Lady Harriett was there to reinforce this doubt?"

"She told me that the two of you are to be married and that you'd left for London in order to make the necessary preparations."

Bloody hell!

The anger that gripped him was unlike any he'd ever experienced before. It curled itself around him, tugging at his very core and demanding him to seek satisfaction for the wrong this wonderful woman before him had been subjected to at the hands of that harpy.

"When I asked her to leave you alone after your hasty departure from the modiste, I did not know the extent of her untruths. Had I done, she would not have gotten off as lightly as she did." He made a mental note to pay a call on the Croonings. It was one thing to have a jealous streak, but to spread lies in which he and Isabella figured was unforgivable and without pale. "Needless to say, I have no intention of marrying her, since there is only one woman for whom I hold an interest. Unfortunately, she is quite determined to marry someone else."

There was a pause as she gazed back at him with endless amounts of regret. Her lips parted slightly and he held his breath, wondering what she might say—if she would refute his statement and tell him what she so obviously wanted to say, that the only man she planned on marrying was him.

"Lord Kingsborough," came a voice from directly behind him. Whatever Isabella might have thought to say would have to wait. Turning, Anthony was surprised to be met by the very curious gaze of a girl who shared Isabella's coloring. Her attire was scruffier, however, and it looked as though there were leaves in her hair. "Miss Jamie Chilcott at your service," she said. "How do you do?"

Anthony stifled a grin and offered her a gallant bow. "I trust you must be Miss Chilcott's . . . sister?"

"I certainly am," Jamie confirmed with a cheeky smile. "And since I've heard so much about you lately, I thought it time I made your acquaintance—see what sort of man has captured my sister's interest."

"Jamie!" Isabella cried, sounding both embarrassed and horrified.

Anthony's grin turned to a heartfelt laugh. "And do you approve?" he asked, his attention still on Jamie.

The girl frowned, as if giving the matter a great deal of thought. "That depends," she drawled with a casualness belying her age. Heaven above, this girl would be trouble when she grew older—Anthony just knew it.

"On what, exactly?" he asked.

Jamie shrugged. "You'll see."

"Jamie," Isabella warned as she drew out her name for emphasis. "What are you up to?"

"Oh, you know, Izzie—the usual." And with that,

Jamie folded her arms across her chest and marched over to the stone bench, where she took a seat, not in the least bit bothered by the cold, it would seem, and looking much too smug for someone who wasn't up to mischief.

Anthony felt an eerie sense of uneasiness wash over him—as if he was about to be made the butt of a joke. There was no doubt the girl was up to no good, and rather than be annoyed by it, Anthony felt rather humbled. She was testing his mettle the only way she knew how, to ensure that her sister made the right choice. It was endearing, really, in a way, though Anthony sincerely hoped he wouldn't end up covered in mud as a result. His valet would have a fit.

Recognizing that there was no point in worrying about what was surely to come, Anthony decided to tell Isabella about his plans for the following day.

"And my mother agreed to this?" she asked as she stared back at him in wonder.

"I don't believe she felt as though she had much choice, given that the invitation was issued by my mother." He decided that it was time to go. She and her parents had a lot to discuss—far more than Isabella could possibly imagine. With a bow, he took her hand in his and brought it to his lips. "Until tomorrow, Bella." Turning to Jamie he added, "A pleasure to meet you, miss."

Jamie nodded with an impish gleam to her eyes. What on earth was she up to?

And then Anthony felt it—a movement in his jacket pocket, as if something was squirming about in there. His own boyish instincts took over, and, acting as nonchalant as possible, he said, "Perhaps I ought to check the time first."

Eyes on Jamie, he stuck his hand inside his pocket until he felt something soft and slippery and very much alive. "What the . . . ," he gasped, feigning surprise.

Jamie's eyes widened while Isabella turned an accusatory glare on her sister.

Staggering backward a bit, Anthony yelled, "Oh my God! It's got me! Help! Get it off of me!" He fell to the ground, pretending all the while to be struggling with the creature in his pocket.

"Good Lord, Jamie," Isabella cried, rushing over to where Anthony was lying. She looked over at her sister with a scowl. "What did you do?"

"I . . . I . . . ," Jamie stammered, standing perfectly still but looking suddenly pale.

"Isabella," Anthony groaned.

"Yes," she said, kneeling down to offer her assistance and shielding Anthony from Jamie's view.

"I think it will take both of you to pull me free from this beast," he said with a wink at Isabella.

She smiled back with sly understanding. "Yes, yes of course," she said, nodding profusely. "Jamie, do come and offer your aid. The duke is in a terrible muddle, and all because of you, I suspect."

"Oh . . . please hurry," Anthony yelled, satisfied to find Jamie springing to his side in the next instant. "Isabella, if you could move aside a little so Jamie here can get a hold of my arm."

Isabella dutifully moved aside while Jamie bent low, a move that proved detrimental, for as soon as Anthony had the girl within reach, he grabbed hold of her with his free hand, yanked the other—which was clutching a small frog—from his pocket and dropped the amphibian down the back of Jamie's gown with a shout of victory.

Jamie yelled with surprise and started jumping about, trying to rid herself of the creature, while Isabella and Anthony both sat back on their haunches and laughed at how funny she looked.

"I'll get you for that, Kingsborough," Jamie grinned as the frog fell from beneath her clothing and started hopping away.

"Not if I get you first," Anthony said, leaping to his feet and chasing after the girl until, catching her, he proceeded to give her a good tickle.

Jamie squealed, laughing harder until she eventually begged for Anthony to have mercy on her.

"It looks as though you've finally met your match, Jamie," Isabella said as she came toward them with a sparkle in her eyes that told Anthony that she highly approved of the way in which he'd handled her naughty sibling.

"And he, in turn, has passed the test," Jamie said happily as she stuck out her hand toward Anthony. "It's an honor to know you, Your Grace."

The girl's words warmed Anthony's heart, encouraging him in his plea for Isabella's hand, for there was acceptance to be found in them. With a bow, Anthony bid Jamie and Isabella good day, whereupon he started down the path feeling both lighthearted and cheerful.

He could feel Isabella's eyes upon him as he strolled away from the cottage and made his way back toward Main Street, where he found his carriage waiting. Climbing in, he settled himself against the seat with a smile. That had gone rather well, he thought, and with the Chilcotts now on his side, there was no question that Isabella would soon be his wife. The day had definitely gotten a whole lot brighter.

Chapter 22

"Heaven above, you can't be serious!" The exclamation came from the duchess a split second after Anthony announced that Isabella was in fact the granddaughter of the Marquess and Marchioness of Deerford, not to mention daughter of the infamous Lady Margaret.

Anthony would not have been surprised if she'd had a fit of the vapors, but instead she just reached for her sherry and took what most would have considered to be an inappropriately large sip. Anthony smiled. He then explained the situation regarding Mr. Roberts, adding that he and Mr. Chilcott would have a word with him together. "So please don't mention anything about my forthcoming proposal when they visit. I'd like to do this by the book and without another man's intention to offer marriage hanging over us."

"Yes," his mother agreed, chasing her previous sip of sherry with another. "I think that's a wise decision—one that will be more likely to ensure Miss Chilcott's acceptance." A crease appeared upon her forehead and she leaned toward him, tilting her head a little as she did so. "What about her . . . identity though? I assume her parents will apprise her of that?"

"I have explained how important it is that they do so immediately," Anthony said, hoping that they would be wise enough to follow his advice. "I believe they were in agreement when I left."

"Good . . . good . . ." The duchess nodded and down went another sip of sherry.

This was clearly a situation that called for fortification as far as she was concerned. *Hell*, Anthony mused, *it's a situation that has made me turn to brandy more than once.*

His smile broadened as he raised his own glass to his lips and swallowed.

"And the letter?" his mother asked, nodding toward the missive that was lying on his desk. It had come from Lucien Marvaine, the Earl of Roxberry, assuring him that the culprit behind the shooting had been apprehended. There was nothing further however, no mention of who the perpetrator was, but a postscript suggesting that Anthony come to Roxberry Manor so Roxberry could apprise him of everything that had happened.

"The earl will have to wait," Anthony said. "As eager as I am to discover why Lady Rebecca was shot, everything else is just a matter of formality. After all, the villain has been caught. I have more pressing matters to attend to."

Leaning back in his chair, he breathed a sigh of relief. It looked as though a positive outcome was finally within reach. Tomorrow, Isabella would come for tea with her parents, after which, he and Mr. Chilcott would seek out Mr. Roberts and tell him that he'd best forget whatever plans he had of marrying Isabella.

Once this was done, Anthony would offer Isabella a proper proposal, and with Mr. Roberts having by then released her of all obligation toward him, she would be bound to say yes. Anthony was sure of it. Tomorrow could scarcely come fast enough.

Isabella was in shock. It was the only way to describe what she felt after everything her parents had told her. It was also the only way to explain why she wasn't furious with either one of them. She was a lady, the granddaughter of a marquess, and they'd kept this from her for eighteen years. Dear God, their existence was probably the best-guarded secret in all the British Isles and beyond. And now she was supposed to hop into the ducal carriage that had come to collect her and her parents, drive up to Kingsborough Hall and sit down to tea with the duke and dowager duchess.

She'd always dreamed of living a fairy-tale existence, but she was starting to think that whoever was penning this one had gotten a few details terribly wrong. What a muddle and what a deception. Yet in spite of it all, she was happy, because for the very first time since meeting the duke, she felt a spark of hope. "Does he know about this?" she'd asked her parents the previous evening, when they'd finally told her the truth. "Is the duke aware of who you are, Mama? Of who *I* am?"

"Yes, my dear, he knows, though he has only discovered it this afternoon."

"When he came to visit?"

They'd both nodded, and Isabella, her curiosity satisfied, had kept quiet. One thought, however, had remained in her head with deep determination: *"There is only one woman for whom I hold an interest. Unfortunately, she is quite determined to marry someone else.*" He'd been hoping that she would agree to marry him in spite of everything. But how could she, with the hold Mr. Roberts had on her? Even now it would be difficult to go back on her agreement, or more precisely, her father's agreement. His honor would be questioned and . . . Isabella dared not think of what might happen if Mr. Roberts revealed himself to be the spiteful sort.

Worse was the fact that if she did accept Anthony's proposal now, he might not think her heart was in it, believing that her yes was determined by her newfound status. Heaven help her, but it was complicated. So she decided not to think about it overly much, enjoying her parents' company instead as the carriage rattled along the road, swaying gently as it turned up the driveway toward Kingsborough Hall.

As soon as the carriage pulled up to the front door, the steps were set down by one footman while another opened the carriage door, each standing to attention on either side as they offered their white gloved hands and helped the guests alight. Gravel crunched beneath Isabella's slippers as she stood staring up at the gray stone edifice, with its sunken windows and pointy turrets, thinking of the man who lived beyond these walls. She decided that the building and the man didn't suit. The building was far too austere for such a kind and quirky soul.

Quirky.

She focused on the word and couldn't stop herself from smiling. It suited him. There probably weren't many dukes around who collected bits and bobs—seeing in someone else's junk the possibility for art.

Artist.

Isabella's smile broadened. Perhaps the building did suit him after all, for she could certainly imagine it as inspirational fodder for his creative mind.

Allowing her parents to lead the way, Isabella fell in behind them and ascended the front steps. As she passed over the threshold and into the grand foyer, she cast a discreet look at the butler, who stood as stiff as a newly starched cravat. And yet when his eyes met hers for the briefest of moments, Isabella saw the mortification there. He was embarrassed by the way he'd treated her when she'd been there last, and so, when he opened his mouth, Isabella was certain that he was about to apologize.

With no desire to further humiliate the man, Isabella gave him a little nod, smiled reassuringly and said, "We're here to take tea with Her Grace."

It was a redundant statement, of course, since the butler would be fully aware of who they were and why they'd come, yet when he responded in the affirmative and asked them all to follow him through to the blue salon, Isabella could have sworn that his features eased a little. She had saved his pride, and he was grateful for it.

They only had to follow him a short distance before they arrived at a room with an open door. With a knock, the butler announced their arrival, then stepped aside and waved them through.

"How kind of you to accept my invitation," said the duchess as she rose to her feet and came to greet her guests. Anthony, who'd been standing by one of the windows looking out, turned, his eyes brightening as they settled upon Isabella.

She felt the heat rise in her cheeks and tried to get herself under control by greeting her hostess. "Thank you for having us, Your Grace," she heard her mother say as she swept into a deep curtsy. "We are most honored."

Isabella followed suit while her father bowed. She'd never seen her parents so formal before, yet her mother in particular behaved with unparalleled grace and etiquette. *She was born to this,* a voice reminded her just as the duke stepped forward to make his own salutation.

Isabella kept her gaze trained on a porcelain lion that sat beside the fireplace. *He knows who I am.* Something even she hadn't known until the previous evening. The thought made her jittery in every conceivable way, for this changed everything between them. She was no longer some simple country miss whom he could take for a tumble without consequence. Indeed, the only way he could have her now would be through marriage.

"My lady," he said, taking her mother's hand and raising it to his lips for a kiss. "We are the ones who should be honored. I know how difficult it must have been for you to come here today."

Isabella could feel her brow drawing together in a crease. How much had her parents told him?

"And Mr. Chilcott," Anthony continued, shaking her father's hand. "We are only too happy to welcome you into our midst."

Isabella's heart pounded as he stepped toward her next. His hair had been impeccably arranged (no doubt by a very patient valet), his cravat was elegantly tied without being ostentatious, and he wore a dark gray velvet jacket with a black waistcoat beneath and charcoal-colored breeches.

He looked impeccable, and as he took her hand in his, sending darts of heat racing up her arm, Isabella met his gaze—hot and smoldering. She could have melted into a puddle right then and there, he was so magnificently tempting. "Miss Chilcott," he said. "May I say that you look exceptionally lovely today?"

It was a good thing that he took her arm then, for she feared she might have dropped to the floor—her knees were too wobbly to carry her weight a moment longer. What on earth was he doing to her? She tried to focus on what his mother was saying to her mother— something about how she recalled seeing her at a few social functions years back, except Anthony leaned close to her ear and whispered, "I always said you had a sparkle about you."

The words softly tickled her skin, and she shuddered as it rippled across the nape of her neck. She could think of no response to such a remark, nor did she dare say anything just now for fear that her words would come out a croak. She remained silent instead, seating herself on one of two pale blue silk settees, her mother and the duchess already occupying the other, while her father had seated himself in an armchair. Anthony, in pursuit of her as always, lowered himself onto the vacant spot beside her. *Dear God.* Was it just her, or did the room seem overwhelmingly hot all of a sudden? If only she'd had a fan.

Matters didn't improve as she sipped the warm tea that the duchess served, and no matter how much Isabella tried to concentrate on the conversation taking place around her, she could think of little other than the fact that Anthony's thigh kept brushing against hers whenever he moved to pick up or set down his teacup—which he was doing far too often, in Isabella's opinion.

At one point, she hazarded a glance in his direction, only to be met with a much too mischievous smile and a pair of eyes that told her he knew precisely what he was up to. She could have throttled him at that moment if it hadn't been for the fact that they were not alone. He was deliberately trying to unsettle her, and the worst part was that it was working remarkably well.

Stifling a groan, she returned her attention to her father, who was now in the process of telling the duchess that he'd once had the honor of saddling her late husband's horse during a visit he'd paid to one of the Deerford estates.

Dear God!

Isabella cringed, though the duchess appeared touched by the story, which included a very fine and flattering depiction of Anthony's father. A lull arose in the conversation as they each considered the man who was no more—a person who'd been so highly regarded that it would be near impossible for anyone else to live up to him.

Isabella eyed Anthony and found in his features a determination etched so deeply that she wondered at how she could have missed it before. Her breath caught, and as he turned his head to face her, she saw him for who he really was—not some pampered aristocrat used to getting his way and willing to do whatever he had to in order to get it, as she'd initially thought.

The Duke of Kingsborough had resolve, but it was born from the love for a man he'd admired more than any other, and a longing to do whatever he could to make that man proud of him, even if he was no longer here to see what his son was capable of. Her heart swelled for him at that moment with a love so deep and pure that it very nearly took her breath away.

"I was wondering if you would permit me to show Miss Chilcott the library," Anthony said, pulling Isabella out of her reverie. "There's a particular book that I promised I'd lend to her."

"How thoughtful of you," his mother said. "I have no issue with it as long as the Chilcotts don't—just be sure to leave the door open, that's all."

Isabella blushed at the duchess's implication that something untoward might happen between her and Anthony if they were left alone behind closed doors. Well, it probably would, considering that they hadn't even required that much when they'd kissed in the middle of the road for all the world to see.

"By all means," her father said while her mother gave a nod of confirmation, "as long as you abide by your mother's conditions—I'm in no mood for a duel." He winked.

If Anthony thought it embarrassing, he hid it remarkably well, helping Isabella up instead and then offering her his arm. Saying something to the effect that they would be back shortly, he guided Isabella out of the room and away from the safety her parents and his mother had offered.

They didn't have far to go, though with each step they took, Anthony became keenly aware of the heat entering his body at the point where Isabella's hand rested upon his arm. He'd enjoyed the discomfort that had emanated from every part of her body as he'd sat beside her on the sofa, for it meant that she was far from indifferent to him. He knew this already, of course, but the confirmation bolstered his confidence. He was grateful for that, considering the conversation he would have with Mr. Roberts later in the day.

Arriving at the library, Anthony opened the door and ushered her inside, only to recall their last encounter here. A similar thought must have struck Isabella, for her eyes immediately went to the shelves where his figures were displayed and blushed. But then her eyes caught something, and she moved forward as if drawn by one singular object of interest. "Is that me?" she asked as she came to stand before the tiny model he'd made of her using the fabric from her gown.

It was Anthony's turn to feel embarrassed, and he masked it by heading for the side table and pouring himself a brandy. For some reason, her opinion mattered more than he ever would have imagined. It was a silly hobby of course, but it was his, and he'd put extra time and effort into perfecting her likeness. It was imperative to him that she approved. "Yes," he muttered, offering her a glass of sherry, but she waved away his offer as she peered closely at the figure, as if imparting every detail of it to memory.

With bated breath he waited for her censure, until she finally leaned back, turned toward him with glowing eyes and said, "You put more care into this one, Anthony. It's . . . I mean, the others are incredible too—I've said so before—but this one . . . it's as if . . ." She hesitated and averted her gaze from his.

"As if what?" Anthony prodded.

She kept quiet a moment, as if taking courage. When she spoke again, her voice was but a shy whisper. "As if your whole heart was in it when you made it. I absolutely love it."

But do you love me?

He could not ask such a bold question without sounding foolishly desperate, so he merely thanked her as relief flooded his body and he decided to address the topic that had floated in the air between them since her arrival, no matter how uncomfortable it might be. "You seem to be taking the news of your heritage rather well—far better than I would have thought, in fact. How do you feel, knowing that you are not simply Miss Chilcott, but the granddaughter of a marquess?"

Taking a deep breath, she walked across to the bookcases and started perusing their contents. "No different at all really," she said as she ran her fingers along the spine of an atlas. With a quick glance over her shoulder at him, she gave him a crooked smile. "Perhaps I ought to be angry with my parents for lying to me all these years, except nothing good would come of that. They are still the same people who raised me, cared for me and loved me. I understand why they did what they did—they loved each other, and this was the only way in which they could be together. Yes, they deceived me, but they were only doing what they thought best; what they believed would protect me."

Anthony stared at her as she stood there, dressed in a simple light green gown, her hair knotted neatly behind her head, though a few loose tendrils curled against her cheeks. "You're a very forgiving woman, Isabella. Your parents are incredibly lucky."

She gave a little shrug with one shoulder. "I think it would be unfair of me to judge them based on a decision they made in the face of a difficult situation so long ago. Everyone makes mistakes, Your Grace, and they are my parents. I won't hold a grudge."

"And what of your grandfather, the marquess?"

Isabella stilled. "He treated my parents most selfishly. My mother refuses to speak of him, so I don't know much. I suspect that it was he and my grandmother who stopped me at the ball to ask about my gown? They recognized it, though I was certain at the time that they were mistaken."

"They asked me to help them find you, hoping that you might be able to give them a clue to their daughter's whereabouts." He watched as her posture tensed. "I haven't said a word to them yet, though I do believe that it would be the kind thing to do. They lost their daughter twenty years ago and have been worried sick ever since."

Isabella nodded, her face still turned away as she faced the many books before her. "So it was because of them that you went looking for me," she said. There was no disappointment to be found in her voice. She simply stated it as fact.

It wasn't true though, and Anthony definitely didn't want her to think that this was the only reason why he'd scoured Moxley for any sign of her. "No, Isabella, I went looking for you because you stirred to life a part of me that I'd long since forgotten existed—a *joie de vivre* I haven't felt in many years, not since my father got sick. In your company, I felt the weight of all the responsibility I've been shouldering for so long lighten, allowing me the opportunity to have fun. But there was also something else—something powerful that drew me to you, and I felt as though I'd be giving up on the best opportunity life was likely to afford me if I didn't do all in my power to at least further my acquaintance with you."

She didn't move, but he could tell that his words had moved her, judging from the slight quiver in her breath. Moving toward her, he reached out his hand and gently traced the line of her jaw with his thumb. Her breath hitched, and though she might have appeared as calm and collected as a stone statue, Anthony could see her pulse racing against her neck, and he knew that her emotions were raging beneath the surface.

If he tried to kiss her now, she would allow it, of that he was certain, but he'd taken advantage of her too many times already and had made his decision—it was time to treat her with the respect she deserved and for him to act the part of the gentleman he claimed to be. How many times had he said he'd reformed during the past weeks, only to have gone and acted on his rakish impulses? It had to stop. And so he stepped away from her and crossed the room to a safe distance. "I believe it was Mary Wollstonecraft's *A Vindication of the Rights of Woman* that I promised you," he said. She turned then, and he suspected from the surprise on her face that she had not expected him to have moved so far from her. She nodded. "It should be just over there to your right—one of those brown volumes on the lower shelf."

He watched as she crouched down to retrieve it, but as she did, he remembered something. "Wait," he said, starting forward, except she'd already noticed the book he'd hidden behind Wollstonecraft's and was presently pulling it from the shelf as well. A wave of heat descended over Anthony as he swooped down in an attempt to snatch the book from her hands. It was too late though. She already had it firmly in her grasp, and he was forced to abandon his attempt, muttering an oath beneath his breath instead.

"It looks as though you've misplaced one of your books," she said, smiling up at him.

"Quite right," he said, hoping that she wouldn't notice the sheen of perspiration gathering upon his brow. "If you'll please hand it to me, I'll make sure to put it back in the right place."

She must have seen right through him, for her eyes narrowed and she frowned, looking from the book to Anthony, from Anthony to the book and back again. He held his breath as he waited for her to make her move, and then she opened it.

Oh dear God in heaven.

"*The Path to Passion*," she read. "By Anonymous. Hmm . . . what a curious name for a book, and how rare for an author to seek anonymity rather than fame."

Anthony felt himself cringe all the way down to the tips of his toes. He cleared his throat. "Er . . . yes. I suppose the author wasn't particularly proud of this . . . ah . . . er . . . piece. Perhaps we should save him from the humiliation of reading any further?" He reached for the book as if it had been the dullest thing he'd ever set eyes on before, hoping she'd relinquish it.

Instead, she clutched it tighter and turned herself away from him. "Nonsense," she said. "He or she is not even here, and besides, I'm rather curious now as to why it's been hidden away like this. I'm beginning to suspect that it was on purpose."

Christ!

Well, there was nothing for it now but to wait for the inevitable, so, without further ado, Anthony finished off the remains of his drink and returned his glass to the side table. He was just about to take a seat in his favorite armchair when a loud gasp stopped him in his tracks. It was impossible for him to stop the smile that sprang to his lips, for he knew precisely what it was that had evoked such a shocked response from Isabella, and he rather enjoyed knowing that he was no longer the only one feeling uncomfortable.

"Oh my," she said in a breathy voice. "These are quite . . . ahem . . . provocative pictures."

"Yes," he said, seeing no sense in denying the obvious.

He expected her to close the book at that point as she blushed and fumbled for some sort of excuse to escape the library as well as his presence. What happened, however, was something entirely different, and it was Anthony who was left gaping as Isabella settled herself on the floor, appearing to study the images before her more closely as she angled the book first one way and then the other, tilting her head as she did so. "How on earth is this even possible?"

Anthony coughed—hell, he practically choked on his own breath in response to her question. "Isabella, I really don't believe your parents would approve if they found you leafing through that particular book. I suggest you put it back where you found it immediately." It had to be done for his own sanity if nothing else, for he knew by heart each erotic position the book portrayed, and watching her study them was doing very little for his tightly reined self-control.

Thankfully she agreed and did as he asked, but when she rose to her feet and turned to face him with the Wollstonecraft book in her hand, she tilted her head, studied him for a moment and eventually said, "I wasn't aware such books existed, though I can certainly appreciate the educational benefit of them. Hopefully we'll have the opportunity to study it together more closely at a later date." And then, as if she hadn't just fired his every desire, she added, "Shall we return to the others?" Upon which she headed for the door, leaving Anthony to deal with the uncomfortable state he was now in before he was once more presentable enough to enter back into polite society.

Chapter 23

"It appears you have a visitor," Isabella said just as Anthony was preparing to hand her up into the carriage. He and Mr. Chilcott had agreed to escort the ladies home before heading over to Mr. Roberts's. Turning his head, he followed Isabella's line of vision until he was filled with tremendous irritation at the sight of Lady Harriett riding up the driveway. *What the devil does she want now?*

He quickly ushered Isabella into the carriage and out of Lady Harriett's assessing sight before stepping away from the landau just as Lady Harriett's horse came trotting up to him. "Your Grace," she said with a pretty smile that belied her true nature. "I came to call on you so we can discuss the upcoming Season."

Surely she must be cracked in the head.

"I thought I made it clear to you when last we met that I have no desire to keep your company."

He watched her bristle, but she quickly recovered, though her smile did strain a little around the edges as she said, "My apologies, Your Grace. I was only hoping to make amends, but since you appear to be otherwise engaged, I shall bid you a good day." She then swung her horse about and cantered off, allowing Anthony to breathe a sigh of relief. It was about time she realized that her backhanded efforts to win him would only incur his wrath. He could only hope she finally realized that she wouldn't stand a chance against the woman presently ensconced in the privacy of his carriage.

Climbing inside, Anthony offered Isabella an apologetic smile as he settled down on the vacant seat across from her and next to her father. He could tell from the wary expression about her eyes that Lady Harriett had managed to unsettle her yet again but she was trying her best to appear unaffected.

"How's your sister faring?" he asked, hoping to draw Isabella's attention to a lighter topic than that of her nemesis.

She grinned openly at him. "As mischievous as usual, I suppose."

"She switched the salt and the sugar on Sunday when Mr. Roberts came for tea," Mr. Chilcott muttered at Anthony's side. "I daresay he didn't find the apple pie as tasty as usual."

It was difficult for Anthony to hide his smile. Young Jamie was certainly doing her part to aid Anthony by trying to discourage Mr. Roberts's suit.

Lady Margaret, however, did not look amused, and no matter how happy Anthony was that Mr. Roberts had suffered an ill-tasting piece of pie, he understood her sentiment all too well, for Jamie's mischief reflected poorly upon her. "Needless to say, her actions have been punished with another day of confinement, as well as helping Marjorie in the kitchen."

"I only wish I'd been there to see Mr. Roberts's expression," Isabella grinned, eyes twinkling with devilish delight.

"You were not?" Anthony asked, a wave of relief washing over him at this revelation. It had irked him to think of the two of them sitting down to tea together.

Isabella shifted a little uneasily in her seat and eventually glanced stubbornly out the window, apparently reluctant to answer.

"Isabella wasn't feeling well that day and remained in her room for the duration of Mr. Roberts's visit," Lady Margaret explained, eyeing her daughter with a touch of suspicion.

Recalling the way in which Isabella had fled from him outside the bookshop, Anthony felt a surge of warmth course through him. Eyes fixed on Isabella, whose cheeks had colored more deeply now, he simply said, "How fortunate it is that she recovered so quickly." He'd unsettled her that day—he was sure of it, for she'd had much the same effect on him—and there was immense happiness in knowing that she hadn't simply gone home to entertain Mr. Roberts as if nothing had happened between her and Anthony.

With each word they spoke to each other and every touch, the connection between them strengthened. It was just as well that the Chilcotts had finally begun to warm to him, for he preferred not to entertain the thought of whisking their daughter off to Gretna Green—an idea that had crossed his mind on more than one occasion. No, it was simpler if everyone accepted his suit, and as far as he could tell, this was thankfully no longer an issue.

Anthony awoke the following morning to a blue sky overhead and rays of sunshine beaming through his bedroom window. His conversation with Mr. Roberts the previous day had gone better than expected, leaving Anthony in an exceedingly good mood. In fact, he'd been pleasantly surprised by how willingly Mr. Roberts had relinquished his attachment to Isabella once Anthony had told him of his own interest in her. Given Mr. Roberts's character, he likely wished to avoid the complication that fighting over a woman would be bound to entail. He'd actually been most hospitable and gracious toward both Anthony and Mr. Chilcott, going so far as to offer them his best cigars and cognac.

With the help of his valet Anthony dressed in a light brown jacket, beige breeches and dark brown Hessians with a waistcoat to match. Placing his fob watch in his pocket, he then headed downstairs, where he met his mother for breakfast.

"You're looking very handsome today," she said, abandoning her newspaper and taking a sip of her tea. "I'm certain Miss Chilcott will be very impressed."

Her secretive smile made him smile in return. "I dearly hope so, Mama, for I've no idea what I'll do if she refuses me now."

"She won't refuse you, my love," his mother promised. "Why it's obvious for all to see that she's positively smitten with you."

"Well, I will be sure to send you a letter straightaway as soon as I have my answer," he said. "You'll probably be halfway to London as I make my proposal."

Once his mother departed with Goodard at ten, Anthony told Phelps to inform the grooms that he would be needing his favorite horse saddled and ready to leave within half an hour. He then finished his tea, met briefly with his secretary and finally departed for Moxley at a pleasant trot. Today he would not rush but take his time, consider the words he would say to her wisely and savor every moment so he'd always be able to recall it in exact detail.

So, as he rode into town envisioning his future with Isabella at his side and their children tumbling about all around them, Anthony failed to notice the quiet looks of disapproval that trailed after him as he went. Nor did he think overly much about the shopkeeper's unwillingness to help him purchase the dark blue gloves Isabella had fawned over when Mr. Roberts had insisted upon the green, or the florist's sour expression as he picked out a large bouquet of daffodils. If these women were determined to have a bad day, then that was their prerogative—his mood, however, would not be ruined by anyone.

But when half the town stood whispering behind him as he opened the garden gate at Isabella's cottage and started up the path that would take him to the front door, an overwhelming sense of uneasiness settled upon his shoulders like a cloak. He tried to shrug it off, telling himself that news of his impending proposal had probably spread and that the inhabitants of Moxley were only eager to discover Miss Chilcott's answer. He might even have succeeded in his attempt if it hadn't been for the sudden shout that rose through the air. "Whore!" someone yelled, and another quickly repeated the insult until Anthony felt his blood boil in his veins. There could be only one explanation for this, and her name was Lady Harriett.

Instinct told him to turn back and face Isabella's accusers, but rationality stopped him in his tracks. Nothing good would come of him beating them all to within an inch of their lives as he wished to do, except that he would feel vindicated. Isabella, on the other hand, would have to suffer further embarrassment. There had to be another way.

Knocking on the door, he waited only a moment before it was opened just enough by the maid to allow him entry. "Thank goodness you're here, Your Grace," she said, her voice shaking as she took his hat and gloves. "The Mister and Missus are in a right state, and poor Miss Chilcott has locked herself away in her room. She refuses to come out!"

"Hopefully I can help," he said in the calmest tone he could muster. "If you'll be so kind as to put these flowers in water, I'll go on through to the parlor and have a word with the Chilcotts."

Taking the large bouquet from Anthony's outstretched hand, the maid nodded, bobbed a curtsy and scurried off. Once out of sight, Anthony took a deep breath, straightened his jacket and stepped toward the parlor door. After a quick rap, he was admitted entrance by Mr. Chilcott, whom he found nursing a large glass of brandy, while Lady Margaret was pacing frantically back and forth. Jamie sat on a chair in a corner, eyes averted and looking miserable.

When Anthony entered the room, Lady Margaret turned toward him, her whole body sagging with relief as she let out a heavy sigh. "Thank God! You've no idea how happy we are to see you, Your Grace. The situation is completely out of control, as you can see. Why, there is the most outrageous rumor circulating about Isabella—people claiming that she's a . . . a harlot!"

Setting Isabella's gift on a corner table, Anthony eyed Mr. Chilcott, who was presently taking another sip of his drink. Christ, this was bad. Rumors could break a person's reputation forever, even if there was no basis for truth behind them. The fact that everyone chose to believe it would be enough for them to forever shake their heads at Isabella every time she stepped outside her front door. Something had to be done.

"Do you have any idea why they're saying this? What has led them to make such a serious accusation?" he asked.

"Our maid, Marjorie, went into town a short while ago to purchase some items for me. She overheard a group of women talking, and from what she could make out, one of them was saying that Isabella had been seen cavorting with a man assumed to be one of your groomsmen or fieldworkers, since the tryst had reportedly taken place on Kingsborough land—in one of your barns to be exact." Sniffling, Lady Margaret quickly dabbed at her eyes with a bunched-up handkerchief. "Everyone in town knows of her attachment to Mr. Roberts, so this is part of it, but what makes it all so much worse is the claim that Isabella accepted money from this man in exchange for whatever favors she allegedly provided. The insult to her name is beyond compare, not to mention the men we've had to turn away in the last hour, all hoping to strike a deal with her. It's disgusting!"

Anthony could practically feel the steam coming out of his ears as the story poured from Lady Margaret's mouth. He wanted to break something or hurt someone—preferably with his fists—but he forced himself to remain calm for the sake of Isabella, Jamie and their parents. A monumental task to say the least. "It's the last Friday of the month today, is it not?" he asked, turning to Mr. Chilcott for confirmation.

Isabella's father nodded grimly. "Yes," he said, his features bleak with despair.

"Then there will be a town meeting tonight—at the assembly hall if I'm not mistaken?" He'd attended a few of these meetings before, since he thought it important to know if there were issues he ought to be aware of. Commerce was often discussed, so if he chose to stay away, he would have no idea of whether or not the people of Moxley were thriving.

Lady Margaret nodded. "Yes, yes of course there will—it's the highlight of the month for most, and with all the baked goods that the wives provide it's turned into something of a social event."

"Right," Anthony muttered, his mind whirling with options. There was only one he could think of that would save Isabella's reputation, though he would in all likelihood find himself hunted down and killed by Mr. Chilcott. That thought alone was enough to stop him from voicing his idea. Instead he asked, "Would you be kind enough to pass a note to your daughter?"

Isabella was furious. She had a good idea of how the rumor had come about, but there was no consolation to be found in that, for it was hardly enough to make it go away. Rumors had a tendency to spread like wildfire, and once they did, they were usually impossible to put to rest. Her thoughts went to Anthony, of what he had to be thinking, and she grew angrier still. Lord help her, how she loved him. She knew he was presently in the parlor with her parents and Jamie, for she had heard him arrive, but she would have to calm down before joining them, since she presently feared she might take out her frustration on the first person she came into contact with, and that would be unfair.

Hands on her hips, she took a steadying breath. The last time she'd seen Anthony, he'd looked at her with adoration in his eyes. She dared not think of how he might look at her now, not because she thought he might believe the slander—no, he was smarter than that—but because he couldn't possibly marry her now without courting scandal of the worst possible kind; the Duke of Kingsborough marrying a common whore.

No, it was impossible, and to make matters worse, she could no longer count on Mr. Roberts either, for he had called on her earlier to free her of any obligation she might feel toward him since he was well aware that her affection lay elsewhere. At the time she'd been overjoyed—no more than an hour later, she'd been filled with concern for her family's future. One thing was for certain in all of this—if vengeance was what Lady Harriett was seeking, she'd struck her target dead center.

Footsteps sounded beyond her door, and Isabella prepared herself to turn whoever it was away, but nobody knocked. Instead, there was a scuffling sound followed by rustling as a white piece of paper folded neatly in two was passed under the door. For a long moment, Isabella didn't move as she just sat there on her bed, staring down at the note that lay upon the floor. She knew who it was from, of course, and feared opening it, wary of what it might say.

Eventually, her curiosity got the better of her and she knelt down to pick it up, climbing back onto her bed and settling herself against her pillow as she unfolded the missive and read:

My dear Isabella,

No matter how dire this situation may seem to you, I believe I can solve it with ease, if you'll only trust me.

I shall await your response patiently in the parlor.

Yours always,
Anthony

With a sigh of relief, she clutched the letter to her chest and allowed herself to relax. He was not about to let this come between them, and she felt suddenly chagrined that she'd ever imagined he might—he, who'd proven himself willing to do anything to make her his. A cautious smile teased the corners of her lips as she slipped her feet inside her slippers, strode toward her door and turned the key. If he still believed they had a chance in the face of all this, then so would she.

Anthony was a nervous wreck by the time he entered the assembly room with Isabella on his arm (her hands elegantly dressed in the blue gloves he'd given her) and her parents following closely behind them. They were the last to arrive, and as they did, everyone else present turned to them with gawking eyes. As Isabella and

Anthony sank down onto a bench that stood close to the door, Anthony felt his hands grow clammy while his heart beat erratically in his chest. Dear God, he felt on the verge of a seizure.

"Are you all right?" Isabella asked in a low whisper as she leaned a bit closer.

"I'm fine," he managed, barely getting the words past the knot that was forming in his throat. She obviously didn't believe him, for she immediately responded with a skeptical frown.

He tried to think of something other than what he was about to do in an attempt to calm his nerves, his mind going to Isabella and the trouble she faced. Even now, as they sat there to one side in the hope of keeping a low profile, Anthony could hear the whispers circulating as everyone's eyes continuously sought Isabella. It was enough to send the most confident person running for the nearest exit, which, incidentally, happened to be right next to where Isabella was sitting—it was a miracle that she was still here.

"Shall we begin?" Father Green, the local rector, asked as he stepped up in front of the assembled crowd as moderator. "I understand the Flemmings would like to suggest—"

"If you ask me, we ought not continue this meeting until that fallen woman over there has left—there are children present!" The words were spoken by a man Anthony did not recognize and followed by cheers of approval, as well as clapping by others.

"She's a disgrace to this community!" a woman added, encouraging the crowd to grow louder still. "One can only thank the Lord that Mr. Roberts discovered her true nature before it was too late."

"How can you say so, Millie?"

Anthony's head snapped around at the sound of Isabella's voice, so full of outrage as she jutted her chin forward, daring the Millie woman to do her worst. Devil take it if she wasn't lovelier than ever as she stood there defending herself before all the townspeople, though there was no mistaking the hurt that shone in her eyes.

"You've known me your entire life," Isabella continued, "and yet you're eager to think the worst of me without a shred of evidence."

Millie looked momentarily uneasy, but then another woman said, "The account of your disgraceful actions has come from a reliable source, Miss Chilcott, and as far as lacking evidence, you're wrong about that, for there was a witness who saw you accepting money for favors."

"Who?" Isabella asked, not budging at all, though her hands were balled in tight fists at her sides. "Who witnessed the incident, Mrs. Garrison? I should like to have a very firm word with that individual."

A hush settled over the room as the townspeople whispered amongst themselves. There were a few shrugs before Mrs. Garrison spoke up again, saying, "That is irrelevant. The point is that you've been ruined—who witnessed the incident is neither here nor there."

"I've nursed your children through bouts of influenza, Mrs. Garrison, when work kept you from doing so yourself," Isabella whispered. "How can you be so cruel?" Her voice rose. "How can any of you?"

To their credit, the townspeople looked well and truly ashamed now.

Anthony clenched and unclenched his fists. He didn't

have to look at Isabella to know that she was trembling, for he could feel her whole body shaking at his side, and yet her courage did not fail her. She remained exactly where she was. Turning his head in search of her parents, he saw that they had both gone pale. He offered them a smile, hoping to ease their concerns, but it didn't look as though it had any effect. Someone else added a comment as Anthony studied those present. He found Mr. Roberts, whose mouth was set in a grim line, his eyes dark with anger, and then, just beyond him, Lady Harriett's smug face. As Anthony saw her eyes sparkle with delight, he shot to his feet and stormed forward. He'd had enough.

Still shaking in the face of her accusers, Isabella watched as Anthony strode toward the spot where Father Green was standing, approaching the rector with the fury of a man about to commit murder. He'd looked terribly nervous when they'd arrived and taken their seats, which was why she'd decided to save him from having to address those present by doing so herself. Watching Anthony now was like watching a man about to slay a dragon to save her, and it spoke to something so primitive inside her that she felt her heart might burst with love for him. Whatever qualms he'd had about coming here appeared to have been replaced by an anger so tangible that it ought to have terrified even the bravest of men.

Sure enough, the loud voices of accusation died as the townspeople watched his progress. One by one, they all shrank away from him, sinking onto their seats and averting their gazes for fear of incurring his wrath.

And yet, in spite of how cowed they all were, Isabella feared that no matter how afraid the people of Moxley might have been of their duke, their opinion of her would remain unaltered. Truthfully, Isabella felt fortunate that a stake was not present, for she was confident that many of those present would have taken savage joy in seeing her go up in a blaze.

Nothing Anthony could say or do would change that. The rumor had taken its natural course, and Lady Harriett had won. Heaven help her, Isabella had even heard a woman claim that Isabella had lured her husband away from her and that he couldn't put food on the table because he was spending all his money on buying favors from Isabella. The lies were rampant, and she in turn was ruined.

Eyes trained on Anthony, Isabella held her breath, unable to determine what he planned to do or say. He was standing perfectly still now as his dark gaze swept across the room, meeting hers across the distance between them. Outwardly, he looked frightening in his apparent ducal confidence, but Isabella knew better, for the way in which he rocked ever so slightly between his feet gave him away. He was as nervous as he'd been when they'd first arrived, perhaps even more so now that he was standing up there with everyone's attention pinned directly on him. This was his Achilles' heel—the one thing that unnerved him more than anything else, and the reason why he'd postponed taking his seat in Parliament: public speaking.

Isabella's heart lurched in her chest. She wanted to leap to her feet and run to him, offer her support as he bravely stood up to do the very thing he always avoided. And he was doing it for her. She'd never thought it possible to love him more than she already did, but she was wrong—this selfless act on his part was enough to melt her heart. Nevertheless, as she moved to do what instinct demanded, he gave her a slight shake of his head, staying her act of kindness.

"It is remarkable how quickly a rumor can spread," Anthony said as he looked at all the people gathered before him. "Especially when it is negative, born of nothing but hatred and jealousy. Did any of you even bother to consider the truth of it? I know that many of you have met Miss Chilcott personally. Did you not wonder how a woman of such decent and honorable character could turn to a life of depravity?

"Yes, it is true that her family is struggling and that she was hoping to marry Mr. Roberts in order to better their position, but I daresay that Miss Chilcott would rather starve than lower herself to the degree that all of you are suggesting." There was a fire blazing in his eyes, and Isabella couldn't help but notice that he was standing perfectly still now. "You may ask yourselves how I know this; how I can possibly be so sure that she did not do what the rumor suggests . . ."

Oh dear God!

Surely he wouldn't. Gripping her seat with her hands, Isabella waited with bated breath for him to continue. She was powerless to stop him.

"I know," he went on with steel in his voice, "because *I* was the man whom she was with at the barn. It wasn't one of my stable boys or fieldworkers as some would like to believe, but *me*, the Duke of Kingsborough."

A cumulative gasp went up from the crowd and Isabella just sat there, stunned and unwilling to turn and look at her parents for fear of the shame she'd undoubtedly see in their eyes.

"But," he was now saying, "contrary to what you may think, nothing untoward occurred between us while we were there. I merely wished to speak with her privately so we could discuss the matter of her becoming my wife."

Another gasp and Isabella's heart was galloping away with her. Some of the people present started to speak, to ask questions, but Anthony raised a staying hand. Good God, it looked as if he had more to say.

"Now, I know that Mr. Roberts has had designs on Miss Chilcott for some time, but he is not in love with her, whereas I am." Were some of the women who'd only moments earlier been willing to toss Isabella to the dogs actually sighing? Isabella blinked, and his words began to sink in. He loved her. Heaven above if he hadn't just said as much to everyone present. Isabella sat in a daze while her heart thumped with delight and her stomach fluttered with anticipation. Anthony loved her, and nothing had ever felt more wonderful. "Now that Mr. Roberts has retracted his interest in Miss Chilcott, she is free from all responsibility toward him, and I am finally able to ask her the one question that I've been so desperate to ask." Meeting her gaze, he finally allowed a smile as he extended his hand toward her, beckoning for her to join him.

Isabella couldn't move. Her mouth had grown dry, and she just sat there staring at him as if he'd just dropped from the sky. This was what she wanted, wasn't it? She no longer had an obligation toward Mr. Roberts, not just because he'd cried off but also because her parents had accepted her right to choose the man she wished to spend her life with herself.

Her mother had realized how wrong it was to keep Isabella from Anthony on the basis of her own terrible experience. Since then, Lady Margaret had warmed toward the duke, going so far as to tell Isabella how kind she thought him to be. And then of course there were Isabella's own feelings to consider. She loved Anthony and had longed for them to find a way to be together since she'd first seen him striding across the ballroom toward her that evening they'd first met.

It all seemed so long ago now, with everything that had happened in between. The fairy tale she'd always wished for was about to be hers, so although this wasn't the private, romantic moment she'd been hoping for, with every gossipmonger in Moxley staring wide-eyed upon her instead, she felt a surge of happiness bubbling inside her. It spread rapidly to every inch of her body until she felt herself growing warm and giddy from it. And when her mother gave her a gentle nudge, reminding her that Anthony was still standing there waiting for her to join him, she knew she must have looked a fool with the loopy grin that captured her lips.

Somehow, he'd done it—he'd discredited the rumor, saving her reputation and offering her his name and protection in one clean sweep. Of course, if anyone ever discovered the truth, his honor would take a severe blow indeed. She knew that Lady Harriett was sitting diagonally to her right, and she fought the urge to look at her, keeping her gaze trained on Anthony instead. Lady Harriett deserved nothing from her, not even the acknowledgement of her presence, but the fact that she had witnessed enough of Isabella's rendezvous with Anthony to base a rumor upon it was most disturbing, to say the least.

Pushing the vile thought aside, Isabella smiled up at Anthony as he took her hand in his and dropped to one knee. Silence filled the air as everyone present trained their ears and listened.

"Isabella, you know that I love you, and I believe I have proven myself willing to do almost anything to secure your hand in marriage. Would you please do me the honor of becoming my wife, my duchess, and in so doing, of making me the happiest man in the entire world?"

As she stood there, gazing down at that handsome face of his, so full of hope and happiness, her eyes misted, and her throat closed against the yes she so desperately wanted to give him, so she nodded her enthusiasm instead as the first tear trickled down her cheek. It was kissed away a moment later by Anthony, who'd leapt to his feet and was presently hugging her against him while the whole room erupted with applause.

Finding her voice, she quietly whispered against his ear, "I love you too, Anthony, so terribly much."

Chapter 24

With Isabella on his arm, Anthony started leading her toward the exit, only too happy to get away from these people who had been so eager to pass judgment on her only moments earlier. As they drew up to where Lady Harriett was standing with her parents, however, Anthony turned a dangerous glare on Lord Crooning. "I did not wish to publically humiliate you, my lord," he said in a muffled tone. "But I think it prudent to tell you that your daughter is to be found at the core of all this spiteful gossip. Had she been a man, I would have called her out. Do whatever you must to keep her under control and out of my sight, or so help me God I'll see her shunned and ostracized to such a degree that her only option will be to leave the country. Do I make myself clear?"

Lord Crooning gave a curt nod of response, his eyes flickering with something akin to fear, and as Anthony's gaze went to Mrs. Crooning and Lady Harriett herself, both kept their faces downcast, the arrogance they'd both displayed in his parlor only a week earlier completely gone. "I hope you'll forgive me for bringing you into all of this," Anthony said as they passed Mr. Roberts in the doorway.

"You did the right thing," Mr. Roberts said, taking Isabella's hand and bowing over it to show his regard. He might have had his ulterior motives for wishing to marry her, but Isabella had had hers too—theirs had *not been* a love match but one from which both parties stood to gain, and however much Anthony had disliked Mr. Roberts's intentions toward her, he'd proven himself a gentleman in the end.

Thanking him, Anthony led Isabella outside to join her parents, who stood waiting for them.

"Congratulations," Lady Margaret crooned, embracing her daughter while Mr. Chilcott shook Anthony's hand. "And welcome to the family, Your Grace," she added, releasing Isabella, whose face was beaming with unabashed joy.

"I should say the same to you," Anthony grinned. For the first time since his father's death, everything in his life felt good and right. Now, if he could only get Isabella off to the altar as quickly as possible, he'd be most content. Of course, there was also his mother to consider. He would have to send word to her immediately, and once she heard the news, a quick marriage by special license would be out of the question.

Not that he minded too much—she deserved the joy of helping Isabella arrange all of those little details that women were so fond of. The only problem this presented was that he'd probably have to wait a couple of months before taking his lovely bride to his bed. He groaned. Somehow, he'd have to find a solution to this unless he wished to subject himself to a constant state of discomfort. Needless to say, he did not. Of course, she'd snuck out of her home before on the night of the ball, so perhaps . . . ?

He escorted them all back to the Chilcott residence, but as soon as Isabella's mother and father had alit from the carriage, he waited a moment before helping Isabella down, affording them a bit of privacy, since her parents had now almost reached the front door. With her hand tucked snuggly against the crook of his elbow, he leaned close to her as he whispered, "Any chance I might convince you to have another midnight escapade?"

Her head turned sharply toward his, and though her eyes were initially filled with surprise, they quickly started to sparkle with mischief. "Why, Your Grace, I do believe you're hoping to seduce me." There was a slight twitch at the corner of her mouth, suggesting that she was struggling to keep a straight face.

"Meet me at the garden gate tonight at eleven?" he pressed, determined to come to an agreement before they arrived at the front door, where her parents stood smiling and waiting for them to join them.

"I'll be there," she promised just as a lovely pink hue flared in her cheeks. And then their moment of privacy was gone and they were being ushered inside for tea while Lady Margaret prattled on about how happy she was for her daughter and how they must sit down together with Anthony's mother and discuss the wedding gown, the flowers and whatever else would be required to make the big day perfect. Anthony, on the other hand, said nothing, his thoughts straying to the promise of what that night would bring.

With a thick, woolen shawl draped about her shoulders, Isabella quietly opened her bedroom window at precisely five minutes before eleven and climbed out, careful not to wake Jamie, who'd fallen peacefully asleep an hour earlier.

Easing herself down from the ledge, Isabella closed the window, jamming a wad of fabric between the two frames to hold them in place while she was away. She then walked brusquely around to the front of the house and down the garden path to where Anthony stood waiting. "My horse is this way," he whispered as he placed his arm about her shoulders and hurried her along. "I thought it best to leave him tethered a short distance from here so his whinnying wouldn't arouse suspicion."

"How thoughtful of you," Isabella said beneath the strong weight of his arm. Heat coursed through her, and for the first time that day, she considered what she was actually getting herself into by agreeing to meet him like this. Her heart's pace quickened with anticipation, for there was no question about it—Anthony would not wish to get her alone like this for a mere chat.

"Where are we going?" she asked as soon as they'd located his horse and were riding along the dirt road, increasing the distance between themselves and Moxley.

"Why, to Kingsborough Hall, of course," he said with distinct amusement in his voice as he urged the horse onward.

Good Lord!

"But that's . . . that's . . ."

"Outrageous?" he offered, his voice still ringing with mirth.

"Well, yes," she said. She attempted to look back over her shoulder at him, but her position made that impossible. "What if someone sees me? The last thing I wish is to incite more gossip."

"We'll just have to be extra careful," he said as he angled his head to place a kiss against her neck, which in turn made her skin sizzle. "And besides, my mother is out of town, and I have sent all the servants to bed."

Isabella actually gulped. The consequence of her actions had suddenly become very real, and for a fleeting second she considered asking him to turn the horse about and take her home.

But then she recalled their time together in the barn—how sensual it had been and how utterly incredible. She loved this man and he loved her; they would be married soon, though probably not soon enough. Did she really wish to wait until her wedding night to be with him? The answer rang loud and clear inside her head, and she shook off whatever misgivings remained. In another month or two (depending most likely on how good she would be at convincing their respective mothers to hasten things along) he would be her husband, but for tonight, he would be Anthony, the Duke of Kingsborough—her lover.

It felt both right and wicked all at the same time, sending shivers scurrying down her spine. But then she recalled the book she'd found in his library, and whatever excitement she felt was replaced by a sudden nervousness. He probably had vast amounts of experience in this area, whereas she . . . dear God, she knew nothing on the matter.

What if she did something wrong? Something that might displease him or, worse, hurt him? Heaven help her if he suddenly decided that they did not suit after all, due to her lack of expertise in the bedroom. Whatever would she do then? It would be too late and . . . and . . . worst of all, he would see her in a state of complete undress.

Well, she might as well call off the wedding now, because she was only too aware of what she looked like beneath the gentle folds of her gown. She wasn't fashionably thin, her thighs had too much meat on them, and her breasts were larger than what was considered proper. God help her!

She was so caught up in her frantic imaginings that she barely paid attention to her surroundings until she'd been lifted off his horse, ushered inside Kingsborough Hall through a back entryway and whisked upstairs to his bedroom. Not until the door closed behind her and the lock clicked into place did it dawn on her where she was, and by then, she was in full panic.

She felt his hands upon her shoulders in the next instant and she flinched, stepping away from him as her gaze wandered the room in search of a chair. If she could only sit down a moment, she was sure she'd feel better.

"Is something wrong?" he asked with a hint of concern.

"Oh . . . er . . . no, not at all." *There!* In one corner of the room was a small seating arrangement—two chairs with a table between them. Isabella hurried toward it, feeling in no small part like a complete imbecile as she hastily seated herself in one of them. She then looked at Anthony, who was still standing exactly where she'd left him, regarding her with a bit of a quizzical expression. "I'm just ah . . . er . . . oh, bother!"

One elegant eyebrow lifted in response. "You don't seem quite yourself. Would you rather go home?"

"No!"

The other eyebrow shot up as well before he recovered from her unexpected outburst, whereupon it relaxed back into its usual position. With slow, careful steps, Anthony crossed the floor to where she sat. He gestured toward the empty seat, and when she nodded her approval, he lowered himself into it. He watched her for a moment before saying, "Something is making you uneasy, Bella. Would you like to tell me what it is so I can help you relax?"

She shook her head. It would be impossible for her to confide the source of her fears in him—or so she thought until she felt his hand upon hers and looked up into his eyes, finding nothing but loving reassurance there. With a deep breath she told him of her worries while he, in turn, sat patiently and listened.

He didn't frown or smile or make any other attempt to judge her, but when she was finished, he raised her hand to his lips and kissed each of her fingertips before saying, "First of all, you must never allow yourself to think that I find your figure displeasing, for I love your lush curves and the softness that your breasts and thighs have to offer. Your body arouses me to no end, Bella, and if you don't believe me, then allow me to show you."

And before Isabella could fathom what he was about, he lowered her hand against his groin. He was hard there beneath the fabric of his trousers, and though her heart was beating wildly in her chest and her mouth had long since gone dry, she found herself unable to pull away. There was something fascinating and empowering about this effect she had on him.

"Second of all," he continued, his gaze locked with hers as he moved her hand over him, "there is nothing you can do to cause me displeasure, nor anything that would ever cause me to think less of you. Just do what feels right, try whatever piques your curiosity . . . experiment in any way you please. This is our playroom, Bella, and as long as we are alone here, there will be no boundaries between us."

His words of reassurance eased away her troubled thoughts, and as he lowered his mouth over hers, she did not pull away but welcomed his kiss instead.

Feeling the hot, moist pressure of his tongue as it traced its way along the seam of her lips, she opened her mouth to allow him entry. A low, throaty groan escaped him in response to her acceptance and she found herself leaning toward him, trying to get closer just as his arms came around her waist, pulling her from her seat and onto his lap.

Not for a second did he disengage his mouth, his tongue roving over and under hers as he pulled her against him. She pressed herself closer, flattening her chest against his and delighting in the wave of heat this simple act evoked. He abandoned her mouth to trail hot kisses along her jawline and down her neck. "Forget your inhibitions," he murmured as he ran his hand up along her side, but then he stopped his progress (annoying man) and said, "Open your eyes and look at me."

On a deep, steadying breath she complied and was instantly stunned by the ravenous look in his eyes. His lips were slightly parted and his breathing was deep and labored. He didn't say anything further as he gently lifted her until she was almost standing, then he raised her skirts until they were bunched around her thighs and turned her so that when he pulled her back down she found herself sitting astride his lap. "That's much better," he muttered with a wolfish grin as he placed his hands against her bottom and scooted her closer until she felt herself pressed against his hardness. "Now move, touch me, let yourself go."

Unsure of herself, Isabella hesitantly raised her hands against his chest. Remaining perfectly still, he watched as she ran her hands over him. She knew he wouldn't mind her touch, and yet something inside her—some stupid, ingrained reservation—stopped her from acting on the impulse she felt to undress him.

She bit her lower lip instead and closed her eyes to draw a deep breath. His lips were on her again, this time lower, against the swell of her breasts, his tongue tracing a trail of embers along the edge of her gown, and when he gently pinched that tender flesh with his teeth, a flood of sensation darted straight between her thighs, and she gasped in response.

"If I can do it, so can you," he murmured as his fingers went to work on the back of her gown. It didn't take long for him to loosen it enough to pull it down, freeing her breasts to his reverent gaze.

She heard him suck in a breath, and in the next instant she felt hot air teasing her perky peaks, dizzying her mind against the onslaught of pulsing energy that strummed through her, pushing her to finally do what she so desperately longed to.

Tugging at his shirt, she freed it from his breeches and ran her hands beneath. With a groan of pleasure he settled his mouth against one breast and began to suckle. She kissed his neck, nibbling carefully while her hands continued to explore. But it wasn't enough—

she wanted more—needed to calm this growing desire that pooled at her core, so she did what instinct told her to do and ground herself against him.

"Bloody hell," he gasped, releasing her breast and squeezing his eyes shut.

For a moment she almost paused, fearful that she might have done something he did not like, but then his eyes opened and she recognized the hunger that was there, and with her gaze locked on him, she rotated her hips again. It felt good—really good.

"That's it," he said on a breath of air as a sigh escaped her lips. "I knew you had it in you."

Encouraged by his words and aroused to the point where whatever inhibitions she'd had had been tossed right out the proverbial window, she pulled her skirts up higher and placed her hand between them. God, she felt wicked, but the fire in his eyes told her that he more than approved of this newfound, wanton behavior.

Gazing at him from beneath her lashes as she stroked them both with her fingers, she found herself saying, "You asked me once if I ever touch myself here, and I said no. I didn't lie to you, but since then, I must admit I've done it . . . often."

His breath grew ragged when he lowered his gaze to watch the progress of her movement, and if she wasn't mistaken, he also grew harder. "And what do you think about as you give yourself pleasure?" His voice was rough as he posed the question.

Bringing her free hand to his cheek, she brushed her fingertips lightly against him and whispered, "You—always you."

With a groan he swept her into his arms and carried her toward the bed, settling her gently on the edge. He didn't speak as he pulled her arms from the sleeves of her gown and lowered the garment to her waist. Getting up, she allowed it to fall at her feet. Her chemise was next, and Anthony didn't hesitate a second to whisk it over her head and toss it aside. Stepping back, his eyes trailed over her, and the look of appreciation she saw there made her feel silly for ever worrying that he might not approve. It was blatantly obvious that he did, his eyes practically sparkling with glee.

"I believe it is *your* turn to undress, Your Grace," she said, offering him a cheeky smile as she stepped toward him. "And I would be more than happy to assist."

He did not move as she pushed his jacket from his shoulders, nor did he flinch as her fingers pulled away his cravat and worked the buttons of his shirt. But when she traced the waistline of his breeches, she heard him suck in a breath and she raised her gaze to meet his in question.

"Allow me to remove my boots before you continue," he said as he went to work on the task—tugging on the stubborn footwear until they were tossed in quick succession across the floor, where they landed with a thump.

Straightening himself, he allowed her to continue where she'd left off. A surge of excitement coursed through her at the prospect of what she was about to do. This man would soon be her husband, and she had every intention of getting to know his body as well as she knew her own.

No sooner had she unfastened the last button holding his breeches in place than that hard length of him sprang free. Curious, she hesitantly curled her fingers around the smooth surface and slowly ran her thumb back and forth, cautiously eyeing him to ensure that he didn't mind her taking such liberties.

"Oh my God," Anthony muttered. The sensation of her fingers upon him like this was divine—she was divine. Heaven help him, but he'd never experienced anything close to this before. No other woman could possibly measure up. In his mind there was only Bella. He took a steadying breath as he looked at her, the expression upon her face so full of passion and focus.

Whatever he'd said or done to bring out the vixen in her had certainly worked. She was incredible, and as she tugged him ever so gently, a surge of heat rushed to his groin while sparks of desire flittered across his skin. He'd never been this aroused before in his life!

Capturing her mouth in a hot and fervent kiss, he ran a hand over her hip, across her bottom and down to the soft flesh of her womanhood. "Yes," she gasped as she parted her legs to grant him further access.

Trailing a finger along her center, he abandoned her mouth in favor of her ear, nibbling gently on the lobe as she trembled against him. "You're so wet, Bella, so ready and . . ." He dipped a finger inside her. "So tight."

"I suppose I want you quite badly," she murmured.

"There can be no doubt about that, and while I want you just as badly, I'd also like to taste you."

"*What?*" she squeaked, eyes wide as she tried to pull away.

He refused to let her go, leading her to the bed instead. "Trust me, love, you'll enjoy this more than you can possibly imagine." Once he'd settled her against the plush pillows, Anthony proceeded to kiss his way along her outstretched body, chasing away the tension that had filled her when he'd told her what he had in mind. It took a while for her to relax, but he enjoyed every moment, relishing the opportunity he'd been given to simply adore each and every part of her. When he eventually flicked his tongue against her place of desire, she gasped and groaned with such pleasure that he almost found himself undone.

He wanted her pleasure as much as, if not more than, he wanted his own, and the more he laved her, the closer he sensed her coming to her climax. Pulling back, he couldn't help but smile at the dazed look upon her face as he climbed up between her legs. "This is bound to hurt a little," he warned.

"That's all right," she said with sincerity gleaming in her eyes as she raised her hand to caress his cheek. "I want this—I want you."

Anthony didn't need a second telling, but he was determined to make this good for her and therefore took his time, no matter how difficult it was for him to stop himself from forging ahead. When he reached the proof of her maidenhood, he stopped, catching his breath as he braced himself above her. His body screamed for fulfillment, but he ignored it, focusing all of his efforts on her instead. "How do you feel?" he quietly asked.

"Strange . . . full, I suppose, and oddly complete."

Reaching between them, he started to stroke her. "How about now?"

"Yes," she breathed, her fingers splaying across his back as she tried to pull him closer. "Oh, God, yes. Please, Anthony . . . I need . . ."

And then she arched her back, pushing herself against him, and he complied, thrusting himself forward, burying himself to the hilt. A small groan of discomfort escaped her lips and he stopped to ask if she was all right. "Yes," she said as she pulled him back for another breathless kiss.

With a sigh of relief, he withdrew from her a little, then plunged back inside. She groaned her pleasure, and he repeated the process until he felt her moving with him, their rhythm carrying them both on a wave of ever-increasing passion as they climbed the steep slope that would take them to the eventual place of ecstasy.

It didn't take long before Anthony felt Isabella shudder as she tightened around him, crying out his name. He followed close behind, the rush of sensation that whipped through him at the moment of climax more powerful than any he'd ever experienced before. Breathing hard, he collapsed on top of her, spent and satisfied as he breathed in her scent.

"That was really quite . . . remarkable," she said as he turned his head to place a tender kiss upon her temple.

Anthony smiled, his lips still pressed against her head. "Indeed it was, Bella, and do you know, I believe it's only the first remarkable moment of many between us." He could feel her skin grow warmer and knew she had to be blushing. Rolling off her, he scooped her up against his chest and hugged her close.

They remained like that for a while, and Anthony was just beginning to close his eyes, thinking her asleep, when she suddenly twisted herself around to face him with a rather pensive frown. "I would like to meet my grandparents," she said, looking him squarely in the eye. "I know that you know where they live, and I . . . well, I'd like to make their acquaintance at the first opportunity."

"I believe you ought to discuss that with your mother, don't you? After all, she's the one who had a falling out with them and ran off. It would probably be best if she makes the first conciliatory step."

Isabella sighed as she relaxed back down against his arm. "She'll never do it. It's a matter of pride for her now, I believe, and while I can understand her reasoning, they're my grandparents." Her eyes met his again in an imploring way. "Don't you think I should have the right to make my own decision—form my own impression of them? Not to mention what they must be going through. They probably think their daughter dead!"

"I can't say that I disagree with you, love, but it's a delicate situation. If you go behind your mother's back she may feel betrayed."

"And what about me?" Isabella asked, her voice filling with annoyance. "Ought I not feel betrayed for being lied to my whole life?"

"You have a point there," he conceded.

"Besides, if I mention it to her she'll only try to stop me—I'd rather she doesn't know until I've met them myself and decided whether or not I'd like for them to be a part of my life."

Anthony nodded. "Very well, then," he said. "I shall send word to them. They are no doubt in London by now, but I can invite them up for the weekend . . . together with my mother and sister, perhaps, since I doubt your parents will allow you to come here alone and unchaperoned."

"But if your mother or Lady Louise ask me to join them for tea, she'll have no cause for protest," she said, warming to the idea.

"That's the plan, I suppose."

Raising herself on her forearm, she gazed down at him and smiled the most dazzling smile he'd ever seen. His heart lurched. "Have I told you how much I love you?" she asked.

He pretended to consider that for a moment before saying, "I believe you may have, though I wouldn't mind hearing it again."

She grinned. "Well I do—enormously." And then her gaze turned hot and she lowered her lashes to offer him a seductive gaze. "Do you suppose we might have time for another remarkable moment before I have to return home?"

Blood pumping in his veins at her suggestion, he flipped her onto her back in one fluid move, eliciting a squeal from her as he placed his lips against her breast and quietly muttered, "I believe we might."

Chapter 25

It took no small amount of organization for Anthony to pull off his plan of reuniting Isabella with her grandparents. He'd sent word to his mother and Louise first, but as eager as they'd both been to jump to his assistance, they'd had social functions that had been difficult for them to back out of without coming across as rude.

Eventually, it was decided that as long as the Deerfords were in agreement, they would come to Kingsborough Hall the following week so they could return to London in time for the Darwich Ball. Anthony's mother had written to him, suggesting that if Lady Margaret and her parents were to reconcile as well, then the ball presented not only a good opportunity for Anthony and Isabella to announce their upcoming nuptials, but to welcome Lady Margaret back into Society with her husband by her side.

His mother signed off by saying that with the limited time available to them, she would place all responsibility of finding appropriate gowns for both Isabella and her mother on his shoulders.

Setting the missive aside, Anthony rolled his eyes and groaned. He detested anything to do with modiste shops, fashion plates, fittings and the like—hell, he himself was barely reasonably dressed at any given time, and his mother wanted him to help Isabella select a ball gown. Eyeing the side table, he decided that there wasn't enough brandy in the world to make this task any more appealing.

Blast!

He loved Isabella, of course, and would do anything for her, but fabric selection at a modiste's? Gah, but it was a most unpleasant thought. Still, it was important that she look her absolute best when she made her first appearance before the *ton*. With this in mind, Anthony found himself escorting both Isabella and her mother to Madame Bertrand's, where he took a stand against a green silk—not that it wouldn't have suited Isabella immensely, but the frost blue he'd seen the last time he'd been there would suit her better. Her mother, thankfully, agreed, and together they convinced Isabella to acquiesce.

For Lady Margaret, Isabella suggested a burgundy satin, and when her mother protested, it was Anthony to whom Isabella turned for support, which he happily gave, since it was a lovely fabric. "A bold color for a bold woman," he said to his soon-to-be mother-in-law with a wink.

In the end, their errand was accomplished in record time—a feat for which Anthony gave the ladies full credit. To show his appreciation, he invited them both for tea at Mrs. Wilkes' Tearoom, ensuring that they both selected a tart and suppressing a smile when Isabella deliberately avoided the one with apples. Seating themselves in a small nook, they each proceeded to enjoy their treats.

"Thank you again for ordering those gowns on our behalf," Lady Margaret said as she took a sip of her tea. "The fabric was very dear, not to mention how much it will probably cost to—"

Anthony waved away her concerns with his hand. "My dear lady, you really mustn't worry about that. It is my pleasure to ensure that you will both be equally stunning at the Darwich Ball. Tomorrow I will send my valet over to your house so he can discuss your husband's attire with him."

Lady Margaret leveled him with a frank stare. "You still haven't told us what you intend to say when people start asking about Isabella's identity and heritage."

"I'm working on it," Anthony assured her, though she didn't look the least bit convinced. All he could do was thank his lucky stars that she didn't know what his plan entailed, for she would undoubtedly quit the country before allowing him to reunite her with her parents or make a public appearance as the long-lost Lady Margaret.

Casting a sidelong glance at Isabella, he steeled himself. This was what she wanted, and he had to concede that if this situation could be resolved, Lady Margaret's reputation could in all likelihood be restored, allowing her daughter to be accepted into Society with honor and dignity. It was most assuredly a battle worth fighting.

When Lady Louise and her mother the duchess stopped by the Chilcott residency two days later, Isabella was about to collapse into a bundle of nerves. She'd been looking forward to this day for almost a week, but now that it had finally arrived, something odd had begun happening to her stomach—as if it had suddenly decided that it didn't belong in her body. Attempting bravery, she donned a bright smile as she wished her mother a pleasant afternoon, promising not to remain too long in her hostesses' company. On quaking legs she then made her way toward the Kingsborough carriage, which stood waiting, and allowed the driver to help her up.

"Dear me," Lady Louise said as Isabella seated herself across from her. "You look as if you're heading to the gallows! I hope your parents didn't notice, or they'll think we have ulterior motives."

"Which we do," the duchess reminded her daughter.

"What I meant is that they might believe we're trying to offer Anthony some time *alone* with his future bride," Lady Louise said.

The duchess snorted. "As if that might be any worse in this instance. As it is we'll be lucky if Lady Margaret doesn't murder all of us once she discovers what we've been up to." Isabella winced, and the duchess immediately turned a kind smile on her. "Not to worry, though. I'm confident that everything will work out just fine, and as for your jitters, they're really unfounded. Your grandmamma and grandpapa are equally anxious to meet you."

"Truly?" Isabella asked.

The duchess nodded, still smiling, and a quiet sense of relief washed over Isabella, which was silly, really, considering how anxious the Deerfords had seemed on the night of the ball when they'd almost blown her cover. She was their granddaughter, for heaven's sake. They would have to be beasts not to want to meet her.

Drawing a fortifying breath, Isabella leaned back against the backrest and braced herself for the afternoon ahead. She had asked for this, it was her idea, and there was no turning back now without looking like a coward, and a coward she was not—she'd meant to marry Mr. Roberts for the sake of her family, after all. As far as heroics went, that ought to count for something.

Eventually, Isabella managed to calm herself, and when she stepped into the parlor at Kingsborough Hall, only to be swept into an immediate embrace by Lady Deerford, she knew her concerns had been unfounded.

"Look at you," her grandmother cried, stepping back for only a fraction of a second before pulling Isabella against her once more. Given the portly woman that Lady Deerford was, Isabella was forced to admit that she did give rather good hugs. "You're ravishing, my dear—a diamond of the first water and I'll shoot anyone who says otherwise."

"Now, now, my dear," a male voice said with a good-humored ring to it. "It wouldn't do for you to kill her when we've only just found her—perhaps you will allow the girl to breathe?"

"Nonsense, Hugh—I've no intention of ever letting her out of my sight," Lady Deerford replied, though she did disengage herself from Isabella and stand aside enough for her to get a better view of her grandfather.

Deerford chuckled. "I daresay Kingsborough may have a thing or two to say about that." He stepped right up to Isabella and smiled—eyes warm and welcoming as he took her hand and raised it to his lips. "It is a pleasure to make your acquaintance." Leaning closer, he whispered, "Please go easy on her—she's been waiting so terribly long for this moment and is full of excitement."

"And why wouldn't I be?" Lady Deerford asked, attesting to the fact that there was nothing wrong with her hearing. "She's my *granddaughter*—fully grown and practically with children on the way, and I've only just set eyes on her now! Of course I'm excited!"

A cough sounded and Isabella caught Anthony's eye. He was trying very hard not to laugh, so she shot him a bit of a scowl, for she actually liked what little she knew of Lady Deerford so far and was touched by her enthusiasm. Lord Deerford seemed equally amicable—not at all the sort of man whom she would imagine to trick his daughter into an engagement by arranging to have her publically seduced. Certainly an explanation was in order.

"Come," the duchess said. "Let's sit and have some tea."

Moving toward the seating arrangement, Isabella purposefully seated herself on one of the sofas, allowing her grandmother the obvious delight of sitting next to her, while her grandfather seated himself in one of the chairs, with Anthony in another and the duchess and her daughter on the opposite sofa.

"Allow me to pour," Lady Louise said, reaching for the teapot while the duchess picked up a plate of scones and passed it to Lord Deerford, who took one with a smile and a thank-you before offering it to his wife.

"So, I understand that congratulations are in order," Lady Deerford said as she took a scone and placed it carefully on her plate, "since you are soon to be married to the duke—handsome fellow that he is. You're a lucky woman."

"Thank you, my lady, I—"

"Oh no, we'll have none of that, my dear. I'm your grandmother—I think we ought to forgo the honorific, don't you? Why not call us Grandmamma and Grandpapa instead?"

"Very well, Grandmamma," Isabella said slowly, gaining an instant squeak of approval from the lady herself. "Your wishes are greatly appreciated, and well . . . it is in part because of our upcoming wedding that I wanted to meet with you. You see, I am hoping that you will be able to join us as our guests, but in order for that to happen, there is a certain . . . situation . . . which will require not only some attention but a great deal of delicacy as well."

"Your mother?" It was a simple question posed by her grandfather and one that cut straight to the point.

Isabella nodded. "Precisely."

Silence reigned as her grandfather stared back at her with a thoughtful frown. He eventually turned to the duchess and said, "Would you mind affording us a moment alone, Your Grace? I would like to explain myself to my granddaughter."

The room must have cleared in less than five seconds, with Isabella catching only a fleeting nod of reassurance from Anthony before the parlor door closed behind him and she was left alone with her newfound grandparents. Not knowing quite how to respond, she decided to do the British thing and offered them both some more tea.

"How much do you know?" Lord Deerford asked,

his voice solemn as he leaned slightly forward in his seat and rested his elbows on his lap.

"Enough, I suppose," Isabella said. Her grandmother had lost her vibrant demeanor and was now sitting very still on the seat beside her. There was no question that this was a subject she'd rather have avoided. Isabella knew that for any possible relationship to flourish between them, they could not ignore the issue. In a steady voice, she began to relate what her mother had told her.

They sat for a while in silence after she finished until, with a great sigh, her grandfather stood, went to the side table and proceeded to pour himself a brandy. "It's all true," he finally said, meeting Isabella's gaze unflinchingly, though the tension that gripped him was visible in his posture. "But you have to understand—I was at my wit's end. She'd just made her debut with great success, garnering no fewer than ten suitors in the space of a week. One of them was even a duke, if I recall. We were thrilled for her—positively thrilled!"

Lady Deerford shifted uneasily in her seat and promptly asked her husband if he would please pour her a sherry. When asked if she would like one as well, Isabella heartily accepted, hoping it would be enough to get her through this painful conversation.

"But would she have any of them?" Lord Deerford asked rhetorically, glancing sideways to where Isabella sat as he poured the dark brown liquid into two separate glasses. With a resigned shake of his head, he set the bottle aside, picked up the glasses and carried them to the table, where he placed one before each lady. "No, she claimed to be in love—with my stable master, for Christ sake."

"Hugh!" Lady Deerford admonished.

"My apologies," he muttered, resuming his seat and leaning back as he balanced his glass on top of the armrest.

Isabella bit her lip. The situation was not an easy one, made only more difficult by the fact that she understood both sides. Her mother had good reason to be upset with her parents, though it would of course have been unheard of for them to encourage a relationship with the man she'd eventually eloped with. "You know," she said, choosing her words carefully, "I think what hurt my mother the most was not so much your disapproval of my father but rather the way in which you tricked her. She felt betrayed, and forgive me for saying this, but she was right to do so."

"What would you have us do?" Isabella's grandmother asked. She shifted a little so she could look directly at her granddaughter. "We'd like to make amends if possible."

Lord Deerford started to say something, but his wife cut him off. "You had your say twenty years ago, Hugh." Her eyes glistened with emotion. "It's my turn now—tell me, Isabella, what do you think would be the right approach?"

The desperate longing on her grandmother's face tore at Isabella's heart, and she found herself reaching for her grandmother's hand and squeezing it within her own. Her grandfather looked almost equally affected. "I believe an apology would be a good beginning, and then, of course, accepting my father as your son-in-law."

"You think Society will be more forgiving now than they would have been then?" her grandfather asked. "The scandal such an acceptance would incur would come crashing down not only on our heads but on yours too—on the Kingsboroughs, as well as on your future children. As it is, I daresay your fiancé has his work cut out for him explaining who you are once you make your appearance at the Darwich Ball, never mind who your parents might be." Raising his glass to his lips, her grandfather took a deep swallow. "As far as I am concerned, I will be more than happy to welcome your mother and your father into my home—we've lost enough years together as it is—but it is imperative that we consider the consequences."

He was right, of course, and while Isabella wouldn't mind being shunned by a Society she didn't even know, she couldn't subject the Kingsboroughs or her unborn children to such a fate. "In that case, we have two options. We can either continue as we are or we can fabricate a story to explain the situation."

Lord Deerford grunted. "Your mother will never agree to lie."

"She might if it is in her daughter's and grandchildren's best interest," Lady Deerford mused. Her eyes lit with renewed enthusiasm. "We must at least try to convince her."

"Very well," Isabella agreed. "In the meantime, I think we ought to discuss our plan with the duke and his mother, for I too am quite curious as to how he intends to introduce my parents and me at the ball on Saturday. He might have an idea that we can use."

"I suppose that might work," Isabella muttered as she considered Anthony's suggestion. She'd imagined him concocting a complex tale as a means to escape their current predicament, only to discover that his solution was pretty straightforward and remarkably close to the truth.

"Honesty is generally the best policy," he said as he strode across to one of the windows and stared out. "Although in this instance I have to say that a bit of elaboration is in order—to protect not only your reputation, Isabella, but also that of your parents and your grandparents. Deerford claimed your mother was kidnapped. I will not dispute that and complicate things further by having him branded a liar. Besides, I believe such a scenario is better than that of your mother deliberately thwarting all propriety by running off with a servant." He met Isabella's gaze and quickly said, "If you'll forgive me for saying so." She nodded, though her lips were drawn a fraction tighter than usual.

"When all is said and done," Anthony continued, "I believe the *ton* will accept my explanation, for they all have two important qualities in common—they thrive on a good story, and they heed rank and authority. As a duke, I doubt they will dare discredit me. Especially not if my family and the Deerfords support my claim."

"You have our complete cooperation in the matter," Lord Deerford confirmed. He looked at Isabella. "He's right, you know. There's no doubt that there are those who will always wonder about the truth, but they won't voice such opinions publically for fear of incurring Kingsborough's wrath."

Looking to Isabella, Anthony felt a surge of reassurance. Her confidence in him was unmistakable—it shone in her eyes so clearly that he knew she would trust him with her life. They'd come this far—he wasn't about to let anything ruin it now, not even the scrutinizing gaze of the *ton*. "Before we do anything further," he said, "we have to meet with your parents and explain the situation to them. We've had enough lies and deceptions to last each one of us a lifetime—it's time we started being honest and frank with each other. Isabella, I realize that this won't be easy for you, but you know that I'm right. We cannot go behind your parents' back, surprising them at the very last instant, when they've no choice but to accept our plan. It wouldn't be right."

"No, it wouldn't," she agreed. But that didn't lessen the bout of nervousness that descended upon her an hour later as she entered her home while Anthony and her grandparents waited outside in the ducal carriage. *Gracious!* And she thought she'd been nervous about meeting *them*. This was far worse.

"Oh, you're back," her mother said, raising her gaze from the piece of embroidery she was working on as Isabella opened the parlor door and stepped inside. "Did you have a nice time?"

Her father lowered the newspaper that he'd been reading and peered at her over the rim of his spectacles.

"Er . . . yes, it was lovely," Isabella said, crossing to the nearest seat and dropping herself into it. There really was no easy way in which to break the news to her parents, so she just blurted, "I met my grandparents."

Her mother froze and her father promptly dropped his paper. "Wh-what are you talking about, Isabella?" her mother asked, her eyes darting toward the door, while her father leaned forward to retrieve his paper from the floor.

"My grandparents," Isabella explained. "*Your* parents, Mama. I've met them. Today. At Kingsborough Hall for tea. They're very eager to see you."

Her mother blanched and was across the floor in an instant, knocking over her teacup in her hurry to reach the window, where she began yanking the curtains shut. "Are you mad?" she hissed as the light dimmed in the room.

As Isabella grabbed a napkin to clean up the spilt tea, she looked up and met her father's accusing gaze. She knew what he must have been thinking, but she chose to ignore him. After all, considering what they'd done to her, she felt rather justified, not to mention that she was well and truly sick of this nonsense and decided to say as much. "You're a grown woman, Mama. You've made your own choice—your own life—but you've made your mistakes too, just as well as they have."

"How can you possibly compare what *I* did with what *they* did to *me*?" Her mother's eyes were sharp as flint.

Isabella didn't back down. Instead she offered her the most dubious gaze she could manage. "You kept my birthright from me, Mama, from Jamie too, and you hid us from them, denying not only them but us a relationship that wasn't yours to deny. And if that's not enough, you tried to discourage my interest in Anthony because you didn't want me associating with an aristocrat. How, pray tell, is that any different from what your father did to you?"

"My father betrayed me by allowing me to think that he would actually let me marry your father, only to have me compromised instead at the hands of a rake."

"And you would have me believe that you would have given me the option to choose my future freely if it hadn't been for Anthony putting two and two to-gether?" She shook her head, angry at her mother's stubborn state of denial. "I don't believe you ever would have told me, and in my ignorance, I would have been just as betrayed by you as you were by your father."

Her mother gaped at her. Finally at a loss for words, she threw her hands in the air, eventually slumping down onto a stool.

"You are right, Isabella, and I cannot possibly begin to tell you how sorry I am for what we did, but you must believe me when I tell you that both your mother and I did what we thought was best at the time." Her father's eyes darted to her mother before adding, "What would you like us to do?"

With a heavy sigh, Isabella said, "Talk to them, allow them to ask for forgiveness, and let's try to move on."

"I cannot," her mother said, finding her tongue.

"You will try," Isabella told her calmly. "Not for your own sake, perhaps, but for me and for the children I hope to have. Once I marry Anthony, questions will be asked, not only about me but about you as well. I would like to avoid scandal at all cost. Do I have your cooperation in this?"

"Yes," her father said before her mother had a chance to reply.

When Isabella looked to her for approval, she said nothing but offered the most reluctant nod that Isabella had ever seen. "Thank you," Isabella said on a sigh of relief as she went to her mother, knelt by her side and placed a kiss upon her cheek. "I know how difficult this is for you."

Her mother nodded, looking not exactly displeased

with the situation at hand but rather exhausted—as if it was all too much for her. It was all too much for all of them, Isabella decided, but for now, there was nothing for it but to muddle through. What a relief it would be to have it all over and done with. "Come along you two," she said, getting up and offering her hand to her mother. "My grandparents are waiting outside with Anthony, probably just as apprehensive about all of this as you are. Let's invite them in, shall we, and see if we can't forget our differences."

Her mother still looked skeptical, but she didn't make a fuss this time. Instead, she returned to her seat on the sofa, waited for Isabella's father to do the same and then nodded. They were ready to take on the past.

Chapter 26

Isabella would forever look back on the two hours that followed as the most emotionally tumultuous of her life. The anger her mother felt had been most apparent in the way she'd yelled at Lord Deerford until the man had actually leaned backward, as if he'd hoped to avoid her verbal assault. Lady Deerford had been the first to dissolve into a puddle of tears, apologizing for her husband's past actions until she must have been sore in the throat.

Isabella had felt terribly sorry for her, but her mother was apparently made of stronger stuff, for she hadn't looked the least bit affected. Anthony had looked as if he'd rather have been anywhere else but in that tiny parlor at that very moment, and he'd retreated to a corner with obvious discomfort.

In the end, it had been Isabella's father who'd intervened and, speaking with more authority than Isabella would ever have given him credit of possessing, had told her mother firmly that it was time to bury the hatchet since, as their daughter had recently pointed out, they had barely treated her any better. "How would you have felt if Isabella had decided to elope with the duke, never to be seen or heard from again?" he'd asked.

Isabella's mother had stopped her tirade and looked at everyone in turn—the first sign of embarrassment showing in the blush on her cheeks.

"In fact, she is better than us, for she was willing to ignore her own happiness for our sake, whereas we put your parents through hell." He'd turned to his father-in-law then and held out his hand, which the marquess had quickly accepted. "I'm so sorry. I wronged you in the most despicable way—we both did—and I can only hope that you will one day find it in your heart to forgive us." Turning to his mother-in-law, who'd been furiously dabbing at her eyes with her handkerchief, he'd apologized to her as well before sweeping her into a tight embrace.

Releasing her, he'd finally looked to his wife, whose own eyes had begun to glisten, and said, "Go on—make amends." Upon which the dam had broken and she'd burst into tears as she'd flung herself into her parents' arms.

Isabella had joined the exchange of embraces, until everyone—save Anthony, who hadn't left the safety of his corner for a second—had looked flushed and puffy. They'd been smiling, though, grinning even, as they'd stepped away from each other with bashful self-awareness. Falling silent as they'd noticed Anthony gaping at them as if they'd all belonged in Bedlam, they'd watched as he'd slowly raised a bottle of brandy and said, "Care for a drink, anyone?" Upon which they'd all erupted in a fit of laughter.

Yes, it had been a memorable afternoon, one which had ended with Anthony relating his plans for introducing the Chilcotts into Society. "Since it was initially put about town that Lady Margaret was kidnapped and nobody knows that she really absconded with Mr. Chilcott, we shall simply elaborate upon the tale, explaining how Mr. Chilcott saved her and took her to his home for recovery. The two fell irrevocably in love and, fearing her parents' disapproval, since Mr. Chilcott was untitled and with no wealth to speak of, she decided to stay away all of these years."

"Until now," Isabella said, liking the simplicity of it and deciding that it was bound to be accepted as the truth.

"Until now," Anthony echoed with a nod of confirmation. "On their way to Kingsborough Hall for the ball," he continued, "the Deerfords noticed a woman who reminded them of their daughter. Having never abandoned hope of finding her, they approached her, discovering to their joy and elation that it was indeed the long-lost Lady Margaret. Upon being introduced to her husband and children, they showed not the least bit of disapproval toward Mr. Chilcott but thanked him profusely for saving their daughter from her attackers and have since accepted him as a valuable member of the Deerford family."

"I have to say that it does sound plausible," Mr. Chilcott said.

"In addition," Anthony pressed, addressing Isabella's parents, "I shall see to it that you are moved either to one of the apartments at Kingsborough Hall or to a larger town house—whichever you prefer. Once we are through, nobody will dare so much as frown in your direction." With a smile he turned to Isabella. "Now then, I believe your gowns will be ready tomorrow. I'll ask Sands, my valet, to pick them up and have them delivered here so you can start packing." Gathering her up in his arms, he then kissed her quite thoroughly upon her lips, not the least bit concerned that they had an audience.

"**A**re you almost ready, dear?" Isabella's mother called from the other side of her closed bedroom door. "The duke is here to escort us, and judging from the way he keeps fidgeting with his cravat, I suspect he's most anxious to see you."

They'd arrived in London the previous day, upon which Isabella and her parents had been taken directly to a town house that Anthony had rented for them. After seeing them in, he'd said his good-byes and left for his own home. Isabella hadn't seen him since and had grown anxious for his company as well.

"I'll be right there, Mama," she called back, unable to keep from laughing as she glanced at herself one last time in the mirror, finally seeing herself the way Anthony probably did—not plump, as she'd always imagined, but sensual in every conceivable way as the ice-blue silk slithered across her every curve, hugging her breasts and hips. There was no doubt in her mind that her fiancé would find it most appealing.

Satisfied, she turned her back on her reflection, opened the door to her room and stepped out onto the landing. With a deep breath, she began her descent, and when she finally entered the parlor, the hum of voices that had busily been discussing some topic or other faded into silence as everyone stopped to stare. "You look incredible," Anthony finally managed, coming toward her as if in a daze. "I . . . heavens!"

"Does that mean you'll dance with me this evening, Your Grace?" she asked, batting her eyelids.

"It means I'll throttle any other man who tries to," he murmured as he raised her gloved hand to his lips and placed a gentle kiss upon her knuckles.

They arrived at Darwich House a half hour later to begin their progress along the receiving line. "I say, Kingsborough! Who is this lovely lady on your arm?" Lady Darwich asked as Anthony bowed before her and Isabella curtsied.

"My fiancée, Miss Chilcott," he told her cheerfully.

"I don't believe I've ever had the pleasure," their hostess said with a frown, raising her quizzing glass as she gave Isabella a head to toe inspection. She nudged Lord Darwich, who was standing at her side, quite soundly in the ribs.

The earl bowed toward Isabella before returning his attention to Anthony. "Your father would be proud of you, and . . ." Lord Darwich's words trailed off as his eyes went beyond where Anthony stood. "Dear me, you look rather familiar. In fact—"

"You remember our daughter, Lady Margaret; Lady Margaret Chilcott now by marriage," Lord Deerford said, stepping closer as he brought the rest of the family with him. "And Miss Chilcott here is our granddaughter."

Lady Darwich looked momentarily as if her eyes might burst from their sockets, but she recovered and, with a smile, eagerly waved them toward the ballroom. "What a pleasure it is to see you again after so many years, Lady Margaret. Oh, we're so happy that you were able to join us this evening, so very, very happy."

Anthony didn't doubt that for a second, for the Darwich Ball was about to become the most talked-about event since the wedding between Cleopatra and Caesar.

"The Duke of Kingsborough and his fiancée, Miss Chilcott," a footman announced in a booming tone, barely drawing a breath before adding, "accompanied by the Marchioness and Marquess of Deerford, along with their daughter, Lady Margaret Chilcott, and her husband, Mr. Chilcott."

The last part was almost swallowed up by the buzz of voices that rose through the air. For the first time since assuming his title, Anthony was happy to be a duke, for as he led Isabella down the steps to the dance floor, the crowds parted as if he'd been Moses.

Nobody quirked an eyebrow at the woman on his arm as he pulled Isabella into his embrace with every indication that he desired a waltz. He gave a curt nod toward the orchestra, the whispers ceased and a hush descended upon them while the first strains of music rose and fell to a steady beat.

"Oh my," Isabella muttered, looking around as Anthony swept her across the dance floor in a wide circle. "It appears you've shocked them into silence."

Anthony smiled down at her. "Quite impressive, don't you think?"

With a grin, she nodded, allowing him to take the lead as he twirled her about, the remnants of the rogue in him holding her scandalously close. The music faded far too soon for his liking, but as they drifted to a stop before his mother, he remembered that there was still one very important matter to attend to.

Everything that was about to happen was for show—an act that would hopefully make it clear to the *ton* that Isabella and her parents were under his and the Deerfords' protection, and that nobody was to say a word against any of them if they valued their own heads.

"Darling," his mother said, her voice higher than usual so as not to be missed by anyone. Nobody moved as she went toward him—not even the rustle of a single skirt could be heard. Smiling, she turned her attention to Isabella, and taking her hands in each of her own she said, "What a pleasure it is to see you again, my dear."

"Thank you, Your Grace," Isabella said, curtsying as well as she was able to with her future mother-in-law holding on to her.

Louise and Huntley approached them next, followed by Winston and Sarah, the Deerfords, Isabella's parents, and even Casper, who looked ever the gallant rake in his evening black.

Flanked by them all, Anthony waved over a footman who was carrying a tray of champagne flutes. Ensuring that each of his family members received a glass, he then addressed the crowd, not feeling the least bit nervous at all this time. He'd won Isabella's heart, and so the fear he'd always had of speaking aloud before others dissipated. None of these people mattered as long as he had her by his side. "It is with great joy in my heart that I not only announce my engagement to the lovely Miss Chilcott but also welcome her mother back into our midst. She has been missed for far too long, but thanks to Mr. Chilcott, she has found her way home." He raised his glass high in the air. "A toast! To the love of my life, a woman with more courage than any I have ever known, and to family, without whom our lives are meaningless."

There was a pause, a slight hesitation, and then

there was a clap, followed by another and another and yes . . . another. Within seconds the whole ballroom was resonating with the beat of it. There was even a loud whistle. Anthony breathed a sigh of relief. Isabella and her mother would be safe, as would her father. The *ton* had given its approval.

Later, when Anthony led Isabella outside for a bit of fresh air (though to be honest, he was far more interested in the privacy the outdoors offered), he felt content. A life shared with the woman he loved—a woman who'd somehow become his friend and ally—stretched before him, and he looked forward to it more than he'd ever looked forward to anything else before.

"Happy?" Isabella asked, weaving her fingers through his.

Not caring what anyone might think or say, Anthony pulled her against him, his lips dangerously close to hers. He could feel her breath upon his chin, and as it whispered across his skin, it left a path of embers in its wake. "With you, always," he murmured right before his lips touched hers, not in desperation but in reverence and adoration. Disengaging, he said, "Though I do feel sorry for our mothers."

"Oh?" Isabella's eyes went wide with wonder.

"For I fear they will have to abandon all hope of arranging that grand Society wedding they were hoping for—I'm getting a special license first thing in the morning." Before she could protest, he kissed her again, more deeply and more passionately, pouring all his love for her into that one starlit moment, reminding her not only how deeply his affection for her ran but also why waiting a moment longer to take their vows would never work.

**Keep reading for a sneak peek
of Sophie Barnes's next novel in the
At the Kingsborough Ball series**

THE SCANDAL IN
KISSING AN HEIR

**Available January 2014
from Avon Books**

Kingsborough Hall, Moxley, England
1817

Daniel Neville, heir to the Marquisate of Wolvington, had removed himself to one of the corners of the Kingsborough ballroom—as good a place as any for a man who'd been labeled an outcast by Society.

Overhead, candles held by three large chandeliers were spreading their glow across the room, the jewels worn by countless women winking in response to the light. This was true opulence, and nobody did it better than the Kingsboroughs. Why, there was even a glass slipper sculpted from ice and a pumpkin carriage sitting outside on the lawn—a touch of fairy-tale splendor indicative of the theme that the dowager duchess had selected for her masquerade.

And what a masquerade it had turned out to be. Never in his life had Daniel born witness to so many feathers. They were everywhere—attached to gowns, on the edges of masks, and sprouting from women's hair.

The ball gowns were marvelous too. These were not the boring dresses that were generally on display at Almack's. Certainly, one could still tell the debutantes apart, due to their tepid choice in color, but they all had a bit of something extra, like crystal beads that sparkled when they moved.

It was refreshing to see, and yet as he stood there, watching the spectacle unfold—the etiquette that formed the backbone of Society being employed to its fullest—Daniel felt nothing but bland disinterest. It was only two hours since he'd arrived, but it felt more like four. God help him, but he'd never been so bored in his life.

Recalling the glass in his hand, he took another sip of his drink as he watched a group of ladies approach on their tour of the periphery. There were three of them, one of them being the Countess of Frompton. If Daniel wasn't mistaken, the two young ladies in her company were her granddaughters—typical debutantes dressed in gowns so pale it was hard to discern where the fabric ended and their skin began. It would do them both a great deal of good to get married, if for no other reason than to be able to add a touch of color to their attire.

As they came nearer, Lady Frompton glanced in Daniel's direction. Their eyes met briefly, then her ladyship quickly drew her granddaughters closer to her, circumventing Daniel in a wide arc that would have been insulting had it not been so expected. He'd known this would happen, for his reputation was so tarnished that he could probably have ruined a lady by merely glancing in her direction. Why he'd bothered to attend the ball at all, when the chance of enjoying himself had been as distant a prospect as traipsing through the African jungle, was beyond him.

Well, not entirely.

He needed to find himself a wife, or so his uncle had informed him last week. "You're a bloody curse on this family!" he'd said. He'd then delivered a long list of reasons as to why he'd thought this to be the case. "It's time you grew up, learned a thing or two about responsibility or you'll end up running your inheritance into the ground after I'm gone. Heaven help me, I'd love nothing better than to disinherit you and allow Ralph to take up the reins, but—"

"My nephew?" Daniel had said, unable to help himself in light of the fact that his uncle would rather have entrusted his entire fortune to an infant.

"I doubt he'll do any worse than you." As deeply as the words had wounded him, Daniel had done his best to hide all signs of emotion. "Your sister's a level-headed woman, her husband too. I'm sure the two of them would be prepared to act wisely on Ralph's behalf, but since the law prevents such an outcome, I rather think it's beside the point.

"That said, your aunt and I have come to a mutual agreement—one which we hope will encourage you to get that head of yours on straight. You will cease your gaming immediately, or we will cut you off financially, which, to clarify, will mean that you will have to work for a living unless you wish to starve. Additionally, you will stop associating with loose women, engaging in haphazard carriage chases, or anything else that's likely to embarrass the name your father left you. And finally, you will get yourself engaged within a month and married by the end of the Season."

Daniel had stared back at his uncle in horror. The older gentleman, however, had looked alarmingly smug and satisfied with this new plan of his. Daniel had turned to his aunt, whose presence had only served to increase Daniel's humiliation tenfold. "He cannot be serious," he'd said, hoping to incur a bit of sympathy from her.

She'd glanced up at him, eyes crinkling at the corners as she'd offered him a sad little smile. "I'm afraid so, love, and I have to say that I am in full agreement with him. You cannot continue down this path, Daniel—it will be detrimental if you do. Please try to understand that we're only looking out for your best interests, as well as those of the family at large." Her eyes had been filled with disappointment.

Of course he'd understood, but he'd still been furious with both of them.

Raising his glass to his lips, Daniel took another sip. A wife—ha! As if finding one here was likely to happen when no self-respecting parent or guardian would allow their daughters and wards within a ten-foot radius of him.

No, Daniel was there because it had been Kingsborough who'd issued the invitation. They'd moved in the same circles once, and Daniel had always enjoyed the duke's company immensely. Things were different now though. The duke had reformed, abandoning his rakehell ways in favor of supporting his family. There was much to be admired in the strength of character Kingsborough had shown, and Daniel had wanted to offer his friend some respect for everything he'd been through—the difficulty he must have endured in dealing with his father's demise. But with so many people in attendance, the duke had only been able to speak with him briefly, as there were many others who craved his attention.

Oh well.

Daniel fleetingly considered asking one of the widows present to dance, but he decided against it. No sense in wasting time on fruitless pursuits, since none of them had any inclination to marry. They'd gained their independence and had every intention of holding on to it. The only thing he could hope to do with any of them was enjoy the comfort of their beds later, but that would hardly hasten his progress to the altar, nor would it improve his aunt and uncle's opinion of him if they happened to find out. Knowing them, they'd probably decide he'd gone too far in thwarting their wishes and cut him off before the month was up—an unwelcome prospect, to say the least.

Across the floor, he spotted Mr. Goodard, another gentleman friend of his. They'd often gambled together, and Daniel decided to go and greet him. With wife hunting being a futile endeavor, sharing a bit of friendly banter over a game of cards would be a welcome distraction.

Squaring his shoulders, Daniel started to head in Mr. Goodard's direction when a flutter of red met the corner of his eye. Glancing toward it, he took a sharp breath . . . and froze.

Who on earth is that?

Next to the terrace doors, partially concealed by a pillar and an oversized arrangement of daffodils, stood a woman unlike any he'd ever seen before. Her hair was black, and from the looks of it, exceptionally long, for it wasn't cut in the style that was fashionable but piled high on her head in an intricate coif. It took a moment for Daniel to come to his senses and realize that he was not only staring openly at her but gaping as well. Quickly snapping his mouth shut, he cursed himself for being such a fool—it was just hair, after all.

And yet he suddenly had the most bizarre and uncontrollable urge to unpin it and run his fingers through it. Of course, it didn't hurt that the woman it belonged to promised to be a tantalizing beauty if the fullness of her lips was anything to go by. Unfortunately, the upper half of her face was concealed by a mask, but if he could only get close enough, he ought to at least be able to see the color of her eyes.

On reflex, he began going over all the ladies he'd ever been introduced to, attempting to recall someone who shared her attributes, but it was to no avail. Clearly, he'd never encountered this woman before, and he found the mystery that she presented most intriguing.

Moving closer, he watched as she tilted her chin in profile, her jawline fine and delicate beneath her high cheekbones. A lock of hair falling softly against the sweep of her neckline had come to rest against the bare skin of her right shoulder, and the unexpected urge he felt to brush it aside and place a kiss there in its stead was startling. Daniel hesitated briefly. Women didn't affect him, and whatever was said to the contrary was untrue, for the charm and soulful eyes he chose to display were no more than tools he applied in his endless pursuit of pleasure. He was methodical in his seduction. If he placed a kiss against a lady's shoulder, it would be for a reason, not because he couldn't stop himself. The fact that he'd felt a helpless need to do so now, however brief it had been, disturbed him.

Stepping up beside the lady, he took a closer look at her. Whoever she was, she couldn't possibly be an innocent, dressed as she was in scarlet silk. He wondered if she might be somebody's mistress, or if not, then perhaps a widow he hadn't yet met—one who might be willing to marry? As unlikely as that was, he could always hope.

Knowing that the only way to find out would be to talk to her, he decided to do the unthinkable—ignore etiquette and address her without being formally introduced. After all, it wasn't as if his reputation was likely to suffer further damage at this point, and considering her gown, he thought it unlikely that hers would either. Dressed in such a bold color, the lady could hardly be a saint.

One thing was for certain however—he needed a wife, and he needed one fast. If her reputation did suffer a little from his talking to her, then so be it. Perhaps he'd marry her and tell all the gossipmongers to go hang. The corner of his mouth lifted at the very idea of it. What a satisfying outcome that would be. Hands clasped behind his back, he leaned closer to her and quietly whispered, "Would you care to dance?"

Rebecca flinched, startled out of her reverie by a deep, masculine voice brushing across her skin, leaving gooseflesh in its wake. Turning her head, she caught her breath, her body responding instinctively as it flooded with heat from the top of her head all the way down to the tips of her toes. The man who stood beside her was nothing short of magnificent—imposing even, with his black satin mask that matched his all-black evening attire.

His jawline was square and angular, his nose perfectly straight, and the brown eyes that stared down at her from behind the slits of his mask sent a shiver racing down her spine—there was more intensity and determination there than Rebecca had ever seen before in her life. He wanted something from her, no doubt about that, and as nervous as that made her, it also spoke to her adventurous streak and filled her with excitement. "Good evening," she said quietly, returning his salutation with a smile.

He studied her for a moment, and then he smiled as well, the corners of his mouth dimpling as he did so. Oh, he was a charmer this one, no doubt about that. "I hope you will forgive me, considering we haven't been formally introduced, but I saw you standing here from across the way and found myself quite unable to place you. Naturally, I had no choice but to make your acquaintance—I am Mr. Neville at your service, and you are . . . ?"

Rebecca knew her mouth was scrunching together in an attempt to keep a straight face. So he was the curious sort. Oh, how she'd have loved to tell him exactly who she was. Would he stagger about with a look of horror on his face before dropping to the floor in a faint? she wondered. Unfortunately, she wouldn't be able to find out, for the risk of discovery was far too great.

For her plan to work, she would have to turn the head of at least one gentleman this evening—preferably some young pup who would become so smitten with her that he'd be eager to do anything to win her hand before the night was over. Not very likely perhaps, but she was desperate enough to give it her best try.

Gazing up at Mr. Neville, she doubted that he would suit. His confident bearing and debonair smile belonged to the sort of man she suspected would seek her company in the name of seduction only, not because he wished to find himself leg-shackled by morning. She ought to discourage him and send him on his way, but since she was happy to avoid venturing out into the crowd a little while longer, she decided to accept the distraction Mr. Neville offered. Until he'd come along, she'd been bored out of her wits anyway. Having arrived through the garden a half hour earlier, she'd spotted her aunt and uncle, the Earl and Countess of Grifton, almost immediately, and, unwilling to be discovered this early on, she'd hidden behind the pillar, waiting for them to retreat to the gaming room as she knew they eventually would.

As predicted, they'd done so over ten minutes ago, yet here she still stood with no idea of what to do next. Ordinarily, she would have tried to befriend some of the other young ladies, then ask them to introduce her to the various gentlemen. The only problem with that plan was the gown she was wearing. When her maid, Laura, had first shown it to her, Rebecca had laughed. She should have known that turning to Lady Trapleigh for help would have had such a shocking result, for she was a widow of the more notorious variety—it was no secret that she kept many lovers, for she spoke of them openly and in much the same way that other women might speak of their bonnets.

From what little she'd shared with Rebecca, it was

clear that Lady Trapleigh's marriage had been an unhappy one. Her husband had been fifty years her senior, so when she'd heard of Rebecca's situation, she'd immediately offered her sympathy, and the two had formed an acquaintance. She'd been the only person, aside from her maid, in whom Rebecca had confided her plan to escape marrying a man old enough to be her grandfather, not because they'd been close friends, but rather because the challenge ahead had seemed so overwhelming that Rebecca had needed the encouragement she'd known Lady Trapleigh would give her.

Rebecca had not been disappointed in that regard, for the widow had not only voiced her admiration but had also promised to help in whatever way she could. She'd visited Rebecca regularly over the last two years, aiding in Rebecca's pretense and doing whatever possible to keep the Griftons in the dark.

When Rebecca had seen the red gown, she'd known that she shouldn't have expected her confidante to be in possession of anything more demure and that she had probably lent her the most reserved gown she owned. At least her breasts would be properly covered, for which she could only have been thankful. Knowing Lady Trapleigh, it could have been worse—far worse.

Rebecca returned her attention to the gentleman before her. "This is a masquerade, Mr. Neville, is it not?" she asked, deciding to keep his company a little while longer. Oh, how pleasant it was to be in the presence of a young and handsome gentleman for a change, rather than suffer the attentions of men who coughed, croaked and hobbled their way through what remained of their lives, as was the case with the suitors her aunt and uncle kept pressing upon her.

"It is," Mr. Neville said, dragging out the last word with a touch of wariness.

"Then part of the amusement, I suppose, comes from the mystery of not always knowing the identity of the person with whom you're speaking. Wouldn't you agree?"

She watched as Mr. Neville's eyes brightened and his smile turned to one of mischief. "Tell me honestly," he said, ignoring her question, "are you married?"

"Certainly not," she said, attempting to sound as affronted as possible, which in turn made him laugh. Surrendering, she allowed the smile that threatened to take control of her lips. "If I were, I would have ignored you completely and rudely walked away."

"Is that so?"

"Quite."

"Well, then I suppose I should inquire if you have any brothers that I ought to live in fear of."

She grinned this time and shook her head with amusement. "You are incorrigible."

"I've been called much worse, I assure you."

"I do not doubt it for a second." And it was the truth, though she had no intention of sharing any of the adjectives that were presently coursing through her own mind, like *magnificent* and *delicious*. Her cheeks grew instantly hot and she cringed inwardly, praying he wouldn't notice her blush. Heaven forbid if either word ever crossed her lips—the embarrassment of it would likely be impossible to survive, particularly since her mind had now decided to turn those two words into one singular descriptive, namely *magnificently delicious*. Her cheeks grew hotter still, though she hadn't thought such a thing possible, but apparently it was.

"Would you care for some air? You're looking a bit flushed."

Oh dear.

She'd rather hoped he wouldn't have been able to tell. Looking over her shoulder, she considered the escape the French doors offered. She wouldn't mind the cooler outdoors right now, particularly since it would probably be the very thing, not only to cure her overheated reaction to Mr. Neville but also to avoid for just a little while longer the task she'd set herself. Looking the way she did, how on earth was she to make a good impression on any of the young gentlemen present? She wasn't sure, though she knew she'd have to figure it out before the evening ended and she lost her chance altogether.

Her eyes met Mr. Neville's, and the promise of trouble in them only compounded her instinct to dismiss him as a possible candidate. But instinct could be wrong, couldn't it? So far, he was the only person she'd spoken to, the only man who'd asked her to dance. Granted, hiding behind a pillar probably hadn't helped her much in that regard. Still, despite her better judgment, she couldn't help but acknowledge that when Mr. Neville looked at her in that particular way, she lost all interest in the other gentlemen present. Perhaps she ought to consider him after all.

Deciding that accepting his offer to go outside with him so soon after they'd just met would probably give him the wrong impression, but intent on having a bit of fun, she looked him squarely in the eye and said, "It's very kind of you to offer, but I must consider my reputation. Why, you look precisely like the sort of man who'd happily kiss me in some secluded corner without a second thought for the consequences."

Mr. Neville's mouth quite literally dropped open. She knew her words were bold and inappropriate and that she probably ought to have been mortified by what she'd just said. But she wasn't. Mr. Neville's reaction was entirely too satisfying to allow for any measure of regret. Folding her hands neatly in front of her, she stared back at him instead, challenging him to respond while doing her best to maintain a serious demeanor.

"I . . . er . . . assure you that I would do no such thing," he blustered, glancing sideways as if to assure himself that nobody else had heard what she'd just said.

It was all too much, and Rebecca quickly covered her mouth with one hand in a hopeless attempt to contain the laughter that bubbled forth. "My apologies, but I was merely having a bit of sport at your expense. I hope you'll forgive me—and my rather peculiar sense of humor."

He leaned closer to her then—so close in fact that she could smell him, the rich scent of sandalwood enveloping her senses until she found herself leaning toward him. She stopped herself and pulled back.

"Of course . . . *Nuit*." His eyes twinkled. "I must call you something, and considering the color of your hair, I cannot help but be reminded of the night sky. I hope you don't mind."

"Not at all," she said, attempting a nonchalant sound to her voice, though her heart had picked up its pace as he'd said it, the endearment feeling like a gentle caress of her soul.

Who was this man? Could she really have been so fortunate to have stumbled upon the man of her dreams? A man who might potentially agree to marry her once she confessed to him the true nature of her situation? She dismissed the hope, for it was far too naïve and unrealistic to have any merit. Besides, Mr. Neville's suave demeanor screamed rake and scoundrel rather than incurable romantic, which was what she would need. In fact, he was probably precisely the sort of man she should try to avoid, although . . . she made an attempt to look beyond the debonair smile and the lure of his eyes. Could he be genuine? Surely, if he really was a rake, he wouldn't have been so shocked by her suggestion that he might try to compromise her. Would he? She wasn't sure and decided to give him the benefit of the doubt instead.

The edge of her lips curled upward into a smile. "How about a refreshment instead," she suggested. "A glass of champagne, perhaps? And then I believe I'd like to take you up on that offer of yours to dance."

"Yes, of course," Mr. Neville said as he glanced sideways, undoubtedly trying to locate the nearest footman. There was none close by at present. "If you will please wait here, I'll be right back."

Rebecca followed him with her eyes as he walked away, his confident stride reflecting his purpose. She was not unaware of the looks of reproach he received from those he passed, though, and she couldn't help but wonder if her instincts about him had been correct after all. Was she wasting her time on a scoundrel whose only interest was in something that she had no intention of offering? She hoped not, for she'd quite enjoyed their conversation. It had been comfortable and unpretentious, spiced with a sense of humor.

As he vanished from sight, she gave her attention to the rest of the guests, watching with interest as the gentlemen approached the ladies. One gentleman, she noticed, was making his way toward a cluster of young ladies with quick determination. She watched him go, wondering which of the women had caught his interest. But right before he reached them, another gentleman cut in front of him and offered his hand to one of them—a lovely brunette dressed in a dusty pink gown. Placing her hand upon his arm, the pair walked off without as much as acknowledging the presence of the first gentleman. Rebecca wondered if they'd even seen him. Perhaps not, she decided, except that the second gentleman suddenly looked back, grinning with victory at the first gentleman.

What cheek!

She was just about to turn her attention elsewhere when a man's voice said, "I don't believe I've ever had the pleasure of making your acquaintance."

Turning her head, she was forced to look up until her eyes settled upon a handsome face, but where there was something playful about Mr. Neville's features, this man looked almost menacing—as though he was not the sort who was used to having his wishes denied. "I really wouldn't know," Rebecca told him, feigning boredom as she did her best to still her quaking nerves. Whoever he was, he was huge—the sort of man who could easily fling her over his shoulder and carry her off without anyone being able to stop him. "Perhaps if you told me your name . . ."

He smirked. "Lord Starkly at your service. And you are?"

She offered him a tight smile in return. She was not about to play the same coy game with this man as she'd done with Mr. Neville. That would only lead to trouble. But she could hardly give her real name either, so she said, "Lady Nuit."

Lord Starkly frowned. "I don't believe I—"

"This is a masquerade, my lord, is it not?" She heard the impatience in her voice but didn't bother to change it. "Where would the fun be if there were not a little bit of mystery attached to each person present? Let's just say that I'd rather not give away my real name for personal reasons."

"Yes, of course," Lord Starkly said, his features relaxing a little. The predatory glimmer returned to his eyes and he said, "I understand completely why a woman such as yourself would prefer to remain incognito, though I—"

"A woman such as myself?" Rebecca asked, unable to keep the blunt tone of indignation from seeping into her voice. She shouldn't have been shocked, considering her gown, but she didn't seem to be able to stop herself.

"Come now, *Lady Nuit*. There's no need for you to keep up your charade for my benefit. I mean, what other reason would a woman possibly have for engaging in conversation with Mr. Neville unless she was already a fallen angel? Not to mention that your attire is rather indicative of your . . . ah . . . experience in certain areas." He paused, leaned closer and lowered his voice to a whisper. "I trust that you are his mistress or perhaps hoping to become so, which is why I decided to hurry over here and proposition you myself."

Rebecca could only stare at him, agog. What was it with this man that he felt he could so blatantly insult a woman as if she'd been nothing more than bothersome dirt tainting his boots? She so desperately wanted to hit him that she could barely contain her enthusiasm to do so, her fingers already curling into a tight fist at her